BAKER'S DOZEN

To A Couple of my
Favourite People

CRITTER

Rick (Critter) Davis
Baker's Dozen

Published by BooxAi

ISBN: 978-965-577-947-9

BAKER'S DOZEN

THE BANSHEE WAILS

RICK (CRITTER) DAVIS

Dedication

I would like to dedicate this book firstly to my wife of fifty plus years for putting up with me and encouraging me to follow my dreams that didn't always pan out, and who stuck by me through thick or thin and good times as well as bad.

And to Donny Petersen HAMC, a much-respected biker, author, Technical writer and consultant, motorcycle mechanic, shop owner, innovator, custom motorcycle builder, World traveler, philanthropist, boxer, weight lifter, friend and a full fledged 1% Biker. His influence and knowledge extended around the World, he was fearless, yet humble, and yet could be shy at times. He was an ambassador of the World of bikers to the outside World and he always did things by his rules, and he did it with class, dignity and style. He didn't back away from a fight, be it with the police and the legal system or some heavies looking for trouble.

His writing took us from the small towns and neighborhoods of Toronto and then around the World, into dense jungles and then to the top of Mount Everest and then into the mean streets, back alleys, slums of some of the Worlds most dangerous neighborhoods.

I thoroughly enjoyed Donny's books and he was the inspiration for me to do what I always wanted to do but didn't know I could. He encouraged me to do it, but told me straight up: "Do it because you love to write. There isn't any money in it!" He read some early drafts of this book as I was writing them, and I heeded his advice.

His presence at the Riders Mag booth at the Motorcycle Shows always drew crowds and the Show had offered him his own space for free. He called me up and asked if he could be at our booth instead because, as he put it, "I'd rather be with the real people."

He called things as he saw them, and didn't sugar coat things, didn't care if you agreed with him or not! He was his own man and a true original!

Donny Petersen
1947 – 2021
Gone But Not Forgotten. Love and Respect. Ride in Peace

As this book is set-in small-town Ontario, Canada, I would like to further dedicate this book to all the Motorcycle Clubs of Southern Ontario, who have influenced me from my earliest recollections to present. In the days when every MC would attend all Club Field meets and participate to the fullest, in times when the games were hard core, gritty, down and dirty and would quickly separate the men from the boys.

Things could get rough, and at times, medical attention was required, but they were a ball and the highlight of the year.

Today, Clubs come and go, sometimes without notice, but back in the early days, you knew who was who and what they stood for, because they made themselves be noticed and their intentions were clear. The old Clubs, whose patches were revered and prized as if they were gold. Clubs had history and pride and wore and represented their patches with honour against all and any challengers. Many of these Clubs still exist today, although mortality has taken its toll and many of the older members have passed on.

Some of the old Clubs have disappeared or were swallowed up by other, larger Clubs over the years. But they made their mark and had their role in the History of Motorcycle Clubs.

I had the honour and the privilege of being able to cover events for many different Clubs over my years as Photojournalist for The Rider's Mag and was treated very well by so many people. 1%er Clubs and non 1%er Clubs and independent Riders alike. It has been an adventure and there are many stories to be told, and I will do my best to relate them to the readers, as these were the best of times! There like will never be seen again!

CONTENTS

FOREWORD

There is one road that leads into and out of the Town of Swanton Harbour. It of course, ends at the lake, or starts there, depending on your perspective and intersects with the main highway. There is a large, attractive, roadside sign at the edge of Town, it reads; Welcome to the Town of Swanton Harbour. It continues with The Town's catch phrase; "The Gem of a Town, that will exceed your expectations!" There are many who live here, who think that something like; "All that glitters, is not gold!" or "All that looks peaceful and serene isn't always a little piece of Heaven." Or even "All dark clouds don't have a silver lining." might be more appropriate.

The town, founded in 1909 by Steve Swanton and family, when they opened a feed mill, general store and post office, down near the lakeshore, which, served the local farming community. It grew from those humble beginnings to a Police Village, then achieving Town status, in 1961. For all intents and purposes, it is a nice place. It was, a small, peaceful, town in the late fifties and early sixties, nestled between the lake and the rich farmland that produced crops of corn, potatoes, onions and provided good grazing for cattle for both beef and dairy products.

It was also appealing to the horsy crowd and was home to many sprawling ranches with large fancy homes along with barns and stables that could often rival the houses, as to habitability. With 30 miles of shoreline on a fair-sized lake, the Town offered excellent fishing, boating, swimming and other water sports so it was also a great tourist destination. The rugged, hilly terrain that was plentiful; also supported many winter activities offering excellent skiing, and snow-mobiling.

They had two Motels, one four-star hotel, two three stars hotels, two laundromats, two Bowling allies, three Movie theatres, a large Community Centre, and fair grounds, plus two Arenas, and seven baseball Diamonds. There was an IGA store, an A&P, a Dominion Store, a Steinburg's, and Loblaws, was rumoured to be looking to open here as well. They had a Canadian Tire, and a United Co-op, and were considered to be one of the fastest growing Towns in the Province!

There was a High School, Public, Elementary school, a Catholic School, and a Private School. All the major churches were represented as well; Baptist, United, Anglican, Catholic, Presbyterian and a Kingdom Hall of Jehovah's Witness, were all here, if you needed to save your soul, or to make you feel blessed!

It was also home to; Gino's pizza and Chinese take out, Ruby's Diner, Chuck's Burger and a Kentucky Fried Chicken Outlet, Grumpy Bob's Garage and tire service, who also ran a fleet of two Tow Trucks and Nick's Full-service Gas Station, and Convenience Store. It was a growing Community alright! It was close enough to the nearby city of Toronto to be considered convenient, but far enough away and rooted in farm Country to still be thought of as Rural.

This was an ideal spot to raise a family and promised good wholesome living. You might expect that the Murder of a Police Officer, Police Corruption, Motorcycle gangs, Political Scandal, Organized Crime, Sex scandals, bribery, gambling syndicates and the like, to be big city crimes, certainly, not the fare for nice, quiet, peaceful, little bedroom communities like Swanton Harbour. You would be wrong!

You may think, in a small Town such as this, Police corruption and such, if it existed at all, would be on a somewhat, lesser scale. However, the size of the Town, doesn't necessarily dictate the size crime it can attract, or impact it can have! Corruption and crime know no borders or boundaries, the insidious seeds, no matter how small and innocuous, they may seem, are cast indiscriminately and can be germinated, take root and thrive anywhere! The impact can be just as damaging and devastating, to the victims, no matter where it rears its ugly head!

The murder of a Police Officer is still, the murder of a Police Officer, no matter where it occurs, and raises the bar substantially, on the scale, of how much media attention it receives, how seriously the Police take it and how extensive the investigation is! Plus, in a small tight-knit community such as Swanton Harbour, where the rumour mill works over-time, and gossiping, speculation, and second guessing is a favourite pastime, and to have truth, compete with conjecture and rumours, can be a daunting task in itself!

Parents, however well intentioned, often, mistakenly, move to these small communities, in hopes of escaping and sheltering their children, from the evils and temptations of the "Big City", only to find that those evils and temptations, have already beaten them here. They find that their kids have readily imported all of the "Big City" stuff so they, could escape the seclusion and boredom of life in the burbs and beyond and not be labelled as hicks!

Some, made an escape from the mundane, by other means! They formed, or joined into groups of those who share similar interests be it music, sports, stamp collecting or whatever. One of these groups, turned to their passion and love of a sport, that was actually, more about love and respect for each other, combined with the love of motorcycles, the motorcycle culture, and lifestyle. They created and modified a lifestyle and a community of their own, that to them, was real, distinctive and tangible and, to them, more acceptable.

However, much of Society, didn't understand, or care to understand, the attraction that some felt towards motorcycles or the motorcycle culture. Those, who adopted that culture, and all that went with it, got to be branded as outcasts, misfits! They were harassed and were bullied and maligned by those who were supposed to protect the rights of all citizens, not just the one's that they (By the authority that they felt the badge entitled them to.) felt were worthy of the rights of citizenship. They did so, with the blessings and full support of the rest of society, who were conditioned to this type of behavior by propaganda by police agencies and main stream media who were more interested in juicy headlines than truths.

That was OK by them, these were Bikers! Or rather, in this case, they were a baseball team, a bunch of kids, who became Bikers and also came to play a prominent roll in the Murder and the investigation.

CHAPTER ONE
THE BEGINNING!

THE LATE OCTOBER WIND, coming off the Lake was cold and bitter and was rapidly performing its task of stripping the trees, of their colourful foliage, now that the first frost, that occurred a few days previous, had taken its toll. It seemed to slice right through Dan's heavy leather jacket and gloves with ease and made him shiver. He, piloted the bright orange, knucklehead, bobber, off the long meandering country roadway, through the beautiful stone archway that marked the entrance to the Cemetery's narrow driveway.

He cruised at an easy pace, the throbbing heartbeat of the big, V Twin motor, breaking through the absolute silence. Nearby birds took flight and several squirrels sought shelter in nearby trees! He proceeded along the driveway, winding between the various plots and monuments, and followed it along until it opened up to a wonderful vista of the lake and the rapidly diminishing cavalcade of colour that was, the surrounding woodlands. This marked the spot where would he veer off, down a small pathway for a hundred yards or so, then glided slowly and carefully across the well manicured grass that was quickly being covered by an immense carpet of leaves, towards a recently occupied gravesite.

The Cemetery, was tranquil, and serene, as well as almost empty, save a few souls who were dressed to suit the inclement weather. It served as fair warning, that Winter would soon hold us in its icy grip. These folks, were visiting loved ones of their own and went about their business of tending to the graves. They did however, cast curious looks towards him, as his arrival had caught their attention, firstly, for being out on a motorcycle, that wasn't exactly quiet, on such a cold, inhospitable day and secondly because they recognised him.

He noticed that some floral arrangements were still in place, as he came to a stop, beside the grave. The cold wind, once again caught him a little off his guard and a sudden chill, ran through his body, as he sat there just staring at the grave for several minutes. He let the motorcycle sit, at its signature, pulsating, uneven idle, before he twisted the throttle a couple of times in quick succession, listening, as the throaty growl reverberated throughout the cemetery, before shutting it down and dismounting. The sound was pleasurable to him and he knew it would certainly appeal to REB, should he be able to hear it. What the Hell? It didn't do anybody any harm even if it couldn't reach REB's ears. He breathed in deeply, enjoying the musky, heady, scent of the decaying leaves, that hung in the crisp Autumn air, filling his lungs and soothing his senses with its invigorating fragrance.

"That should get your attention!" He said out loud, and

slowly walked over towards the grave, until he was standing directly in front of the handsome, large black marble headstone, that marked the place they had laid his friends body to rest just a few short weeks ago. He reached out and touched it, perhaps hoping to feel something other than the cold hard surface and then examined the offerings that had already begun to accumulate atop the grave marker. Different, personal items, that had been left there as tokens of love and respect, by friends, who, like himself, had come here for some private time with him, and to make peace with his spirit. There was a small Inukshuk, possibly, built and left there by Tramp, or perhaps his Uncle or other family members to mark this as a sacred place in accordance with the ways and beliefs of their indigenous culture.

Some of the items, could be considered to be junk to some; various bottle caps (Guinness mostly), pocket knives, buttons, patches, locks of hair, lapel pins, rings and other various jewelry items and trinkets that had some connection or meaning, between them and their departed Brother. There were also envelopes, containing various amounts of cash, obviously, to settle debts owed, and were now considered to be paid. He left everything undisturbed, other than leaving an item of his own, an old, Swanton Harbour, Chief of Police shoulder flash that he had encased in clear acrylic resin.

On the tombstone, it was inscribed; Robert Edward Baker, Sept 12, 1945 – Sept. 12, 2020 – R.I.P. – G.BN.F. – L&R – A&F. Loving Son, Husband Father and Brother. There was the Club Logo emblazoned on it with; The Bakers

Dozen in a rocker above, and below, it said; President and founder. He will be missed!

"Well old friend; It has been quite a ride and an adventure! And we've certainly come a long way, on roads that I ever would have imagined I would travel, and to destinations that I hadn't planned on going! It has been quite a transition from Chief of Police, to where I am now! I guess, I really have turned the page."

Dan took off his gloves, unzipped the front of his jacket, and extracted a bottle of Wiser's Deluxe, Rye Whiskey, that he had tucked in there. He unscrewed the cap and poured some of the potent liquid on the ground just in front of the headstone. "Sláinte, Mo Chara!" He then raised the bottle to his lips and took a long pull. He could feel the comforting warmth, as the strong liquor made its journey to the depths of his stomach. He would repeat that procedure several more times during the course of his visit.

"I got your message the other day! Trust you, to throw one last curve at me, you, old coot! You know I'm a sucker for an inside curve, and I guess I should have expected it!" He said with a grin while shaking his head.

He poured them each another stiff shot, and just sat there on the ground, with his old friend, while looking out at the lake, watching the white caps form on the waves, before they crashed against the rocky shoreline. The wind, suddenly picked up, sending leaves scattering between the graves in little eddies and another shiver ran through Dan's body. He quickly did up the jacket, and then just sat there, leaning back against the black marble monolith, in silence.

That is something that they did quite regularly

throughout the years, just sitting in silence, together, gathering their thoughts and formulating their conversation, until one of them figured that they had thought long enough, and decided it was time for discussion. They found that often, silent time with someone that you've bonded with, could often be as comforting and as stimulating as conversation! Sometimes, words are just so unnecessary.

For Dan, now, it was time to ponder, reflect, and assess the things that had occurred over a lifetime, along with recent choices and decisions that were made. Right or wrong, good or bad, would be determined by others, after life had left his body and his time on earth was done. This would be based on how these people, perceived him, personally, weighed things out, and calculated his worth as a human being. He hoped they would approve, but as REB would say; "Fuck 'em if they don't!"

For men like he and REB; they just tried to do the best they could, and lived the best they could by their own rules and the standards, that they set for themselves. In the end; what if, you could take one final look back and make a final assessment, what would you change, if you could? That was a question he had no answers to.

Shaking his head, and smiling, he rose to his feet, and they shared one last shot of the whiskey! He then said out loud; "Your secret, is now our secret, my friend, and it goes to the grave with me! I'll leave this, here with you, Mo Chara, so you'll have something to share, with me or the next person that comes up to visit you! I will bring more." He then placed the half empty bottle on the grave, leaning it against the fine, black marble marker.

This place, held more cherished memories for Dan, and he was not done visiting quite yet. He solemnly, made his way down to the next plot, where the bodies of his wife and two children also lay. He was now crying, as he sat on the cold ground, amongst his family, overwhelmed by the sense of loss and sadness. He had no words, he just sat there for and immeasurable amount of time, sobbing and trying to make sense of it all. He again, rose to his feet, regained his composure, but still not able to bring voice to the words that stuck in his throat. Not wanting to just leave without expressing something, he simply, blew a kiss towards the graves, turned and quickly walked away, a lump burning in his throat like he'd swallowed a blazing ember!

Dan, then, walked back to the orange motorcycle, that he and his friend both loved, and one kick brought it back to life! The harsh bark of the short exhaust pipes, breaking the silence and sanctity of the place once again. This, was a far cry from the sound of the massive Funeral procession, that had filled this place, not so long ago.

He then raised his right hand pointed towards REB's grave, in a familiar, one finger salute, which he quickly converted to a thumbs up. Smiling broadly, he gave the throttle a good twist, before heading back through the rustling leaves, and off into the chilly late afternoon, Autumn splendour! The rumble of the exhaust marked his passage and soon faded off letting silence and serenity once again be restored.

Dan's journey through life continues, however, there is a void that could never be filled. Although, his family's and his friend's body, may well lie cold, and lifeless, beneath the hallowed ground of this place, their spirit rides away with him on that bright orange bobber. He could feel REB's presence as he turned from the driveway onto the paved road, twisted the wick and roared off with the cold wind stinging his face. That was the winds kiss, and that, brought him to life and he twisted the throttle even further, leaning into the turns of that winding road like it was a challenge! He could almost hear his Brother urging him on! REB may be gone from this Earth but his, legacy, memory, and his achievements will live on in the hearts and minds of many for years to come.

Robert Edward Baker, was born to Francis and Edna Baker, on a bright sunny late summer's day on September 12th in the year 1945. They were of solid Irish stock, who left their Native Ireland, to forge a better life here in Canada. They had very little in the way of money, and very few possessions, upon arrival in the Country, and worked at whatever jobs they could find, until they could get enough to open the Bakery shop of their dreams. Jobs, was the operative word as they both worked multiple jobs, and it seemed that they were always working.

They had rented a small house, from a farmer, just outside Town. It wasn't much more than a shack, but it was a roof over their heads, which they desperately needed as Robert was due any time. They even had a spot to grow a small garden, which was essential to their survival.

Francis, got hired on as a carpenter's helper, and put in long, hard, tiring, days, then pitched in, to help his landlord with chores, in the evening and on weekends to help pay the rent. He would chop wood, worked in the fields, harvesting crops, and loading hay onto a wagon with a pitch fork. He was hard working, tough as nails, multi talented and determined to succeed. There was no day of rest for these folks, and they didn't expect one.

Edna, cleaned houses, took in laundry, helped picking crops, and would bake, cookies, scones, cakes, bread, biscuits, pies and tarts, that she would load into large wicker baskets, and trudge ten miles into Town and sell to the General Store. Her baked goods, got to be very popular, and sold out almost as fast as she could put them out. Francis made her a small wagon, to transport her goods and in winter a sled that he fashioned out of scrap material served her well. They weren't getting rich, but they were managing to save some money, and when a shop in town, with living quarters above came available, they were able to put a small down payment on it, and that was Baker's Baked Goods first home.

Edna, gave birth to Robert at home, in that ramshackle, little shack, with the help of a Mid wife, and just never seemed to miss a beat, in her busy life, and was back working, just as soon as she could. After he was born, the Midwife who was cleaning him up, noticed that he had a small red and very distinct birthmark on his left chest just above the nipple. She remarked at the time, that it resembled a wailing Banshee! She, being of old Irish stock, had experienced a life, rife with, and steeped in, old beliefs, superstitions, folklore and tales of the supernatural and such. She was a little unnerved by the discovery at the time, but no one else gave it any consideration and any concerns she might have had, were dismissed as happenstance.

He was to be their only child, and although Edna never

complained, it was hard on her, as she and Francis, had both hoped for a large family. They would have liked more children, but they didn't have much choice, money was tight, times were hard, work had to be done, and they chose to be thankful with what they had.

Young Robby, was a blessing to them, and he had such a good temperament, and could amuse himself for hours with the simplest of toys, was well behaved, mindful, and respectful of his parents. He, as well, seemed to pick up on his parents work ethic, and was always eager to pitch in wherever he could, even as a toddler.

But, he had a rebellious side to him, and as well, he possessed a fearsome temper! He was absolutely fearless in his approach to anything and everything. There was always a bit of a hard edge to him, although, it was undetectable most of the time, but it was definitely there. It lay, just beyond what was visible to the eye, so, if you looked closely enough, you knew that something ominous, dark and dangerous, lay dormant within, just below the surface. That, could, and did, cause some problems for him and his parents, from time to time. Robby was also very analytical in the way he dealt with things, and his actions even as a young lad, always seemed measured and well thought out. He very rarely, just charged into anything, without giving it some solid thought and consideration first, as to how he would go about things.

He, also had a true "Poker Face" even in childhood, and his facial expressions, other than pure joy or happiness, never betrayed his true emotions, thoughts, or whatever action or reactions lay in store. Emotions such as anger, fear, disgust, or hurt were masked and obscured by that "poker face". His ice blue eyes, were his most dominant feature and, he could lock into an intense stare, that could make most people uncomfortable. Some said if he was pissed off, he would fix you with a look that while not showing any emotion or intent, would send a chill down their spines as if someone was digging their grave. He was skilled in letting the other person's guilt, dishonesty, fear or anger betray them with just a look from him.

Robby was an average student in most subjects, but excelled in art, music, and sports. He was an excellent athlete and displayed natural abilities in any sport. This presented a challenge, to the hard-working family, for whom every penny was needed to keep their fledgling business going as they needed to expand their little shop, to keep pace with demand. Sports equipment was expensive and while they didn't want to curtail their son's involvement, it did present a problem. But things had a way of working out for them, as they had made fast friends in the community, through their honesty, hard work and their generosity.

When someone in Town got sick, or injured or had fallen on hard times; the Bakers were the first ones to offer to help. They would drop off large baskets of baked goods or a pot of home-made soup, or stew. They were always careful and mindful of their money but would occasionally miscalculate an order and drastically undercharge for goods for someone who was facing hard times. People would try to make them aware that a mistake had been made, but they would just get a smile in return, and know that it was no mistake. Often, they would add items to someone's order and tell them that it was older stock that they didn't want to stock any more, but it was still good, and they would rather, give it to them, rather that throw it out. Their customers certainly appreciated them.

One such customer was Police Chief, Stanley Marshal, who had known the Bakers since they first came to Town and was very impressed by the hard-working couple, and the way the fit into the Community. He also saw something in young Robby that he felt needed nurturing.

Stan Marshall, was not a big man by any means, and certainly, not typical of those hulking six foot, plus, ex football players, who usually were attracted to this type of work. He only stood five foot, seven and a half inches tall, and weighed in at one hundred and fifty-five pounds. He was well muscled and was as tough as they come, when he needed to be, and was certainly capable of making his presence known, again, the key words apply; when he needed to. His size and demeanor were deceiving and many a big tough man, was quickly made aware of his ability to scrap and take care of himself. He was totally fearless when faced with any situation. However, in his entire career, he never drew his gun, other than to clean it, practice or lock it away. Secretly he hated guns! He knew how to use one as verified by his performance at the gun range, he appreciated that guns had a purpose and were often necessary to have, but he still hated them! I guess his wartime experiences, led to his aversion to them. He was prepared however, and would do what he needed to.

He was affable, had a kind nature, a soft voice and an easy-going mannerism and attitude, which was sort of unusual for someone making a career in Law Enforcement.

He had an avid interest in sports and was a contradiction to that old adage about coaches, that stated; Those who can play, play. Those who can't play, coach!

The coach, could play as well as anyone, and in rough and tumble sports, like hockey, when someone would think that he could rough Stan up in the corners, taking him in hard against the boards, they were in for a surprise! Instead of an easy target, they found a formidable adversary, skilled in applying elbows and knees to vulnerable and painful spots on the body and the refs and linesmen were mostly oblivious to it. They thought twice about trying it again.

Stan however, found his true talent, was in coaching, teaching the game and its fine points, shaping future all stars and even had a couple of his charges make it to the NHL. He had a way of getting the absolute best performance from his players, be they top calibre or mediocre. He loved what he did and put his heart into it.

The same applied to his approach to Law enforcement, he did not regard his badge, as a privilege that gave him authority, with which to rule over others in the Community, but considered his job an honour to be charged with the responsibility to help and protect as many in his Community as he could. He preferred to be liked, and earn respect through his deeds and performance rather than by demands or fear and intimidation. You could always expect a fair shake from Chief Marshall, as long as you were up-front and honest, however, he could also be harsh, when and if he needed to be!

He took a real interest in young Robby Baker, and from time to time, could be seen, just sitting on the steps of the store with him, just having a conversation. The feeling was mutual, and Robby was thrilled when he got to be on coach Marshall's Hockey team or when "The Coach" would drop by one of their baseball games or practices.

When Robby went to sign up for the Baseball team, he found out that his only nemesis, Danny O'Reilly, was on the team already, and they didn't get along, and rather than get the whole team involved in their rivalry, he decided not to play. Coach Marshall could understand his position, and sought him out, and it was his suggestion, that Robby start a team and league of his own. He knew Robby had the initiative, the drive and the ability to make it work, and he would be there to mentor him all the way through it. He had no idea, at the time, but Chief of Police, Stan Marshall had inadvertently set things in motion that would eventually lead to the formation of The Bakers Dozen, Motorcycle Club!

He recognised in Robby, a natural leadership capability, and charisma, and he also noticed, that many of the kids in Town, who did not come from affluent families, had fallen through the cracks, in the current sports programs that currently existed in the community.

Many of the more well-heeled parents, and politicians, were more obsessed with winning, championship pennants, trophies and the like, than having their children learning and playing, for the pure love of the game and just playing! Playing sports, was expensive, or at least, too expensive, for many families to buy equipment, pay to register, and all the rest!

Stan did what he could, but, he was far from wealthy himself, and just didn't have the time it would take. But, he saw in Robert Edward Baker; the makings of a protégé and he did have many contacts and quite a bit of influence, with many of the major Sports franchises in the Province, and they came through for him. Robby was a natural, and he did the rest, with a lot of help and guidance from the Chief.

Stan, had two boys a little older than young Robby, and one slightly younger, and they were all into sports in a big way. He, himself, was coaching, baseball, football, soccer and hockey. He would drop off boxes of sports equipment, like baseball mitts, skates, balls, bats, pads, hockey pucks, hockey sticks, helmets and other items that he said his boys had outgrown, at the Baker's house or shop.

Despite his assertion, as to the source of this much needed and appreciated equipment, by the sheer volume of stuff, you had to know, that he had sourced them from other places, as well, as his own collection of hand me downs and cast offs! This was especially evident, when shoes and skates in sizes like 14, 15, and larger which, co-incidentally happened to fit the "Beanpole", Chuck Taylor, who, was always outgrowing everything he had.

Robby always found the right recipients for every piece of equipment and collected outgrown stuff and in turn found new owners for it as well. Stanley Marshall was pleased, as more kids who otherwise would do without, and not play, could! He figured, what goes around, comes around and always liked to pay it forward. Besides, if these kids were playing sports, they weren't getting into trouble and making work for him and his Department!

Robby liked to play, but he had the ability to realize, that the game, always came first, and winning was just something that happened, when you played the game properly, and things went your way. He was patient and kids, of all ages, loved and respected him. He displayed no ego, and the other kids recognized that he was a truly gifted athlete, who chose to hang out with them, when he had the ability to play with those, older, and far more talented, than themselves.

His parents, sponsored the Team, The Bakers Dozen, but Robby was pretty sure that Chief of Police was also behind that it in some way, as well. He knew his parents could not afford to buy the boxes of new baseball gear and uniforms that were dropped off at their door on occasion. He knew, that they couldn't afford a lot of the other expenses that were paid either. He also knew that the old Chief was happy to see a bunch of kids, who would not have otherwise, be able to participate and have fun, and doing just that! Robby recognised early, when you have a true friend, you just have to treasure that friendship and that friend for what, and who they were, and that there are people who just try to do what is right, just because of the way their heart feels! He could see that look, in whatever you wanted to call him; Chief Marshall, Coach Marshall, or just plain Friend, Marshall's, eyes, when he came out to the games or practices. Chief Marshall was the first and only Cop that he trusted, respected, admired and truly loved for many years to come. The Chief, to him, was a man and a humanitarian first, the Cop thing was how he made a living!

Robby loved playing hockey, and his natural athleticism and ability to read situations and plays, suited him for the game and his position at centre. And his leadership abilities, made him the obvious choice as team Captain. He could make some brilliant plays all on his own, as he could stick handle, and skate circles around most of the other players, but he was always willing to set up a goal and make a pass rather than try to showboat.

He was happy when the teams were put together that he wasn't on a team with Danny O'Reilly as he was a Showboat and they were constantly fighting. It wouldn't have been much fun. It was hard enough when the two teams played against each other, because he would know for certain, that they would clash and they would spend more time in the penalty boxes than on the ice, and the fun was playing, not sitting in the penalty box! He wasn't sure what Danny's problem was, but he would come after him whenever they were on the ice together. He wasn't afraid of him and had nothing really against Danny, but he wasn't about to take any crap from him. He wished he would just go away and leave him alone!

The first year Robby and Danny both made the All-Star team. Robby found out that he would have to not only be on the same team, but Coach Marshall had put them both on the same line together. He was at centre and Danny on Right Wing, he went to the Coach to tell him that he wanted to drop off the team.

Danny was equally upset, not because he was on the same team and line, but because he felt he should be at Centre, because that was his normal position, and that is where he shined, and could best outshine Robby Baker.

The coach, took them both aside, separately and talked both into just giving it a try and promised, that, if it didn't work he would change it up! But he told them, that they had to give it an honest effort. He told them not to think about who they were playing with, but who they were playing against, and just play hockey, the way they both knew it should be played. He told them not to plan plays, that the plays would just happen naturally.

Both, Dan and Robby, as well as all of their teammates, most parents and other coaches, thought the old Coach was nuts! The other teams, were in Heaven, because they figured that those two, who were considered to be two of the best players in the league, would spend more time fighting and trying to out-shine each other, to actually play the game, and that they would just have a cake-walk to the Championship.

It was awkward at first, as there was still a real tension between them, but, after the first couple of scrimmages, the natural chemistry started to manifest itself, and the magic started to happen, and they weren't even aware that it was happening, it all just started to flow. Natural instincts were now at play and it was a sight to behold! The two were working together as if they had played together all their lives.

They were making plays that looked as if they had been carefully and meticulously choreographed without any fore-thought, simply because that was the way to do it, that is what their natural instincts told them to do. The two just seemed to sense that they were in sync, and playing along-side a player of equal calibre and ability and took full advan-tage of it. The others on the line, and the rest of the team, also picked up on the vibe and they too, played in unison, with heart and conviction, in a way that they never had before. Danny and Bobby could even be seen smiling at each other once in a while, and caught themselves doing "High Fives" even an occasion impromptu hug was exchanged.

The opposing team, could not believe what was happening. The game was a complete blow out! As was, the rest of the series and The Swanton Harbour, All-Stars, went on to win the Championship in glorious fashion! When the MVP award was to be decided, they couldn't pick only one and for the first time, two MVP awards were presented to both Dan and Robby!

You might think, that, that experience, would have marked the end to the rivalry between the two. It did not! The next two years All Star Games were a repeat of that first year's victory. The two could play in complete symmetry on the same line as if they were meant to be, but when the series was over, they went right back to the status quo.

CHAPTER TWO

SHIFTING GEARS

THE WHOLE MOTORCYCLE THING, started innocently enough, but would evolve, and in turn, shape the lives of many, for years to come.

It began, when REB, showed up at the property, that Robby's parents owned, and the kids now used, as a hang out spot, one afternoon. He said that he had found an old, what were called; Pie Wagons or Servi cars, and he had it bought off some guy who owned a gas station down on River Street, cheap and rode it there on the QT, avoiding Cops. He didn't have any ownership for it, as it had been lost years ago, but didn't care, they weren't going to plate it, or take it on the road! It was nothing to look at, but it ran OK, and they all loved it!

REB's folks owned quite a bit of land out this way and this was a parcel that REB really took a shine to, and they he and his friends use it. His folks, were figuring one day, they might move out of Town, and be farmers one day, as farm land, around here, back in those days, was plentiful and cheap! This parcel, that they bought, even had a rickety old house, a dilapidated old barn and a drive shed that were still standing! When they died, they left everything to REB.

This was the perfect spot for this bunch, to hang out and riding the Hell out of that old Trike was a bonus. They took the lid off of the box and would load everybody they could in there and just tear around the fields, bouncing through ruts, ditches and small creeks, terrorizing groundhogs, rabbits and other assorted woodland creatures, and just had a ball.

It would break down on occasion, because of all the hard use and abuse, they put it through, and, by necessity, they all, even the girls, learned how to fix everything from ignition and electrical problems, to tires and wheels and welding stuff back on. Snagging gussets and brackets in place became a regular pastime and occurrence and they were also always on the lookout for hunks of metal. Calamity, was probably the best of the bunch when it came to fixing those old buckets of bolts.

Then someone else, found a deal on an old Indian Chief, that had been chained up to a telephone pole or something on this service station parking lot, for years. It was painted bright orange with black stripes like a tiger. The motor was seized and it took a lot of effort just to load it into the back of an old pick-up truck, and get it back to the property. It was a real challenge, but they got it done. Now to get it running!

They did all that they could, but to no avail. One day, a few of them stopped into a small motorcycle shop down on

Elm St., and chosen spokesperson; Calamity, went in and talked to an old mechanic, who worked there, by the name of Tony. Tony didn't seem to mind answering their questions and giving them tips, he even loaned them a couple of manuals and parts catalogues. He was rough looking, swore a lot, had a bunch of jailhouse tattoos, chain-smoked cigars and constantly and regularly could be seen swigging from a large bottle of tequila, that he kept in a drawer in his tool chest.

He seemed to like them, and even loaned them some of his specialty tools like pullers and wrenches, some of which had been modified just to work on one specific part for one specific job. Many of these tools had been designed and fabricated right in the shop, welding, heating, bending, cutting, filing, and twisting or whatever was necessary until the tool worked. Sometimes it took longer to fabricate the tool than it did to do the job that it was designed it to do. The magic, came in the fact, that without that tool; the job wouldn't have been able to be accomplished. Patience, ingenuity and knowledge were key and they learned that from Old Tony and others whom they had yet to meet.

This old Indian, though, appeared to be well beyond their skill level. Calamity went back to this mechanic and told him the situation, he agreed that it just might be more than what they could handle at this time. He said that he would come by in the evening after work and take a look."

"He showed up, just like he said he would, driving this old Chevy panel truck, that was his main transportation. His absolute pride and joy, however, was a 1949 Panhead FL Hydra glide, that he treasured. At first glance, you wouldn't know that anyone cared about, or for, his motorcycle, judging from the bike's appearance!

We learned, that this particular, style of motorcycle became affectionately known as a "Rat, or Rat Bikes". These bikes had a distinct appearance that could be easily be mistaken as neglect! The one thing these Rats had in common, is that they were interesting and had a charm, character and personality that was as individual and personal as those who rode them. They came to love and appreciate them both.

Tony's bike and he, suited each other well, the bike, had character all its own, and got as much or more attention, wherever and whenever he rode it, than those with the fancy paint and kept in pristine condition. It was always, very dirty, the leather and padding on the seat was worn and tattered and almost non-existent. The bike, had, over the years, gathered many stickers, pins, bottle caps, sports pennants, raccoon tails, rabbits' feet, and anything else, that captured Tony's imagination, or unusual sense of design and it could be glued, taped, screwed, bolted, or otherwise attached to the body of this unusual motorcycle! He even had the actual skeleton of a dead rat in a sprung trap, that he had glued in place on top of the front fender. A Davy Crocket lunch box sat where the tool box used to sit, a wooden Coca Cola crate was bungee corded to the rack over the rear fender and it was full of odds and sods. Derby covers, fabricated from old canned ham cans replaced OEM covers. Tons of little things that could keep you occupied for hours and you still would probably have overlooked something.

That damned motorcycle was fun, and fun was supposed

to be the objective! Was it not? Sometimes, friends would just stick something on, that they spotted on their travels and Tony would always be able to spot it right away, and was appreciative of his friend's contributions to his labour of love. He could identify where each and every item had come from, and for him, every look at that old motorcycle was like a ride down memory lane!

It was however, in perfect running condition, and mechanically, was well maintained. But it also, naturally, because of its appearance, got the attention of Law Enforcement, on a regular basis, and he would get pulled over, often.

Initially, they'd looked over the bike to see if it was roadworthy, and then, the inspection could go on for an hour or more, as the bike inspired interest, and closer examination, as it captured people's attention and appealed to their natural curiosity, sense of humour, and could be a real conversation starter!

These inspections usually just turned into a gabfest with old Tony shaking hands with the Coppers at the end of it, and they would part company on good terms. Sometimes, the Cop, would have something that he thought would add something to the bike and occasionally he would get stopped just so the Cop could give it to him! Tony, was only too happy to attach it! It was indeed a labour of love and a bit of a Community project!

He had painted it yellow, although, over the years, the paint had become faded, chipped or worn off in places. He had given it the name, or it just became known as "The Dirty Rat" which was hand painted in white and black paint on each side of the tank, above that was a caricature of a Rat, dressed in a dark, pinstriped, double-breasted suit, wide colourful tie, wearing a wide brimmed Fedora hat and holding a revolver in his hand, which he had also personally, hand painted, showing off his artistic flair and talents as well as things, mechanical. The rat was done to resemble actor "James Cagney" who was often misquoted for the line "You dirty rat! You killed my Brother" from the 1932 film Taxi! The actual line was "You yellow bellied dirty rat," Tony had the kind of unique character and personality that he could carry over to his motorcycle and visa versa and they were like a matched set.

Anyway, he gave that old Indian that they had named "Tony Tiger", because of it's black and orange paint-job, a once-over, and just shook his head. He then, went back to his truck and when he returned, he was carrying a complete Indian motor in his arms! "This one works fine and it will fit in here nicely! You can have this one and I'll take yours back to the shop and rebuild it, I have all the parts, you can help if you want, and learn how to do it yourselves. Then you can have it back as a spare. I got enough old crap taking up space at the shop!" he told them. He then, proceeded to swap out the motors and started to give the bike a real good look over. He'd shake his head, take something off and go back to his truck and get some other parts and replace this and that or he'd swap out the wheels and tires.

He was working away for about four hours and they were starting to worry. No one had asked about what all this would cost, as money, they had none! They were hoping that he could just give us advice, not do all the work! He was rough looking, and there was talk that he was a member of a motorcycle gang. Were they nervous and more than a little scared? Damned straight!

"Cal was picked to talk to him, and in spite of being scared stiff, just walked up, and flat out told him, that they were just hoping for advice, on what to do, and how to do it, but had no money to pay him for motors and all the work he was doing."

"He suddenly, threw his tools down into the dirt in disgust, and looked her straight in the eyes. "No fucking money eh? No money? Who, the fuck mentioned money? I sure as fuck didn't! The loud tirade brought the others rushing into the shed, but no one spoke! "You needed help! I'm helping, or trying to, if you fucking kids would stop fucking interrupting me! If a helping hand from a friend, for some friends isn't good enough for you, Fuck you all!" They were all totally taken aback by the outburst, and didn't know what to say.

Old Tony continued! "Now this thing is almost ready to go, do you want me to continue, or do you want to fucking insult me some more?" With that he, chomped down hard on his cigar, picked up his tools and continued to work. A half hour later, the Old Indian responded to his kicks, by springing to life, for the first time in years.

Tony Boiko, was their new friends name, a Ukrainian, who had Immigrated here just before the war, and joined the Canadian army and served as a despatch rider, which is where he hooked up with many of his buddies, and formed a real bond with them, which just carried over into civilian life. He was a highly intelligent man, mostly self educated, but he was an avid reader with an insatiable thirst for knowledge and the ability to retain absolutely everything he ever learned, read, saw or heard about with a photographic memory and natural intelligence, that knew no bounds. He was fluent in eight different languages, including profanity!

Tony seemed to know something about absolutely everything, it didn't matter if it was, World history, local history, geography, how and why, something was made, anything! He was a wealth of knowledge and information and they loved being around him and he seemed to like them pretty well too! When that old Indian fired up, he was as excited as the kids were, perhaps even more so because he got to see the look of pure joy on their faces.

Old Tony, was their first introduction to anyone remotely resembling a "Biker". They were impressed! They then learned that all "Bikers" were not the same, and the same holds true with people, animals and anything else, he would tell them! "Always look for what lurks beyond the surface. Look past what appears to be obvious." He told them over and over, that in general, no matter what race, creed, colour, job, education, religion or profession, there was always going to be a mix of good, bad and sometimes evil. The trick he said, was to be able to spot the difference and avoid whatever or whomever before they could do you harm. If you think someone is going to hit you and you can't get away, hit first and give it everything you got and don't stop until you can walk away!

Just because someone rides a motorcycle, doesn't mean that they ride it well, or has the same values as you. Just because he or she says they are your friend doesn't always mean that they are! Don't call him a biker, until you've seen him ride, and don't trust anyone until they have proved themselves worthy of your trust! Words that they all learned to live by!

They learned a lot from Old Tony, and loved hanging around with him. "They practically haunted the shop where Tony worked, until one day, when they got there, he wasn't. Mr. Johnston, the owner of the shop, was there sweeping the place out, and he told them that Old Tony was really sick and couldn't work anymore. He was going to close up the shop, as without Old Tony, he just couldn't do it himself! Tony, as it turns out, didn't just work there, but was his partner. He was a keen, highly skilled motorcycle rider and racer as well as an excellent mechanic.

Looking back on it, they had all noticed that Tony was losing a lot of weight, and was always, very tired, and that had been the case, for some time. He would get winded, just doing something simple, and would have to sit down a lot, to catch his breath. Although he never mentioned it, he always seemed to be in a lot of pain, was taking a lot of pills and was no longer, indulging in his usual hearty slugs of Tequila. In fact, the bottle was no longer in the drawer of his tool chest. His ever-present cigar remained clenched between his teeth, but he never lit it anymore.

"Although young, they were now, thanks to Tony, some-what capable and quite comfortable with wrenches and equipment and were quick studies and could now troubleshoot and detect many mechanical problems and even fix them. They were more than willing to help out wherever and whenever they could! Old Tony gladly took them up on their offer to help!

He offered to pay us one day. That, was a moment, that Calamity had been secretly hoping and praying would come! It was her turn to be the Cranky fuck! So, in her best possible, impersonation of Old Tony, she threw the tools that she had in her hands, hard to the concrete floor and they made a Hell of a racket! That startled Old Tony, and got everyone else's attention too, including Art Johnstone's! She, then, launched into a tirade.

The others, didn't know what she was going to do until she began. In fact, she didn't even know she was going to do it, it just came out! "Money? Money? Who the fuck mentioned fucking money?" She shouted! "We sure as fuck, didn't! We came here to help, so we are fucking helping, or trying to, if you fucking old codgers would stop fucking interrupting us! If fucking friends can't help fucking friends, when they need it, just to fucking help, fuck you then! Now we've got more fucking work to do here, so unless you want to fucking insult us some more, we will get back to it!"

Old Tony just stood there, absolutely stunned at first. His mouth hung open and the cigar dropped out and fell to the floor! Then, he started shaking, trying to stifle and contain the laughter that was building, before bursting out with a big hearty laugh! Everyone, was laughing so hard, their sides felt like they were going to split! Old Tony too was in tears, partly from pain, but mostly from laughter. A short time later they noticed he was weakening substantially, and knew it was time to leave and let him close early. Art Johnstone witnessed the whole thing and had almost pissed his pants, he admitted later!

One thing was certain, he was their friend, and they were

his. Calamity, remembers the big smile he had on his face and the look in his eyes, as he said goodbye and closed the shop door that afternoon. That was their last time in that shop, with their friend, and in their element. Thanks to Tony, they now had an element.

They all went to see him in the Hospital and he seemed to enjoy that. He looked really bad and had tubes running into him. They didn't stay long, as he was extremely weak and very tired. When they returned, the next day, they were told that he had died during the night.

They all went to his funeral, and except for them, Mr. Johnston; his partner, and several old bikers, (That was obvious as they were riding motorcycles.), no one else attended. The bikers, all came over afterwards, and introduced themselves to them and shook their hands! They said that Tony talked about them all the time, and that they made him very happy and they wanted to thank them personally!" These guys, even knew them all by name, yet they had never met any of them until that day.

"One afternoon, Calamity and a group of the regulars, went by the property and were just hanging out when they heard a bunch of motorcycles, and looked up to see them, following Old Tony's beat up old panel truck along with three other trucks coming up the driveway. There was about a dozen of them, some of the riders, were the ones they had met at Old Tony's Funeral. There was a couple of younger guys riding with them, not much older than themselves. One of them turned out to be Mr. Johnston's son Bill, a big, tall, lanky guy with an unruly mop of red hair, he had an easy smile and Calamity took a shine to him right off! The other younger guy was his pal Reggie, they all were just hanging around checking out some of the project bikes that the crew had on the go.

By now Mr. Johnston, or Art, as he now, insisted he be called by them. As he put it to them one day; my Mother, bless her soul, called me Arty, some of my customers, may call me Mr. Johnstone, some people, who know me better, call me Arthur, my friends call me Art. You can call me Art. unless you don't consider me a friend, and then you can all go fuck yourselves!

Until that moment, Calamity, had trouble imagining him and Old Tony as friends or partners as they always seemed to be so different, but there was one of the links that bound them! They both, apparently, shared that same caustic mannerism and dry sense of humour and when combined with mutual respect, and love for motorcycles and each other and that was their bond. He had pulled up the old Chevy panel truck up beside the concrete pad and the three other trucks had parked in a row beside it as per Art's instructions.

He called them over, opened the back doors of the panel truck, to reveal an absolute treasure trove of parts, some old, some new and still in boxes. All of Old Tony's tool boxes, chests and cabinets were crammed in there as well. They moved on to the next truck, a much larger, around five or possibly ten ton International. It, also, was old, and kind of beat up. It was a stake and rack unit, with a tarp covering the tops of the high wooden racks that enclosed the back. Art untied the ropes holding the back of the tarp, while his Son Bill, climbed up and pushed the tarp back so that they could access the heavy wooden back racks and he then wiggled and wrestled the back rack from its moorings and swung it open.

Inside, were a half a dozen motorcycles that had been at the shop, including Old Tony's "Dirty Rat.". Some were complete, while others were in various stages of repair, assembly, or disassembly. There were frames, front ends, saddle bags, tool pouches, windshields, boxes and more miscellaneous parts, as well as a huge assortment of tires, exhausts and under a large tarp were four complete, Harley-Davidson motors, a knucklehead, a flathead and two panheads complete and in stands. There were also, many pieces of equipment. Drill presses, a large hydraulic press, a small metal lathe, welding tanks with torches, tire equipment, and a large air compressor. One of the motorcycles, a 1947 Knuckle head was eventually claimed by REB, and that motorcycle was his pride and joy and was with him for the rest of his life. With the help and tutelage, of those "Old Bikers" he tore it apart and completely rebuilt it! Painted it bright orange with Rattle cans, from the hardware store and several coats of clear lacquer also from rattle cans, outside when the wind died down enough that he wouldn't put a coat of orange paint on anything that was downwind. He put it back together and rode her and that is the way she is today!

The third truck, another panel truck, was opened to reveal boxes and crates full of various parts for a wide variety of motorcycles. Plus, several batteries, drums and cans of oil, and other fluids.

The forth truck was a large flatbed with a black tarp

covering its cargo that turned out, was lumber, shingles a keg or two of nails and other building materials.

They just stood there looking at all this stuff, with their mouths hanging open and not knowing what to make of it all.

A couple of new guys and some women rolled up in a couple of cars and started to unload some coolers and a few buckets of Kentucky Fried Chicken. There were soft drinks in one cooler and Beer in the other. And it was a bit of a free for all, for five or ten minutes as everybody grabbed what they wanted and found something to sit on. Then, when they had all got fairly well settled in, Art began explaining what this was all about.

He explained. "As you know, I shut down the Shop! After Tony passed on, as just it wasn't the same, and I didn't want to do it anymore, not on my own! He wanted you kids to have his half of the inventory and his half of the proceeds from the sale of the business and the store! He didn't have a wife or kids and no relatives, that he wanted to share anything with, or even acknowledge. They didn't even bother coming to his funeral, and wouldn't be interested in old motorcycle shit anyways. You were like his kids, he loved you all, and you brought him great pleasure, just being around. He loved your enthusiasm and your interest in motorcycles and the lifestyle. He loved coming out here and he figured you could use a little help."

"I started to sort through it all, separating my stuff from his and I just couldn't do it. It was never mine or his, it was ours! I just couldn't think of it any other way, so I talked it over with my boy Bill here, as he should be able to claim something. He didn't want to run the business with me, and especially not by himself, but did want an old panhead FLH that he had always admired. He has it and he's riding it today! He understood what I was saying about you kids and your relationship with Tony, and how I felt. He's seen you around school and such and knows a lot about you. He said that I should honour Tony's wishes and give you Tony's half! Since I can't separate the two halves, you guys get it all! We will work out the legalities and stuff later. I understand your leader and owner of this property is Robert Baker, I'll need to talk to him, as well as whomever else you want to be your legal representative. You can have full access to our Lawyer, on our tab, as well."

They didn't know what to say but just stared, at the stuff that they had just been given, then at Art, at each other, at all those wonderful bikers and were totally speechless. Calamity, however, was checking out Mr. Bill Johnston who now seemed to be noticing her as well.

"These first two trucks belonged to Tony and you kids can have them as well. The other two are mine and when they are empty I will pick them up or one of the guys will bring them back."

"The building materials are for your shop which some of these gentlemen will help you build. Tony had some plans made up for a proper shop and there is a small amount of cash, to cover expenses, like permits, and hooking the hydro back up, and so on. Also, he said while the pond was nice, lakefront would be better still, he knew that the lake was just a short distance from here and Tony had bought the parcels of land that separated this property from the lake, It used to be commercial Campgrounds and is zoned as such, with all the permits, so that might come into play in the future, when you merge them you will have lakefront property as he left them to you kids through Robby Baker as well."

Just then, REB and Tramp had rolled in and they were immediately set upon by the whole crew who all tried to tell them what was going on, all at once and they couldn't understand any of it. Other than it, seemed to be good news and they were all excited. Art then called him and Tramp over, they accepted a beer and some chicken and listened intently to what Art was explaining to them. However, it was hard for them to drink or eat with their mouths hanging open like that.

So, the crew of old bikers did as they said, and over the next while, helped them build an amazing shop and they now, even had electricity. That was the beginning of our property that they all enjoy today. Those "Old Bikers" just sort of adopted them and visa versa. Incidentally, those "Old Bikers" that they keep referring to, were only in their thirties and some in their forties at that time, but as kids who were only fifteen or sixteen at the time, they were old.

"Big Bill, who was around nineteen or twenty kept hanging around too, and he and Calamity were getting along very well, right up until he and Rose Marie Higgins, who is now better known as "Gypsy", met! Bill and Cal were talking one day when she walked up, and it was like Cal didn't exist anymore. He just stopped talking and stared at Rose Marie! That was OK, Calamity had tons of stuff to keep herself occupied, what with all these parts, she was going to be busy and she too had picked out the bike that she wanted to build!

Calamity too, had noticed that Rose seemed even more distant and troubled and wondered what was going on in her life and had asked but also, been shut out! She needed something or somebody in her life, and something was definitely happening between the two of them, and in an instant and definite spark had occurred! It was noticed by everyone there. But something was up with Rose Marie lately and she behaved much different than usual, very distant, and withdrawn. She seemed reluctant to start anything with this handsome young man who was obviously was attracted to her. She tried to reach out to her but she wouldn't talk even to her and they were close friends. She just couldn't understand what was going on with her.

REB graduated from High School and then worked odd jobs, but had developed an interest in motorcycles, which carried over well and he was good and had gained quite a reputation for not just being a great wrench but for designing and building Custom bikes as well. His artistic flare and creativity also played well into that vein and he became well known for custom paint too. So, the shop and the property were serving him well. If things got tight or he needed some extra cash he would drive a truck for a buddy who owned a fleet of trucks or do odd jobs. He also had picked up some silk screen printing equipment and with his artistic flare also proved to be useful and lucrative.

Then the motorcycle phase, had now proved itself to be more than a mere phase, but an entity. It became the main focus of young Robert Baker and his followers, and it looked like it had a firm hold on them and would determine what was to happen next!

By now, things had started to change, as many other kids were aging and seeking out other activities and interests, aside from sports, but many followed the lead of Robby Baker and his crew of misfits who were now being referred to collectively as "The Dozen". The property that Robby's parents had bought, that had sat vacant and unused for so long, had now become quite a gathering place for all these kids.

It took some time, but Robby, who, had a keen mind and vision, had a good sense of the direction he wanted to take things and eventually it became a reality.

Chief Marshall, was well aware, that Young Robby along with his followers, were taking a new path and kept a close eye on things, but really had no objections. He had known all of these "Kids" their whole lives and knew what they were made of!

He was aware too, that there were always those who liked to stir things up, or liked to play fast and loose, with the truth and other people's property, who were showing an interest in the Dozen. Robby and his crew proved themselves to be more than capable of handling any problems that arose. Those who caused trouble and did not fit, were promptly made to feel extremely unwelcome, sent packing and sometimes, were limping when they left. The Dozen didn't put up with any crap! The old Chief approved of the way things were handled.

CHAPTER THREE

DISCOVERING THEMSELVES

IT WAS a good fit with these older guys being here, with these kids, as they knew lots about everything, and especially about motorcycles. These men, many of whom had no families, or any, that they ever mentioned, were generally, the black sheep of their family's, misfits, and rounders, many, fresh out of the armed forces and thrust into manhood in perhaps, the worst possible fashion!

They, having to experience the horrifying realities of war, with nothing to prepare them for the horrors that they would witness and participate in! Worse still, these men, now, were thrust back into society with nothing to prepare them for the harsh reality of civilian life. They now, wanted to just get out there and see all they could see, and experience all that they could, before death came looking for them. They understood and respected the finality and the certainty of death. Most didn't fear it, but tried their best to avoid it for as long as they could.

This place, served as a base for them and they ranged out from here, many, leading Nomadic lifestyles! For some, it was a sanctuary, for others it became a home, the only home that they had known for a while, as many came back from the war, tired, tormented by things they had endured, experienced, seen and done and were emotionally, worn out!

They had no idea what PTSD was in those days! You just manned up and did what was expected of you as a soldier and a man. Some, found that wives and girlfriends, hadn't waited for them, as they had promised, and had moved on with their lives without them! They discovered, in none too kindly a fashion, that human emotions such as lust and loneliness, can often outweigh, loyalty and fidelity, when it came right down to it. Many sacrificed their young adult years, to this tragic event and they knew nothing other than military life and were now cast back into a society, that wasn't ready to deal with them, and they knew not what to do as civilians!

What they had seen, experienced and done in the name of their Country, during relatively a short period of time, would haunt some of them for the rest of their lives, and, while few, ever talked about their wartime experiences, we could tell that these things always weighed heavy on hearts and minds and they were confused and conflicted! The consequences of their participation in something and events that they neither caused or had any control over, had considerable weight, and not everyone carried that burden well! Some relied heavily on alcohol and other substances as an escape or a crutch.

This older crew, separately, in pairs, or in small groups, would span out from the property and travel all over Canada and the United States on their Motorcycles, for most of the year and come back with tales of the road, the people they met and things that they did and experienced, that had everyone of the young bloods, enthralled! They knew that they could never forget the horrors and inhumanity that they had seen, but hoped that if they could see and experience enough good that they could overwhelm the bad! These kids benefitted from the knowledge and experience that these men had to offer.

Many, of this rag tag bunch of individuals, started dragging in a few old travel trailers, that they picked up for cheap, and parked them here, by the pond, and then just stayed here most of the time. Some like Lenny, Stretch, Tiny, and Fancy Pants have long since moved into the Community now and live like Citizens, but keep in touch with the Club and attend most events and functions. Others like Big Frank, Lucky and Red had passed on within the past seven or eight years. Chico, one of the originals, who they met at Old Tony's funeral, died in a motorcycle accident the first year he was here! His leather jacket and his boots still hang on the Clubhouse wall.

Yeah, all these kids, had pretty much got bitten by the motorcycle bug, and soon, they all had motorcycles of some sort. They had a couple of old Harley flatheads, three Indians, two Triumphs, a BSA, a Norton, and Ariel square four a Matchless and a Ducati. That is just the original group. They were gathering quite a crowd of like-minded kids and soon started doing shit, like hill climbs and Moto-cross as there was some really great terrane on this property. One of the guys that hung out here's father, had a big old Grader and he came in and carved out a flat track, for a case or two of beer, and that was a blast. He also cleared the section of land down towards the Lake and it was gorgeous.

It seemed that there was always something going on out here, and everybody just started camping out much of the time. They had the pond that was spring fed so we had a place to swim and clean up after a hard day wrenching, now they had a lakefront to enjoy as well and a few old boats started to appear along with a makeshift dock. It was a good spot just to be, and to be together.

REB's folks were only too happy to see the property put to good use. And chipped in where and when they could. Sometimes they would donate some baked goods for their parties, but the absolute faith and trust they put in them as a group, and their undying support, is what really mattered and really solidified them. Not all of them had that kind of relationship with their parents and appreciated what they saw, and experienced and it gave them a true sense of self worth.

Now, the property started to fill up with stuff that they, and the people that hung out there would find a deal on, or scavenge from junk yards and they would drag it here, to store, or work on or with, and for use by anyone who needed to use it. It became Community property even before they fully understood what Community property was! It was right!

These kids, were smart and resourceful and learned to adapt and improvise, and could turn just about anything into a tool capable of performing any task that needed to be done, even if it only was only needed to do it once, it had served its purpose and often that is all they needed it for was once, it just had to be done. Jacks, assorted tools, Oxy/acetylene cutting and welding equipment, from here, there and everywhere had a way of finding a home here! They didn't have any neighbours, close by so, no one complained about the clutter or the noise from the work sessions or parties which often ran into the wee hours or days.

It had also, now become known as a great stop over for many Bikers and like-minded souls, as they made their way across the Country or across the Province and is wasn't unusual to have a visitor set up camp for anywhere from a day, a night, two or three days, two or three weeks or even two or three months. There were some very gifted craftspeople that stopped by here! Leather craftsmen, people making and selling trinkets' and jewelry, artists, tattoo artists, singers, song writers, or just rounders. They were all welcome here if they got along and didn't cause trouble.

The Cops knew about them of course, but, being that they were way they Hell and gone out in the Country, and they had enough stuff on their plates without worrying too much about them and mostly left them alone. That didn't mean that they escaped the attention of certain Cops, like Dwight Higgins and a new Cop on the job by the name of Dan O'Reilly, took every opportunity to give them grief. Dan O'Reilly was new and pretty much, too far down the ladder, to cause major problems, but it was clear he had a long-standing grudge and hatred for REB in particular, and by extension, anyone remotely connected to The Dozen.

Officer Dwight Higgins, on the other hand, really turned up the heat, as he claimed that his step Daughter, Rose Marie was being corrupted and abused by the low-lives, who frequented this place! He even conducted a full-scale raid, which ended very badly, in that he shot and killed REB's dog. It all got conveniently swept under the carpet, as these matters concerning Police, often do.

A few years later, Dwight Higgins was found murdered up at his cabin, and the body, the cabin and everything had been torched and went up in smoke.

That really brought the heat down on them. REB was strongly suspected, and spent a good deal of time in the company of The Swanton Harbour PD. Dwight Higgins' step daughter; Rose Marie, as well and other people whom were at the property were questioned relentlessly, until Old Tony's and Art Johnstone's Lawyer, caught wind of it, and stepped in and stepped up, challenging the Cops at every turn, standing up for their legal rights. The whole incident, was let to die away, in the unsolved case file, due to lack of evidence and no clear suspects.

Soon they were doing repairs on their own vehicles, which, as those kids, were now aging, working, earning money and getting their drivers licenses and they were now acquiring quite a variety of cars, trucks, motorcycles! Even an old School bus or two ended up here and they, along with a couple of old camper units that they dragged there and parked to be utilized as shelter from weather place to crash if whatever project they were working on lasted too late or if a party just got out of hand and a few too many beers were consumed or just storage sheds!

Yeah, they usually had a good supply of beer as well as soft drinks on hand, in some old coolers, until they scored a beer fridge or two. If it was there, and you were thirsty, you helped yourself. If there was none, you went without, or went out and got some more! They had a couple of barbecues and kept some frozen burgers and hot dogs in an old chest freezer that they picked up real cheap from a garage sale. Simple rules, simple times! Eventually, they also had discovered Marijuana, although at first, only a few indulged. These trailers and busses also made for great "Make out spots" as they also discovered hormone's, and why girls are designed differently than guys and approved!

There was always something to do at the property as someone was always having to fix something on some vehicle or other and would come here to do it. They had tools and space and they pooled their knowledge and their resources and got it done. They even laid out some forms out of old lumber and one of the hang around's, girl's uncles ran several cement trucks. If he had extra concrete left over from a job he would get his drivers to swing by and unload into the forms for them and smooth it out. They now had a great concrete pad to work on that made it easier to roll jacks, creepers and hydraulic lifts around!

The shop really helped, but much of the time it was occupied with projects already on the go. So, they would use that concrete pad. Calamity Jane, really shone when it came to mechanical stuff and she was always covered in grease, usually in baggy coveralls with shop rags hanging out of her pockets along with various hand tools, and she always wore a big black bandana tied around her head to keep that long luscious mane of hair in check. She was not self conscious or shy, and not adverse to stripping down to her bra and underwear when the sun got hot, or if it started to rain, as there was no shade or shelter from the elements over that pad and there definitely was no air conditioning.

Calamity, was, even back, in those early days, the most self assured, self confident, unpretentious person that most had ever met, male or female, bar none! Her walk was almost manly, her long legs took long confident strides and was a real presence when she entered a room. To these kids, she was as close to being a female version of John Wayne as you could get, You, almost expected her to speak like "The Duke".

To say, that there were lots of guys willing to work with her, but none daring, or stupid enough, to step over the line with her, was an understatement and she always had an audience as guys were always interested in getting some valuable mechanical pointers. She was a very competent wrench as well and she could and would work on anything with favourable results. Cars, motorcycles, trucks, tractors, lawn mowers, anything, nothing seemed to phase her. she was drop-dead gorgeous even covered in grease wearing those filthy coveralls, cleaned up she was ravishing! Everyone realised that, except Calamity.

One time, a large fully loaded tractor trailer unit, broke down just up the road, late one night and one of the guys; Andy, spotted it and stopped to see if he could help. The driver was pretty bummed out, and desperate for help as he was far from home base, but he also didn't have much money and didn't know who to call.

Andy, came back to the property and Calamity was still here finishing up a brake job for another friend. He told her about this stranded trucker and it was decided that she would go and see what she could do. There were a few guys and a girl or two still there as well. They started throwing tools, flashlights and a cooler full of iced beer and soft drinks in Andy's old pick-up truck, they all piled in as well, and headed back out to the highway where this truck and a very dejected driver sat on the side of the road.

This driver wasn't exactly overjoyed to see a pick-up truck loaded down with teenagers pull up like they were his saviors. He was even less impressed, to learn that this pretty, young girl was going to be working on his truck!

"Have you ever worked on a truck this size before." he asked.

"Nope! First time!" she replied, nonplussed as she tried to get past him to the truck.

"How do you know you can fix this?" he asked, getting more nervous all the time!

"I don't! I haven't even looked at it yet! How do you know I can't? You just figure I can't, because I'm young and a girl?" Suddenly, very angry she was up in his face! She shot back, not even trying to mask her emotions! "Do tits make you uncomfortable or me incompetent? She shouted and was now only several inches from his face! If, you've got a better plan, or someone that you have more confidence in, nearby, tell me now and I will go back to what I was fucking doing!" She was right up in his grill, her right-hand tightening menacingly around the long handle a long, heavy flashlight, as she had reached the end of her patience and her tolerance for bullshit had also reached its peak! "If you want, I will take a look and I will tell you if it's something I can fix, and then I will tell you, yes or no! If yes, I will go ahead and fix it, if no, I will fucking leave you to it, fuckface! You've been doing a stellar fucking job, up to this point! You can just carry on with that!" At one-point Andy had reached out and grabbed her shoulder trying to get her to back off a touch and he was almost nailed by that long heavy flashlight. He didn't try to intervene any further, if that driver insisted on pissing her off; it was on him!

The shocked driver, quickly backed out of her way, and he told her briefly what the truck was doing before it shut down on him. Someone handed him a cold can of beer, and Cal, Tramp and a couple of other guys went over to look at the truck.

A couple of the guys started running back and forth from the tractor trailer to the pick-up, relaying tools and such, as Cal requested. Tramp held the flashlight! The driver, wisely, was just sitting on a guard rail, out of the way looking very worried but not daring to even look in Cal's direction!

About a half hour later Calamity climbed up into the cab of that truck, they heard the sound of the motor turning over and the driver perked up. Seconds later, it roared to life, black smoke billowed from the twin stack exhaust in response to her foot on the throttle and then it settled in to a smooth idle!

"Holy shit!" The elated driver shouted! "Oh my God, you fixed it! Thank you so much! How much do I owe you?"

Cal just glared at him as she stepped down from the cab. "Andy here, said that you don't have much in the way of money, so just be on your way and enjoy the rest of your trip! Thanks, will do fine!" She stopped suddenly and turned to face him, looked him square in the eyes and added emphatically "Don't judge a book by it's fucking cover! It is insulting and demeaning!" She then turned back and stormed to the waiting pick-up truck which was all loaded up and ready to go, hopped in the back with her friends and they left the driver standing there, embarrassed but appreciative and most importantly, mobile once again! Old Tony would have been proud!

CHAPTER FOUR
FINDING THEIR WAY

THE BAKERS DOZEN wasn't established as a Motorcycle Club. It was, just what it started to be, a baseball team. But the people who made it happen, just stayed together and formed a bond and a trust, and that was the glue that held them together through thick and thin, through good times and bad times and everything in between. As they aged, their attention and focus turned eventually from baseball to motorcycles and the biker lifestyle appealed to them so they adopted it. Others were drawn to it and them as well, and they were accepted without prejudice, until when and if, they were found to be unworthy and they were summarily ejected. It just evolved naturally over time.

It soon attracted more, like minded and spirited souls, into the fold. There was no recruitment, no effort to build their numbers. People were just simply drawn to them for what and who they were and what was formed was more than a club, it was family and it then developed into a small but distinct community.

Those who came to them, were often, the Black Sheep of their natural families. Often, runaways, escaping abuse at home and found sanctuary and peace within this community that they could not find elsewhere. Some, suffered from substance abuse and while their parents may have wanted to help, they were ill equipped and totally in the dark as to what the warning signs and effects of drugs were and unable to deal with them. Many who came to the Club, previously had been down the same road themselves, and they knew how to deal with the problems and could recognize signs when their charges slid backwards, and could stop it before it spiralled out of control. They knew how to spot lies and behavior, that only someone who had behaved that way or told those same lies and excuses would recognize. Like they say; you can't kid a kidder or con a con, they were wise to the it all! They could help and often did. Many people credit the support they got from the Club with coping and cleaning up their dependence on alcohol and drugs!

The Bakers Dozen was the Baseball Club who occupied the property, courtesy of Robert Edward Baker who owned it all. What formed around them, was a group that they referred to collectively as the Bakers Dozen Crew or simply the Dozen. Like we are going to see the Dozen or the Dozen's property. It was informal and unofficial, there was no membership beyond those who were part of the baseball club. But it was most definitely, an entity. There was no official patch or colours even for members, however, some had taken to wearing a crude little green Shamrock patch with a

13 in the middle somewhere on their garb as a show of respect and support for their hosts and to display their commitment. Some even started getting that design tattooed on themselves, because it was cool to be cool and the Dozen were cool.

There were a couple of nice young girls, who were also incredible artists and tattoo artist as well. They had showed up one day, and decided to stay on. One of them; Little Lisa, a petite little brunette with big brown eyes and a smile that could light up the darkest room, changed up, that little patch design into a Shamrock, with a red heart and the 13 in the centre of that and made it into a tattoo. Those in the Club saw the design and had no issues with it. In fact, several like Gypsy and Calamity Jane, and even REB had that design tattooed on themselves as well. That was as close to Support gear that existed from that era.

Lisa and Dominique were their names and they were long-time friends from the Montreal area, who were heading for Vancouver, but heard about this place along the way, and decided to check it out. They set up a crude little Tattoo studio in one of the campers, using an old generator, to provide electricity. Lisa hooked up with one of the hang-arounds, named Jingles, and Dominique, a diminutive blonde of four foot five inches in height with a natural pair of breasts, that had to have been intentioned for someone twice her height, as her bust measurement, was almost equal to her height. She, apparently swung from the other side of the plate, and took a shine to one of the ladies who was also just passing through and then also, stuck around until after the disappearance.

One day, people noticed that the girls were not there. All their stuff, clothes, tattoo equipment, photographs, memento's, and other personal stuff was there, but they weren't. Clients showed up for their appointments for tattoos, and the girls were a no show. People began to worry, as that, was very unlike them. Jingle's and his old pick-up truck were also missing, but his old Triumph, was still parked beside the girls trailer and it was established that he and the two girls had left for town in his old pickup truck the night before to pick up some beer and stuff, and not returned.

They were about to go out and look for them, when they saw several Police Cruisers coming down the driveway and knew something bad, had happened.

The Police had found Jingle's body, he had been beaten to death, and left, along with his pick-up truck, in a ditch, out on one of the back roads, north of Town. But there were no girls anywhere to be seen. They said they were searching, but had turned up nothing. They said, that if we needed more information we could check with the head of the investigation; Officer Dwight Higgins. They were never seen or heard from again. Dominique's little friend searched fruitlessly for them as well and moved on. Jingles death was written off as probably the results of a drug deal gone bad.

There were a couple more girls who mysteriously disappeared from the property and elsewhere in the Community without a trace, but head of investigations, now, Sargent, Dwight Higgins, put it down to; as he so delicately put it; "They had probably just wandered off with whatever swinging dick came along, with some drugs, and they were probably in Yorkville Village or Rochdale, with the rest of the degenerates!"

None of them ever surfaced again. Neither these cases, or others, similar in nature, were ever solved and quickly found their way to the dead case files as none of these women were from affluent families. Some were indigenous women, others were just girls from the Community, some were known to work the sex trade, while some others were just nice young girls, but none of those disappearances, got much attention from either the mainstream media, or the Police and the general public seemed to be largely indifferent. The only ones who noticed them missing were family and friends and those who loved them. They had many questions and concerns but received no answers!

The Club and the property became a melting pot, as more and more people started coming here and all were welcome, until they proved themselves unworthy of being there, and were ejected. This property was not going to be a flopping ground for the dregs of Society. You had to fit.

The crew, just pooled their skills and talents, and worked together to get things done, not just for themselves and their Community but for the outside community as a whole as well.

There are all kinds of things that motivate Bikers. Fun is one of things that draw them together. Why go to someplace that isn't fun. It is easier to have fun with people of similar likes and interest than someplace with people who don't. Clubhouses can pretty much guarantee that you will meet others like yourself and you can sit in a spot that has atmosphere that you feel comfortable in! You can shoot a game or two of pool, play some darts, or cards or just sit and enjoy a few pours with some friends. There are usually good tunes playing and you can kick back and relax without some punk getting up in your grill because he thinks he is a tough guy and can beat on a biker.

It is a place where like minded folks hang out. But many of these Clubs do lots of stuff out in the Community as well. If they see a need and a cause they are usually the first ones who try to help, for no other reason than just to help! Someone, has a fire or an accident or gets seriously ill, they are willing to help and have access to a network of people who can and will help in whatever way they can. Anyhow, there are lots of ways to be charitable and to truly benefit those who slip through the cracks in society, that don't make the local news!

Calvin and Chuck Taylor, both original members of the Bakers Dozen BC, had gone on to start a small, but very successful, Motorcycle shop, on the east side of town. They came around the Clubhouse one night and started telling a story about this old guy who did odd jobs for them. The old guy, was a pensioner whose wife had died just recently. He would show up each day like clockwork, to do odd jobs, cleaning, stocking shelves, do a few deliveries or pick ups, or just sweep up, or clean windows and worked for cash. They really didn't need him much of the time, and it was an added expense that they really couldn't afford, but gave him work, because he needed the money. He hadn't showed up for a couple of days, and they got worried, but he had no telephone so they just stopped in at his house to check on him one day. It was storming out.

When the old guy answered the door, they were immediately taken aback by the musty smell that came from the house. They could hear running water, looked past him and saw buckets, pails, pots and pans scattered around the floor in an unwinnable effort to collect the rain that was pouring in through the many holes in the roof. The gyprock that once, was the ceiling was piled up against the one wall in a soggy mouldy heap.

They immediately took the old guy, along with his dog, from his home, drove him to a local motel and put him up in a room.

They dropped by the CH, as they knew that some of the guys who hung out there were into construction and other trades, and figured they would ask if anyone could help them out as they'd rather give the work to folks they knew. The urgency was understood and phone calls were made immediately, and soon a crew was assembled to go and investigate. Calvin and Chuck told them to send all the bills for materials and labour to them and they would look after payment.

The house was inspected and the work was then divided between several individual crews all with particular skills and they were on it like a fat kid on a pork chop! In some cases, they pulled workers off paying jobs, to help out, because they needed to get something done on this house that fit that particular skill-set. Within a day, a large dumpster had been brought in, the house was completely gutted and the old roof removed and replaced with a new one. The inside was remodelled, refinished and refurbished, including the floor, plumbing and the electrical service and the old panel, was torn out as well, and replaced with new everything from top to bottom it exceeded normal building codes as it had to now meet their, more demanding, standards and codes! Two and a half weeks later Calvin and Chuck got a call, and were asked to bring the old guy and his dog home again. All involved were there, waiting, when they drove up. The old man looked troubled, as they escorted him to the front door. He just about fell over as he walked through the threshold.

The place shone like a new penny! Everything was new, furniture, appliances fixtures, everything, even the dog, got a nice new bed and new toys. They even went so far as to replace clothing and linen that was severely water damaged. Pictures and artwork had been restored as well. The old man burst into tears and it must have been contagious as there was nary a dry eye in the place, tough old bikers crying, what a sight. He was desperately trying to thank each and everyone of them and was trying to hug them all and shake their hands!

Calvin and Chuck, were almost as surprised as the old man, as they had received no updates on the job, and figured that these guys had things well in hand, and if they had come to a problem, that they couldn't handle, they would have called. They were blown away by the level and quality of workmanship, and the amount of work that had been done. All they were hoping for was to give the old guy a roof that didn't leak.

They shook everybody's hands and thanked them all. They asked for bills and invoices so that they could pay them. They got the same answer from each of the contractors; "Oh yeah! We will write something up and get it to you!" Those invoices and bills never came. While it was Charitable, nobody thought of it as Charity and preferred to chalk it up to doing what was right and enjoying the way it makes you feel when you can pay it forward and truly benefit someone who needs a hand up. Anyhow, there are lots of ways to be charitable and to truly benefit those who slip through the cracks in society, this was just one.

That story never made it to the local newspaper, it was never on the local television news, there was no photo-op and most of the general public were never aware of it! It wasn't done for notoriety or publicity that would change the image of Bikers. It was done because it needed to be done! That is humanitarianism and Brotherhood! That is what the Club was about! It was experiencing, recognising and prac-tising Brotherhood!

This was just one of the things that this Club, and other Clubs, did and do, without fanfare, or publicity. Bikers are happy with the image they have as motorcycle enthusiasts, most have no criminal records, and strive to live up to what a real Biker really represents, to other real Bikers. Not what the media or the police or the movies and TV shows claim they are, but what they know they are! They like, and are proud of who and what they are, and they know who their true friends are. They work real jobs, earn a living to pay their bills and raise their kids! They are no different than any other Citizen of this Country, pay taxes, vote and the whole nine yards! They just like motorcycles and hang out with others who are compatible!

For the most part, the Clubhouse, was just a gathering place for kindred spirits. You could, pretty well always, find some one there, as someone was either working on his or her car, truck or motorcycle and if you ran into a challenge or something that you didn't know how to fix, there was usually someone else there who did and most any job became a community project if required.

They again, pooled their time, resources, skills and their talents, and dismantled much of the old farmhouse, but used original framework to reconstruct it and remodel it, into what served them quite well as a Clubhouse. Giving them a spot for a pool table, dartboards and of course a large bar. The kitchen was also rebuilt to be able to handle large gatherings. There were four, small, bedrooms, upstairs, along with a large, full, shared, bathroom. A couple of rooms were presently, occupied by a couple of the members, who had taken up temporary residence due to unforeseen changes in their lives, or in the case of Calvin, refuge from his wife, who was on the warpath, after finding a lady's lace panties in the back seat of his car.

It was far from being a mansion, but it was functional and comfortable, as was, the once again, expanded shop, which was busy most everyday and night.

There was always beer and other beverages readily available. The pond was there and the lake so you could swim and cool off in the summer. In the winter, the pond would freeze, and many an impromptu hockey game broke out, and they even had teams formed from members of the outside community who would come to play against the Dozen's team. It was a shinny League but it was fun! So, the place offered a real retreat from the mundane or the structured lifestyle that often, existed beyond those property boundaries.

The Club, also provided employment opportunities, as many of those who came here also owned, ran, or worked for companies who were constantly looking for workers. The Club had a wealth of skilled trades-people or those willing to learn, and work hard at its disposal. That is the type, that the Club attracted, those with strong ethics and convictions. Most everybody, that came around here, were compatible and if they weren't this place served as a place where they separated the wheat from the chafe, and for some, this was a far as they ever got and were never welcomed back.

You didn't just show up and say here is my money, where do I sign and where is my patch? Can I make up my own Nickname now? It wasn't about a patch, it was about fitting in with the others in the family. Family was the operative word.

If you were on board, you were on board for everything and anything. Be it a burst pipe at the Clubhouse and wading in a pool of raw sewage, trying to fix something that you'd never worked on or with before or whatever. You adapted and did what you could and what needed to be done to the best of your ability, while looking for someone who did know what they were doing. There was a wealth of knowledge and experience here and it never took that long to find the right person for the job. I say person, because many of the women who hung out here were, capable of handling most any situation as well. Members cut the grass, clean the place up and look after all the other chores that go with having a house.

The Club also offered members, proper legal assistance as they had the Club Lawyer on retainer and could be reached for consultation, 24/7 and could offer reliable advice and assistance for a member or by referral by a member but not on the Club's bill. Good, knowledgeable, solid recommendations and advice were essential before proceeding with anything.

Then there is the issue of death. In many cases, there were some guys and gals that hung out at the property, who were single, with no family who would claim them or didn't want anything to do with them, in life or in death. The Club, and the people there, were as close to Family that many of them had and the Club and that adopted family, did not let hem die alone. They often, arranged a stay in a hospice which was often in the home of a member or a friend. Someone, was with them night and day until they passed.

If you were regarded as a true Brother or Sister, you were that, until the life left your body! You were given a proper send off and paid proper tribute. Sometimes, the Club, did not have enough in its coffers to cover the tab for the funeral. Members and hang arounds often, pooled their resources and dug deep into their personal funds to try and meet the obligations. More than once, they had to get an emergency meeting together to get enough co-signers on a loan, to pay for a funeral or they would hold a fundraising event and use the proceeds for that cause! So much for all the massive, illegal wealth that was allegedly, abundant with Bikers.

The Clubhouse, was a place where you could feel comfortable and be amongst your own kind with little fear of having to fight your way out of there! Which did happen on occasion, in locations, outside their comfort zones, as being different and dressing different, and having long hair and beards didn't always sit well with some in the community and they made it clear that "Bikers" were not appreciated or wanted in their midst!

This was a time when Bikers were not always well received in small town bars, or big city bars either for that matter, many Legions didn't allow them in their buildings at all, while wearing biker attire, even though many of them were Veterans. If you were wearing a Club Support or even just a Harley shirt they often made you turn it inside out in order to get in. This remains a sore point with many old bikers to this day, now that many, Legions who found their membership dwindling, looked for other methods of raising funds to keep their doors open. They started to hold Show and Shines, that raised thousands of dollars in one day and they condoned the bikers for that day. Then, the next day, they were once again banned and branded as undesirables.

CHAPTER FIVE

ADVENTURES SOMETIMES JUST HAPPEN!

SOMETIMES BIKERS just had to stand their ground. One incident, comes to mind, where, some time ago, back in the late 60's, to the early to mid 70's. Some members and a hang-around or two, on their way back from a field meet, somewhere in Eastern Ontario, stopped in this little Hotel, in a small town, for a bite to eat and a cold beer or two. It was a farming Community and this was a hot Sunday afternoon, and the place was pretty busy with the members of the local, Rubber Boot Brigade!

They all went in, took a customary seat, with their backs to a wall and ordered their beer and whatever. All seemed fairly copacetic, although, there were some particularly, nasty looks and comments being cast in their direction from every corner of the room. You could feel the tension level rise, and the muttering got louder and the looks of disgust, turned to angry stares and many of the men were now puffing out their chests and strutting by the bikers, looking as mean as they could muster. The guys all figured they should drink their beers and eat their food as quickly as possible and hit the road, as the hospitality factor, and ambiance now, left a lot to be desired.

Then, Tramp got up and wandered into the washroom, and he was followed in by a half a dozen burly men in coveralls and red necks.

There was a sudden commotion coming from the washroom, and when the bikers all jumped up to investigate. They were blocked by a dozen or so of the locals who now looked totally unfriendly, and formed a formidable wall, to someone who was not a biker!

The crew were outnumbered at least, three to one, not including the half dozen that were in the washroom with Tramp, but they were not intimidated! Just then, the washroom door was knocked off its hinges and two farmers came through it, backwards, the hard way, followed by Tramp, who had two others, firmly in the grasp of the meat hooks he called hands. The other two, could be seen, sprawled on the floor just inside the door, seemingly, out of commission.

These farmers were not fairing so well, but they had numbers in their favour and were a determined lot, who weren't about to let these filthy Bikers feel welcome in their Town.

Being Bikers, who don't really know how to retreat (They had heard the word, but were not entirely familiar with the concept.) and when faced with trouble, there is only one direction, that they do fully comprehend, forward, but, forward, meant scrapping with all these local farmers. That was fine with them, and they attacked, kicking and punching anything in coveralls and rubber boots! It wasn't hard to find one, as they were so drastically outnumbered.

Since the odds, were so unproportionate, some of the bikers started to improvise and used what was at hand to compensate! A chair, a table leg once it was removed from the table, and converted for use as a club was good, or an even an empty beer tray would do, in a pinch. They were good at improvising! One, had a belt, fashioned from a chromed, Harley primary chain, which had an enormous, very heavy, Harley-Davidson buckle and he was swinging it with authority. When it made contact you could hear the impact clear across the room, and they knew, whomever was the recipient, would be feeling the effects for a long time.

Soon, it got sort of quiet, as everybody was either worn out from fighting or out of commission. Only a few, were still locked in combat. Others from each side took a short pause, looked around assessing damage and while some of the Bikers were bruised and some bleeding and nursing bruised fists, twisted knees and ankles, they were all still standing! Some, then took advantage of the lull, and stepped back to finish what beer remained in their glasses and bottles that hadn't been spilled on the floor, while the locals tended to their injured. They had not faired anywhere near as well, as intended. The Cops had been called but the nearest one was about an hour a way, investigating a few cows that had broken through a fence and had wandered out onto the highway and since radio communications, weren't then, what they are now, the Cop hadn't even heard about the melee yet. It was clear however, that this battle was far from over!

The farmers still had a distinct advantage, in that, this was their town, and, for them, reinforcements were only a phone call away. They made the call, and before the bikers could make their way out, the new recruits came plodding in, some, with fresh cow shit still on their rubber boots. They must have been thirsting for a fight more than a beer because they wasted no time in getting down to it!

Many, of the first wave of the agricultural community participants, had, had enough fighting and preferred to watch this round. So, the odds while still in favour of the RBB, didn't change much for the bikers, but, they once again, beat the opposition back handily, as they were a game and scrappy bunch.

There was another brief pause in the action, and a couple of the bikers ordered another round or two, of beer, which was reluctantly given to them by a frightened bartender, who didn't want these bikers to turn on him. The fight was far from over, although, rather than a full pitched battle, there were several skirmishes that broke out at various places at various times. A trip to the washroom by a Biker was bound to spur another ambush and bikers started going to the john in pairs or groups of three.

This battle went on like that, for what seemed like three or four hours, before the Bikers finally got up, paid their tab, fought their way out the door, to their motorcycles, which were surprisingly, untouched, and rode off out of Town just as a lone Police Cruiser, manned by a single Cop, who, having wrapped up his wrangling duties, roared into Town with his lights and sirens going and came to a screeching halt in front of the Hotel! The crew of bikers, did get jacked over, but that lone Cop, who, having no reinforcements on their way, being out in the country, with a dozen or so, very pissed off bikers, who, still looked like they could have some fight left in them, wisely, let discretion be the better part of valour, and sent them on their way with, a stern warning!

These were wild times, and perhaps, the best of times. Times, that will never come again. They were different times, and the people were different as well. There was a code, that governed behavior of Bikers, and it was respected, right up until it wasn't, by some at least. The solid guys and gals were getting fewer, attitudes changed, and so did loyalty and respect. Beefs, were generally settled with fists, and boots, and seldom went beyond that, until that too changed. Those were the days! The young bloods of today, know not what they missed, and have a hard time believing that those days and those times ever existed!

Drugs were not a huge concern back in the early days and when they did arrive on the scene, Clubs tried their best to control and regulate their use by their members. While Marijuana and hash were the party favours of choice, other things like crystal meth, LSD and other drugs started to become more prevalent and controlling them became a real problem. Many Clubs, had rules put right in their charter to deal with things that needed to be dealt with, and things were spelled out clearly and voted on! So, you knew the regulations and you knew the consequences. Needles and hard drugs were strictly prohibited and members would be 86'd from the Club for their use. Some found it an easier way to earn money and got involved but it was never dealt through the Clubs themselves, but rather individual initiatives! The Police however, were always trying to make a connection to the Clubs themselves and further their quest to have the Clubs deemed to be Criminal Organizations.

There were so many different and colourful characters that you could meet at the Clubhouse, at any time and it could be very entertaining, to say the least. Someone, one time, showed up with some perfectly legal explosives called Tannerite which is used for exploding targets for firearms and they decided to try it out. They had a fair amount and decided to mix the whole thing!

"What's that?" You ask.

"Did anyone have any experience with this substance or did anyone read all the instructions?" What would be the fun or adventure in that? That, would likely be the astonished, response to that foolish question if anyone had thought to ask it! As the saying goes; "You can't be old and wise, without first, being young and foolish!" There was an abundance of young and foolish and a distinct lack of old and wise, that afternoon and for many afternoons to follow.

They had one old car laying around the property at the time, that was on its last legs, and was destined for the junk yard anyhow, so they drove it out into a field as far as it would go on its own steam, but, being somewhat, safety conscious, they figured that it should be a bit further out than that, and hooked a chain to it, towed it with a pick-up truck, further but not too far as none of them were that good as marksmen, and some beer had been consumed.

They got it set up, and then took turns trying to hit the target, using the one and only gun that was on the property.

It was an old 303, picked up at the Army Surplus store and they used it for shooting groundhogs.

Finally, one of them hit a bullseye, which was good, because they were almost out of bullets, and some with short attention spans were already, quickly losing interest! However, no one was prepared for the ensuing explosion, or the shock wave and the ton of shrapnel that flew back at them. Nobody had bothered to take cover, as they didn't know what to expect. They were just lucky that no one got hit by any of it. That was their first experience with Tanner-ite. It would not be their last, although a few were assigned to research it a bit further and they were far more selective as to how much should be mixed at a time, and where they would play with it! Suffice to say, A lot of junk got blowed up really good!

There were two Brothers, who showed up there on a fairly regular basis, Bob and Don, were their names! They were a couple of real nice guys, who rode, and also ran a small trucking outfit. Whenever they showed up, the one Brother, Don, the older of the two, was always injured, he either had a cast or two or had multiple bandages on some part or parts of his anatomy. There was always a story that went with the injuries of course. The telling of these tales, was always entertaining and it had everybody clinging to each and every word! Even before a tale was finished, people would be looking at them and then at each other in total wonderment, and disbelief and were undecided as to if these two guys were for real or not. Seeing how it was only Don who was getting injured they had to question his powers of reasoning or did he just do whatever his younger Brother suggested.

For example, the two brothers were working with their father, taking down fifty feet of television tower, complete with antenna and rotor from the side of their house, which was being sold to a neighbour. It was Bob's job to climb the ladder, beside the tower, unfasten it and then slowly, lower it down by a length of rope to Don, who was on the ground and would then grab it when it was lowered within reach by Bob and he would then just walk it back and then lay it gently on a tall, sturdy, upright piece that they had fashioned, so as to not damage the tower, the antenna, or the rotor. Although they were quite thorough in preparing a safe place for the tower to rest once it was brought down, even down to the point of placement and height of the upright piece, which would keep the antenna and rotor from actually touching the ground. They had even cleared the pathway of branches and other such things that would impede the towers safe decent.

They had however, made a miscalculation or two in the planning of the operation (henceforth referred to a "The Plan") itself. They had greatly underestimated the weight of the tower and its attachments and overestimated the actual physical strength of the two brothers especially Bob who was the man on top with the rope. The amount of strength that he would require to perform his part of the plan, which would have an effect on how his ability to effectively slow the assent of the tower and attachments.

The unfastening of brackets went well, but that is where (the plan") started to fall apart! The weight of the tower on the rope, proved to be far, far, too much for Bob to handle and the rope quickly, and effortlessly, slid through his gloved hands with little or no resistance! The tower, however, continued unbridled, on its travel downward and was now in total freefall.

This, left the ever valiant, and vigilant Don, who had calculated the trajectory perfectly, and stayed true to his task and tried his damndest to bring "the plan" to a safe and successful conclusion and salvage "The Plan" but the weight of the tower, was just far too much, as was the speed at which it was falling, and once again, it was proven, beyond a doubt, that Don was a mere mortal, not superman and no amount of determination was going to save "the plan".

The Father, who was the supervisor for this operation and mastermind and orchestrator in enacting "The Plan", was in total shock and dismay and quickly ran over to see what damage was done. He ran right past, where poor Don lay under the tower and checked out the antenna and rotor. He then happily announced; "It's OK I think the rotor and antenna are fine!" Bobby was too busy trying to get his brother out from under that aluminum tower to care about the fucking tower or anything connected to it! Donny was trying desperately to get his wind back. It was soft ground which provided some cushioning and Don had also beefed up a bit lately, so injuries were held to a minimum. He only sprained a wrist or two and had a few scrapes, bruises and contusions and his ribs were only sore for about six weeks or so.

It seemed that every time they came by, Don had some new injury and some outlandish tale about how it happened.

If they weren't well known, to the crew here, some would say they were just making it all up. Now, as soon as anyone saw them arrive, everybody was alerted and immediately ran to get fresh beer, because they didn't want to miss, seeing what injury had occurred this time, what kind of brace, cast, bandage or appliance Don would be sporting, and on what part of his anatomy, or to miss any part of the stories. Neither Brother, ever paid for a beer, ever, it was a small price to pay for the entertainment!

There was the tale of Don trying to get a boat motor started and somehow it blew up in his face! It didn't just go poof and create some smoke and maybe a little noise, it didn't just make a lot of noise, and catch on fire and create a lot of smoke! That, might be what may happen to anyone else on the planet, but wouldn't be anywhere near good enough for our man Donny! It was a full-blown explosion! Fireballs, shooting 50 feet in the air, lots and lots of smoke and a large piece motor that nearly, took his head off on its way out into the lake.

Its recovery, was assisted by the oil slick left where it had splashed down a considerable distance away. The explosion could be heard for miles and shook nearby buildings. The fireball singed Don's hair, beard and eyebrows as well as his arms and chest hair. Plus, he was covered from head to toe in soot and oil spatter. He couldn't hear properly for three weeks after the incident! Just, another day at the Beach for the guys we lovingly called the disaster Brothers!

Then they got into telling the story of when they were fixing the roof on and old barn which had a real steep pitch to it. Being safety conscious, Don tied one end of a very long length of rope to the trailer hitch on the truck and the other he fastened around his waist, he was then confident that he would be well anchored and he wouldn't be getting hurt today! No sir! Everything was fine as wine, right as rain and a bunch of other things you sometimes tell yourself, just before shit happens! Shit happening, was a regular occurrence with these two, as they often let their guard down, and didn't allow any margin, for error.

"This Plan." was, that once he was on the roof he could work on the far side and he would let out just enough rope from the coil attached to his waist, to gain access to the parts of the roof that needed tending to with lots of stability and without worry of falling. Now, this, was "A Plan!"

Funny though, when he reached that point in the story, everybody listening, instantly identified definite flaws in that particular "plan", and were already thinking; Naw! Don't do that!" There was an audible groan from the audience, and many, were already standing there, mouths agape, and shaking their heads in disbelief.

Everything was fine and the job was going well and accordance with "The Plan", then he heard Bobby, who hadn't been brought up to speed on his Brothers "Plan", holler up, that he was going into town and asked if Don needed anything. "Maybe just a pack of smokes and grab me a burger and a Pepsi!" he replied.

Then, he heard the sound of his truck starting, and he remembered that they had both come in one vehicle. Don, now realized what was about to happen, and he opened his mouth to call down, just as the truck motor, revved up, and he felt the rope quickly tighten around his waist.

That was the last thing he remembered, until he woke up in the Hospital two days later. Bobby was sitting there, waiting anxiously, for his Brother to regain consciousness.

The first words out of Don's mouth were; "Did you get me my smokes, and no mustard on the burger!"

People often asked Don, if he ever thought that he should stop working with Bobby! "Why would I do that? He's my Brother!" He would respond. Incidentally the Brothers were never asked to participate in the many Club workdays, or other work projects. They were never invited to the Tannerite parties either!

The stories and the people were largely, why people went there and why they kept coming back. It was fun! People were genuinely happy to see you arrive and if you'd had too much to drink, they always got you home safely along with your vehicle. Stories, were an inexhaustible commodity at the Clubhouse and the more people who came to gather, the more stories there were to share.

The Club property was a safe haven where people could be around kindred spirits.

There were a lot of great souls who made this place a sanctuary, and looked at the people here as family, and some strong bonds and lasting friendships were created and cherished. They shared in happy times and the satisfaction and happiness derived from joyous occasions and events. They watched families grow up, in the warmth of this Community, and the family that grew from humble beginnings.

They watched the children, of Brothers and Sisters, grow to adulthood, with many of them, clinging to the Club and its traditions as well. They in turn, had kids and the circle was often left unbroken for several generations or more.

They shared in happy times like Christmas when the Club always had a Children's Christmas party, complete with a Santa Claus and presents. Easter, saw egg hunts! There were fishing derbies, in the stocked pond, Halloween parties, and graduation parties, all hosted here on this amazing piece of land. There were also several weddings held here as well. Adult versions of those special parties occurred there as well, and money was raised for the designated charity or charities of their choice.

The property and the Club, also hosted many funerals, as they suffered the loss of many friends and family, over the years. Everybody was emotionally involved and often, loved other members, parents and family members, like they were their own. They saw their share of tragedy, felt much sorrow, pain, and heartbreak due to human frailty and happenstance as the years rolled on by!

They paid proper respect and tribute to those departed souls and had a memorial wall erected on which each fallen member's name was inscribed. They held a funeral run, each year where, they would ride to where each fallen Brother or Sister was buried. Those cremated, would have their ashes, if the Club had possession of them, taken along, strapped to a motorcycle, in some fashion, and in the end, were given traditional tribute before the day was done. The urns containing those ashes, were then returned to a place of honour in the Clubhouse.

One Member who had requested that his ashes be loaded into a shotgun shell then fired out over the pond that had brought him so much joy and peace in his younger years, and comfort, as well, as that same peace, when he knew his time on earth was winding down, the Club honored his request and each year another shell is loaded with some more of his ashes and the ritual is repeated. "Gone but not forgotten!" were not just words that were spoken at this place!

One old friend, who had been a fixture at Club events for years, and would appear regularly at Show and Shines and other such gatherings riding his 2003 Kawasaki Drifter, that was fashioned after a 1937 Indian. He fell in love with that bike from a picture and his, was the last one ever produced, and he had to have it shipped from B.C.! It did not disappoint and it was everything he ever wanted in a motorcycle and more. He rode it everywhere and collected a sizable collection of trophies and awards at Bike Shows and Show and Shines, far and wide. It was his solace in his later years, which he needed desperately, when life kicked him in the teeth several times in quick succession.

First, cancer, took his Son, then his wife, then he was diagnosed with it, and just when he was at his lowest and looking at facing a hard war alone, he met a younger lady at a Club event, who was a rider and a kindred spirit and they fell in love, married and for six years were incredibly happy. She helped him every step of the way, in his battle with the disease and they actually won several rounds and he was in remission.

Then death came calling once again, and this time, took this fine old gentleman, not from Cancer, but by means of a deadly virus, that was sweeping the Globe, claiming millions of lives. But this kind-hearted soul who was now a widow, who, saw this friend through to the end, and was a comfort to him until the death claimed him, saw to it that he didn't die alone!

Now the Club and friends, that she had made there, helped her through her pain, and dealing with her loss. They learned that true love, can be elusive and some never find it, if you are lucky enough to find it, you cherish it, and nurture it, because love, like life, can be fleeting, and you have to enjoy it while you can.

There were two men who had first met here on this property, during a Club Poker run. They hit it off instantly, and were almost inseparable, for thirty years, they worked to together, and for the last twenty years of their lives and if one of them quit or got fired, they would both leave and wouldn't take another job, if they wouldn't hire both of them, together.

They even dated and ended up marrying twin sisters. They bought houses beside each other as well. Eventually, they built and opened a small motorcycle shop on a lot across the street from where they lived. They did good work and treated their customers with respect and charged fair prices for what they did! They in turn were treated with respect.

The two Brothers and their wives, were out for a ride one evening, when some drunk crossed the centre line with his car, and hit the foursome head on! All but one Brother were killed and while he survived physically, he was dead inside. He didn't ride his beloved Matchless motorcycle any more, although, he was able to rebuild it, it lost its lustre, and held no "magic" for him anymore. He sold the shop and the houses, along with all his tools and other possessions and the night before he was to vacate the house, he went out to the garage where his last possession, his Matchless motorcycle, was parked, closed the door, fired up the bike and sat there, on it, until his friend and Brother, came to take him away to join their wives. He had left all his money to the Club!

Those, were funerals, that weighed especially heavy, on the hearts of everyone. It was difficult to comprehend that people with the kind of love, joy and spirit that these people exhibited throughout their lives, could end in such tragedy.

Often, during these story telling sessions, when the names of those departed souls, were mentioned, as part of the stories, a sudden cool breeze would blow through. It was as if, their spirits had been awakened and they were making their presence known. It would often send a chill down the spines of some and raised those tiny hairs on the backs of the necks of others. Some thought it to be unnerving, yet, to others, it was a comfort, in the notion, that their spirits lived on within the boundaries of this property and they still felt comfortable and welcome. It wasn't a haunting but a visit. "A hug from the other side!", as some put it!

Pretty much, without fail, at some point, during these sessions the names Black Bart, and Tonto were brought up and that opened the "Story Telling, Floodgates from Hell"! It seems everybody and his Brother had a story about that pair of characters. They were not bad guys in terms of being mean, dishonest, brutal or evil or anything like that! But they were Hell Raisers, pure and simple! Many of the stories about them, usually ended with one, or both going to jail for a period of time! Not for anything criminal, and usually non-violent, shit, but jail seemed to just societies way, of trying to curtail some of their antics, as they had no other way of dealing punishment to souls such as these!

They were also, almost inseparable, other than, when they were serving out sentences in different facilities. Their exploits, were almost legendary by any standards, simply because many were so fucking outrageous! You could never tell what they would do next, but you knew it would be memorable!

Late, one Saturday afternoon, the two were out with their wives for a ride and stopped into this restaurant in a small Town about thirty miles from home. It wasn't a terribly fancy spot, but when the foursome came in and seated themselves at a table close to the bar, the waiter approached them and they were informed that the establishment has a strict dress code and the jeans, t shirts, boots and leather jackets that they were wearing, wasn't up to their standards or dress code.

A proper shirt, jacket and tie and formal pants would be necessary for admittance. He then asked them to leave. Which they did, much to Black Bart's displeasure. They went outside and Tonto started off down the street, motioning for the others to follow.

He led them to a second-hand store and they wandered inside to find a huge assortment of used clothing. The place had a musty smell to it, but that was fine. He went right to the men's section telling the ladies to pick out a couple of dresses from the lady's section.

Tonto then grabbed a jacket he felt would fit him and tried it on. It was ill fitting and was well out of style but he was satisfied with it. He then went in search of a white shirt, tie and pants. He motioned for Black Bart to find something too. "Fuck that! I'm not buying special clothes and getting dressed up just to eat in that snobby shit hole!" He protested.

"Trust me! This will be worth it! The clothes and the evening are on me!" Tonto told him.

Bart was still reluctant, but went about finding a suit a shirt and a gaudy tie.

The girls had already picked out their own, somewhat outlandish, and slightly bizarre outfits, and had put them on in the change room.

He and Black Bart went off to change as well, and emerged from the changeroom looking somewhat garish but passible. Tonto's shirt was slightly too large and the collar was quite loose.

He paid for the clothes and they wore them outside and he motioned for the others to stay where they were and told them he would be right back. He sprinted to a General Store, a few doors down, and came back with a bag full of stuff, then they went back to the restaurant.

The snooty waiter greeted them at the door and looked them up and down with a disdain usually reserved for dog shit on a shoe! Very well, come with me and was leading them to the back, where he was going to seat them at a table by the washrooms.

"This will do nicely! announced Tonto and quickly plunked himself down at a table in the centre of the room the rest of the foursome, followed suit. The waiter started to protest but Tonto immediately stood up, his face was inches away from the waiter's and asked loudly, in a threatening tone; "Is there a problem?"

They were served their meals and they were spectacular! Everything was cooked to perfection but the waiter kept the attitude in full gear! At one-point Tonto called him over and asked quietly, If the owner knew that he was such a fucking prick or if he hid it from him.

The waiter stiffened and indignantly replied huffily; "I am the owner!" then stormed away. The meal finished, they enjoyed some after dinner drinks. Tonto suddenly got up and went to the washroom taking the large bag with him. In the bag was a large rubber hot water bottle which he completely filled with one can of chunky vegetable beef soup and one of cream of mushroom soup. He screwed the cap back on and shook the water bottle up really well before stuffing it down the front of his shirt suspended it by a length of cord, around his neck, with the top positioned right at collar level.

The place had now, filled up with diners and now, most every seat was taken. The Owner/waiter was looking at them impatiently and starting to pace back and forth past their table. He had already presented them with their bill, but kept cruising past, hoping to hasten their departure.

Tonto who had returned from the washroom but without the large bag and now, casually, reached up and removed the cap from the hot water bottle, the neck of which, was now protruding slightly above his collar. None of the rest of the bunch were in on the prank, and looked as shocked as anybody else in the room when Tonto stared to wretch, loudly, and while he was doing the sound effects so well and so convincingly, and then he started squeezing the giant hot-water bottle, forcing the liquid from the open top of the container and out from under his chin as if he was actually hurling. No one in the room was looking close enough to spot the ruse! The reactions were almost instantaneous. The contents, that now were spewed across not only their table and themselves, but tables, servers, and guests within a 15-foot radius, maybe more, from their table!

As if on cue, and like he was in on the joke from the start, Black Bart picked up his fork and started to pick large pieces of meat and vegetables from the mess that now completely covered their table-top and ate them.

That was the topper! Patron's were now heading to the doors, in a stampede, as if a fire alarm had been activated in a place already filled with smoke. The place emptied quickly and the shocked and stunned, owner/ bitchy waiter, stood there in disbelief as Tonto threw two hundred-dollar bills on the table in front of him to cover the bill and the tip, smiled broadly wiped his chin and in unison the foursome rose from their seats, and walked out without a word. They mounted their motorcycles and rode off!

Another night the two were out for a ride. They had stopped for a meal at a little roadside bar and grill. There was an obnoxious, fat, blonde in there who had obviously had way too much to drink and she was behaving badly, and they had cut her off at the bar, this displeased her somewhat, and she was now, loudly, ranting that her boyfriend was some bigshot politician and he would shut them down, if they didn't treat her with respect! The guys, had enough listening to her shit, got up, paid their tab, and left. They stopped to fuel up their bikes at the adjoining service station, and noticed that the drunken blonde was being ejected from the bar, and wasn't taking it well. She staggered, cursing and swearing, to her car and tore off into the night, in a gorgeous, white, 56 Thunderbird, barely missing a couple of cars and people on her way.

Bart and Tonto just shook their heads and carried on with their own business of fueling their bikes.

They rode off in the same direction as the drunken bitch in the T bird had gone, hoping that she was well on her way to wherever, and wouldn't be a concern to them

About ten miles down the road they spotted the white T bird on the shoulder of the road. The fat blonde was standing at the passenger side, obviously ridding herself of her last meal and whatever quantity of booze she had washed it down with.

They gave her a wide berth and carried on down the highway.

It was a gorgeous night for a ride, a big full moon illuminated the sky and the road that stretched before them like a magical silver ribbon. A million or so stars, twinkled brightly, in the purple sky. A purple haze seemed to envelop everything, as well as the two riders who rode silently onward, blissful and contented, together, yet alone, the notes of their V Twin engines harmonized perfectly, providing an overture that rose into the heavens announcing their presence! It was a tad chilly but it was a nice sensation when they would ride through a pocket of warm air and then back to a chill. Light fog patches started to form here and there, adding a mystical vibe to everything. The air smelled sweet of cedar and pine and the musky scent of the woods and swampy sections along the way added to the heady mix that was almost euphoric.

Black Bart was the first to notice the headlights, fast moving up behind them, they seemed to be weaving from side to side. The trance was broken, and the two seasoned riders knew to be cautious and slowed to the shoulder of the road and stopped to let whatever, go on by.

The white T Bird rounded the sharp corner, going much too fast! The driver lost control just as it got close to the two bikers.

Both bikes and both riders were struck, sending them, and their bikes, careening across the highway! Bart and his bike went into the ditch! He was shaken up, but otherwise OK. He clambered up the embankment back to the roadway, and hadn't even checked on his bike yet, as he was more concerned about Tonto. He immediately saw that the T bird had come to rest against a concrete abutment at the side of the road. The boozy blonde driver was slumped over the wheel, her tangled mop of hair was dripping blood that was flowing from a gash to her forehead.

Bart then spotted Tonto, who had also been sent flying, and had landed heavily, against a guardrail, just before his motorcycle finished tumbling across the road, towards him, seemingly, in pursuit of its rider, and it crashed into him crushing his chest, and somehow, shearing off his left arm just below the shoulder. He was dazed but conscious, and was just gazing around the scene in a state of shock, trying to make some sense of it all. Tonto then spotted his arm laying on the pavement a few feet away and looked down to see the damaged stump that stuck from his tattered shirt, blood was pouring from it. He knew it was his arm because he recognized the watch and his turquoise and silver rings! He saw Black Bart staggering out of the ditch from where he had been thrown. He tried to speak but couldn't! He tried to point towards his left arm, but his right arm was pinned under his motorcycle.

Bart made his way to his old friend and wrestled the motorcycle from on top of him. He took off his belt and fashioned a makeshift, tourniquet to what remained of his friends left arm with it. He could see the flashing lights of Police cars, Fire trucks and ambulances in the distance and the sound of the sirens were welcome.

"Help is on the way man. Hang in there!" He tried to reassure his friend.

The Cops arrived on the scene first, and one Cop, came over and gave them a cursory once over he saw the tourniquet and that Bart was tending to him and then joined his partner, who was working on extracting the drunken bitch from her car! They had recognised her, as someone they knew personally, and were tending to her as best they could. She had come to, and was now loudly ranting and babbling, mostly incoherently, about how these maniac Bikers came out of nowhere and slammed into her car! She wanted them arrested!

Bart tried to comfort his old friend, who was finally able to speak. He said in a weak voice; "Grab my arm eh! Someone will steal that watch and my rings! I'd like them to go to my wife and kids! He then spotted one of his boots lying off in the middle of the road, he looked to see if the other one was still on his foot. Satisfied, that he still had one, he sent Bart to retrieve it as well. "That's a new boot! I've only had these boots for a week! Someone will steal them sure as shit!" Bart complied, then tucked both the arm and the boot under his right arm as per Tonto's instructions, and that seemed to give him comfort.

They sat there by the curb watching as the boozy blonde was being tended to. She was pointing at them, crying hysterically and the Cops seemed to be buying into her story, judging from the angry looks that they were receiving.

Tonto, clutched at Bart's jacket pulling him in close, so he could hear what he had to say! "Brother I usually don't approve of a guy hitting a woman, but if anyone is deserving of a punch in the teeth, it is her, I would be eternally grateful if you would go over there and punch that belligerent, drunken cunt, right in the mouth! Not just a gentle little tap! Put some zing in that thing!"

Bart sat back up straight, looked his friend square in the eye and asked; "Seriously?"

Tonto smiled back and nodded!

Without another word, Black Bart smiled, winked, stood up and strode directly over to where the EMS team had finally gotten her out of the wrecked T Bird and to her feet and were about to load her on the stretcher.

"Just a minute" he said to her. "My friend has a message that he asked me to relay to you."

"If he wants to say he's sorry, he's too late! You two, have already caused enough damage!" She spat the words at him!

"Naw, that isn't it!" At that, he hauled off and punched her with every bit of strength he could muster and landed a punch, that was probably the best he had thrown in his life-time, right in her mouth! The blonde's head snapped back and the only thing that prevented her from going down was the burly ambulance attendant who had a hold of her and when her head sprang back forward again, her eyes had rolled back in her head and she was out like a light, and ready to fall, but his right arm was already cocked and ready and he let go with that as well, he could feel the shockwave clear back to his shoulder so he knew it too, was a solid hit! This time, she went back and took the ambulance attendant with her. She slumped to the ground and lay there like the big lump of shit she was.

That, as expected, earned him the full attention of every Cop on the scene. They all wanted to get their licks in against this animal biker. Bart, was pretty busy trying to fend off the boys in blue, but managed to look over at where Tonto lay, unattended, propped up against the guardrail, his left arm and his boot tucked under his right arm, for safe keeping. He was smiling! He managed to raise his right hand slightly and gave him a thumbs up, then the hand and the arm dropped lifelessly to his side and his left arm and his boot tumbled to the ground, beside him. He slumped forward and Bart knew that he was gone. That sparked a new intensity in Bart, that he had never had before and the fight was on in earnest! It ended when one of the Cops landed a solid blow with his nightstick to Bart's head and he fell to the ground. The fact that he was out, didn't stop these overzealous coppers from getting in a few more punches and kicks while he lay unconscious on the ground.

He awoke in jail the next morning, no one had seen fit to

get him medical aid for his obvious trauma, until the Club's Lawyer came on the scene. The Club, had heard about what went on and retained him on behalf of Bart. That was a good thing, as he was a good Lawyer and was quickly able to sort out the Bullshit from the facts and was able to build a strong enough defense that the charges of dangerous driving and other nonsense dropped. Bart still had to answer to the assault charges against the Blonde and against the Police.

The Judge was being reasonable and considered, the circumstances and the emotional stress at the time and let him off with a small fine and a warning!

The drunken blonde, beat all charges against her, largely because none of the Cops bothered to do a sobriety test or get a blood sample from the Bitch.

Bart was never the same after that, he sold his bike and his house and quietly moved away and no one ever saw him around or heard from him again. There were rumours that he ended up, homeless, living on the streets, then, dyeing of an overdose in some mangy alley, in Hamilton, one cold December night!

Members, and those who considered themselves to be part of the Dozen Crew and family had certainly seen a mix of characters over the years. There had been a real assort-ment of people and personalities ride through their gates. Not everybody was allowed to stay. Not everybody fit! Over the years, they saw some of the most dangerous and meanest people on the planet, some of the weakest, some of the strongest, some of the meekest and mildest, some of the absolute toughest and those who were far from tough, but always willing to stand up, and some of the most brazen.

They had the most honest and trustworthy, and some of the worst, thieving, lying, cheating, and conniving, fuckers imaginable make an appearance at one time or another. It could be an adventure!

Some drank socially, others heavily, and others didn't drink at all. Some liked to gamble others did not! Some liked to carouse with the wilder ladies. Some were the wilder ladies! Some were sweet, shy, bold as brass and some were timid! There were some who were very skilled riders, some were not! Some were complete novices and there were some girls who just liked to go for a ride with someone with no desire to pilot their own. Some were married or had steady girlfriends. There were relationships that failed and others that lasted for decades! Some were deeply religious and others not at all. This place and these people were no different that any other part of Society. The Club and the crew and those they associated with it, were a microcosm of Society as a whole. The one thing that these folks all had in common; was the love of motorcycles and respect for the rights of Brothers and Sisters who came here and were accepted into the fold, as the individuals that they chose to be.

They Club, sifted through all the different personalities, dispositions, flaws and attributes in deciding who was welcome and who was not! Similar traits, and personalities were common among most who were regulars here. They were all individuals but compatible.

The folks who frequented this property, had experienced lots of emotion and seen many different situations, over the years, both, good and bad, and would see more of the same for years to come! If these people could hold the faith, keep traditions and core values alive, and educate the young properly this lifestyle will survive. The youth is the future. But those good old days are history and will never come again.

Those days and those times, however, live on in stories that are recanted over and over whenever the older guys and gals would get together.

They would listen intently and laugh and then tell their own stories. That story might remind someone else about a similar situation. Everybody took turns telling theirs and the someone else would have one and on and on it went. Hours would drift by without notice.

Tales of the road, the travels, the adventures, things learned, things experienced, the different Towns, Cities, villages, campgrounds, breaking down in the middle of nowhere, and having to scavenge for parts and fixing their rides with the most meager of tool kits imaginable. Embellishment and exaggeration were not only condoned, but were expected, and encouraged and some stories just improved with age and each telling! The roads and conditions got worse, the opposition stronger, odds were greater, bigger, better armed and heroics on the part of the teller were legendary!

These stories of bad roads, good food, great food, bad food, fucking horrible food, mean cops, decent cops, good people, bad people, bad weather, good weather, horrible weather and encounters, close and otherwise, with everything from locusts, bats, birds, like wild turkeys that can knock a rider off his mount quicker than you can blink, insects, spiders, deer, moose, bears, antelope, alligators, snakes, caribou and buffalo and just about anything else, that walks, flies, swims, slithers, or crawls.

They spoke of ranging out through Florida, In the Florida Keys, in Earnest Hemmingway's old stomping grounds, eating large quantities of lobster, freshly caught fish and shrimp, from a shack on a Pier, experiencing North and South Carolina, New Orleans and Mardi Gras! Drinking moonshine, drawn right from stills in West Virginia and Kentucky and falling asleep beside their bikes, on a stretch of road known as Alligator Alley, which was allegedly, appropriately named, until a State Trooper happened along and found them, before the alligators did, and had them move along. They told of partying with different Clubs in different States and Provinces from east coast to west coast, south to Mexico, and North to Alaska and were always (Well mostly) treated with respect!

When these stories were being related, you could see the look in certain people's eyes and could almost feel the Wanderlust swelling in their souls. If you looked into the faces of riders like Gypsy and Bill Johnstone you had to know that, that was the life that they would adopt one day! They really didn't get to choose that life and lifestyle, as the Wanderlust had taken a firm hold on their souls and the lifestyle had already chosen them. Everyone knew that it would be just a matter of time until they would hit the road.

CHAPTER SIX
LOVE AND RELATIONSHIPS

FOR REB THOUGH, his incredible shyness around girls was painful for him and resulted in a lot of teasing from his friends, then one day; a new family moved to town. They were the Murphy's, a family of Irish decent who had made a couple of stops and a couple of attempts at settling in, after their arrival in Canada from Belfast. First in Halifax, Nova Scotia, where the father was employed by a small boat builder until he got a job offer from a Company in Toronto, Ont. an automotive firm. The father, Patrick who was an excellent and extremely creative, engineer and a brilliant planner and organizer, also tried his damndest to uphold the reputation of the Irish as the best drinkers in the World. His aspirations fell short of his abilities and he died shortly after the families' arrival in Swanton Harbour. Beforehand, he had managed to garner a sizeable estate, that enabled the family to sink some deep roots into the Community and establish a home here.

There was a daughter, by the name of Linda, an adorable young lady, with a long mane of flaming red hair, a complexion as fair as the morning dew and eyes of green that would challenge the finest fields of green on earth, as to which was finer! Her smile would rival the sun as to which was brighter and warmer. This, in the eyes of two young men who were already intense rivals! From their very first glimpse of her, on her very first appearance at school! Both were forever, smitten! One would win her heart from their introduction, the other would be bitter and jealous, before learning that true friendship is something to cherish and should be considered priceless!

Such was the case with Linda Louise Murphy and Robert Edward Baker. It was love at first sight, however, it was conflicting for the painfully shy young man, who on one hand couldn't keep his eyes off her and made every excuse possible, just to be around her, he purposely, avoided actually speaking to her for Months. And while this lovely young lady with the ravishing red hair and flashing green eyes had definitely captured his attention and his heart, his usual bravado was no where to be found. If they chanced to actually meet face to face, he would restrict the greeting to a quick, awkward, smile and a wave and then blush and slink off somewhere to admonish himself for being such a wuss. Somehow, she sensed his true feelings, and would keep her eye on the bashful young man, as she had very strong feelings for him as well and was persistent.

One evening, at a small get together, at a beach party, at a small park down by the lake, where they were both in attendance, she managed to corner him. Once they were together, alone, the rest of the World no longer existed in their view, he could only see her, he could hear only her. He was lost in those mesmerizing Emerald green eyes. He could see her lips move but couldn't really concentrate on her words. She was his enchantress, his queen, and his World from that moment forward!

They sat there talking for hours. Unbeknownst to either of them, everyone else, had long ago, gone home. The dawn had arrived and they were still there, talking! They were oblivious to all else, just sitting there under a large maple tree near the beach.

She was the first to notice that the sun was coming up and that they were all alone. She looked deep into his eyes, and asked; "Do you want to feel something strange?"

She took his hand and placed it gently under her left breast!

He was startled at what he felt! Her heart was beating a mile a minute, racing like crazy! He looked into her eyes and asked; "Are you OK? What is that about?"

She smiled, gazed sweetly into his eyes, and replied; "Darl'n, it has to be you, because it has never done that before!" She then leaned in and kissed him deeply!

It was now REB's heart's turn to beat frantically, and his head was spinning as they fell backwards to the ground. What happened next, could best be described as absolute frenzy! Clothes were hastily cast aside and they sought each other's most intimate areas in what may well have been, the most clumsy, inexperienced, encounter ever.

For someone who had always seemed to have his shit together and control of his emotions in most any circumstance, he had never in his life, felt less in control of anything! It was hard to concentrate, everything was moving way too fast, like a freight train out of control!

He wanted desperately to be cool and seem like he knew what he was doing! He couldn't, because he didn't have a clue! He had dreamed about this moment so many times, but now that it was actually happening, it was like something totally unimaginable! He was in a panic, "Don't fuck this up! Don't fuck this up!" Those were the words that kept repeating themselves over and over in his brain!

For Linda as well, she wasn't sure what to grab, what to kiss or whatever, she loved the feel of his hands on her naked body. She shuddered and quivered and almost exploded when his hand slipped between her legs and strong fingers found their way to the quick of her! She sucked in a hard breath, as his fingers slipped inside her. She kissed him hard, her tongue darted in an out of his mouth. Her hand reached down and grasped his fully erect and throbbing penis and she could hear him moan.

They just rolled in the grass, heads spinning and bodies aching with desire! Each, secretly hoping that the other knew what they were doing and when to do it, what would be the next step, but REB was hoping that it would happen soon, very soon. Apparently, Linda was thinking along those lines as well and finally took charge, rolled him onto his back and mounted him. It was like a million flash bulbs went off in their heads. They were caught up in the rapture of the moment, as nature took its course. Thrusting and grinding themselves together, in a pure, act of passion, driven by animal instinct alone, because any classy romantic notions and plans they might have had, went out the window at the first kiss and finally, climaxing, then collapsing, entwined together in each other's arms and falling into a gentle slumber, still locked in embrace.

They awoke a half hour or so later in that tranquil spot, under the tree to the sound of the birds chirping and feeling the gentle summer breezes blowing over their naked bodies. They were oblivious to everything beyond that shady patch of grass and did not want to move so as not to disturb the magic that they had just experienced.

REB's hand gently caressed her delicate breasts that looked so tantalizing in the soft glow of the early morning sunlight! He tweaked her nipples gently then leaned in an gave each one a tender lick and chanced a small suckle. She just murmured and stretched out spreading her legs, inviting him to explore further. He did, his hand slid gently down into the moist tenderness of her groin and she sucked in a sharp breath at his touch and began to move and gyrate her hips slowly in response to his probing fingers but suddenly stopped him. She suddenly realized that they were in a public place and she sat up trying to cover herself with her hands while she quickly took stock of their surroundings. REB also, had lost track of everything and now, the two rushed to retrieve the clothes that had been so carelessly cast off, while trying to sneak glimpses of each others naked bodies and got dressed before the place got busy.

That was the beginning of a relationship that survived all the usual ups and downs, fights and squabbles, turmoil and trouble that all normal relationships go through, along with a few extra that were unique to them alone, as they were unique.

Dan O'Reilly, soon realized that he'd once again, shown up a day late, and a dollar light, to win over the petite young beauty and Robert Edward Baker had bested him once again. However, strangely, he saw the way the two of them looked at each other and their love was obvious. He, was surprisingly happy about their relationship, from the outset. In later years, after REB and he had buried the hatchets he appreciated it even more, as he got to share in their love as friends! Fate had dealt them a good hand and he was happy for them. Dan went on to marry, and have a great relationship and built a life with his childhood sweetheart; Nancy Knott. They had two wonderful kids and everything worked out.

REB and Linda's love and their commitment, lasted more than fifty Years, until death changed the game. In that time, they married, raised five wonderful daughters and went well beyond the call of duty, one night when they were paid a visit.

REB and Linda, both of whom were humanitarians and had hearts as big as all outdoors. They had a house outside of town, nearby, but separate from where the Clubhouse and what was considered to be Club Property were situated. They lived there with their five daughters.

It was a large house well off the beaten path and given REB's reputation as a cantankerous old biker, plus all the very large signs warning; that trespassers, would be pissed on and then shot, dissuaded lots of folks from making random visits!

Late one night, they heard a car pulling up their long

driveway. REB stepped out onto the front porch. It turned out to be Chief Marshall.

"Kind of late to come visiting isn't it Chief?" I see that your gun is still in the holster, so I assume it isn't a raid!" he said with a chuckle!

"REB, I need to talk to you and Linda." He said solemnly.

He motioned towards his Cruiser and the passenger door opened and someone emerged and started towards them.

A large woman stepped into the light and the Chief introduced her as Tanya Evans, from Social Services for the Ontario Government.

"REB, Linda," He began. "We are faced with a very delicate situation and I am going to ask for your indulgence. We have a bit of a crisis. Ms. Evans' Department deals with domestic violence and the safety of women and children who need to escape from violent and extremely dangerous situations. They set up safe houses, where families in need, can be taken and kept safe until more permanent settings can be arranged."

"These houses, are operated in complete secrecy and anonymity."

The only ones who have any knowledge of these homes or who runs them are the Chief of Police and any trusted personnel in my Department and top officials with top security clearance in the Social Services Department of the Provincial Government!

"We recently had one such safe house compromised and it turned into an extremely violent situation."

"I was asked if I knew of anyone else that would qualify as potential safehouse operators. I said that you two and your family would top my list as you had good hearts and could keep a secret."

"I know that you have five daughters, but I know you and I know your daughters and I know how tight knit you all are."

"The program involves getting the endangered family out of harms way, often on little or no notice and getting them to a place where they can be safe until we can make other, more permanent, arrangements!" This can occur at anytime day or night!" The operators are reimbursed for expenses but there are no actual wages being paid or money earned. These families are desperate and often leave with just the clothes that are on their backs. No toys, no food, no possessions. They are scared to death, and all they want is shelter and safety.

REB and Linda both looked at each other, shrugged and replied in unison. "Yeah, OK, if you think we can help! Sure! The girls will be cool with it."

The Chief then nodded to Ms. Evans who retreated to the Squad car and returned, leading a young mother in obvious trauma sporting bloody bandages wrapped around her head, a large bandage on her cheek and across her nose and her left arm in a sling. There were two siblings who appeared to be in their early teens one of them was carrying a young toddler. Linda guided them into the house while REB stayed behind to talk to Chief Marshall.

That was the beginning of a long-standing relationship that provided much needed shelter for hundreds of families over the years and a relationship with families who realized that there were good people out there who did things because it was the right thing to do, and not for profit or notoriety!

They continued on with the program and did what they could and what they said they would. Their girls were instrumental in calming children who were traumatized by the way life had unfolded for them. They shared their toys and their clothes; their pets also helped to soothe frazzled nerves and restore trust in others. They knew that what was being done was top secret and no one should ever know about their guests!

Their involvement also made them aware of things to watch for that were signs of domestic abuse and things that could escalate into dangerous situations. They would tell their parents if they saw some tell-tale signs and they in turn would pass the word to Chief Marshall so that he could investigate. They occasionally would bring troubled children from school home with them to get them away from abusive situations.

CHAPTER SEVEN
SAD ENDINGS, NEW BEGINNINGS

THE SUN WAS SINKING low on the horizon, casting long shadows and painting a wonderful mosaic on the sky from Mother natures full pallet of colour, ranging from bright crimson to vibrant orange! The wispy clouds picked up hints of blue, green and purple and cast them, in a velvety haze and were just scattered around in a mesmerizing, random pattern in a vibrant, everchanging, enchanting masterpiece. It was relaxing, yet stimulating, and it lifted the spirits of a worn-out Chief of Police who had just spent an exhausting day at a Police Conference in the city.

Dan O'Reilly, was feeling every single minute, of his 75 years on the planet and it was his birthday today so it was somewhat appropriate that he felt or at least, acknowledged his age, but even the comfortable seats of his truck didn't diminish the ache that he felt in his back and butt from too long on those hard fold up chairs, that had surely been designed and built in Hell, by Satan, himself.

He skirted the construction on the main road opting for a couple of lesser travelled secondary as well as a few interconnected, dirt roads, that would, perhaps, shorten his journey a bit, or at the very least, he would see a lot less traffic!!

It had been a long day and he was glad to be finally heading home! He hated those damned seminars! Each one was just like the last, and boring as Hell, but he had to go! As head of his department, they expect him to stay current with all new methods of Law Enforcement and learn to be sensitive to changes in the Community and Socially Woke! If that were really the case, you'd think they would actually come up with something new and update the material that really reflected true Community issues.

He always got a kick out of the ones specifically dealing with Outlaw Motorcycle Clubs as it was amusing yet, disturbing to see and hear the kind of stuff they were filling green recruits' heads with, and it was no mystery as to why there is tension in interactions between the two groups! It was virtually unchanged from what he was taught as a recruit and it took years before he found certain truths and thought for himself, outside of the perimeters of what was being taught. He could really open some eyes if they would let him speak of the things that he had learned over the years, but those in charge, did not want to hear any of that. They did not want to listen, they were here to talk and teach the same, tired, stereotypical crap, drivel and rhetoric that they have been spewing for years! They had already established an agenda and approved methods and were content with it.

His big, black, pit bull, Zeke, who, had been his constant

companion the last six years, since his wife died and he didn't like leaving him alone at home. Not that he couldn't be trusted to be by himself but Dan's days were often unpredictable and could be long and it would be unfair to Zeke, to be left alone. He was excellent company, loved travelling in that big black truck, and loved the varied, but, far from veterinarian approved diet, being on the road provided like burgers and especially chicken fingers or tenders or whatever that particular place chose to call them. He would lie back in a corner of the room, during the conferences, as he was designated as a Service Dog and would wait patiently for them to end. Mostly he just slept through them. Dan often looked at him laying there content and peaceful and wished that he could curl up on the floor beside him and sleep as well. The Chief, even had a special collar with a badge on it custom made for him. His big head was now resting on the centre consul of the truck, and every once and awhile he would nudge Dan's arm with his nose, wanting a pat on the head or a scratch behind his ears! Dan would absent-mindedly stroke his soft smooth coat as he drove and it brought both of them peace!

His mind was busy trying to piece together tomorrows schedule, which he should have been doing all day, instead of attending some mind-numbing seminar. His cell phone broke his concentration. It wasn't the Department's phone, but his personal phone ringing and vibrating in his right-front pants pocket! This was worrisome in itself, because very few people had his personal number, fewer still, actually called it. He wiggled around until he could extract it from his pocket and glanced at the call display. It identified the caller as "Linda Baker", he accepted the call!

"Hey Linda, what's up?" he asked, his tone betraying the troublesome feeling that came from the pit of his stomach, as it was very unusual for her to be calling him, and he knew, it couldn't be good news, that he was about to hear.

"It's REB, Dan. He's not doing very well at all, and asked, actually he demanded, to see you ASAP." The worry was very evident in her voice and Linda was not the kind to be rattled! She was one of the most truly, self reliant people he had ever known, and had an inner strength that seemed to know no bounds! Now, her voice was cracking with emotion and he could tell that it was serious!"

"I'm just on my way home Darl'n! I'll swing by the house, drop Zeke off, get a change of clothes, grab the bike and head right over!" Shouldn't be much more than an hour!"

"Can you please come right over now?" She stammered "Just come as you are! We're at the Clubhouse! I'll let them know at the gate!" Please! Come right away!" He could tell that she was now crying and on the verge of hysteria, which is something he had never seen her do or even heard of her doing in the many years he had known her and REB! "On my way! Five minutes!" With that he switched on his flashing lights and siren, did a quick u turn and put the gas peddle to the floor! He could hear the clatter of loose gravel from the soft shoulders of the road being spewed from the tires hitting the fender wells and could see the large cloud of dust that his maneuver had created! Hell, it might be against protocol but what the fuck? He hadn't broken protocol for quite a while now! He was over-due, thus justified!

He skidded to a halt at the gates as a couple of very large men stepped out in front of his truck, blocking his entrance.

"What the fuck do you want here?" said one of them, as he walked menacingly up to the driver's side of the truck and peered in the window, the other came up on the right side, Dan couldn't say for sure, but, both appeared to have something in their hands hidden behind their backs. Zeke had risen up from his slumber on the passenger seat when Dan had hit the siren and was now, alert and ready for action and these two didn't look like anything he wouldn't or couldn't take on!

"I'm here to see REB!" he announced!

"Well REB isn't taking visitation right now! Especially not from a fucking Cop unless you have a fucking warrant!" The tall one at his driver's door snickered and sneered and looked to his partner for approval at what he had just said!" They weren't wearing patches so Dan figured them to be hang arounds from some visiting Club that were just helping out.

"Look, REB'S wife Linda just called and asked me to come! She was supposed to let you guys know! Man, it's urgent!" he tried to explain.

Just then, someone shouted from the shack at the side of the driveway! "It's OK let him in! But tell him to shut off the lights and siren for fuck's sake!"

Dan immediately, shut off the offending lights and killed the siren! Truthfully, he had forgotten that he switched them on. The two, stepped aside and opened the gate so he then, sped off in the direction of the Clubhouse! Hell, it used to piss REB off when he showed up in his official Cop vehicles, wearing his official Cop Uniform, on the few, very rare, occasions that he had done so, he was pretty certain that showing up with lights and siren on, would be something that the crusty old fuck would consider to be over the top!

On his way in, Dan had noticed a lot of bikes and a lot of people hanging around, some were setting up tents some were gathered in little groups, most were wearing their cuts, proudly emblazoned with their Clubs Colours or insignia. He noted many of the Big Clubs, were here as well as many smaller, lesser known Clubs, and lots of independents but they were arriving here in droves, from all over Canada and the United States! There would be many more arriving soon depending upon REB's condition. The final outcome had already been predetermined, the factor, that had yet to be established was when. People wanted to say goodbye and pay their respects to a man they had long considered to be a Brother.

He, in his Police vehicle, wearing his full uniform did get some attention as he made his way up the driveway to the Clubhouse, but nobody challenged him. They figured the guys at the gate must have cleared him, but he made them nervous and they kept an eye on him.

As he walked up to the house he recognised many faces that he hadn't seen in quite a while. It looked like all hands-on deck as far as the Dozen went! At least, most of what was left of the original 13 members of The Bakers Dozen, appeared to be here! They wouldn't all be there of course, as time and circumstance had cut into the roster somewhat and their numbers had dwindled considerably especially over the past ten years or so. REB'S immanent death would be another blow and there were many who wondered if anyone would be able to keep things going after REB was gone. He had always been the stabilizer and the spark that kept things alive! Would the Club be able to survive the loss of their leader and what would happen next were questions that weighed heavy on many minds?

All seven, large barbecues that the Club owned, had probably been going steadily for days now and he could see a lot of propane tanks in the cage. That cage would be refilled constantly over the course of the next several days! Whatever they had on the grill, sure smelled good and the fragrant smoke wafted through the whole property and lingered tantalizingly in the air, stimulating taste buds and appetites with the promise of good food! Fried onions, he was sure was one of the items being grilled and that aroma was to the Dan's olfactory senses, what the Siren's song was to sailors' ears! The huge smoker was being readied for action and he was pretty certain that a whole hog and probably a hip or two of beef would be on the spit before too long.

He'd say; "Look we can't be having you come around here, driving that fucking thing and dressed like that! You trying to drop the property values? Are you trying to ruin our reputation and lower our standing in the Community? You want our neighbours to think we allow low class Cops to hang around? It's bad enough that you ride that fucking Geezer Glide" in here all the time! We have a fucking image to uphold for fuck's sake! He could, and often did, go on like that for hours!

"Maybe he was sleeping and didn't notice!" he thought!

Linda was on the front steps along with her and REB's

five natural daughters who were trying to calm their obviously, very distraught Mother. She looked at him and the
tears that were welled up in her big green eyes, burst into full
flow and poured down her cheeks! She tried desperately to
speak, but couldn't get a word out of her mouth. She broke
free from the girls and flew into his open arms! She was
sobbing violently and uncontrollably, trying unsuccessfully,
to get some words to come! They would not! They stood
there, her face buried in his shoulder, he could feel the
warmth of her tears as the were absorbed into the material
of his shirt! He said nothing, he just held her tight until the
sobbing subsided, and she was now slowly but surely,
starting to regain her composure! Rachel, the oldest daughter, now about 50 years old, a frail but very pretty girl who
was a trained, and certified nurse, and who had been there
since REB's condition took a sudden turn for the worse a
few Months back, the rest of the girls had arrived within the
last few days. She stepped forward and comfortingly pulled
her mother away from the embrace! She pulled her close to
her and then passed her to her sisters, who were hovering
close by!

Linda suddenly broke free from all of them. Took a sharp,
deep breath, exhaled slowly and Dan and the girls watched in
disbelief as she metamorphosized, back into the composed,
dignified, tough as nails woman that she had always faced
the World as! She certainly, would never have let REB see
her like that, displaying that kind of vulnerability and
emotion! It just isn't what they did! She wasn't going to have
his last image of her as that of her being some of a weak-
assed woman, who let her emotions get the better of her! All

the stress and the strain of the last few Months had just been building up and she needed a release! That was done, and it was time to get back to the business at hand and headed back inside the house to tend to her husband.

Rachel stopped and turned towards Dan. "Thanks for coming so quickly!" she said softly. The stress and strain were evident on her as well! She told Dan how REB's condition had gone from bad to worse and then, much worse! He's been a fucking bear! He knows that his death is close at hand and he's doing stuff that he's not supposed to be doing, because according to him, that it just has to be done! He's got a list of stuff that he insists on getting done right now! Everything has an urgency to it! He's driving the Hang arounds and the construction guys nuts! He's got them running all kinds of errands, and has been hounding, those working on that new edition relentlessly! He still won't tell anyone what it is, or what it's for. Only the construction guys are allowed anywhere near it and the workers have been sworn to secrecy! He says it has to be ready for tonight!

He's supposed to be resting! He's coughing continuously, spitting up blood and he rattles when he breathes! He almost doubles over in pain every time he coughs or moves any part of his body and that, is almost continuously! He won't take the pain pills because he says that they put him to sleep and he has no time for sleeping. "I'll take a big nap when this stuff gets done, I promise you!" He says! It seems to be his new, favourite saying, and we're all getting very tired of hearing it!" Apparently, he called his lawyer and had him come over a few hours ago, and locked himself away with him a few hours. That was, earlier this afternoon and no one knows what that was all about. Not even Mom!

You see the state that she is in, and Dad looks like he will collapse at any moment! He insisted that we call you right away as he had some shit to give you in person! I don't know what it is, he wouldn't tell us! It's in a big bag and a large box that one of the Club Brothers brought to him late this after-noon! There are about twenty boxes and a bunch of bags and envelopes, they are all sealed and no one has any idea what is in them, but he looked really happy when he looked at the and especially the one with your name on it! He even smiled when he saw it!

That, is when he really started to fade and he was having a lot of trouble getting his breath! He's on the oxygen bottle now, and Mom managed to slip him some morphine and it seems to have helped. He was really getting upset, so Mom called you! We told him, that we could give whatever it was, to you and that you were on the road! He screamed and cursed at us and he's never done that, ever! He hollered "Fuck that! I want to see that Irish Mother Fucker here in person, right fucking quick! Call him! Tell him it's fucking important, Damn it!"

Linda took his hand and led him into the room that had been serving as a hospice for REB for the past week or so! It was adorned and decorated with all his favourite things! They even had his old Knucklehead set up on one side of the room so he could look at it. Pictures and memorabilia were everywhere! It was supposed to give him peace in his final moments but at times it served as more of a source of irrita-tion to him, as truth be known, he yearned to throw his leg over that Knuckle that he loved so much, kick it over and just ride the Hell out of here! He longed to feel that throttle in his right hand and twist the wick and listen to the sweet music exiting from her exhaust in response. He needed the sensation of the wind in his face, the fresh air filling his tired old lungs and natures sweet fragrances stirring his senses. If they could have somehow figured out how to recreate that for him, that would be comforting to him! He knew that he was simply riding out the clock here. He had a lot that he still wanted to squeeze into whatever time he had left on this Earth and that he was rapidly running out of time to do it!

Dan could see REB laying on the hospital bed from the doorway where he and Linda had stopped momentarily. The nurse, named Veronica, who actually, was the wife of a hang around, who had volunteered her time as she was off on vacation and he was barking orders at her, cursing people out and generally being an asshole and a complete pain in the ass!

The trouble was, the big man wasn't feeling very much at peace right now! Given the situation, that was quite under-standable. There was stuff that he felt was important that he had to see to! He wasn't going to let anything, including his own death to prevent him from accomplishing all of the tasks he had set out to do! Victoria along with his daughters, all were trying to get him calm down! "Fuck calm down! I have no time to calm fucking down! Death will have to wait until I have time to deal with it! It can wait it's fucking turn!"

He was gaunt and had lost a lot more weight, since Dan had last seen him just two days ago. The usually tanned and taught flesh of his face was now slack and covered in a thick, white, stubble, and sagged from his jawline, and accentuated the folds, wrinkles and creases. His eyes were sunken back in his head and no longer had the sparkle that they had just days ago, either. He now looked skeletal! It was hard to watch this once, enormous man, deteriorate to this degree, so quickly!

His head snapped around as Dan entered the room! "What the fuck? Did someone call a fucking Cop? Do you think that you're going to get me to take these fucking pills because you have a badge and a fucking gun?" He swatted the pill bottle off the table scattering its contents all over the floor! Veronica, who had just placed that bottle there, moved in quickly to gather them up.

To everyone's surprise, including REB, Linda, immediately launched herself from where she had been standing in the doorway, across the room, to his bedside, a distance of around ten feet, in three quick, menacing strides! Her green eyes were blazing in anger, and glaring as only she could! She got within inches of his face, so close, that their noses were almost touching! She unloaded on him, hot and heavy, both barrels, as if she was a mother scolding a misbehaving child! She hissed; "Robert Edward Baker! You fucking apologise to Veronica, right fucking now! She is here on her vacation to help you! You do not fucking treat her or anybody else like that! Everybody is doing all that they can to help you! You fucking behave yourself! Or you might well be stuffed into a closet and be left to die on your own, by your fucking self, in the fucking dark, if you ever talk to these nice people like that again! Then again, I may just speed up the process! I do have a fucking gun and know how to fucking use it! Tell me, just how are you going to get all that important shit that you have to do, accomplished then? You are behaving like an unappreciative, disrespectful asshole! Smarten up!

The entire room fell dead silent! Nobody in the room could believe what just happened and what they heard come out of this sweet little woman's mouth! You could have heard a pin drop!

"It's Ok he's under a lot of stress!" Veronica started to say as she gathered up the pills.

REB interrupted her. "No, she's absolutely right Veronica! I behaved like a dick. Please forgive me." He the turned back to Dan who stood in stunned silence, after the outburst from Linda! REB still considered him, to be fair game however!

"What the fuck are you doing, coming here dressed like that and driving that fucking Cop Truck to boot? What the fuck was with the lights and siren? You're going to piss off all our neighbours and drop the property values!"

"So much for being asleep." Dan muttered to himself. "Sorry! I forgot I had them on! I had to make a u turn on the highway after Linda called and said that you wanted me here pronto, and never turned them off until I got to the gate and was told about them. Besides you don't have any fucking neighbours! The closest one in ten miles South!"

"And we'll never have any, with, all these kinds of goings on! I thought you Cops were supposed to be respectful of the rights and sensibilities of the citizens in the Community!" He countered, never wanting to let someone else get the last word or off the hook too easily!

"Why the fuck would you come here dressed like that? That's a Hell of a way to come to see a dyeing man who is

supposed to be your fucking brother! Change into something respectful and more appropriate for your surroundings! Show a little fucking respect! Typical of a cop! No one
else's feelings mean a fucking thing! Show some respect and
some sensitivity for crying out loud!"

"I didn't bring a change of clothes, I was working, didn't
have time to go home!" Fuck! This was awkward! He knew
REB was mostly pulling his chain but he did hate it when he
wore his uniform and such! He knew he should have gone
home first!

"Shit! At least take off that fucking shirt, I'd rather see you
naked than wearing that shit! But there are ladies present
and we don't want you putting them off men altogether from
the sight of you naked!" REB cursed, still shaking his head.
He reached into the bag in front of him and extracted a
balled-up piece of black fabric and tossed it across the room
hitting Dan right in the face! "I think that will fit you!" Dan
quickly unfolded it and stood there dumbfounded!

It was black t-shirt, a logo had been silk screened on the
front, left breast position with a modified version of what
had been the baseball team's logo for years, that had
consisted of a small green shamrock over two crossed baseball bats with a small black spade in the centre with a white
13 in the centre of the spade. Also, on the old baseball shirts,
the teams name Bakers Dozen was emblazoned in big capital
letters above the logo. This image had the crossed baseball
bats being replaced with crossed pistons and instead of
saying Baker's Dozen this shirt simply said "Better by the
Dozen" in a rocker above the main design. The word
CHARA arched across the top petal of the shamrock in white

lettering. The back of the shirt was the same but much larger.

REB was extremely proud of his Irish heritage and integrated many Irish words and expressions into his day to day language. "Chara is Irish for friend! Of course, you know that!" REB announced. An enormous smile had formed on REB'S face! "Something new, I'm going to try and get this approved as a support item as we have never had any. I think, it's long overdue! I wanted you to have the first one. You've been a great friend and I love you! It's a shame we wasted all of those early years hating each other! Fuck it! Mo Chara! Bràthair gu bràth! Bràthair gu bràth! Water under the bridge! Go get changed out of that Cop shit and put on a real shirt! Grab a beer and something to eat! I've been smelling some great aroma coming from that barbecue pit for the last while! It smells good but I can't bring myself to eat anything! I can barely keep soup down. Hang around awhile! I have some things to say and some business to attend to, and we are going to have a meeting and I want you there! Now get out of here! I want to see if I can get a short nap, clean up and maybe even get a shave if I can trust Linda and Veronica here not to cut my fucking throat with the razor for being an asshole! I might even get into some real clothes before the meeting!" He winked, a big grin, again, spread across his face! The sparkle had also returned to his eyes.

As he left the room he noticed a line of REB and Linda's other "Kids and family" lined up waiting to get in to see him.

There were around twenty of them and he knew there would be more showing up soon!

Dan walked out to the truck after getting a large bowl filled with nice cold water he got from the bar. He filled another with some potato chips and even found a couple of hotdogs and a hamburger that had been left there unattended and put them in there as well. He presented them to Zeke on the ground by him and he devoured it all, almost instantly before shoving his muzzle in the cold water splashing much of its contents all over the place in the process. Dan let him off the chain to run a bit, and to do his business, in the little knoll, by the creek. The property was well lit so he didn't worry too much about him running into critters like skunks, porcupines or coyotes. His stripped off his uniform shirt, folded it neatly, and along with his gun, gun belt, bullet proof vest, and other gear that he wouldn't be needing here tonight and locked them in the back of the truck!

He got a chance to admire his new t shirt in the reflection of the trucks side window! He then attached a long chain that he kept in the back of the truck for occasions like these, to Zeke's collar and then clipped the other end to the Truck's bumper hitch, moved his dish of closer to him and turned to walk back towards the house. He had barely taken three steps when suddenly Zeke let out a deep, throaty, growl and stood stark still, his hackles were up and he stared off towards an under crop of bushes under a large oak tree. A soft sounding wolf whistle, alerted him to the fact that he was not alone out here! His eyes peered into the dark shadows He could now make out the glow of a burning cigarette held by an indistinct silhouette and he could now detect the unmistakeable scent of marijuana as the smoke drifted towards him.

"Hey, Dan the man!" He instantly recognized the voice, despite the fact that he hadn't heard it, in perhaps five years. It had mellowed slightly with age, along with the gentle abuse of good liquor, and strong marijuana. The playful lilt still remained, but now had a husky, sultry, sexy tone that resonated in something similar to a cat's purr, that would have stirred the loins of most men just by listening to her talk. She sure could talk!

There was a rustling of brush and a tall slender female form emerged from within the shadow. It was Mary Jane McGuire, better known, to people around here, as Calamity Jane. Her signature long black tresses that used to flow tantalizingly to below her drop dead, gorgeous butt were now cropped to shoulder length and had steaks of grey. She was wearing very little make-up, and she was still absolutely stunning!

"What do you know for sure?" She asked playfully, and held the joint out to him, but he declined!

"Oh yeah, still a Cop, even without the badge and gun! Sorry I forgot!"

"That's not it!" He replied. Not just right now.

"I'm doing OK under the circumstances!" He stated." What about you Calamity, what's shaking and baking in your World! I haven't seen you since Big Frank died! What's that, five years?"

"Yeah something like that. Been out in BC, running a small, hunting and fishing camp, I have a small fishing boat that I charter out too, so now, that is; Captain Calamity to you! You wanna come aboard, Matey?" She said with a wink, a smile, and a quizzically, raised an eyebrow. "AArrg!" Even in this light Dan could see her big brown eyes twinkling!

There had always been a not so subtle, hint of a strong spark, between them, both of them knew it and felt it, but timing and circumstance had never been right and neither had crossed that line, yet!

Calamity, had always talked a mile a minute and without any punctuation! She jumps from one sentence or subject right on to the next without a pause and sometimes it is hard to keep track of what the original subject was, and what she was talking about now, as it changes so abruptly, so often, without warning. She looks you straight in the eye the whole time she's talking and she is just so damned pretty, and so sincere about everything she tells you, it is a pleasure just to be in her company! Talk is often, just an excuse to look at her. It is also hard to fit a word in edgewise, or at all, until she has finished what she had to say. With her, that could take a while. She was also one Hell of left fielder or any other position she chose to play!

"I'm also growing some dynamite weed and operate a small still, producing some excellent shine, but very small scale, special orders, for special people. It's all absolutely, on the down low, so as not to draw heat! I finally got to use those recipes that those good 'ol boys we met on that Club run, down in West Virginia in the seventies, traded me for a few blow jobs way back when! They still call me every once in a while, inviting me back! I guess, I must have given memorable head, back in my day! Of course, you, wouldn't know that, would you? You never did step up to the plate, when I was pitch'n!"

She took a short breath and continued. "You know, I'm getting by, enjoying myself, but it always feels like I'm missing something! The asshole I went out West with, turned out to be just that, a complete asshole, much like every other man I ever hooked up with! I ditched his pathetic ass after just seven months! I had more than too much, of his act and told him to get the fuck out! He didn't take it well, and came at me, intending to beat and kick some sense into me! I beat him to the punch though, and as he came through the doorway of the house, I hit him square in the face with an axe handle! Broke his fucking nose, jaw and took out three teeth, all from the front too! He's damned lucky the head of the axe had come off the day before, and I hadn't got around to fixing it yet! He would have ended up dead, I would either have had to find a place to bury the motherfucker or I would have gone to prison, but I would already be almost done my sentence by now and it would have been worth it!" The look on her face, told him that every word was true!

She took a big long toke off the joint, coughed a little, and continued. She certainly had Dan's attention! "That hunk of hickory did the job, pretty good and I didn't have a body to bury! I got my point across, and he must have figured out that I was serious and I wasn't anywhere near calming down, tired, or losing any steam or objectivity, and he ran like Hell for his truck! For good measure and add a little extra meaning to the words; "Get the fuck out of here!", I grabbed my 30/30 and put three rounds right through his windshield as he made his escape! He backed right over the trash cans and took out about twenty feet of cedar rail fencing on his way out! He was damned lucky that he didn't hit one of the dogs or I would have put one right between his eyes! No, Hell, I wasn't even close to hitting him. I know how to handle a fucking gun!" She interjected in answer to Dan's Quizzical expression but continued; "I could have! I didn't want to kill him, just wanted him gone! That was the last I saw of him! Fuck him! We had used my money to buy the place, not his! I did all the work while he sat around smoking weed that I grew, and drinking shine that I produced all fucking day and went out whoring all night! I figured I owed him nothing, but I gave him a going over with that axe handle and the bullet holes in his windshield as my version of lovely parting gifts!" Then she let out a hearty laugh and took another toke.

I thought long and hard about packing up and coming back here at that time. But I had fallen in love with the mountains and being by the ocean. I get to see some whales from time to time!"

"This really sucks with REB! I thought that big Motherfucker would live forever! Linda called and told me, and I couldn't fucking believe it! I was going to ride, but when she called again, and told me that he was deteriorating rapidly, I caught the fist flight I could get on and rolled into town last weekend! Linda let me stay at her house. There are a few of us oldies staying there. Linda and their girls are staying at the Clubhouse to be with REB. I figured you might be retired by now!" They did a ton of work to fix up the old meeting room to make him comfortable and allow for a lot of visitors. What's with the construction and why all the secrecy about the addition?

Dan seized the opportunity of a short pause and managed to say something, but it was hard to decide what to respond to, react to, or question to answer. "Yeah, they have it fixed up real nice for him. I wish he could unwind a bit though! He interjected when he got the opportunity. He's a man on a mission and this whole dyeing thing is cramping his style! He likes to be in charge and the thought of some grim reaper horning in on his action has him a bit on edge! You're still riding eh?

"Yep still got the old shovel! I did the bottom end over the winter and she's running as good as new! I wish I could have ridden here, but what the Hell! I love that fucking shirt! It's about time! A bunch of us wanted to get REB to do something like that years ago. We have so many supporters, I don't know why we didn't have something like that sooner! Wait until people see it, they will go fucking nuts!"

"Are you going to be in town long? I still have my old shovelhead that you're more than welcome to use, and I have plenty of space at the house if you need a place to crash."

"Oooooh? Step into my lair said the spider to the fly!" she teased. "You Cops can be devious motherfuckers eh!" In this light, she couldn't see if he was blushing but just knew he would be! She playfully punched him in the right shoulder. You know I may just take you up on both of those offers. Linda and the girls will, I'm sure, want to get back home soon and by the way he looks and from what Linda tell me, it looks like it will be very soon. I think the only thing keeping him going right now is he is just too fucking stubborn to let death interfere with his plans! Who knows what they are? But he has, some apparently. I'd like to stay around for a while, maybe two or three weeks or a bit longer if it won't be any trouble for you. I'd love the use of that old shovel! That was M's old ride! I didn't know you still had it! She's a great old bike and she's almost identical to mine.

"Done!" "You can come back with me tonight if you want, or whenever you want!" You didn't know about the shirt then?"

"Hell no! I don't think anybody knew! The sneaky old fuck! It sure looks like his artwork and he still has all that old screen-printing equipment and shit in his Studio. Linda told me that he'd been spending a lot of time out there with the doors always closed and locked, before he got really sick! She tried to get him to take it easy but he'd still be constantly sneaking out there! No, it looks great! Glad he was able to get it done and give it to you in person! You mean a lot to him!"

"Let's grab a beer." he said, taking her by the arm "I'm starving and the smell coming from those barbecues has been driving me crazy since I got here! I haven't eaten since breakfast! My stomach was rumbling so loud I could hardly hear REB's rant!

"She laughed and as they strolled off towards the house, arm in arm, Calamity, told him she'd stay at Linda and REBs house tonight and get her stuff over to his place tomorrow. She, of course, monopolized the rest of the conversation, which was just fine with Dan, he wasn't much in the mood for talking and her sultry-lilting voice was relaxing, refreshing and comforting, like a glass of fine Whiskey!

They had grabbed a couple of burgers loaded with fried onions along with a couple of cold beers and had just finished eating, when Linda and the girls came out and asked that we all go back inside as REB wanted to get things started.

A lot more people had arrived and were crowded into the large room. REB looked good considering. The ladies had gotten him cleaned up and had all that, stubble shaved off leaving his customary Goatee which was pure white as was his long mane of hair, that had been painstakingly combed back and gathered into a long braid that hung to his mid back. He was dressed in a fresh, short sleeved, black, button up club shirt, a fresh pair of black denim jeans and his black cowboy boots that had been shined to perfection. He was in his wheelchair with IV tubes hooked to multiple IV bags hung on an IV tree that in turn, was attached to the chair which all were hooked into his deteriorating arms that bore no resemblance to what they once were. He was alert and upright, his eyes were sparkling and he had a glow about him that nobody had seen in at least two months.

Dan knew everybody in the room and he and Calamity went around the room to say hello to as many as they could, before REB started the meeting. He loved this place and the people that came here! They loved what this club stood for its core values and the intense loyalty and respect that was always displayed here along with honesty and integrity! The club did a lot of charity work and was always giving back to the community but never lost sight of the original purpose of riding a motorcycle was to ride a motorcycle! If they could help somebody along the way, that was fine but they were always "Bikers" First, charity fundraising was a sideline! They, were well respected by other Motorcycle Clubs as well. Dan had come to realize all that, but it had taken him a while to learn and appreciate all that it was!

REB had been wheeled into the room by Linda and Veronica and set in front of the boarded-up doorway to the new addition that nobody other than REB, Linda and those who where working on it had seen or had any knowledge of. The doors and windows were all covered with sheets of plywood and had been, since the project was started five months previous. Everyone was curious! He kept looking impatiently at his at his watch. Dan was sure he knew who and why they were waiting, as one of the Dozen was no where to be seen!

He announced in a voice that was strong and clear, although there was still a hint of discomfort that could be detected! "Well I'd like to get started now because I'm not sure how long the pain-killers that the lovely Nurse Veronica has running through this fucking IV are going to last! She promised she would give me something to allow me to function and not be fucked up and a complete embarrassment! So, if I start to drool and fall out of my chair, you'll know that she fucked up! Let's get on with it!"

"First off, this room is just too fucking small!" He announced loudly, with great panache! He then motioned to two of the work crew who had been part of the project since the start of it, and they moved in and quickly removed the boards covering the wide doorway. They then, threw the heavy doors open, to reveal a very large but extremely dark-ened room. There was a momentary, murmur of confusion, as eyes strained into the darkness to make out what was in there, but that was soon silenced. "Perhaps, some light will help!" Reb announced, and a flick of a remote switch that REB held in his hand turned on a bank of lights that illuminated an enormous and spectacular space. It was all done in Douglas Fir boards and beams with very high ceilings, three large ceiling fans hung down from the massive, over-head beams which would be great for circulating the air during large parties and functions.

A large stone fireplace with a heavy wooden mantle running the entire width of it, occupied one whole end of the room. There was a beautiful wet bar at the other end of the room, that certainly looked capable of accommodating large crowds. A wide array of pictures that would require days of constant studying, to fully absorb, were hung in every available bit of wall space. Old pictures, new pictures, and some that hadn't had eyes set upon them in decades along with memorabilia, such as pieces and parts that had come off various motorcycles in the many hill climbs, drag races, biker games, flat track adventures and many other events that they had experienced over the years, that few if any, other than REB and Linda knew existed anymore!

In the centre of one wall, were another set of double doors, that opened into another large adjoining room. Above the door, carved out in the centre of a large piece of Douglas Fir was an incredible likeness of Old Tony. Under the picture were the words; This room is dedicated to the Memory of Tony Boiko, the man without whom, this would not exist. Immediately, as you walked in the room you came upon a huge glass showcase that was revolving, slowly, and continuously, inside the case, sat "Old Tony's, Dirty Yellow Rat" motorcycle. Yet another tribute to a man that they all admired! Art Johnstone was invited as a special Guest, as was his Son Bill. They had just arrived and you could tell that they were overjoyed, overwhelmed, and thrilled by it all!

"You've come a long way!" was all that Art could say, before breaking down in tears. Proper tribute and respect had been payed!

Big Bill, however, was preoccupied, scanning the faces in the room but not seeing the one he was hoping to see.

This room, had enormous picture windows on three walls, that now had the outside coverings removed, to a afford the gathering a spectacular vista, of the rolling hills and heavily treed countryside on two sides, and the lake on the other. In front of the windows sat a massive, round, oak, table that was about twelve feet in diameter, the table top itself was draped with an enormous sheet of black fabric. There twenty-two, matching, high-back oak, upholstered, chairs arranged around the table with one larger and slightly more ornate chair at one side. At each place setting was large black box and an envelope!

"This, ladies and gentlemen, this, is mine, and my lovely Linda's gift to the Club and to you!" REB continued in a grandiose manner! He was loving this and his smile couldn't have gotten any broader!

"Now if you will kindly proceed to the table, some will find their names at a spot at the table, when and if, you do, please sit there and do not open or examine what has been placed there for you. If you do not find your name at the table, please take a seat at one of the chairs on the perimeter which will be designated as your seat by the name on the envelope which you will find on each of those chairs. Please do not open, or examine these envelopes, until I tell you to and no peaking under the fucking table cloth either! We have some business to attend to first!"

He looked behind him and smiled broadly at Linda, who was beaming with delight, as she wheeled her man to the head of the table, as they waited for others to take their places! He again, glanced at his watch then up at Linda who gave his shoulder a comforting squeeze.

"Mo Chara! My friends! Thank you so much for joining us here tonight! It is with great pleasure that Linda and I offer the Club and all of you the use of this room, which we hope you will enjoy for many years to come! You have all given of yourselves, freely and generously, for many years and this is a token of our appreciation and utmost respect!"

"Given my current circumstances, I am relieved to be able to attend, as I wanted desperately to share this with you! This will probably be my last opportunity to be with you all, in the flesh! It was touch and go if the construction could be completed in time, or, if I would last long enough! There are still a few finishing touches to be done before it is complete. Please don't look behind things as they might be hiding uncompleted work or blemishes! They will be dealt with, I fucking guarantee that!" he cast a quick, but distinct, frown towards at a couple of the workmen who were standing back in the corner, on troubleshooting duty! "Someone, please get those poor fuckers a drink! They worked hard to get this done and put up with a lot of shit from me! In fact, give these men a hand too! You all did a fine job gentlemen! Thank you, please pass this along to your entire crew and you will also be given parcels for yourselves and your crew, from us, to show our gratitude!"

An ovation erupted and the two embarrassed workers smiled and waved awkwardly and tried to sink further into background.

The larger chair had been moved aside to accommodate REB and his wheelchair and Linda had now taken her seat beside REB and opened a large ledger, her reading glasses were delicately perched atop the bridge of her nose, her pen was tapping nervously on the surface of the table as she waited for REB to get down to business! Those drugs that were now the only thing other than his adrenaline were all that was allowing him to function and could only last just so long, and she didn't want him collapsing or anything, at least, until after the meeting!

"As it stands, we are lacking one member of "The Baker's Dozen, Baseball Club" to have quorum!" he paused as if on cue, the sound of a motorcycle roaring down the driveway and sliding to an abrupt stop at the front steps interrupted him! There was the sound of hurried footsteps on the heavy planks of the front porch, before the door burst open and a beautiful lady, dressed in black leather and denim, a frenzied mop of long, luscious, blonde hair flowing from beneath a black bejewelled, bandanna which framed a tanned smiling face. She came striding into the room, with all the presence, aggressiveness, and confidence of a Grizzly bear or a moose in heat! Gypsy, AKA Rose Marie Fitzpatrick, had arrived! A cheer erupted! She was accompanied by a midsized black and white dog resembling a Border Collie, that had a bandanna matching the one she wore on her head hanging around her neck, following close by her side!

"Sorry I'm late! I'm having problems with that bucket of fucking bolts they call a fucking motorcycle, again! I knew I should have bought a fucking Indian! Naw, buy a new Harley, they told me! You'll love it, they said! Fucking jerks! She scanned the room, smiled and waved at no one in particular, until her eyes settled on Big Bill Johnstone! They locked eyes briefly and she may have even blushed. She smiled and got back to her little rant and said "Nice fucking digs!" Someone win a lottery or rob a bank or something? She then bounded right over to REB and gave him a huge hug, a kiss full on the lips, then reached down, gave his crotch a gentle squeeze, looked him in the eye and said "I love you, you mangey old fuck!"! Then she added; Holly shit! You're like skin and fucking bones here! Eat something, for fuck's sake! You look like death warmed over!" She then gave Linda a quick hug and a kiss on the cheek, waved to and blew kisses at a few more people and then sat down on to a chair that Dan had pulled out for her. "What have we here? A fucking officer and a gentleman! Richard Gere hasn't got nothing on you Darl'n! No uniform tonight? Saw your truck and your dog parked out front! I figured it could be a raid and almost didn't come in! Nice fucking shirt!"

The dog followed right along and sat down beside her!

"This is Skooter! She adopted me a couple of years ago, unlike certain men, she has taste and stays with me!" She announced, with a huge smile, while looking directly at the blushing face of Wandering Bill whom she had instantly picked out of the faces from around the table!

A grinning REB, waited until the laughter subsided, and Gypsy finally settled into her seat and shut the fuck up long enough for him to get a word in!

"Welcome Gypsy! Quite the entrance, and fashionably late, to boot! You have flair sweetheart, if nothing else, you have flair! Now, if you will allow me to continue, I've only got just so much time, you know! I only can only stay warm for just so long too, and I don't think they will be able to warm me over again!! We now have Quorum and I'd like to begin, before you wander off somewhere for another five- or six-years, Gypsy! She smiled petulantly back at him, raising a one finger salute and stuck out her tongue at him for good measure! Laughter erupted one again.

"OK! I'd like to call this meeting to order! Only Members are allowed to vote, guests are not allowed to speak unless called upon to do so! Please respect our rules and protocols and keep talking amongst yourselves to a bare minimum, if at all!" He announced gruffly!

"I would like to ask my fellow Members of the Bakers Dozen BC, when the last time was that we brought new Members into our Club was?" People looked around at each other somewhat confused at the question as everybody knew the answer!

"I can answer that question!" He continued. "Never! Never have, and never will! Those of us surviving members are what remains of The Bakers Dozen, BC and there is and always will be only one. There is no adding to what is a defined entity, only death can take us out of that roster and at that point, our number will be retired. However, we, as a Club, have gathered many solid friends and supporters through the years and never even hinted that they would ever become members because, we, and they knew that that was never going to happen.

"Fair or not, these fine, like-minded folks and Kindred Spirits, stuck with us through thick and thin, Hell and high water and most are still with us today just happy to hang out, party their asses off and be part of something good! You've all worked hard at our parties, our poker runs and other events and help make them successful! We thank you! I thank you! However, that doesn't seem anywhere near good enough to me! Thank you, and a dollar might buy you a chocolate bar down at the dollar store! Not good enough! Not anywhere near good enough!"

"Earlier this evening I gifted my dear friend and Brother, Dan O' Reilly, a shirt that I personally and selflessly, designed and silk screened while in excruciating pain, and much discomfort with my own two rapidly, weakening hands, all the while, with the Angel of fucking death hovering behind me, peering over my shoulder, constantly asking me; "Ain't you done yet?" This, caused a ripple of laughter and chatter throughout the room. I heard many favourable comments on the shirt throughout the evening! I hope you all like it!"

"Dan, could you please stand up and try to make the shirt look good!"

Dan stood up and did a little twirl, bowed from the waist and sat back down! There were catcalls and wolf whistles from the crowd! Gypsy reached over and gave him a little slap on his ass!

"OK next order of business! I must apologize to my Club Brothers and Sisters, as I went ahead, completely on my own accord, and modified our logo and printed this shirt without the approval or permission from you. I was wrong and apologize profusely! So, to save me embarrassment and loss of revenue and time spent producing this item, I'm throwing my artistic and creative talents as well as the intensive labour in at no charge, as a donation! Could I PLEASE, get a motion to approve the design and production of this item? I figured we were long overdue to have support items that can be purchased."

"So, moved!" shouted Gypsy!

"Seconded" Tramp added!

"All in favour?"

Hands shot up in response!

"Passed unanimously!" He shouted!

"Could I also get a motion to approve printing enough for everybody in the room?" REB continued!

That motion was also carried unanimously!

"Whew! I thought I may get stuck with a whole wack of t shirts!" said REB, smiling and wiping imaginary sweat from his brow in feigned relief!"

"OK, if you will all open the large envelope on the table in front of you or on your chairs, please enjoy! Courtesy of myself and Linda!"

The room was now abuzz as people ripped open the envelopes, removed and admired the shirts, some, were immediately tearing off the shirts the had been wearing and slipping into the new ones. One big cheer, led by Gypsy, resounded through the room!

REB waited until things started to settle down and he banged his gavel on the sound block on the tabletop to restore order! He wobbled slightly in his chair, Linda was the first to notice, followed by Veronica, who had been hovering behind him and just off to his right, watchful for indication, that he was weakening. Dan too, had also noticed a slight change in REB's energy and demeanor in the last ten minutes or so. REB stopped them all, with raised hands and a stern look. They let it pass, and he continued, but he knew, himself, that he would have to speed things up!

He continued, his voice broke a little, which again prompted movement towards him by those vigilant few who had tasked themselves with his care. Another, stern look from REB made them stand down.

"The Bakers Dozen, started as a makeshift Baseball Club in 1955, made up of misfit boys and girls, playing pick up games in the neighbourhood just for fun, before we formed an actual baseball league! The existing League, with the likes of Dan O'Reilly here, as members, really didn't want us, but we were not going away!

Figuring that we would be eliminated quickly and just go away, they just humoured us at first! We were ridiculed and disrespected every step of the way in the early days! However, we were determined and didn't really give a fuck what they said, and we got good, and kicked some serious ass out there! Eventually, we even established a small, but loyal and enthusiastic, fan base! We all had a good time, but more importantly, through it all, we had each other! Even after playing baseball took a backseat to other interests we were still together as a group of friends. We had this property as a home base and I think that lent some stability.

We stayed together, and over the Years, one by one, we

started riding motorcycles, adopting and enjoying what could best be described as the "Biker Lifestyle"! We have been accused, particularly by Law Enforcement, of being a "Motorcycle Gang!" he paused and stared directly at Dan for an instant! Laughter erupted in the room, as Dan, again, stood up, took at deep bow, and sat back down smiling! Perhaps our resident Chief of Police, could explain to us at some other time, why and how we achieved Gang status!"

"Although we never proclaimed ourselves to be a "Motorcycle Club" We have always conducted ourselves as if we were an MC, and gained respect from most, if not all, recognized Motorcycle Clubs from far and wide! Many of them, have attended, participated in, and enjoyed the parties and events that we hosted here, such as our field event day, Hill Climbs, Poker Runs, funerals, weddings and other celebrations" that we held on this property.

We, years ago, formed The Bakers Dozen Baseball Club, with members of that team, on the advice from our Lawyers, for legal and Banking purposes, again with the advice from our Lawyer. Now, with the Members of that Club dwindling and with my imminent departure for Valhalla, the membership, will further decline and could cause us more issues down the road. "I would like to put a motion on the floor, at this time, that "The Bakers Dozen, Baseball Club's" name be changed to "The Bakers Dozen, Motorcycle Club" and that we adopt our own patch and insignia forthwith!"

While he was speaking, two of the work crew carried in a large display easel, covered with large black sheet, and stood it just behind him and where REB could reach it by turning in his wheelchair`. "I have taken the liberty of designing an insignia, or essentially, I redesigned the logo I created for, and has been used by the Club since it's inception 60 odd years ago, into a patch that I felt would represent the history and traditions of our Motorcycle Club, should my motion carry and this insignia be approved! If carried, current members will continue in their present rank and position, until a formal election meeting can be held, to elect who the members feel would serve them well! You can also write your own bylaws, set terms of office and other such things and our Lawyer will advise you each step of the way!

Now this caused a real stir in the room!

He then reached up and pulled at the sheet that had been draped over the illustration! REB went on to point out and explain the symbolization, that each part of the crest was. "The large Green Shamrock (Which was also the Logo of Bakers Baked goods, his parent's business back then, and they were the only Sponsors of the team.) represented the Irish roots that most of the original founding members shared. I know many of you here today are not of Irish decent, but those were our roots when we started out and made us what and who we were then, and what and who we are today!

The Shamrock is to the Irish what the cross is to other religions. Where the stations of the Cross are; the Father. Son, and Holy Ghost. The three petals of the Shamrock represent Head, Heart and Soul! Tradition and knowing where you came from, I feel are important! In the centre was a black spade with a white 13 in the centre! The 13 represents a baker's dozen as in the Thirteen original members, and the spade I used because I just happen to like spades as an image, and I needed something to contain the 13. The letter M in white is on the left petal and the C also in white is on the right. Those letters are self explanatory. There a pair of crossed pistons behind the shamrock. Two separate green rockers with white outline and white letters stating Swanton Harbour on the Bottom Rocker and the Bakers Dozen on the top rocker. The bottom rocker alone, would be worn by prospective members until their one-year probationary period had been successfully served and they are voted into the club as full members and they would receive the full patch!"

There was a murmur around the room as people discussed what had been presented.

"What about the crossed pistons? Do you think that The Outlaws MC will have a problem with it? asked Big Jake, a long time hang around, from his place at the table, wearing his brand-new Bakers Dozen T shirt with the sleeves already cut off in order to accommodate his massive biceps! The guy beside him elbowed him in the ribs and told him that he didn't have permission to speak! "Oh Fuck!" he exclaimed "I'm sorry!"

"It's OK! The Chair recognizes Big Jake Connor! Hell, I don't think so Jake! I did think about it, but lots of Clubs and organizations use crossed pistons, as well, as skulls, wings and other similar shit! There isn't a smiling skull on there, or any skull at all, for that matter and it doesn't even slightly resemble their patch. Ours is bright fucking green for fuck's sake! I know some guys up near Ottawa that wear a lot of green, and I'll talk to them! In fact, I think I saw a few of them ride in this afternoon. It shouldn't cause any comparison between the two, or any confusion. Depending on how the vote goes, I saw some Outlaws here this evening as well. I'll ask, and they can run it through their room." We will let all the Clubs know, if the vote goes in favour!"

"Gypsy stood up and stated. "That is a fine-looking patch and I would be proud to wear it! However, before I make a motion to approve!" She quickly continued, "Knowing REB the way I do, and his tendency to just bull forward with whatever ideas come into his pointy head, I'm willing to bet that I should add to, or amend the motion, to also say "and produce sufficient patches and other paraphernalia to supply members and future members and save us all the trouble of having to listen to his tale of woe, as to how much time effort and expense went into the creation of said merchandise!

"Second!" Tramp added forcefully!

"All in favour?" hands shot up!

"Carried unanimously!" Reb brought the gavel down on the sound block so hard, that the shaft of the gavel broke and the head sailed back almost hitting Linda before coming to a clattering landing, over in the corner behind some unoccupied chairs! "Cheap piece of shit!" He muttered, examining the piece of wood he was left holding and recognized that if was just a decorative thing not for serious meeting stuff and tossed it back to join the other part back amongst the chairs!

"Thank you! Members only, if you will now open the big white envelope in front of you! In there you will find a large patch and a small patch resembling the illustration behind me, a dress shirt and two T-Shirts also emblazoned with the same image as well as some stickers of various sizes that I threw in because I was in a creative mood and generous mood! Oh yeah, now that the patch design has been approved, please remove this black piece of shit off this fine table." It was then slid off to reveal that under a heavy sheet of glass, the logo of The MC had been skillfully and beautifully carved in the surface beneath it!

"I would now like to call to order the inaugural meeting of The Bakers Dozen, Motorcycle Club!" he said hitting the sound block protecting the table top with a rubber mallet that one of the workers had handed to him! "We will also need a new gavel! A real one!"

The motion was quickly seconded and also approved unanimously.

"OK, new business, all others at the table, please open the small white envelope! Would you please read it and if it is agreeable, sign it with the green pen provided! It is a Club Pen so if you sign, you can keep it as a souvenir. This is your application to join The Bakers Dozen Motorcycle Club. By signing it, you are agreeing to the terms and conditions that are listed on the application. You will be expected to behave in accordance with all Cub rules and policies. It is the same terms under which you have conducted yourselves as hang arounds for The Bakers Dozen. Once you have signed them please pass them to Linda, Our recording Secretary.

Dan shifted uncomfortably in his seat! Fumbling with his envelope and looking to his friend REB for some guidance.

REB could see him sitting there, squirming and fidgeting and doing all that he could to get his attention and ignored him! This was something he would have to decide for himself!

He waited while the process took place, applications were accepted as received and counted.

Linda leaned over to him and whispered after counting, the completed applications!

REB looked disappointed but looked up from the pile of paper before him. "We handed out twenty-two applications and received twenty-one ba…" stopping, mid sentence as the twenty second application was slid in front of him, signed Dan O'Reilly! He looked up and smiled broadly into the face of his friend! Gotcha, finally! Mo Chara! Bràthair gu brath!

"I guess the Town will be getting a new Chief of Police!" He said wry fully!

"I now make a motion that we accept those who have filled out and signed these application as Full Members in the Bakers Dozen Motorcycle Club!"

"Seconded!" Screamed Calamity!

Hands shot up! The Gavel fell!

"Welcome Brothers and Sisters!"

A cheer along with many whoops and hollers that shook the building went up as people hugged and kissed!

REB allowed several minutes for the emotion to subside and called for order, and you didn't have to be watching him closely to notice his discomfort level had risen. "You can now open the boxes!"

"Again, I was being presumptuous by producing this stuff, but I didn't and don't have a lot of time, so I took a shot! Inside each box, is an envelope containing your new member patches and also a package of member shirts in your sizes, along with stickers and some pins. We have brought in several sewing machines, and have volunteers to sew patches on if you like! Please tip generously as it is hard work! We also have several of the best local Tattoo artists on site! It will be an open bar, so enjoy Brothers and Sisters! He announced.

You will also find a wooden presentation box with a laser engraved image of the new emblem and the name of your new Club! Inside the wooden box you will find a bottle of; Pure old Panther Piss, with custom made labelling, which depicts a cartoonish Black panther standing beside a jug, his dick in hand and pissing into a funnel atop a gallon jug, created by myself, plus a handsome pair of shot glasses each engraved with the same stunning artwork as the botte and custom made and engraved presentation case.!

The contents of the bottle was distilled and shipped here especially for this Club, by our Sister "Calamity Jane" out somewhere in the wilds of British Columbia, where she fought off Grizzly bears, poisonous snakes, over-Zealous RCMP officers, poachers and other such things, that lurk in the forests our that way, while under the influence of some killer weed or shrooms, or both, so we will just have to take her word for the fact that quality control was top notch!

I took care of the bottling process myself as I had to do some random sampling! Rumour has it, that Calamity also brought along with her, some of that aforementioned, wonderful BC bud, shrooms and various edible items, that she allegedly produces and can be purchased from our newly opened, Club Support store, at Club discount prices. I also understand she may also, gladly, share her personal, private stash and womanly charms with some lucky guy." He looked directly at Dan, smiled and winked and added; "If he treats her well! If he doesn't, we'll have to help her hide the body in the morning, but don't bury him with me, my coffin only fits one!" He laughed and shouted, "Can I get a motion to adjourn?"

So, moved! someone yelled back. Second! Came another voice! The poor recording secretary strained to see who made and seconded the motion but, in the end, just guessed as to who they were for the record!

"All in favour signify by raising your glasses in a toast to the newly formed The Bakers Dozen, Motorcycle Club! Long may you live, love and ride! Meeting adjourned!"

With that, he reached for his own bottle and glass that sat in front of him on the table. Linda quickly and spontaneously reached out and grabbed his arm, but immediately pulled back, when she saw his reaction. He had stiffened, fixed her unblinkingly, right into her eyes with an intense, smoldering look, from those ice blue laser eyes. He then, defiantly, poured the strong liquor into a shot glass, then poured another for her. Their eyes locked, as if a battle of wills was about to occur! He slid the second glass in front of her, only breaking that intense stare, when he suddenly winked and smiled! She picked it up, winked back, raised it, and clinked her glass with his, in a personal toast, just to them and the life they shared together for the past 50 odd years! Their eyes still locked, they both smiled and flung the harsh liquid back and down their throats! His eyes began to water and he was about to cough but resisted. He took a minute or two to recover and he poured them each another. He looked deep into her eyes, once again, smiled, winked at her again, and said in Irish; Go raibh maith agat mo ghrá! (Thank you my Love!)It's been an adventure!

He poured yet another full shot, raised his glass one more time, tried desperately to stand, but his legs weren't up to the task and he slumped back! "The Bakers Dozen forever and forever The Bakers Dozen!" he bellowed. Welcome Brothers and Sisters, to the Bakers Dozen, Motorcycle Club! I bid you all goodnight and goodbye! I'll wait for you all in Valhalla but don't be in a hurry to join me! He once again, drained his glass, then, collapsed back into the wheelchair, coughing uncontrollably. His arm fell limply to his side and the empty shot glass clattered to the floor, Linda and Veronica immediately and simultaneously swooped in to collect him and were tending to him, as they rushed him back to the hospice room, Dan was close at their heels!

A hush fell over the room, then nervous chatter and they all stared at the now closed doors to the Hospice room. That was the first down beat to an otherwise, fantastic evening!

REB was transferred him from the wheelchair, which they literally had kicked out of the way and it was sent careening into the corner of the room and now lay on its side against the wall, to the bed, by skilled and practiced hands as they worked frantically to keep him alive!

He had regained consciousness, but was now wheezing and shaking uncontrollably and in obvious pain! Veronica injected drugs into his IV, but he wasn't immediately, responding. A couple of other ladies with nursing experience also jumped in to the Frey, in an effort to stabilize him.

Slowly, he started to improve to the point, where the nurses retreated to huddle at the far side of the room, to compare notes. Dan could see them and could tell from their body language that they had exhausted all of their treatment options, and the plan now, would be to just make him as comfortable as possible for the rest of his time here on the planet! Dan moved quietly to the bedside and looked down at his friend. He fought the overwhelming urge to break down and cry! A huge lump had risen in his throat and burned uncontrollably! He, felt so helpless and useless, knowing that there was absolutely nothing he could do to help him.

REB's eyes were now open once again, he was looking around trying to get his bearings. He focussed, and asked in a low weak voice; "Are you pissed at me old Friend?" looking Dan straight in the eye. That was his way! He always looked people straight in the eye, as it was his belief that the eyes were the pathway to people's souls and where the truth of any matter lay. People always felt uncomfortable when he locked them in that probing stare. It was like he was peering directly into people's minds with those piercing blue eyes.

"I kind of trapped you tonight! I forced your hand! I shouldn't have done that to you, but I was on a bit of a roll." At that, his face crinkled up and his mouth formed a huge smile that spread from ear to ear, briefly, the twinkle came back into his ice blue eyes and he let out a chuckle then a full out laugh! Then the laugh transformed into a coughing fit that just seemed to go on forever! That, of course, alerted the ever-vigilant Linda, Veronica and the other ladies and they started towards him, amass, REB raised a hand, shook his head, and he waved them off! He gave them a thumbs up gesture and a smile, in answer to the worried look Linda gave him in return.

He turned back to his old friend, his face, red, grimacing from the pain that wracked his whole body with each and every cough or movement. His eyes were watering and sweat trickled from his forehead and down his cheeks! He forced another big smile, rolled his eyes, and continued. "Wow! I can't believe I got that done! Seriously, if you want to back away, just say so, I'll talk to the rest, they won't hold you to anything you don't want! Tell them I said it is OK! I just wanted to belong to the same Club and share the same patch as you and be true, official, Brothers, just once before I died! We've been on different sides of the fence for way too long, I knew I was never going to be a fucking Cop, so it had to be you coming my way! Again, I wish we hadn't wasted all those early Years hating each other! What an incredible waste of time and energy that was, and you would have made a fantastic short-stop! He paused to reflect and smiled. "Anyhow, that was quite the night!" A look of total satisfaction had now come over his face. He was at peace and it wasn't the drugs!

"Yeah, you were on your game and it was incredible!" Dan interjected. "FYI, you, didn't trick or trap me into anything tonight or ever, you fucking old coot! I've had my resignation typed out, filled out and signed for about six years now. I just haven't dated it and handed it in yet! When that jackass, Dwight Higgins got elected Mayor, and I knew how much he despised me, and you, I just stayed on just to torment the Mother Fucker! I guess, tomorrow is the day, I'll hand it in!

I'll have to return the truck too, I love that damned truck and I will miss it!" He smiled at his deeply troubled friend, perplexed that he couldn't help him.

The drugs that had gone into his IV were now starting to have a strong, very noticeable effect on him he stopped shaking and his speech became slower and he was slurring. His eyes would flicker open and closed as he was fighting to stay conscious and cheat death for a just a little bit longer and try to steal just a few more precious moments of life! That was his true self, a fighter until he very end! His facial expression would revolve, unconsciously, between a smile, a smirk, a grimace and a frown. He motioned for Linda to come to him and she was there in an instant. She leaned in close and he said something that made her stand back for an instant and she looked deep into his eyes. Tears flowed down her cheeks as she leaned in and removed the talisman from around his neck and placed it in REB's hand.

"I think I've got to give this to you in person to make it official and transfer the magic, so lean in here my friend, I can't get up, and no kissing! At least no fucking tongue! He joked!

Dan leaned in and REB used every once of strength he had to drape the ornate object that he hadn't taken off in years, around Dan's neck. Linda helped him with the latch.

Dan rose up, REB looked at him and said; "This will protect you, better than it did me, I hope!" He chuckled!

"My friend, my Brother, Mo Chara, I think its time that you turned the page and begin a new chapter in your life!

Veronica came over and put her hand gently, on his shoulder and he knew that she wanted to for him to leave so they could work on the patient, who had once again, drifted off into a drug induced sleep. It, would have been a taxing time for anyone let alone, someone in the final stages of an insidious disease that would soon claim another victim! Those straight shots of shine, certainly didn't help his condition either, but at that stage of the game, it couldn't really hurt either! In fact, it was his final release and his final time to look life and his immanent death straight in the eye and shout fuck you! My life! My death! My terms! What's next?

"Fuck cancer!" Dan muttered out loud! Veronica heard, smiled weakly and nodded as she moved closer to REB to check his vitals.

"See you, Mo Chara!" He said, as he rose to leave!

"Come by tomorrow, we'll talk." REB mumbled, his eyes, half open, and still fighting to stay in this World, and it was evident that there weren't enough, or potent enough, drugs to put him to sleep, yet, as he knew that the next time he closed his eyes for longer than a quick blink, they would not reopen. He tried to wave goodbye but couldn't raise his arm, he wiggled some fingers instead, summoning enough strength to raise just one finger, the middle one, pointed up, in salute then switching to a thumbs up!

Dan, returned the gestures, then quickly turned to leave. As he headed for the door, Linda, had once again, regained her composure and was headed over to be with her husband for as long as she could. She had REB's little dog Gidget in her arms and was about to put her on the bed with him. But first, she gave Dan a big hug and thanked him for coming by.

As he walked out the door he noticed a line of newly patched vests on the member's backs and could hear the whirr of sewing machines as patches were being attached. There was a large table piled high with vests and envelopes against the wall. He absentmindedly slid his envelope containing his patches on the table, and one of the ladies looked up from her work and acknowledged that she had seen him and smiled. "I'll pick it up tomorrow. Just leave it with Linda." He instructed, as he withdrew three $100.00 bills from his pocket and stuffed them into the Tip jar in front of her. She thanked him and said that would be fine, it would be ready.

There was some serious celebration happening and he could see that a pile of pure old Panther Piss bottles had already been drained of their content. There would be some foggy heads around here tomorrow, he thought to himself. He descended the steps and walked out into the crisp autumn night and to his truck where Zeke waited patiently. He could hear the loud thumping of his stubby tail and butt against the truck's tires as he acknowledged Dan's appearance joyfully. He fired up the truck and headed for home, waving at some members as he exited through the gate.

He was lost in thought, subconsciously, fingering that stunning, silver and turquoise Talisman, the whole drive home, and he didn't even remember driving, but there he was, walking through the front door of his house. He went immediately to his study, to his safe, entered the combination and pulled the heavy metal door open. He took the clip out and deposited it and the gun in a box on one of the shelves and extracted two large envelopes, one had The Mayor and Town Counsel written across it. The other, was addressed to Deputy Chief Angela Jackson! He opened the two envelopes pulled out the documents contained in each, signed, dated them, replaced them in their respective envelopes and sealed them before returning them to the safe and closing the door. "Well that is that!"

He then pulled that wooden box from the box that he'd been given, towards him on the desk, extracted the bottle of Pure old Panther Piss and the shot glasses, poured himself a full shot and slammed it back! He could feel the warmth of the liquid as it journeyed all the way to the very pit of his stomach. He poured and drank one more, before heading off upstairs for a shower and then to bed, Zeke was right at his heels. It had been a long and eventful day. That, and the alcohol were really having an effect on him and now, the bed was certainly looking inviting! He stretched out under the covers, Zeke pushed tight against his side and the two were out like a light!

CHAPTER EIGHT
SHOWDOWN AT HIGH NOON!

THE EARLY MORNING SUN, hung in a cloudless, bright blue sky, and cast its rays, warm and welcome on his face. The old Duo Glide rolled along the seldom travelled piece of blacktop and effortlessly climbed the hills and maneuvered like a dream through the curves, twists and sharp turns that made it more of an adventure than just a ride. He would twist the throttle and take it to the next level, challenging his abilities and skills and having to apply them to make it through. He was in no hurry, the miles melted away and the beautiful scenery, presented a slight distraction as he tested himself, his skills, his nerve and his motorcycle to measure up to the task at hand! To him, that was what riding a motorcycle represented; life and the pure pleasure of just doing it! Dan was enjoying the bright, warm sunshine and the wind flowing over his face and through his hair like the gentle touch of angel's fingers caressing him! The wind was like a siren's call, beckoning him forward. He was as close to

Heaven as he could come without having to actually die! The magical, throaty, rumble of his bike's exhaust coming from the fish-tail pipes was music to his ears and it reverberated majestically with authority, through the quiet countryside.

He glanced in his rear-view mirror and noticed another motorcycle coming up very quickly behind him. He, being in no particular hurry to be anywhere at any particular time, backed off the throttle a bit and pulled slightly to his right to let this other motorcycle that was quickly overtaking him pass unobstructed to his left.

To his complete shock and dismay, this other biker chose to pass him on the right side, running on the loose gravel on the shoulder of the road rather than the paved surface of the roadway! "Fucking Nut!" Dan sputtered. Then! As the other motorcycle came up directly alongside, the rider actually reached out his left arm and slapped him gently in the back his helmetless head! His head snapped quickly to the right, towards this idiot, anger and disbelief, quickly changed to shock and confusion, and he looked into the tanned, ruddy, face of REB, who looked back at him with a huge smile spread across his handsome face. He was riding his big, bright orange, Knucklehead bobber, wore no helmet, and his long red mop of hair flowed freely in the wind. He had his little black and white dog stashed in a sling that was slung over his shoulder and hung diagonally across his chest in front of him. Her long fur was blowing back, she had goggles on to protect her eyes from the wind and she looked as comfortable and content as she always did, when in REB's company! Something, was different though! This didn't make any sense! He then realized, that he was looking at a younger version of his friend, as his hair and beard were both long and very red, not white! No words were spoken, just a big smile, his left hand raised in the one finger salute but quickly changed to a thumbs up and with that and a sudden twist of the throttle with his right hand, a wicked roar erupted from the shorty exhaust and he accelerated quickly on past, shooting loose gravel and dust back at Dan from his wake! He was now totally, dazed and confused to the point that he almost crashed! It all happened very quickly and all Dan could make out on the riders back was a flash of green from the back patch that looked like a shamrock.

Dan cracked the throttle wide open and took off in pursuit, but could not catch the other bike! He could hear the familiar bark of the knuckle's exhaust fade and soon the bike and rider disappeared in in the distance.

"What the absolute fuck?" he heard himself saying out loud, as he woke and found himself sitting bolt upright in his bed.

He sat there bewildered and confused for a minute or two, before focussing his attention on the familiar, and distinctive, low growl and rumble of several big v twin motorcycles coming from the road out front of his house, as they passed. "Wow!" he said as he shook his head yawned and stretched. "Now I'm dreaming about the fucking guy, and I was riding the Duo Glide, and no helmet, fancy that!". He listened intently as the sound of the motorcycles faded into the distance, but soon, several more could be heard as they moved by. This was not a main thoroughfare, but did hook up with a couple of main arteries that led in and out of Town. It was used mainly by locals who were familiar with the streets of the Town as a short cut. This much traffic, this early, was very uncommon!

The cool, September, morning breeze, coming from the open widow of the spacious bedroom, sent a shiver over his body, as Dan, somewhat reluctantly, eased himself out from under the covers and lowered his feet to the large, comforting shag rug that occupied that side of the bed, shielding them from shock of the harsh cold that the bare plank flooring that would have otherwise welcomed them with. He didn't even look at the clock on the bedside table, as he knew it was close enough to 6:00 AM and he was awake, so he shut off, the still set, but totally unnecessary alarm before it had an opportunity to do its job. The early morning sunlight beamed in, bathing the room in its friendly glow.

He stretched and yawned some more, still trying to decipher the strange dream he just had and felt the presence of his constant canine companion, Zeke, as it cuddled up beside him, he stirred slightly, but, was in no real hurry to leave the comfort of that big old King-sized bed, the plush, warm comforter, blankets, cool sheets and pillows that had enveloped them throughout the night.

But, another day beckoned, and when he heard that long groan, accompanied by a few choice cuss words and occasional gastric noises that were sometimes emitted by his bedmate and true friend, as he rose to an upright position, and was now peering out through the window to gain some perspective on what kind of a day was in store for him today. He could still hear the distinctive sound of many motorcycles coming from the highway and knew something was up.

Zeke waited patiently still snuggled deep in the covers as

the morning ritual of visit to the bathroom, sit-down on the toilet, again accompanied by those gastric noises, as well as the sound of his bodily functions happening in the toilet bowl! The ritual continued with a close inspection of his weathered old face in the mirror, followed by a shower that eased his tired old body back into reality. He dutifully brushed his teeth, swished some harsh tasting mouth wash around and spit it out into the sink. "Fuck! That stuff is fucking horrible! Why do I keep buying it!?" He muttered out loud. He looked in the mirror as if expecting his reflection to provide the answer, then shrugged and moved on to the next task.

He stopped to admire the amulet that now hung around his neck and would remain there until he too passed it on when his time came. He thought of the events of the previous day and the commitment that he had made and his decision to resign as Chief of Police. He thought of his friend, whom he was going to miss. He thought of the times that that man had saved his life, and how much his life had changed because of him and how many others had benefited from him as well. He felt himself starting to get emotional and he had to get on with his day.

He shaved, as he had always done, raking first, the right side of his face with the familiar five bladed razor that performed this same task on a daily basis for the past 30 of his now, 70 years. He was well aware that the stubble being scraped from the surface of his weathered old flesh was more, shades of white and grey, than anything else. With each stroke revealing the many scars on the well tanned face, scars consistent with having a job where the main task is enforcing rules and regulations on people, with some, being not too inclined to following them.

He trimmed his large mustache with a small pair of scissors. The mustache too, was now white but it matched the full head of hair on his head. He had been tempted to shave it off many times over the years but it had been on his face for almost 50 Years and he kind of liked it and was used to it, so it stayed. Each scar on that face had a story and he reflected on each and every one of them as he performed his task. Some he would think about and smile, others made him wince! He would then step back and take in the reflection of his still somewhat fit body! He wasn't a particularly large man, standing just over six feet tall and weighed in at just a tad over two hundred pounds so he was no shrimp either! He was well muscled, but had a bit of fat gathering around his mid section. It used to bother him quite a bit but he just, sort of got used to it, and over time, made peace with the fact that it was there and probably would be with him for the duration!

A far cry from what he looked like in his prime, but still respectable, given his age, the torment that he put his body through and the life he had thus-far, survived! He examined more scars, some sports related, that sometimes had required surgery to repair from his days playing football, hockey, baseball and other rough and tumble activities! Other scars were the result of the oft violent career that he had chosen. Two from gunshots, one in the left shoulder one in the chest just above his heart (Both pre-bulletproof vest days!), sustained when he unexpectedly, interrupted a bank robbery in progress and one of the would-be bandit's reaction to his arrival was to shoot him from a distance of eight feet. Dan's subsequent reaction was to pull his own weapon and squeeze off three shots, as he fell. Each bullet found their mark in the centre mass area of the bandit's body and he was dead before he hit the ground! From where he fell and lay bleeding profusely and in a great deal of pain, Dan had still had enough presence of mind or survival instinct to pick out the other two culprits as they raised their weapons and he fired three more rounds wounding the other two miscreants badly enough that they were easily disarmed and restrained by citizens and bank personnel. Something had to be said for pure stubbornness and stamina! He didn't remember much after that but he was told later that he had actually flat-lined twice on the operating table, but they were able to bring him back.

Then there were the scars from three knife wounds one to his right forearm and one to his left bicep from fending off attacks and one to the abdomen when he wasn't able to react in time to deflect the thrust! He knew the source of each and every one of those scars, and could assign blame and visualize their origin and how long each recovery took. It certainly wasn't an easy life that he had chosen but, all in all, it had certainly been an eventful and memorable one!

Now the dressing ritual, starting with underwear, some of which were almost as old as he, but they were comfortable! Then the sock selection from another drawer that like his underwear drawer, offered only one choice of colour, black! The mandatory bullet-proof vest came next, he hated wearing it but it had saved his life on a couple of occasions so he put up with it and it was mandatory. He then reached into the closet and extracted a crisp clean uniform shirt from where it hung amongst a row of identical shirts and put it on, then a fresh pair of trousers and aside from the affixing of his badge and gun belt, he was ready to go!

Zeke, recognizing that the final stage of the ritual had been accomplished, leaped cheerfully from the bed and watched anxiously from the top of the stairs as Dan strait-ened the covers and put the pillows back in place before following his impatient friend who had now reached the bottom in one mighty bound! The scatter rug at the bottom did nothing to impede his dash progress! In fact, it was perhaps, one of his favorite things to do, and he would ride that little piece of rug, across the hallway, and crash into the wall! He stood there now, (It is unclear whether the dog was wagging the tail or if the tail was wagging the whole back end of the dog.) emitting little whines and chirps totally inconsistent with the size of the dog and all four feet were already in motion, running in place. His head constantly looking back to see what progress Dan was making as he reset the magic carpet in preparation for his next decent of the stairs.

When the door finally opened, he bounded out in the yard sending several squirrels and a couple of Mourning Doves seeking cover in the nearby maple and white birch trees. He didn't really didn't have any intention of harming them but the sight of a pure black, a hundred and some, pound, over zealous and very enthusiastic pit bull in full flight gave them reason to err on the side of caution and take flight.

He went about his own ritual while patrolling the

perimeter of the spacious yard inspecting everything for signs of intruders. This was a task that he took very seriously and if he detected that those pesky raccoons had been around he was even more vigilant, every once in a while he'd catch a scent, stop and peer into the trees and perhaps, even stick his big snout into bushes and shrubs until he was satisfied that the masked beasts were no longer in the immediate area, before bounding back to the house where his breakfast would be now waiting in the huge stainless steel dish next to his freshly filled water bowl.

By now, Dan had made his cup of black coffee, toasted his usual sesame seed bagel, buttered it and spread a coating of cream cheese on each half and was scanning the morning newspaper that he had retrieved from his doorstep. After wolfing down his own breakfast, Zeke assumed his usual position at his feet ever watchful for a stray morsel that might accidentally fall to the floor or much appreciated handouts.

With breakfast out of the way and dishes washed and put away, Dan stopped at his small office, practiced fingers dialed the combination to the gun locker/safe and he extracted the Glock automatic weapon and ammunition clips from within, along with the two large envelopes. Just a quick buff of the black boots a final inspection in the full-length mirror by the door, a final approving nod and a quick wink at his reflection and he was ready to go.

Zeke was already at the front door where he waited excitedly for Dan to open it and they could get to whatever adventures lay in store for them today. As they made their way to the awaiting, unmarked, black, Ford F150 that served as his patrol vehicle they were both aware of the distant sound of multiple motorcycles. Dan frowned and habitually bit gently on his bottom lip and an uneasy, uncomfortable feeling crept over him as he eased himself into the seat with Zeke assuming his usual post in the passenger seat.

He didn't bother to radio in, as he was on time, as always, and he was the boss so he didn't feel the need, plus if they needed him the would have called his cell phone. He glanced down to see the phone on the consul, not plugged in and drained of all it's power! "Fuck! That's helpful!" "Fuck!" He threw the phone into the back seat! "Fuck it, I'll charge it when I get to the office!" He muttered out loud.

They headed off down the quiet street and made it to the highway. It was then, that he saw the first of many packs of motorcycles, mostly Harley-Davidsons. Many of the riders sported cuts with Club colours and insignia, lots of different Clubs, and they were everywhere! Restaurants, motels, hotels, all along that stretch of road, with parking lots packed with motorcycles! Now the uneasy feeling had moved to the pit of his stomach and he was pretty sure he knew what had occurred over night!

He drove to the Stationhouse and parked in his usual spot and made his way inside, Zeke trotted at his side, past the front desk and the rows of cubicles that served as offices for the twenty officers that were employed by the Department! There were greetings all along the way with the chief acknowledging them as they went. Zeke however had his destination in mind and proceeded immediately and duti-fully to his big plush bed to the right of Dan's desk in his office, this included stopping enroute, at Angela's desk for his usual petting, fussing and praising of how good a boy and how handsome he was and of course, a large dog biscuit!

Angela, an attractive woman, now in her early to mid fifties, had been with the Force for around twenty-five years and his assistant for the past fifteen years. She had taken a couple of bullets about ten years into her career. Unlike Dan, she was unable to fully recover from her injuries and she was left with a permanent limp and pain that never really subsided. The one to the knee, was the one that affected her most! Dan was able to get her assigned to him as an assistant, at full pay and benefits! She was efficient, bright and pleasant and quite a handsome woman, with a dark complexion common to her native heritage, deep brown eyes, long black hair, trim figure and an infectious smile that made her dimples quite prominent in her cheeks. She looked up, and smiled but something in her big brown eyes, betrayed the fact that she was obviously, deeply troubled by the news she must now impart. She answered the troubled expression on Dan's face without the usual cheerful "Good Morning"!

"I'm so sorry, but REB died last night!" She announced. "Linda called, she said she tried to reach you but your phone went right to voicemail!" Her voice was shaking and her eyes were filled with sadness. She knew that they were close friends.

Dan just nodded, smiled weakly and proceeded to his office, closing the door behind him. He dug into his pants pocket and found his personal cell phone. Yep, it too, was drained and totally unresponsive to his frustrated taps on the screen! He sank into that big black leather chair, he plugged both phones into the charger on his desk, slumped back, and just sat there, staring out the window at the street that was getting busier by the minute as more motorcycles and assorted other vehicles arrived. He knew full well that this was just the start of it. There were going to be a lot more motorcycles and he knew as well, that that many motorcycles and hard-core bikers all in one place, at one time, was going to attract attention from the media and others along with various law enforcement agencies. It was going to be a busy time!

He looked up in response to Angela's gentle knock on his office door and he motioned her inside. "The Mayor is on the phone!" she announced apologetically.

"Tell him I'll call him back!" Dan muttered

"He said it was urgent!" She continued weakly!

He simply cast a harsh look in her direction, that told her all she needed to know on that subject, but she had her job to do and was going to do it!

"Also, Counselor Green and Counselor Steve Smith want to speak to you immediately!" She blurted timidly yet clearly before, retreating hastily back to her desk and tried to appease an obviously angry Mayor!

"Fuck that pompous prick and his sidekicks!" He muttered under his breath and he continued staring out the window, focussing on nothing in particular while trying to collect his thoughts. He glanced longingly, at the lower right drawer of his desk that contained a bottle of Wiser's, Deluxe, Rye Whiskey and a glass. "Too fucking early! But I'll definitely be seeing you later!" he said softly with a grin. Hell! It just occurred to him that he never drank whiskey before he met REB who had introduced him to the habit and that brand years ago and it now would seem to be very appropriate time! "Later!" he muttered again, giving the still closed drawer a little pat.

Zeke, recognizing his friends' distress, quietly walked up and rested his large black head on Dan's lap for him to pat absentmindedly, as he tried to deal with what had happened at what was about to transpire because of it. It was peaceful for the moment, but that was about to change!

He was just reaching for his phone to call REB's Wife; Linda to offer his condolences and get details as to what the arrangements would be, when he heard the commotion from out in the outer office and looked up to see the hulking presence of Mayor Dwight Higgins, obviously, very angry, storming through the office with two of his puppy dog Town Counselors, Green and Smith, following close behind him! They had stormed passed the front desk, to the protests of the officers, manning that station and he was now heading in the direction of his office! He could see Angela rise to her feet and position herself in the Mayors intended path!

The Mayor, a very large man, standing around 6 foot, four, and weighed around three hundred and sixty pounds. He had grown up in this Town and his father served as a Police Officer for about fifteen Years at the same time as Dan's dad did. Dwight Sr. was also a large, slovenly, very unpleasant individual who, one night, was brutally murdered, bludgeoned to death, in his cabin which was then set ablaze. This took place, just after Dan had joined the Department, and the case was never solved! Dwight Jr., who is the spitting image of his father, blamed REB Baker and his Bakers Dozen for the murder.

REB, and other members of the Dozen, including Rose Marie Higgins (AKA Gypsy), Dwight Sr.'s step-daughter, were the focus of an intense and thorough investigation but, in the end, they were never able to prove any connection and the case remains in the Cold Case file to this day! So, to say that he was motivated to cause whatever problems he could for anyone even remotely connected to The Dozen (As they were commonly known.) would be an understatement! Plus, the fact, that his older, step-sister had been strongly suspected as being involved in the murder and still chose to hang around with that bunch, yet, no longer associated with him or anyone in their family didn't help any!

His once blonde hair was now showing a lot of grey and definite signs of advanced pattern baldness. He also displayed signs of obvious blood pressure issues, as his entire head had a constant red hue and it would turn bright red when he was stressed, angry, or flustered and given his disposition, it was red much of the time! He was definitely one or more of those things at this particular moment!

He was also extremely overweight, sweated profusely and constantly. He didn't carry the weight well at all, sported a huge pot belly, wore cheap, ill-fitting, suits, ugly ties, and seemed to outgrow his shirts as he wore them. There was always a button or two missing from his shirts and his skin and hairy belly would be exposed, most of the time just below his where the gawdy ties he wore didn't reach. His beady little eyes that were almost unseen due to his fat cheeks and bushy eyebrows. To top off the total look of success, he wore, white high-top running shoes which he would take off when he was in the office and would put on a pair of red plaid fabric slippers!

Then to add to this whole spectacle, he also, waddled instead of walked! Waddled, is about the kindest way to describe his ambulatory efforts. He lacked grace, or smoothness let alone any sort of cadence or co-ordination so waddle might best describe his movement. Someone once said he walked like the A&W Root Bear and got no argument from anyone. Then one day, some prankster had hidden a speaker in the hallway and played that old jingle, that A&W restaurants used with a tuba part that went "Bump pa bump pa bump ba bump, bump." to represent the mascot bears waddle, as he walked down the hall! Old Dwight was ready to fire everybody in the building that day and there were many taking bets on the odds of him having a stroke or heart attack!

To say he was not well respected, would be a gross understatement. He was the constant target of pranks. Then of course, there were all the very nasty cartoon images of him that were constantly circulating around city hall or being scribbled on the washroom walls in both the men's and Women's facilities all over Town. They could be extremely cruel as well. None of this had a positive effect on his mood swings either! He had come from a banking career, working at several local banks where he wasn't especially liked either, before taking to politics!

One time, unbeknownst to him, one of his staff replaced his regular sneakers, with an almost identical pair except, the replacement ones had those lights in the heels that lit up with each step! He wore them all day, wondering what everyone was laughing at before discovering the joke.

To some, his bulk was intimidating and threatening, and he was constantly rude to his staff and anybody else who he dealt with for that matter. From wait staff in restaurants, parking attendants, secretaries, truck drivers or anyone else, whom, he considered not his equal! He was the Mayor after all and in his mind was due absolute respect at all times! The Bakers Dozen, and REB (Robert Edward Baker) were a particular thorn under his saddle and had been for quite some time!

Now, his two constant, sycophants, and allies, Counselors Richard Green and Stephen Smith, two nondescript individuals, who somehow, got people to vote for them and intended to stay in municipal politics as they were even less suited and qualified to do anything else, in any other field! They hung so close to the Mayor that they were often seen as one entity! They were part of the "New Breed" of local politicians that had squeezed out most of the "Old group" some of whom, were or were related to the founders of this Town. History means nothing to these new people who viewed history as something to be forgotten, quickly.

As Swanton Harbour grew in size over the years, going from Police Village when it was founded in 1909, achieving Town status in 1961 and to date had resisted merging with other municipalities. Politicians such as Mayor Higgins and his cronies were aware of the Big fish little pond, theory and knew all too well that if they were put into a bigger pond where bigger fish ruled they would be considered to be small fry and gobbled up quickly so they did all that they could to avoid that scenario. They were content to be a rural bedroom Community, with no real industries to speak of and other than a few small factories, it was considered to be a farming community.

High housing costs in communities closer to the industrial and social hub, had driven many to seek housing in these rural areas and small villages and Towns. There was an exodus, with many moving here to allegedly, get away from the hustle and bustle of the larger Communities. However, they then busied themselves trying to recreate what they were trying to escape in their new surroundings. They wanted to bring these local, hicks and hillbillies into the 20th Century! Municipal politics, moved too slow and the older locals, were often unreceptive to proposed changes and growth, so these new residents, with support from the large influx of new residents, slowly but surely squeezed out the old guard. Small Town values, and history were cast aside and the Town lost its flavour, character and identity in the transition. Dan had no use or respect for any of them, especially the three who were attempting a coup here and now! He often referred to them as Curly, Larry and Moe. The, Three Stooges of City Hall.

He watched now, as the Mayor came trudging up on Angela, who was now standing, blocking his intended path. Mr. Mayor was having none of that, and basically, straight-armed her in the shoulder, with his big, beefy, outstretched hand, without breaking stride, sending her stumbling backwards and crashing into her desk! Counselors Green and Smith also pushed by! "Out of the fucking way, Bitch!" Counselor Green could be heard hissing as he went by! She shot Dan an apologetic look and mouthed, "I'm so sorry!" Dan just winked at her through the window and she was now suddenly puzzled by a strange, playful, little grin that had formed on his face, and his mustache twitched slightly as he leaned back in his chair, his arms folded across his chest awaiting the spectacle that the Mayor and his minions had planned! "What the fuck is he up to now?" She wondered as she sat down at her desk, eyes fixed on the Chief to see what was about to happen!

Mayor Higgins, now reached the closed office door flinging it open with such force that the glass window broke when it crashed into the wall behind it, sending shards of glass spewing all over the office! The breeze that was created, by this grand entrance, sent loose papers from atop the nearby filing cabinet flying as well! He was in full fury, mode! Standing hovering over Dan who sat stoically, with his arms still folded!

Zeke, startled by the explosive nature of the sudden entrance, and who was certainly not used to his friend being spoken to in such a manner, let out a series of loud barks and quickly and purposely, rose to his feet and was about to go into full on, attack mode. A snap of Dan's fingers, stopped him and he reluctantly, went back to his bed as per Dan's silent command. He kept up a deep throated growl and an intense stare fixed on this fat intruder who dared to speak that way to his friend! Every fibre in his being wanted to tear into the fat fuck!

"What the fuck is that mutt doing in here? Who the fuck, do you think you are?" He demanded! "When I call, you fucking well, pick up the phone!" I'm the Mayor! You work for me!" He screamed at the top of his voice!

Dan glanced discreetly at Angela, where she sat, completely dumfounded, at her desk, and motioned for her to come see him. She slipped unnoticed in and out of the room, examining the quickly scribbled note the Chief had handed her. She now knew that there was a plan in the making, and hurried off to comply with his request!

"What the fuck are you doing about all these hooligans, these dirty, filthy bikers and criminal gangs? The Town is full of them!" He was now just getting warmed up, and he was already mopping copious amounts of sweat that ran freely down through the thinning hair on his head, over the bright red forehead and puffy cheeks and now mixed with spittle that sprayed freely over what ever and whomever was in front of him! His attempts of mopping the moisture, with the large white handkerchief were unsuccessful as it was now completely drenched!

To Mayor Higgins, it was like a dream come true! This was his stage and his show! He had come to have a showdown with this Chief of Police, and if he could knock him down a peg or two, in front of his entire staff and fellow officers, it was just so much better! He would make it clear to one and all, that he was a force to be reckoned with!

Everybody in the room, including those who, were in the process of being booked, filing a complaint, or whatever, stopped what they were doing and had their full attention focussed on the Chief's office with the door still wide open the floor covered in broken glass and strewn with papers! They didn't want to miss this! Counselors Green and Smith, were loving this as well! They knew not, what would be the appropriate expression to put on their faces; anger, shock, or just grins! They chose smug little grins but stayed well back from the Mayor's spray zone! The big Chief of Police was being put in his place today, once and for all! Now he will know that he has to show them respect!

"You have to round these people up and run them out of Town immediately! The good Citizens of this Town deserve to be safe!" He continued, now buoyed, at getting this far in his rant, still on a roll and the Chief had yet to utter a word! "You need to assign someone to this "Biker Situation" that can handle them, and knows how to deal with that kind of scum!" My Son Walter, (The Mayor has a Son that shares many of the Mayor's characteristics and attributes as fat and dumpy seems to have been traits, passed down from generation to generation; probably due to some genetic mix-up somewhere down the line! And the Mayor had gotten him hired on with the department, while Dan was away on a motorcycle road trip a couple of years back.) the Mayor continued after looking around the room making sure he had everybody's attention. Walter graduated top of his Class at the Police academy! He would be perfect!! I want him to be put in charge of this fiasco immediately! I understand that you are friends with this REB character, so this would be a conflict of interest for you! See even his name is disrespectful to society and decent folks! REB, for Rebel, no doubt! I hear he is still the leader of this Gang of Criminals, "The Bakers Dozen"!

He was now pacing back and forth in front of the Chiefs big desk! Waving his hands in the air, pointing fingers in the

Chiefs face, occasionally pounding his fist on the desk for emphasis and effect, which got another rise out of Zeke, who had resumed an upright position in his bed every muscle was now just tense and twitching, waiting to be set loose on the fat, loud, man in the soaking wet shirt, and wilted suit who was ruining what should be a good day at the office! The constant low growl emitting from deep in the now very alert Zeke, grew slightly louder! "Why is this fucking dog on premises? Shouldn't he be muzzled? Can someone take him out of here!?" Pleaded the Mayor, he then resumed his rant, but kept a constant eye on the now snarling and drooling, Zeke.

He was putting on quite a show, to be sure. His chest was pumped right out there! The shirt tail on his left side had come untucked from his pants and now hung out and below the bottom of his jacket! Veins were now very prominent and pulsing, on his beet red forehead. He was giving the whole Police Department notice that he is the man in charge in this Town and that this Mayor doesn't take shit from anyone, not even the fucking Chief of Police! There wasn't a sound from the outer office as everyone was just staring in silence and disbelief! They had never heard anyone ever speak to the Chief that way! Ever!

Now, the Chief, who had just remained seated, expressionless and totally quiet throughout the whole spectacle, and had simply leaned back in that big comfortable chair, with his arms folded across his chest! Other than what seemed to be a slight, bemused, grin that was mostly hidden by his large moustache, he showed absolutely no emotion, no anger, no shock, nothing!

He now, smiled, unfolded his arms, rose slowly to his feet, walked over directly in front of the Mayor, cleared his throat, seemingly, totally oblivious to the spray zone. He looked the Mayor square in the eye, and began to speak in a calm, slow and quiet manner. This had many of the observers totally bewildered. Had their Chief met his match in this blustery, dumpy, Mayor? Had he mellowed? Several "WTF's" could be heard in the otherwise hushed outer office as this wasn't the Chief that they had come to know.

"I will first speak to the matter of all the Bikers being in Town. It is not an invasion! It is a Funeral! These men and women are here, solely to pay tribute and give their respects to a friend who just passed away, in a way that Bikers have been doing for many decades! I have no just cause at this time, for me, personally, or for me to ask the officers under my command, to round up random Citizens of this Country, and run them out of Town because they make you, person-ally uncomfortable!

You may well be the Mayor, but you are not the law and you do not supersede the rights of Citizens of this Country given to them and guaranteed by the Charter of Rights! Your assertions, that these people are all hooligans, criminals and members of criminal gangs or organizations is merely your opinion! They will be treated as law abiding citizens by myself and my department, until they prove to be otherwise or someone supplies me with warrants or documentation that proves otherwise! They will cause no trouble, if left alone. The funeral, I hear, is on Saturday, I will be joining them at the funeral and for the tribute ride to the Cemetery, on my motorcycle wearing Club Clothing and Club Colours!

Most of them will be gone by Sunday!" The Chief announced, and he continued; "Further more, the gentleman's name is Robert Edward Baker. REB is an acronym. Do I have to explain to you what that is? He, was a close personal friend of mine and if you ever slander him or besmirch his name or character in my presence again, you may have to press assault charges against me!

"As to your Son Walter, he has been a Member of this force for two years, and has yet to prove himself to be particularly apt, responsible, capable, or competent enough to be assigned anything more complicated than the traffic duty assignments, he currently is being assigned to. However, I will continue to give him a fair chance to pull up his socks and get with the program!"

His voice was now rising in volume but the pitch remained low and ominous, like distant thunder "Mr. Mayor, with all due respect to your Office, I will do my utmost to all answer your questions to the best of my abilities! First off, I do know who and what the fuck I am! I am the Chief of Police in this Town! According to the terms and conditions of my long standing, Contract and Job descriptions, until I am removed from this position, by order of the entire Town Counsel, at a duly called meeting, where I, along with my Lawyer, and are provided adequate time to state my case, address any concerns and defend myself against any charges brought against me! I will continue to make decisions on how things are done in this Town, in respects to Law Enforcement without input from you! I have the authority to promote, hire, fire, and assign duties to the Officers in my charge as I see fit, and I will decide who does what, when and where in this Department! If you choose to fire me, fine! Have at it! But, there are procedures that you must follow to accomplish that! Do that! I will gladly see you in Court! For now, I am still in charge! Then again I may just resign!"

"Speaking of Court, we may see you there, sooner rather than later! He stated almost cheerfully! "I have assigned one of my Senior Officers to be Acting Chief of Police, or Deputy Chief, if you prefer, in my absence, as I am going on vacation effective, a half hour from now! The duties will include dealing with the current "Biker Situation'" should it turn out to be more than just large Funeral! I will be available to The Deputy Chief alone, for consultation should the need arise! This Officer, has served this Department faithfully and diligently for more than twenty-five years. And is eminently qualified to do the job. I would also strongly recommend this officer as my replacement should I leave, or be unable to fulfill my duties for any reason."

Now this had the whole room buzzing, as no one had heard anything about this, until now. There were no postings. Who is this Officer? The twenty-five years of duty narrowed the field down substantially but still, at this point, no one would hazard a guess as to the identity of this mystery officer.

"Officer Jackson, do you accept the position I have offered you?" He asked loudly, never taking his eyes off The Mayor, who now was standing with his mouth agape, sweating even more profusely that usual, and struggling to regain his composure! Even after he had announced the name, there was confusion as no one saw this coming! Even Officer Jackson could not believe it!

"Sargent Angela Jackson, do you accept the position I have offered to you?" He bellowed!

Angela's jaw dropped, her knees buckled slightly. She spun to look at her Chief and glanced around the room too in absolute disbelief, to assure herself it was real! She was well liked, by everyone and more importantly she was respected, as a person and a police officer! "Yes Sir!" She managed to blurt out!

"Please, step over here Sargent Jackson!" Dan demanded!

"Mr. Mayor, this is Sergeant Angela Jackson, henceforth, Deputy Chief, Angela Jackson! She is a twenty-five-year veteran of this Department and has served as my personal assistant, for the past fifteen years, since she was forced to do desk and administration duties due to an injury sustained in the line of duty! She is fully qualified to do this job and I have the utmost confidence in her ability to serve this department with honour and integrity! By accepting this position, she becomes the first woman and the first member of the indigenous Community to be promoted to this level in any Department of this Municipality or in the entire Nation!"

At that, he reached around his desk and pulled a file folder and a large envelope, out of the open top drawer handed it to her and extended his hand for a congratulatory handshake. Angela didn't know how to respond; her knees were shaking and she fought back tears of joy as she grabbed the Chiefs hand and shook it vigorously. "

"Congratulations! Look over your new job description and your new wage package, sign it and give it back to me!" Dan said, having finally broken eye contact with the Mayor for the first time since he stood to speak! The chief leaned in close to her ear and asked quietly; "Did you get what I asked for?" She handed him a small thin envelope and retreated almost giddily to her desk to see what was about to happen!

A roar of approval erupted from throughout the office!

The Chief, now turned his attention back to the Mayor, who was now desperate to re-gain his composure and control of this gathering! This, was not going according to his ill-conceived plan! It was about to get worse! Much worse!

It was now, Dan's turn at centre stage and he was now speaking for the benefit whole room and continued; "Now, a short while ago, I, as did many other people present in this room and outer office, witnessed a violent, physical assault, perpetrated on the person of Sargent Angela Jackson by yourself Mayor Higgins!

Your accomplices in this violent act were Councillors, Green and Smith! While they actually did not physically touch Sargent Jackson themselves, they did nothing to prevent the assault, or assist Sargent Jackson and were clearly encouraging the Mayor to gain entrance to my closed office door, despite Sargent Jackson's best efforts to prevent that from occurring, as per my orders! I will deal firstly, with the assault on an Officer of the Law, as she attempted to carry out her duties! I will deal with the refusal to obey a direct and lawful order from an officer of the law, damages to public property and behavior unbecoming to an official of the Town later!

"As a duly sworn, officer of the Law, in this Town, I am obliged to charge you gentlemen with Assault, Assault on an Officer of the Law, and failing to obey a direct order issued by a Police officer in performance of her duty! I will immediately, place you all under arrest and hold you all, without bail until your case can be heard by a Judge in the morning!" At that, he removed a USB flash drive from the envelope, inserted it into his desktop computer, hit a couple of keys and the large monitor on his office wall came to life with the images from the Mayors entrance, complete with the assault on Sargent Jackson, and everything else that transpired!

"How about that? We even have video, in colour, complete with sound! My God! Your face gets really red Mr. Mayor, you really should see a Doctor!" Dan announced, and a huge shit eating grin had spread across his face, as he again sat back in his big black comfortable chair. "How shall we proceed, Mr. Mayor? You can call your lawyers now if you wish, from the pay phones, in the booking area! Could someone please apply some handcuffs to these gentlemen's wrists, and collect any personal property, oh yeah and get their belts and shoe laces, we don't want any suicides?"

"Now, Sargent Jackson is due an apology from all three of you! If she accepts your apology, while I can't speak for Deputy Chief Jackson, but I, myself, may be inclined to put the whole incident down to an unfortunate loss of temper and temporary lack of judgement and ask for leniency from the Courts! It can happen to the best of us at times! I may even recommend to the Judge that the three of you must attend and pass anger management and other courses that teach proper social skills and interaction with people both inside and outside the office and let it go at that!'

He now paused for a moment with a pensive look on his face, he rubbed his chin and scratched his head and then continued, "You know what? Assault and many of the other charges that you gentlemen face are serious crimes and are considered to be felonies as opposed to just misdemeanors! Now I will check to be sure, but I think that somewhere in the statutes and articles and oaths of Office that one of those requirements for officials such as yourselves, states that you cannot be a convicted felon! Does that ring any bells for any of you three?"

"Sargent Jackson, oh excuse me, Deputy Chief Angela Jackson." Dan smiled broadly and looked at Amanda who was now, almost in tears. Kind of just rolls nicely off the tongue eh? She may, indeed, choose not to accept your apology and press charges of her own and further seek damages for any injury that should arise from this unfortunate incident!" He continued. As well, any of these officers and or citizens who were present in this room and witnessed the assault may themselves, wish to lay charges! Man, I'd hate to be in your shoes right now!" He looked down at the Mayors sneakers and smirked. In fact, I wouldn't be caught dead in those ugly damn things! Do they at least, light up when you walk?" There was much, not so, muffled laughter throughout the room at the last statement.

He now turned and glared directly at the three men who now stood completely silent in the middle of the Chiefs office. They were blanched and Counselor Green looked like he was going to be sick! Counselor Smith had committed fully, to that action, and had his head stuck in a nearby wastebasket, his retching was off-putting to many in the room but no one dared leave for fear of missing something!

The Mayor had now lost all of his former bluster, the

colour had completely drained from his normally ruddy face and looked like he was about to have a stroke (Which would have been considered a kindness at his point!). He looked meekly at Amanda and stammered out; "I'm terribly sorry for my actions and my behavior Deputy Chief, Jackson! I hope you will accept my apology!"

Green and Smith smiled weakly, while rapidly nodding their heads and produced noise that resembled that sound turkeys make when they are trying to attract a mate!

The Chief the looked up at the clock on the wall, loudly, and dramatically, slapped his hand on his thigh and with an enormous smile he announced; "Damn! Look at that, Twelve noon on the dot! I'm now on vacation! Deputy Chief Jackson you take your time, say, until morning, before court and make your decision on how to proceed with this matter. I will support your decision, whatever it is! Try to find some compassion! The careers of these gentlemen hang in the balance! In the meantime, book these fine and distinguished gentlemen into one of our finest rooms in our humble facilities here! Gentlemen, enjoy your stay!" He cleared a pathway through the broken glass with his boot, then snapped his fingers and Zeke with one more glare at the Mayor hurried to his side and with that he announced to no one in particular; "We have left the building! If the President or Prime Minister should call take a message and tell them; I'll call back at my earliest convenience! If they balk just ask him; "Who do they think they are? the fucking Mayor?" He tossed the two addressed envelopes in the out basket on Angela's desk on the way by and the two, then bounded through the doors, down the stairs and disappeared into the parking lot!

CHAPTER NINE
DEALING WITH THE PAIN

IT LOOKED a bit like rain as Dan and Zeke got home and while Zeke went about his business of patrolling the perimeter of the yard Dan grabbed his phone and dialed REB's cell phone number. "Stupid Fuck!" He spat the words out loud, giving himself a hard slap to his forehead for good measure when he realized his mistake! "How fucking stupid can you be?" He loudly, admonished himself further.

He was about to hang up when he heard a startled woman's voice on the other end of the line! "Pardon me?"

"Oh shit, Linda! I'm so sorry! I dialed REB's number by force of habit! I didn't expect anyone to answer it." he stammered!

The sound of her laughter and her voice immediately lifted his spirits! She was quite the lady and he loved her dearly! "I understand! You aren't the first and likely won't be the last, to do that! I am carrying all the phones in a large bag, with me wherever I go. Mine, his personal phone, his

Club phone, the business phone and one or two that I just found in a drawer, probably old or broken! I'll figure it out! Keeping them, all charged is a job in itself!

"So how are you holding up? You need anything?" he asked

"Too busy to think about it much! So much to do! The whole crew is still here helping out and more are arriving all the time so it takes a lot off my plate! In fact, things get done before I even know they need doing! I feel I'm in the way most of the time! I can't sleep at all, and my stomach is always churning! I'm so tempted to grab a bottle of Jack, a big bag of green and just kick back in some quiet spot, if I could find one, until it's all gone and maybe join the old coot! If I do it quickly, I can probably still catch him, it always takes him a while to kick that old Knucklehead over when its cold, and that is what he would be riding!" she replied laughingly! Dan could visualize her smile and expression as she was saying it!

"I wanted to call earlier but I had a bitch of a morning! I threw our Mayor and his two stooges in jail for the night, so it ended on a happy note! I handed in my retirement papers and resignation today as well! I'm going to take a ride over there this afternoon, I tell you about it then!"

" Yeah, I heard about that!" she answered with a laugh.

"How did you hear? It just happened less than an hour ago?"

"Good news travels fast, Dan! Did you forget that the new; Deputy Chief of Police; Angela Jackson is Tramp's little sister? Everybody is talking about it! I've heard at least 10 different versions, so far! I can hardly wait to hear you tell it!" "I wish REB could have heard about it before he died! He hated that fat son of a bitch! Then again, knowing our Mayor and knowing that the hatred went both ways, I have a feeling that REB's death, and all these goings on, played some part in this story!"

"I'm glad I stopped in to see him last night and got to see him one more time! He looked like shit, and it was sad to see that he had deteriorated so badly, so quickly! When did it happen?"

"Probably not ten minutes after you left! In fact, he watched out the window until the taillights of your truck disappeared over the hill and then got all peaceful and quiet, his dog, little Gidget, that you gave him eight years ago, came up and cuddled right up on the pillow beside his head, with her little head pressed tight against his cheek like she always does! She was such a comfort to him! She licked him once on the end of his nose, he smiled, coughed once, closed his eyes, and he was gone! Gidget let out a plaintive wail like I've never heard before, and it made the hair on the back of my neck stand up! She furiously licked his face as if trying to bring him back, or have him take her with him! She even nipped at me when I tried to collect her, and she has never nipped at me or anyone else before, ever. I picked her off him and put her in another room! She just mopes around now, whimpers constantly and won't eat or drink and I figure that she is next to go! They were so attached! REB was glad to see you too! I know he wanted to say goodbye!"

Dan's emotions started to come into play and he was now starting to tear up and he could feel a lump rising in his throat and he knew he could not talk anymore, not right now! "Hey Darl'n, I think Zeke has a racoon treed or something! Gotta go! See you soon" and hung up! He sat here at the kitchen table, put his head between his hands and cried, deep, long and unashamedly!

He left Zeke a big fresh bowl of water, and after he changed into his jeans, pulled on one of his new, Dozen, MC, T shirts, and that nice custom-made leather vest with all the custom stitching and braiding that Linda had made by hand and given him 10 years ago! "This thing wears like iron." he said to himself as he slid it on and admired how well it fit and looked! "It will look even better with his patch sewn on it! He said to himself. "Shit!" He cursed! Suddenly realizing that he had left the envelope with the patches with the sewing crew, but didn't leave them anything to sew them on! He hoped that they were still at it today and he could get them on there before the day was out! He figured he should take along a jacket as well as he would likely be late, and the nights could get pretty cold this time of year!

The garage door opened in response to the code he entered on the keypad and there sat his growing motorcycle collection, the old 1958 Duo Glide which was still a project bike but it was his pride and joy. Then there was the 1976 shovel head that he bought from a down on his luck and very troubled, friend, that he and most everybody else, just called; "M", ten years back. "M" didn't make it through the hard times and the subsequent depression and ended up cashing in his chips at the end of a hand fashioned noose under a railway trestle one night. It was always a great runner and whenever he rode it he could see the sad face of that old buddy in his mind's eye! He had "In memory of M" painted on the tank just above the seat.

The iron head Sportster that tended to break down a lot and had been a real challenge for him to keep on the road! He had painted "Bitch" in bright white paint on the tank one particularly, infuriating night, when nothing he did would get that thing to run properly! He was ready to roll it out into the yard and just pour gasoline over it and set it afire! REB rode up and saw his frustrated friend pacing back and forth kicking at the dirt and cussing a blue streak! He walked in looked at it, adjusted something, kicked it over and took it for a ride a smug look on his face and said the words "It seems fine to me, it must be that it doesn't like Cops"!

His dirt bike that he would run around on the trails that ran all across the 50 acres of land that he owned. His "daily rider" a 1995 Electra glide Classic that he'd had since new, and rode everywhere, putting many thousands of miles on it each Year. He loved nothing better than to get out there and explore the roads and back-roads. He took a lot of good-natured flack from lots of the guys who were mostly, into the old-style bobbers and choppers! They called it a "Goober" and a "Geezer Glide" and teased him mercilessly, but when they were out on a ride somewhere and they were tired of their 'ol ladies purse pressing into their backs or they wanted to stash their jackets, it was a different tune that they were singing! It's all in fun!

He usually chose to ride on his own, as he liked to set a pace he was comfortable with, and see what he wanted to see when he wanted to see it! But he loved to ride with REB! They were so much alike and so in tune. They seemed to have so much in common, speed preferences, type of roads, food, and bladder functions, they even shifted in unison. It was like they shared the same mind most of the time!

He readied his bike for the ride. Checked his oil, air and all the fundamental things you should check but lots of the times you forget or just neglect to do. He had long-ago gotten into the habit of doing it, mostly because REB could be a real nag, and he was a stickler for routine maintenance!

It was about an hour later and he was heading down the driveway to the road he turned left and was on his way. He could see Zeke's big black head in the window, watching him as he rode away, from his perch on the couch that he wasn't supposed to be on, but, it did have the best view and there was no one there now, to tell him he couldn't.

The temperature had dropped significantly over the past several hours, dark ominous storm clouds were gathering and you could smell the rain in the musky air as he made his way down the winding road to the Club property which wasn't hard to spot as there was now a phalanx of at least a dozen police cruisers from different forces and LE agencies complete with cameras positioned on the road near the entrance to the driveway as well as an assortment of news crews from Newspapers, TV and radio stations because Biker stuff always raised their ratings and there were a lot of bikes and bikers here now and would be more soon. The Cops were stopping all "motorcycle traffic" in and out of the property as they performed "routine checks" for sobriety and violations of the "Highway Traffic Act" and they were handing out citations right left and centre to riders for everything from helmets, loud pipes, high handlebars or anything else they could think of! They were pretty creative when it came to inventing offences when they wanted to be.

Many of the cops who were regular "Biker Enforcement squad guys and gals," were actually not too bad. They knew most of the bikers by name and treated them respectfully or as respectful as could be expected. This was what, in all actuality, was already an infringement on the rights of these bikers. It was harassment and profiling, plain and simple, and it was discriminatory, but they were "Bikers" and that made it OK! One Club from Toronto's East end, had launched a Law suit years ago and had done a "Right to Ride" Campaign and they were going to The Supreme Court with it, and things were looking promising but they abruptly dropped the case before it got there, for a variety of reasons!

Some of the young, over-zealous Cops, took full advantage of such stops so they could assert their authority. They took great pleasure in issuing tickets for ridiculous shit. They seemed to take pride in coming up with really obscure infractions of whatever they could think of. One biker had some snake skin or alligator skin inserts in his leather vest, and they charged him under the endangered species act. Another, whose Harley leaked a few drops of oil on the pavement, was charged for violating the Environmental Protection Act.

A simple folding pocket knife earned another, criminal charges for possession of a dangerous weapon charge, and while the charges were being laid, another Cop stood there, leaned up against his cruiser, cleaning his fingernails with the exact same knife! It is these types of things that causes animosity between Cops and Bikers and the public doesn't see this kind of behavior!

It took awhile, but he finally was cleared by the check-point and his presence, particularly wearing his new t shirt, had caused quite a stir and lots of confusion, as Cops and the newshounds recognized him.

He turned into the long driveway rode on past the gate, where those on gate duty recognised him, this time, and waved him through. He proceeded down the narrow driveway that led to the Clubhouse, noticing many more bikes and people had arrived and were busy setting up tents, some had set up full on camper units and toy haulers and had generators going, so they could enjoy the comforts of home while on the road. The large property was perfect for gatherings such as these.

It had more than enough space to accommodate hundreds of guests, there was a good-sized pond that was stocked with bass and trout and was handy for a refreshing swim on a hot day if you preferred that over the large in-ground pool or stroll down to the lake! There were several outdoor bars that had been set up and they provided serv-ings of beer, wine and liquor for a small donation to the hosts to cover their expenses. There was also a tuck shop where you could purchase items such as ice, cigars, ciga-rettes, condoms, assorted snacks, sunscreen, soft drinks, toiletries and other such items, so you didn't have to leave the property if you didn't want to and have to face the onslaught of Cops, camera crews and what-not anymore than you had to.

The barbecues, were all working to full capacity and

probably hadn't been shut off other than to change the propane tanks for days. Now several Food Trucks had joined the scene offering different fare than regular barbecue. Tacos, burritos and Mexican from one, Gyros and submarine sandwiches from another, pizza, panzerotti, or other Italian cuisine, fish and chips, or ice cream, you wanted it, it was likely there. The gentle breeze caught the smoke, from the cookers and carried the tantalizing aroma throughout the entire property, stimulating appetites of the gathered folks.

There were also dozens of portable toilets that had been conveniently placed around the property. And the crew had also constructed several outdoor shower cubicles in some shady spots with pumps providing fresh water from the pond or the lake through long hoses. These folks, were certainly organized and more than capable. Especially now that they were officially representing their motorcycle Club. They were determined to show the Biker World what class looked like in this neck of the woods!

Dan rumbled into the newly created area, cordoned off and designated as Club Members Only, Motorcycle Parking. He parked and hung his helmet from the mirror on his bike and made his way to the Clubhouse, but stopping every five feet or so, to hug, shake hands or talk to someone. He spotted the same girl he'd seem the night before, still at a table full of vests and jackets he caught her attention and held up the vest, she in turn, sorted through a pile of envelopes, smiled, and held up the one with his name on it! She came forward and collected the vest from him and returned to her station.

Finally, making it through the crowd, Linda and he

spotted each other and she headed over his way. She looked worn out and just sort of collapsed in his arms. She felt as fragile and weary as she looked and as she pulled back from him he could see dark circles under her eyes.

"Have you slept at all?" he asked but already knowing the answer which she reaffirmed with a shake of her head.

"OK, what you need to do right now, is get your ass upstairs and get to bed for a while, have a nice hot shower and change your clothes! Take a few hours for yourself, there are many long hours ahead of us, and if you don't, we might as well just drop you in the box with REB!" He scolded! "Now go!"

She smiled weakly, nodded and headed for the stairs. She almost, veered toward the door as new people came in, but a glance back at Dan, standing there with a stern look on his face and pointing towards the top of the stairs, and she thought better of it. She climbed those stairs, opened the door and when she saw the bed she just rushed toward it and just kind of dived on top of it fully dressed and was asleep in seconds in the exact position she was in when she hit the soft comfortable quilted surface of the bed.

Rachel had seen her mothers exchange with Dan knew what he had told her, which was exactly what she and many others had tried unsuccessfully to get her to do for the past twenty-four or more hours! She watched as she mounted the stairs and made a slow and wobbly assent. She followed her up and was glad to see her there on the bed sound asleep. She padded quietly across the room, removed her Mothers shoes, gently covered her frail body with a blanket, stooped over planting a gentle kiss on the forehead. She then found a sheet of paper from the nearby desk, and scribbled "Do Not Disturb" in big letters underlined them with an iridescent highlighter which she the affixed with tape to the outside of the door, which she quietly pulled closed behind her. She looked down the stairs to see Dan standing there smiling! They exchanged smiles and gave each other a thumbs up!

She then nodded towards Victoria, who was still there also looking bedraggled and worn. He nodded and moved to her side and gave her the same instructions as he'd given Linda and was happy to see her comply. Rachel was waiting for her at the top of the stairs and ushered her into another room and got her settled down as well.

She turned to go back down stairs but stopped when she saw Dan at the foot of the stairs just standing there shaking his head, a stern expression on his face and his finger pointing towards another room. She started to protest but Dan was having none of it! He knew that she hadn't stopped and rested for quite some time as well! She smiled and then did as she had been told as well falling into a deep sleep as her head touched the pillow!

Dan, wandered into the new meeting room to find that more chairs had been brought in to try and accommodate the many visitors who would be coming to pay their respects over the next several days. The room was filling rapidly as people watched the many widescreen monitors, as there was a slideshow of pictures running continuously. There was much for everyone to look at, what with all the pictures and stuff on the walls of this room that had been chosen by Reb and Linda.

He looked around the room but avoided looking toward

the fireplace, as that was where REB's coffin had been placed in front of it surrounded by huge flower arrangements. He reluctantly stood in line with other mourners who were filing past paying their respects. He looked at all the pictures that had been arranged on several large display stands throughout the room. REB'S leather jacket, vest, favourite hat, along with many other trappings of his time here on earth were on display to show the man that they all knew, loved and admired. All this evidence that he had lived a full and very active life, full of adventures, misadventures, ups and downs, good times and bad. He had accidents and mishaps on his way through his life! He had many successes and wins evidenced by the many trophies and pictures of him in the winner's circle at many a bike race, hill climb or show and shine. But there were not enough pictures or personal belongings on earth that could possibly accurately and completely sum up the life and times of this unique individual life, or could convey what and how much he meant to people!

Linda had asked him to do the eulogy and he told her that he didn't think he could! She insisted, and said that REB had "TOLD" her to "TELL" you that this would be the last request he would ever ask of him, unless he can find a really good medium who worked for cheap and he would let him know!

Finally, he found himself standing beside the casket and looking at the face of his friend lying so still, and peaceful. Curled up on the pillow beside REB's head, was the delicate body of "Gidget" a black and white Chihuahua/Yorkshire Terrier mix, whom had been moping around since REB's

death, not eating or drinking and true to Linda's predic-
tion, she was, indeed, the next to go. Somehow, she had
managed to get into the casket with him and had assumed
her usual bedtime position, on the pillow beside his head,
her face, tight to REB's cheek and that is where she died.
That is how they found her and that is where they left her,
in life and in death, she would be with him. Nobody
checked the legality, they just did it! REB looked good, free
of tubes and wires and was dressed in his new embroidered
Club dress shirt, his vest with the new patches sewn on was
draped over a chair beside him. A small table had been
placed beside the coffin, on it was a large bottle of Wiser's
Deluxe. Rye whiskey, (REB'S favourite) equipped with a
pump and a box full of Shot glasses, each inscribed with the
words "Remembering REB. Sept 12, 1945 – Sept 12, 2020."
A sign was affixed to the front of the table which read.
Please have a drink on me. Keep the glass! Slainte Mhath!
(Good Health).

He reached into the box took a glass, filled it, raised it in a
toast. "go dtí go gcomhlíonfaimid arís!" (Until we meet
again!) He tossed that shot back and felt the burn as it
worked it's way to his core. He refilled the glass once again.
"And one for you Mo Chara!" He drank that one down as
well, slipped the glass in his jeans pocket and without
looking back, turned and walked out of the room and went
in search of a quiet spot where he could be alone with his
thoughts!

He walked, past Calamity, totally oblivious to her presence, let alone, much of anything, or anybody else. She had
started to say something to him but recognized the look

which spoke volumes about his present state of mind and let him go uninterrupted.

He hurried off, out the door, strode aimlessly, across the vast lawn and after about a half an hour, found a shady spot beside the pond and just sat there thinking of all of the adventures that he and his friend had shared over the years. He thought back to where it all started and realized the wild ride it had been.

He got lost in those thoughts and his mind slowly drifted off into a haze or a foggy state. It was almost like he'd gone onto a trance! It was peaceful.

Suddenly the trance was broken. He was yanked back into reality by the grinding of worn out plastic wheels on a bruised and battered, worn out blue and white, plastic cooler held together largely by large quantities of silver duct tape. It was emitting a constant clinking of glass bottles from within accentuated by the regular ka-thunk sound that came from one of the wheels that wasn't anywhere near round on and axle that was obviously bent.

Even the handle and lid were held on by large strips of duct tape. This was being piloted along the path by some lanky kid with long scraggly red hair with a green baseball cap and large green T shirt. The Kid did a bit of a double take when he spotted Dan! He, then stopped and asked; "Hey, aren't you the Chief of Police in this Town?"

"Huh?" was all that he said. He looked up angrily at first, looking to see who dared to interrupt and disturb time that he needed for himself!

"I was, up until yesterday." He stated matter of factly, and gruffly, hoping to dissuade further conversation. while straining to make out the young man's face, that was silhouetted against the bright background. Trying to drop a not too subtle hint that he preferred to be alone right now! The youngster either missed the hint or he just chose to ignore it.

"Aren't you Red Green's illegitimate kid? He reluctantly, but sarcastically, answered the brazen young man in green cap and shirt, pointing at all the duct tape on the cooler. "I'd say it's about time to invest in a new cooler, it looks like that one is on its last legs!"

"Its not what the outside looks like old man. The beers nice and cold on the inside and that's what really counts!" apparently not afraid to speak his mind or slow with a comeback to a jab.

Newby or not, he knew that Cops in general and especially Top Cops, were not usually welcome at "Biker Get togethers" and he was curious. "Just how the fuck does that work? One day you're a cop protecting society from the likes of us, next day you're one of us? That's a bit hard to wash!" a pained look spread over his face. But he came forward and uninvited, sat down opposite Dan on the ground, waiting for a response! He tore back a piece of duct tape that held the lid closed and stuck his hand in the cooler and extracted two bottles of beer dripping wet and well chilled, and handed one to Dan.

Dan was initially going to turn down the offering, being annoyed by the intrusion into his much sought after, and much needed, solitude in the first place. He looked at the bottle that was being offered. "Fuck? Labatt's 50? That's what

I drink! What's a young guy like yourself doing drinking an Old Guy Beer!" He asked, taking the ice-cold bottle from the young man's hand and twisting off the cap! He raised the bottle in a toast, then poured the cold ale into his mouth, swishing it around, savouring the taste, before swallowing. The next time he raised the bottle to his lips he drained the bottle completely!

The young man stared in disbelief, then reached back into the cooler and extracted another one and handed that to Dan.

"Wow! You must have been some fucking thirsty! Good thing I came along when I did! You might have died of thirst!" He laughed, and continued. "My Dad drank 50 and I'd steal them from his beer fridge in the garage and I just acquired a taste for it! I loved my Dad and when I drink it or just look at the label I think of him. That's all I drink now. Besides, I can bring it to a party and leave it unattended in the fridge and none of my friends will touch it!"

Dan smiled, raised the bottle, and the two simultaneously clinked their bottles together and then settled back and he was suddenly at ease and sort of glad that this young man with great taste in beer happened along. Maybe, he was wrong about needing and wanting solitude, perhaps this was what he really needed good company cold beer and relief from his thoughts.

"Incidentally, don't let anyone see you with bottles in here, no glass! Only cans on the grounds!" I'll keep your secret, this time!"

He studied the young man's face and features. He was. by his estimation, around 25 years of age. He had a very relaxed yet a kind of cocky, self confident mannerism and an easy smile and green eyes that sparkled when he talked. He had a long mop of unruly red hair that he tried to contain under a green baseball cap. It was then that Dan realized that the cap had a Labatt's 50 emblem on it and was wearing a green t shirt with a large Labatt's 50 logo emblazoned on the front!

Dan laughed out loud! "Talk about brand loyalty or is this a fashion statement! Cheers!" tilting the bottle towards the young man, smiling and draining that bottle as well." To your Dad!"

"Dan O'Reilly, The Bakers Dozen Motorcycle Club, Member, and former Chief of Police of Swanton Harbour, now retired!" He said, extending his hand. That was the first time he had spoken those words, and it felt good saying them! He smiled and leaned back on an elbow stretching his legs out and enjoying the warm sunshine!

"Terry Fox!" Pausing for the bemused expression that he knew would follow his introduction! They call me Foxy and I prefer that, Yeah, my folks named me after him. He ran through our Town and the folks were really impressed by him and his cause!" Terry said blushing slightly. He then knocked on both legs with his knuckles, showing that they were both real flesh and blood. "No other similarities." He said with a big grin, and shook Dan's hand, and pulled another cold 50 from the chest, and tossed it to Dan." Hell I don't want to drink all your beer!" Dan protested, and tried to pass it back to Terry but he wouldn't accept it!

"That's what its for, isn't it? It doesn't do you any good in the cooler with that caps still on! Beer is always better when you get to share it with someone, it just makes it taste even better." Was his response.

Wise thinking for someone so young" He thought to himself. He reminded him of someone but his thoughts right now were muddled, and he just let it go.

"Come down to the bar later." Dan told him. "If you don't see me, just tell one of the guys that I said to drag a case of cold 50 out of the cooler for you and to put it on my tab."

"Naw, you don't have to do that! I got plenty" Terry protested. "Not if you hang out with me much longer you won't and you can never have too much beer!" That was something REB would say, often! "He didn't drink 50 though, he'd always have a case of warm fucking Guinness close at hand.

The two laughed and just sat there enjoying some cold ale, the company that Dan didn't know he needed and the day. It took Dan's mind of all the troubling thoughts that were messing up his thinking! Terry, it turned out, was sort of a hang around for a small Club out near London, Ontario, but lived in nearby Ingersol. He explained that the older members of the Club have been partying here for years and knew REB well. They rode out to pay their respects and wanted him to come along so they could introduce him around and see how he behaved and if he might be a good fit as a Probate or a member one day!

He had an old dyna and he did most of the work on it himself, to keep it running and worked as an apprentice mechanic for a small motorcycle shop out that way. He said he'd always loved motorcycles and that his Dad and Mom rode too, but some old lady in a Volvo turned left, right in their path one day and killed them both! He was 11 at the time! He went to live with his Grandparents until his Grandfather died two years ago. His Grandmother went to a senior's home shortly after and she too died a short time later. His older Brother ended up with the house and the two of them didn't get along so he found a little basement apartment to rent and is now just doing his own thing trying to find his direction!

"Wow! You've seen a lot of changes and experienced a lot in a short period of time!" Dan replied solemnly.

"So how does this work with you being Chief of Police? Did you know this REB guy well? What was he like?" These were just a few of the questions he had to ask.

"My life just, sort of evolved that way! I guess, you can't really plan your life if your life already has plans for you! You may think that you are in charge but, in reality, you just play the cards you are dealt, my friend, just like you did. My Dad was a Cop as was his Dad and I just sort of grew into it." He then smiled and said, I've known REB since we were three years old, I'm 75 right now, so 72 years or so."

"Wow! 72 years! You were friends for 72 years?"

"No, I said we knew each other for 72 years! We hated each other for the first 30 or so years, then we were Brothers for the last 43!" Dan said matter of factly.

"The young man now looked seriously puzzled!"

It wasn't Dan's custom to open up to people, especially strangers, but this young man with a cooler full of his favourite ale had put him at ease. Maybe the ale had just hit him right, or maybe it was just time to unburden himself. So, he continued to speak and young Foxy was riveted to his every word.

"REB and I were the same age, same day, same Month, same Year. We determined later on that he'd beaten me into this World by three hours, even with the time difference. That was the first time he beat me and, we weren't even aware of each other at the time, and we weren't even on the same continents but it seemed to be the start of a trend! We went to the same schools, in the same classrooms, had the same interests in sports and in girls! We were both extremely competitive, both of Irish decent and we both had bad tempers and precious little patience! We also both hated to lose, particularly to each other.

"From the very first moment we set eyes on each other it was like a war had officially been declared between us, or maybe feud would be more accurate a term. Yeah, kind of like a milder, modern day version of The Hatfields and McCoys. No guns!"

"I don't really remember this, but my Mom told me about it so many times, it seems like a memory. REB says he vaguely remembers what happened, but somehow, I doubt if he recalls it at all either. Still, that competitive thing some- times rears itself up now and then!" Dan smiled, chuckled, and continued.

"I have the scar right here!" He pointed to a jagged white line, about three inches long, on his forehead just below the hairline! That was from my very first encounter with REB". His real name was Robert Edward Baker, He was the Son of Irish Immigrants, who came to this Country back in the mid forties just after the war. They didn't have much more than incredible work ethics, and determination and undisputable skills in baking, but got through it by working hard, loving each other and this Land that they now called home. They started a small bakery; "Baker's Baked Goods," that was down on Main St. for about 60 years. They were always just scraping to get by and Bobby was their only child! He was tough as Hell and a really good athlete who always played hard but fair, they were proud of him!

"Me, on the other hand, I came to this Country with my parents, as my Da, was a Policeman back in Ireland, and his Da was also a policeman. The war in Europe was just ending and there was a growth spurt in a lot of Towns and Cities as all the young men returned home. My Da had seen an ad for a Police officer for a Town in Canada in the Police Gazette and applied! He got the job, and we immigrated here.'

Having a Policeman for a father who in turn, had a Policeman for a father, you have to know that he was very big on authority and discipline and not particularly well versed in displays of affection! Also, my folks could be a bit snobby, and while they were all of Irish stock, they regarded other Irish Immigrants, like the Bakers, to be somewhat lower class! My folks, especially my Da, took the fact, that they came to this Country already with a job, a good salary, and a nice home to live, and there was also, the fact that this job put him in charge of others as an authority figure, and that, in their minds, automatically put them in a higher class and standing in the Community than mere common immigrants. That is just the way it was back then, and still is today, to some extent.

Da, could also be somewhat brutal and narrow minded in

his thinking, and enforcement of the law and keeping of the peace. Many in the Community, thought that his methods could border on, and a lot of the time, exceeding what could be considered to reasonable force, legitimate, or entirely legal. He believed that whatever force he figured he needed to use was his choice, by virtue of his badge and could not possibly be considered excessive or unnecessary and certainly not, questioned!

He would walk into a Pub or bar and proclaim loudly; "If you lads don't want a good thumping, you should fucking well do as I tell you, and behave yourselves!" This was usually followed by him smacking his custom-made leather encased truncheon (His, consisted of a five- or six-inch length of lead, probably about an inch in diameter and weighing in at about a pound or three, that hung by leather strap from his right wrist.) hard on a table just for effect! It could put a man's lights out in a hurry! He was my Hero, I admired him and I knew, even at that early age, that I was going to have a career in Law Enforcement and be just like my Da when I grew up!

I was also an only child! I was very much into sports and also very competitive. I would do whatever it took to win! So, the stage was now set for the Baker/O'Reilly feud, round one.

The way I heard it, was my Mother and I were in the General store the same time as Robby and his Mom were there. Apparently little Robby was playing quite contentedly, with a small metal hammer, I think it was used by welders to chip slag from their welds, that he had picked off a low shelf, his Mom noticed but figured that he couldn't hurt anything with it (Or so she thought.) so she just let him carry on, while she explained to the store clerk how many bolts of cloth and other items that she needed.

I apparently, came up to Robby and decided that I wanted to play with "that" hammer. Not "a" hammer, as there were lots of others within easy reach, as we were in the hardware department, "that particular hammer" and proceeded to try and take it from him. I was a spoiled brat, used to getting what I wanted and to date, had never came up against a worthy adversary or anyone who would dissuade me. He didn't want to give it up and I allegedly, punched him in the face, hard, or as hard as a three-year-old could punch. My Mom told me, that Bobby never blinked, yelled, cried or anything, however, he did look confused! He then instantly drilled me in the forehead with the claw end of the hammer and opened up a nice sized wound!

I was bleeding like a stuck pig, but picked myself up off the floor, and charged right at him, until my Mom dragged me away, kicking and screaming, to get me stitched up, before he could hit me again, as Robby allegedly, had his arm cocked back and was entirely ready to deliver another blow! His Mom, stripped him of the hammer, and was shouting apologies to our backs as we left the store. From that point on, the Bakers were out of favour with the O'Reilly's and subsequently, much of the Swanton Harbour Police Department as well. The feud was on and it lasted just over 30 years. I showed that scar to REB more than once and rekindled the story for him and others, time and time again! He offered to autograph it for me on more than one occasion!

Terry's eyes, were fixed on Dan as he talked. He definitely had his attention! He fished two more beer out of the ice in the cooler and put the empties in a nice neat little pile. Dan was now just automatically accepting them. He was comfortable, and totally at ease as something about this young man put him off his guard, so, he continued;

"So, that is the way it was! We'd fight anytime, anywhere and mostly with no real provocation. We only had to be near each other and the fight was on! It didn't matter what the sport, hockey, soccer, basketball, baseball or a game of ping pong! If we were both there, it was only a matter of time before the fight would start.

"Now I mentioned earlier that Robby was tough as nails and could scrap with the best of them. I was good, and tough, but any fight we ever had, he edged me out on every count, except for tenacity, determination and hate, the actual fights, were always won by him, probably 99% of the time! That 1% represented the time when I snuck my Da's truncheon that I'd borrowed without permission, into a fist fight and opened up his forehead for a change! There were so many loud protests and everybody who wasn't avoiding me for several weeks that followed, were threatening to gang up on me! Some have never spoken to me since, to this day! They took it out of my win column, for certain. That didn't put me off at all, and instead, made me more determined to kick his low-class Irish ass into next week and each defeat also increased how much I hated him and I made no secret of the way I felt about him."

"There was one thing about our fights and the outcomes, Robby, or REB as he was becoming known as, always just did just enough to beat me, or anybody else he ever fought for that matter. He, most-times, left some dignity for his opponent, if he felt that they deserved any. Where in, if it were me, that was on top I would always go the extra distance to humiliate my opponents, I'd throw in a couple of extra punches or kicks. I'd rub their faces into the ground or deliberately try to break a bone or mark them up in some way, so that it would serve as a permanent reminder of the time they fought Dan O'Reilly! Something, so anyone I fought would have a memento of the occasion." He pointed to the scar on his forehead. "Most, never wanted to fight me again!

REB was different, he was always up for a fight, even when he wanted no part of a fight! I heard plenty about how many battles that he'd had, and the outcomes, I never saw or heard of him picking a fight, yet I never saw or heard of him backing away from anyone or anything either. I saw him fight older guys, almost twice his size, guys, I wouldn't even have taken on and while I was hoping he'd get his ass kicked, he always came out on top. I begrudgingly and secretly, admired him, but not enough to lessen the pure hatred I had for him."

Dan recognized the bewildered expression on Foxys' face, the one that says "And you're proud of this, you prick?" and carried on.

"This went on for years, all through elementary school and high school and I went on to college and then the Police Academy. I finally realized my dream, and became a Police officer, that is where I really shined, or so I thought!"

"Watch out now, REB!" Here I come! Your low life, low class, Irish ass is mine now!" I thought to myself, the day I graduated. Using my father's influence, I had already, secured a job with the Swanton Harbour Police Department,

I could hardly contain my glee and couldn't wait to start work! Make Robert Edward Baker's life, a living Hell, was my goal! That was my mantra, my main motivation! My hatred for one individual was what pushed me to succeed and rise to the occasion. That was my edge!"

He could see young Terry raise an eyebrow and saw a look appear on his face that was no longer one of interest but one that said he now had serious doubts about his choice of drinking companions!

"Yeah, yeah, I was a complete and total asshole! It took me quite a while to figure that out, but I did eventually! Relax! It's a long story! You got time? Do we have enough beer?" It was now do "We" have enough beer, as opposed to "You" so it was evident than Dan had committed to the telling of this story and was in for the long haul!

Some of what he had already said and what he was about to say, hadn't been spoken about or discussed with another living soul, even REB! It needed to be said! He opened the lid on the cooler and peered inside, fished out two and handed Foxy one. Foxy relaxed again, and the saga continued.

REB and I were both athletic and both good. The difference, was that REB was a natural born athlete, he was good at everything and anything he ever tried! He didn't train, he didn't work out, he just did it! Me, I was working out constantly! I trained hard, I studied play books, took lessons from pros and I still couldn't beat him. That made me resent him still more! He was a natural born athlete who had no desire to be an athlete! He never went out of his way to get into a sport but if a challenge presented itself, he was game! With REB, he regarded everything as a challenge!

This was the late fifties and early sixties, there was no internet, cell phones or video games. We played outside and we would gather together as friends! We created our own fun, rode our bicycles and played games, some that we just made up that fit the numbers we had on hand, we improvised and as long as we had fun, it was all good!

Then, there was baseball! REB loved baseball and put together a team. The fucking "Baker's Dozen" they called themselves! It was a patchwork team, made up of misfits and hooligans from the neighbourhood, but a team, none the less, and they took it seriously! It was like the league of fucking Nations for fuck sakes! They had all these mutt, Irish, a couple of Italians, two black kids, a Jew, a few Indians and two fucking girls!

There were thirteen of them and while they all weren't on the roster, they had enough to field a team! Plus, they had back up players and a manager. The regular league that I played in, wouldn't let them in, mostly because of the girls. So, with Robby Bakers persistence, his boldness and resourcefulness, they formed and ran their own league. It should have been, really Mickey Mouse but it worked well, even though they weren't officially recognized. They didn't care, if they were officially recognized, or not, they were playing ball and by their rules and were having fun!

They had a good team and got noticed and they soon started getting a lot of teams signing up and had a good schedule with good, exciting, baseball. We all scoffed at them at first, but soon found that they were drawing some small crowds out to the games, that were growing, because there was some real talent on display! They were tough to beat!

They were getting attention, spectators and all and there were even rumours of some major league scouts coming around, to take a cursory peak at their games too. This really pissed me off, because in our league, I was like a superstar and these mutts were getting more attention!

We challenged the Dozen to a couple of exhibition games! I figured we would humiliate them and they'd skulk off with their tails between their legs and just fade away, but they ended up winning. They didn't blow us out of the park by any means, but they did win, and the games were truly interesting, and showcased some real, young talent. The spectators loved it and whenever we played, the stands were full and soon, some hotdog vendors started to show up and they were selling out! They and we, had really lucked into something good! But all good things eventually come to an end!

I still despised REB and by association, his entire team. He played catcher and whenever I ran the bases I would be sure to slide hard into home, whether it was necessary or not, cleats up! I got a lot of boos from the stands and even some of my own teammates were questioning me about my behavior! I didn't care! Hatred is an awful thing and it can spread and infect people and things faster than any disease or virus, if the seeds are planted well and deeply. I planted the seeds well, and soon, my entire team, including the coaches soon hated the Bakers Dozen almost with the same intensity that I did, and they had no reason to do so, other than the seeds of hate that I had sowed to do so, along with a couple of lies!

Games would quite often turn into nothing more than donnybrooks with players more interested in fighting, than playing baseball and the games soon lost their lustre and occasionally the Cops showed up. The Bakers Dozen went back to just playing pick-up games, now and then but still having fun.

But the comradery, between each and every one of the thirteen originals, remained, and they could always be seen together and more would join them because they all had fun, together. They would gather in parking lots and fields, as it really didn't matter as to the location, and play games. If not baseball, football or tag or they'd just sit and talk for hours until the street lights came on and they'd head for home. They had quite a variety of kids that could be found hanging out there. There was no discrimination other than me and my crowd who were definitely, not welcome! Then, they started hanging out at some property that REB's parents owned, this property.

There was the original thirteen members, who, other than REB, who was now fifteen at the time, were all around between nine and fourteen years of age at the time. They even had some as young as seven and eight, like Calamity Jane, waiting in the wings and REB, made them all feel part of the team as well be assigning them little jobs to do and made them feel important!

They were a solid crew, and a tough bunch, including the girls and if you were going to pick on one, you had to contend with all of them and they were never afraid to get into a scrap. That damned Calamity Jane in particular, could be particularly vicious! She could accidentally nail someone who had stepped over the line with a wild throw. Let me tell you she had an arm!

Starting with REB, who was recognised as the undeniable and undisputed, yet, still, unofficial leader of the team and the group. He also served as the catcher. He was a heavy hitter and could fill in as a pitcher when needed but he tended to be erratic and needed to work on his pitching skills and develop actual pitches rather than just throwing the ball as hard as he could. Every pitch was a fastball with REB so he was very predictable.

He acted differently than many other kids his age, for one thing, his hair was long by that era's standards, and that really set him apart. It was always combed but it flowed behind him when he ran or rode a bicycle and later motorcycles. He was cool before kids discovered cool! He was James Dean before the World was introduced to him. I hated him even more because, I could see it, even if REB didn't! He didn't as he just did what felt right to him, not to create a look or anything.

He always showed great confidence, poise and had a quiet dignity about him, even as a kid. He seemed totally fearless, except when it came to girls, as he was painfully shy. Girls could make him blush, if they showed the slightest interest in anything, that was beyond just friendship or sports related. There were many girls who were interested but nothing ever developed because REB would avoid being alone with them. It wasn't that he wasn't interested in girls, were one of the very few things that made him feel terribly uncomfortable and awkward.

While others, some, far younger than he were discovering and exploring their sexuality, REB found other things to do. Then he met Linda Murphy and all that changed. I liked her too but it was obvious by the look on their faces whenever they saw each other that I didn't stand a chance. I had a girl-friend whom I had known since the first grade and I married her and we had a couple of great kids!

Nicky Romano, played third base, and was a decent hitter, who's real talent was running the base pads and could steal bases like no one had ever seen, from a kid that age. A short, stocky Italian kid who had a quick, very violent, and explosive, temper even back in those early days. He was extremely tough and most kids were justifiably afraid of him, it was even being said, that hot head, Danny O'Reilly, wouldn't mess with Nicky. I would have, but he could be really intense and he was nuts, and would never quit, ever. So, I avoided him. I was stubborn, not stupid!

There was a story circulating, how Nicky had exchanged words with this big, drunk truck driver, as he passed by a bar, while walking home alone, from a ball game one night. The drunk responded by slapping little Nicky around a bit, not real hard, with fists, or anything but just enough to humiliate him. He then picked him up and threw him in a ditch full of stagnant water.

The drunk thought it was a big joke and had a big laugh at this little whop kid's expense. To his surprise, the now, furious Nicky came out of the ditch faster than he went in, full of absolute and total blind, fury! He charged at the big man, leaped on his back and was hitting him with all his might all over his head and face!

The drunk was easily Six foot, three inches, tall and weighed in about three hundred and fifty pounds and he easily, peeled Nicky off his back, held him out it front of him with one hand and punched him full force, in the face with the other, knocking him back into the ditch.

He then went back into the bar and resumed drinking and laughing with his buddies about what just happened. He was still laughing, when Nicky came up behind him with a baseball bat and clubbed him square on the top of his head with all the strength he could muster. The drunk went out like a light and immediately slumped from his chair to the floor in a pool of blood that poured from his ears, nose, mouth and even his eyes! It took a few seconds for anyone else to even realize what had just happened, and by now, Nicky had got in a few more good licks in with the bat! Blood was spattered all over everybody within the radius of few tables. It took two large bouncers, the owner, and a couple of patrons to restrain him for the Cop, who also had his hands full, getting him into the squad car.

The Cop as it turns out was none other than, Dwight Higgins, a Cop who was much despised by many in the Town, including other Cops, and while nobody actually saw anything, but everyone suspected, that the big Cop, who was known to employ and enjoy, rough tactics, cracked Nicky in the head with his truncheon, to make him easier to handle! Nicky never talked about what happened that night, after he got put in the squad car, but when his folks got him out of jail, later that night, he was bruised up pretty good and was limping badly for months to come!

Officer Higgins, claimed that Nicky had fallen down the stairs at the station house, on the way to the cells. It was also rumoured that Officer Seamus O'Reilly was on duty that night and also put his truncheon to use in teaching this little whop kid, some Social skills! Back in those days, there was no video and who were people going to believe? To say Nicky hated that fat Cop an my Da, in particular, and most all Cops, in general, after that, would be a huge understatement! The drunk at the bar recovered from his injuries but was never seen in that bar or anywhere in Town again.

The other Italian member of the happy crew was Anthony DiMucci who they all called Dion as in Dion DiMucci, the singer who had hit songs like "Runaround Sue and The Wanderer" back in the 60's and is still very active in music to this day. He used to comb his hair back just like Dion and he was pretty smooth! The girls all liked him and he was a nice kid to be around. He played centre field and his speed and skill with his glove made him formidable. He was just an average hitter though.

At first base, was a pretty little blonde-haired girl; Rose Marie Higgins, who was the stepdaughter of one the Town Cops, Dwight Higgins Sr. She was a good player, great hands, fast feet and instincts and was a reliable, consistent hitter and had real skill at laying down a bunt. She was very quiet, reserved, almost timid and always seemed to be nervous and preoccupied much of the time, but baseball seemed to help get her mind off whatever was troubling her and while she was engaged in the game she seemed fine. REB had tried to reach out to her many times but she would deny anything was bothering her and just run off by herself! She would later become known as Gypsy to one and all. It was more than a little obvious to REB and others, that Rose Marie Higgins was a very troubled young lady at that time, although she seemed to come out of it

after a while and today, you wouldn't know she was ever
troubled.

Second base was where Chuck Taylor held court! He was
a wild kid, tall and lanky and his pants were always a whole
lot shorter than his legs were. They didn't have budget
enough to keep that lad in proper baseball pants so he just
wore whatever pair of pants fit him that day. I don't know
how his folks could afford to clothe him! He was one of the
fourteen-year old's and had seen a huge growth spurt when
he was twelve that still hadn't stopped. The growth was all in
height and everybody called him "Beanpole" because he was
so skinny. It was like he could outgrow a new pair of pants
overnight, shoes were also an issue as he was already
wearing a size fourteen. He was over six feet tall at fourteen,
and showing no signs of stopping. He was an incredible
hitter and could field a ball well too. He was constantly
stealing plays from Dion, as with his height and ability to
jump, it was hard for any opposing hitters to get one over his
head at second.

His younger Brother, Calvin didn't have any of the height
of his Sibling, in fact, he was just the opposite, short, but he
was very fast and could snag a ball with the best of them and
made some amazing catches in right field and was also a very
capable hitter. He also benefitted, from his big brother's
growth spurts because he would end up with a lot of new
pants! He would go shopping with Chuck and their Mom
and help them pick out the clothes as he knew that they
would be his soon! Later in life, the two brothers opened a
motorcycle repair shop at the edge of town and developed a
real good reputation as being fair, honest and great

mechanics and the business is still around to this day although Calvin got cancer and died in 2005. Chuck is still a member of The Original Bakers Dozen.

Left Field was Mary Jane McGuire's normal territory, once she came of age, as she was among those eight-year old's that just refused to go away. She was already being called Calamity Jane by her friends and pretty well everyone else who knew her, for no other reason than, it was a lot more fun name, than just; Mary Jane and she loved it! She evolved from this scrawny, little eight-year-old girl who REB let hang around because she showed real interest, into what could best be described as; a sight to behold! Stunningly pretty, six feet tall, slender, but shapely, with a fair sized bust and a mane of long black hair that she somehow got stuffed through the opening in the back of her baseball cap and it still hung down past her butt in a mammoth ponytail. All this was set upon two, very long, and shapely legs. She was an all-round firecracker. Calamity, however, was pretty much unforgettable, for more reasons than the obvious, physical and superficial ones.

At first glance, people would probably assume that she was all show! They would be wrong, dead wrong. She could play any position on the field with equal skill, intensity and enthusiasm but she really shined in left field as those long legs would propel her across the field in long graceful strides, she looked like a gazelle! Her long black hair, was so dense, it barely moved as she ran. She could jump as well and watching her field a high fly was a feast for your eyes because for one, she made it look so easy, and she looked so fucking good doing it!

She was also a real chatter box, even before she was old enough to play. A constant barrage of comments and banter flowed from her mouth, and she could rattle even the calmest players, be they pitchers, batters or fielders or even Umpires, she got to them all. She even continued while at the plate, and could throw a pitcher off his game so badly that she pretty well always got a hit or got a walk and made it to base regardless.

Her voice carried so well, you could hear her from anywhere in the park, like she was standing right beside you! It wasn't shrill or a screech or anything that was really annoying or grating, she could just be extremely loud and very effective!

Then there was her whistle. She could pierce an eardrum blocks away with that fucking whistle. It's good they didn't have car alarms back then because they would be set off for sure! Nobody wanted to sit directly near her because of it and when she was on the bench, she was relegated to the far end of it. Jane didn't care! It was all about fun, and that suited her just fine! Nobody had any trouble making out what she had to say and you never knew what was going to come out of her mouth next, so you paid attention. She was funny and entertaining! Her enthusiasm, spirit and humour, were infectious and her love for the game and her team mates was obvious.

Tramp Jackson, was a full-blooded Ojibwe whose family lived in this area for generations. His parents ran a very successful sporting goods store just outside of town, and set aside a large area of the store for the sale of indigenous crafts, clothing and leather goods by members of the tribe rent free. They encouraged and supported native industries and manufacturing. Tramp worked with his folks and was a quiet fun-loving kid, although, very big for his age and stories about his incredible strength were already circulating throughout the area.

The local High School was trying to get him to come out for their football team and the wrestling team even before he graduated into High School. The rumour was that even at the age of fourteen, he could pull a full-sized car with ten people packed in and on it for 100 yards. He could have pulled it further as he was just gathering momentum when he ran out of road. It was a dead-end road and it was only 100 yards long! He was the utility player, who could hit a ball a mile. His fielding mostly sucked though, and he wasn't terribly fast, so they would put him in if they needed a heavy hitter. Tramp is still a member to this day!

Tramp had a younger brother, Anthony, who could pitch like there was no tomorrow. He had a fast ball that was pretty much unhittable by anyone in that age group at the time. He had a wicked curve and a decent slider. These were all pitches that he had been working on since he was seven. Anthony went on to become a pro ball player and went from player, to assistant couch, and various other jobs until his death in 1990 from a massive heart attack!

Moise was the manager, a small but very sharp kid who had a great knowledge of the game and was very strategic but had no talent for actually playing the game what so ever. He was constantly trying to reposition players around to satisfy his desire to actually feel he was participating in the team positively! But the players, other than, Calamity Jane, liked their positions and balked at his suggested changes and he figured he would just leave them alone as everybody knew what they were doing, but he still got to wear a shirt that said manager on it and he was officially on the team, and that satisfied him. Moise went on to run a couple of bars as he had a mind and a talent for that kind of stuff, and eventually became the owner. His business occupied much of his time and he came around less and less as the years went by but he still kept in touch. He still has the BSA motorcycle that was his first bike and it looks as good today as when he first bought it.

They had a couple of other utility players like lefty who was a decent pitcher with a couple of good pitches and as his name would suggest, was a left hander. He didn't really care if he got in the game at all but he liked to watch and the girls liked his cool shirt and like Moise he was satisfied with that.

When not in the game, these utility players would serve as first and third base coaches.

"Pauly, was something else entirely, he was a big loveable kid but had many emotional and mental health issues, having being born with Down's Syndrome and was also epileptic and prone to seizures. Pauly's actual age placed him in his thirties at that time, but he functioned at a level of a pre-teen. He absolutely loved to watch the games and had his parents bring him out to the ball park so he could watch. REB had noticed them and approached them as it was so obvious that Pauly wanted desperately to play. His parents wouldn't have dared to ask. They were thrilled, Pauly was over the moon! So, REB and the rest, at REB's insistence, voted Pauly in as an official Member of The Bakers Dozen.

It could be a pain in the ass at times, because, winning or losing, REB would insist that he get in the game, and let Pauly have an at bat. The other teams were usually good about it too, and got into the spirit of it all. More often than not, their pitcher would lob a pitch in and strike him gently, so that Pauly could get on base, then he would be told to steal second, which would result a wild throw that would be mishandled by the second baseman, the shortstop and the centre fielder, and that would move him to third base where another wild throw moved him to home plate where he would slide in, just avoiding a tag from the catcher. Pauly's parents thanked the group for what they were doing, as it meant so much to him and to them because when "The Dozen" had him they knew he was safe as they gave them instructions on what to do in the event of a seizure or anything.

It gave them a break for themselves, personally, as it could get exhausting caring for Pauly's needs. The whole team would rush out surrounding Pauly they would all cheer and jump up and down. They would all slap him on the butt as he made his way back to the bench, and all those in the gallery seats would cheer and applaud. The other team would even come over to their bench and congratulate him shaking his hand and patting him on the back telling him he was the toughest player that they had ever faced.

After the game, REB always presented him with a small, MVP trophy it was inscribed with his name on it, and had a figurine of a baseball player on it. Pauly, cherished those trophies, and kept them on a special shelf that his Dad made for him! He was always polishing them and couldn't walk passed them, without stopping to look at them. REB was buying them from a trophy shop in town about a dozen or so at a time, and would buy more as he needed them. They weren't very expensive, but when the trophy guy caught wind of what he was doing with them, he dropped off about a hundred or so of them already engraved, at REB's house free of charge! What comes around goes around and there are good people in this World."

When baseball became less of a focus for the Club, and interests turned to motorcycles, Pauly was even more thrilled, he loved to ride and the Club fixed up that old trike into something that could safely accommodate him as a passenger on rides! They eventually modified, it just for him and they even let him ride it around the property with someone on board with him in case he got into trouble! His parents would come out to watch and often broke down in tears at the sight of their son, actually totally, enjoying himself! Here he fit, amongst this group of people, who were often referred to as misfits and social outcasts. Pauly died back in 2002 and REB and the Club gave him a full on "Biker" Funeral, complete with a full pack escort to the gravesite! Who, would actually care, or take the time to accommodate a lad such as Pauly? REB and the Bakers Dozen.

Young Foxy, was now looking really bewildered. "This fucking REB guy and these Bakers Dozen people sound like really great people. You hated them, why exactly?" he asked in total disbelief!

"I didn't know about any of this then. I guess I didn't

want to know either! Why let the nice actions of the people you hate, ruin a good hatred?"

Foxy just shook his head, drew a long haul on the joint that he pulled from his shirt pocket and that they had started sharing a while back. This might be thought of as a bonding experience, but Foxy was now very unsure if he wanted to bond with this weird old fucker, or punch his lights out!

"Beer?"

"Absolutely!" and he tried to carry on with the story after they had both, stumbled over to an outcropping of shrubs to drain some ale and make room for more!

"How many 50's do you think we've drank in the last while" Dan asked out of the blue.

I don't know for sure I had several dozen in the cooler but I'd say around 24 -30! There isn't a whole lot of them in there now." Was the reply!

"If we had enough empty bottles we could produce probably 100 Canadian and Coors Lights from our recycled 50 and it would taste better that what they get from the Beer Store!" Dan commented. He was wobbling, as was Foxy and they giggled, chuckled, farted and snorted their way back to their spot by the pond.

"You want to hear anymore of this?" Dan asked.

"I guess I should get the whole story, because right now, you look like the biggest asshole that ever walked or rode this Earth. I do find that hard to believe however, because I usually am choosey about who I hang out with and don't believe I would ever sit and drink with anyone who is as big and asshole as you appear to be right now! We should get to the part where you stop being a prick soon though!" Said the young man in earnest!

"Point taken! I will do my best to redeem myself in your eyes!" as he deposited another empty bottle on the growing pile that hey had now fashioned to resemble a pile of firewood, and fished out two more from the rapidly depleting cooler. There was now more ice and water than beer in there by then. Which was just as well, as the ones they each had in their hands went mostly untouched as they both slouched over and fell into a stupor. It wasn't certain which one passed out first but it looked like it could have been a draw.

It was now pitch black out, drizzling rain and starting to cool down pretty good, so a small search party consisting of Calamity, Gypsy, Linda and Tramp, accompanied by Gypsy's dog Skooter, set out in search of Dan, who had been MIA for about or seven or eight hours now! Calamity had seen the basic direction that Dan had set off in so with flashlights they were combing the area for signs of him.

None of them had any idea who this young guy wearing all the Labatt's 50 gear was, but they figured they must have been getting along, as neither was bleeding or had any marks on them, they were both smiling from ear to ear as happy drunks often do. And judging from the size of the pile of empty 50 bottles that had all been piled very neatly nearby, they had drunk plenty and by any definition, could be officially classified as totally drunk!"

Gypsy and Tramp began gathering up the near dead, for transport to more comfortable spots! Linda and Calamity headed back to the Clubhouse parking lot, to get REB's old truck and Tramp's as well. Tramp and Gypsy readied the bodies for relocation! The plan was that Calamity would take Dan in REB's truck and Tramp would drive the young stranger back to Dan's place as well and put the drunks in a safe place and sort the rest out in the morning.

"Do you think we have to explain the "No Glass" rule to Dan? Tramp asked while preparing the empty bottles for pick-up as he would have somebody swing by and get them before they had a chance to get broken.

"Naw I think Dan just forgot he was no longer Chief of Police, and was probably making an arrest, and was actually, confiscating that beer as evidence, but decided that he needed to taste it to see if it was genuine 50. This guy was probably going to verify the findings. They drank them all, just to be really sure!"

At that, they both started laughing so hard that hey had to sit down to stop from falling! I can see the headlines;" Gypsy interjected. "Chief Dan's, last official arrest, thrown out because of lack of evidence, and he was charged with imper-sonating an officer of the Law! They are now trying to do tests on the urine samples to build a solid case against him!"

"Who the fuck is this guy?" Gypsy said, pointing at the young Foxy, who they now had propped up against a tree with his cooler He's got to belong to somebody, and some-body's got to be looking for him! A stranger isn't getting past the gate on his own say so. He's got no patches or tattoos, so there is no telling who or which Club he came here with. Regardless, we can't leave him here! He had a full cooler of beer until he ran into Dan or Dan ran into him! It was 50, but that's still an asset in some circles. She giggled!

"I'll tell them at the gate to spread word around that if any group is missing someone with poor taste in beer and clothing that we have him and he is in good hands and that we are trying our damndest to get him to drink a Canadian!" They again, howled in laughter. "Damn, we are funny fuckers eh?"

That is how Linda and Calamity found them, when they made their way back with the trucks, along with Calamity's luggage, the two lost souls, oblivious to anything that was going on around them, and Gypsy and Tramp almost hysterical with laughter, Gypsy's dog Skooter curled up with the drunks, sound asleep and contented. They loaded their cargo into the respective trucks, buckled them in and headed for Dan's house, somewhat worse for wear but still alive, and tomorrow was another day.

Back at Dan's place, Calamity was appreciative of Tramps size and strength, as he effortlessly hauled the still comatose bikers from the trucks, over his massive shoulders and deposit them where she instructed! That process was stalled, as there was an obstacle that they hadn't considered; Zeke, 125 lbs. of fury, teeth and muscle covered with thick black fur, who was less than impressed with what showed up at his doorstep. He really regarded it as his doorstep as this was his watch, and he was taking his position as watch dog, quite seriously!

It did take a while to establish Zeke's trust, as he had charged out of the front door when it was opened by someone other than Dan, with authority and he was as serious as a heart attack. He didn't try to bite yet, but his teeth were bared and his hackles were up and he made it quite clear that he was prepared do, whatever he had to do!

They wisely, kept their distance, while they tried to calm him down and assure him that they meant no harm. He recognized Tramp, as he had met him many times, that gave him pause, and he calmed down slightly, he'd only just met Calamity once, the previous night, but seemed to remember her as well, so he was analyzing the situation and trying to rationalize things.

Once Zeke spotted Dan slung over Tramp's shoulder and after he had a chance to cautiously approach and sniff him, he somehow got the idea that everything, was sort of OK, and allowed entry, but kept a close watch on everything and was never more than a few feet away at any given time and his mouth was formed into a permasnarl.

Calamity had never been there before, and did a quick walk through, to get the lay of the place and directed Tramp to dump Dan on his bed while she tried to figure out where best to put the drunken young stranger in the 50 shirt and where she, herself, was going to sleep. She picked the couch for the young guy, as there was a washroom is close proximity and picked a bedroom for herself. The rest of the details could be worked out in the morning. Tramp deposited the young Foxy on the couch and she thanked him for all his help, and watched as his truck disappeared into the night.

She then figured out where the dog food was kept and fed a very confused Zeke and let him out to do his business. She turned her attention to Foxy first. She removed his cap and boots and slid off his jeans, draping them over a nearby chair. She found a blanket to cover him and turned off the lights. She opened the door to the bathroom and left the light on so the young man might have a fighting chance of finding it if he came to during the night! He was bound to be confused but a bathroom would probably be one of the first things he would need.

Zeke came back in and headed directly to the bedroom to check on Dan. Calamity followed him up. Dan lay there face down, exactly as how he had landed when Tramp plopped him there. She turned down the covers, rolled him over pulled off his boots and his socks, unbuckled his belt, undid his jeans and slid them off! Then struggled to get the T shirt off. Now she pushed, pulled, rolled and otherwise maneuvered the dead weight until she could cover him and he never woke at any time during the process. Again, she turned the bathroom lights on and left the door open so it would serve as a beacon in the otherwise dark room. He was bound to be a tad hazy when he woke.

She then, toted her luggage to the room, she had picked for herself. Grabbed a quick shower in the adjoining bathroom and slid into bed to reflect on the day and tried visualise what lay ahead.

Dan awoke to daylight streaming in his bedroom window. He knew where he was, but had no idea how he got there, or when. He could smell bacon cooking and toast, and coffee. He looked around for Zeke but he was not there. He glanced at the bedside clock! Shit, 8:30 AM! He could hear muffled voices coming from downstairs. Stumbling quickly to the bathroom for a much-needed, urgent, visit to the toilet, he caught a brief glimpse of himself in the mirror on the way past it.

"Oh God!" He was not a pretty sight.

"He threw some cold water on his face, ran a comb through his hair, took a mouthful of mouthwash a swished it around in his mouth and spit the repulsive tasting stuff into the sink. He then slipped on his pants and an old flannel shirt that was hanging on a door knob and headed down stairs to see what was going on.

Zeke met him at the doorway his tail wagging a mile a minute, the he rushed back to where the Young man in the Labatt's 50 t shirt had been feeding him scraps of bacon and toast. Foxy looked alert and none the worse for wear, far better than how he, himself, felt.

"Morning!" he said cheerfully.

Dan Smiled, and nodded, trying to remember what had happened.

"Good Morning" said the lilting female voice, complete with the husky undertones, as a smiling Calamity came out from behind the open refrigerator door. She looked radiant, her hair tied back, wearing a long button up white shirt that was in sharp contrast, with her long, tanned legs with a pair of white woolen socks on her feet! It wasn't a sight he wasn't used to seeing in his kitchen.

"Coffee? I made bacon, scrambled eggs and toast and was just going to cook up a couple of waffles!" she announced as she pranced to the counter.

"Zeke, has had his breakfast and been out!" she continued as she handed Dan a mug of coffee and gave Foxy a refill!

He still looked bewildered, so she explained! "You disappeared, and were gone a long time, so we went looking for you. We found the two of you passed out beside an almost empty cooler chest, amongst one Hell of a pile of empty 50 bottles! Oh yeah, and I'm supposed to remind you of the "No Glass" policy! Anyway, we couldn't leave you out there sleeping on that cold wet ground as it started to rain, and the mosquitoes and blackflies would have eaten you both for their breakfast. Tramp, brought Foxy, here, and I borrowed REB's truck and hauled your sad old ass here. Some fucking watchdog you got there, tried to lick us to death. She smiled at Zeke and gave him a playful scratch behind his ears. Actually, he really wasn't sure about us at all and I thought that we all might be sleeping elsewhere for a while."

Foxy just sat there grinning, amused by Calamity's rapid-fire way of talking! Zeke was keeping a close eye on him as he still had food left on his plate.

"So how are you making out?" Dan asked him, as he took a sip of the hot coffee and sat down at the table. He had barely sat down and Calamity set a plate in front of him and was now busy filling it with food! He had to hold a hand over top of it to tell her that he had plenty already.

"Doing good now! Thanks for putting me up! Great house! Great dog! You've got great friends (Nodding towards Calamity)! Best breakfast I've had in ages!" he said

"No problem but I didn't have much say in you staying here. I wasn't even sure how I got here either until Calamity just explained it to me. I take it that you have introduced yourselves?

They both nodded. Dan had moved his hand from over his plate to take a sip of coffee and Calamity immediately moved in trying to top it up with more of everything. Foxy accepted another heaping plate full, much to Dan's amusement! He sure could eat, for a skinny guy, he reminded him of REB and his voracious appetite. The long red hair, the easy-going manner, the inquisitive nature, a big liking for large quantities of beer, thank God it wasn't warm fucking Guinness!

He looked over at Calamity who was standing there smiling, she seemed to already know what words were going to come out of his mouth. "Does Foxy here remind you of anybody?" Her smile broadened and that answered his question.

"So, did you find a place to sleep? You sleep OK? Do you need anything?"

"Yeah found a room across the hall from yours, if that's OK. I slept like a log and woke up ready to rock and roll. I love cooking and I love bacon and eggs and found some in your refrigerator! You're going to need more, I can run into town and do some shopping when we've finished breakfast. Foxy says he needs to replenish his beer supply, because some old guy drank most of his!" She said with a laugh.

"Yeah that is the room I was going to offer you. It's yours for as long as you need it, I'll find you a key! He pulled several hundred dollars from his jeans pocket slid a hundred towards Foxy which he tried to refuse, a stern look told him he was to take it. Cans!" He added emphatically, with a grin. He turned back to Calamity. "OK that will be fine get whatever you think we are going to need!" sliding the rest of the money towards her! She was also about to protest but got the same stern look that was given to Foxy so she tucked the money in the waistband of her shorts or whatever she was wearing under that white shirt. "Can you pick me up some decent fucking mouthwash? I hate that shit I've been using for years, I keep buying it out of habit!" She nodded and said that she would check what he had in his bathroom. He started to tell her to take his truck but remembered that, that was the Departments truck and they would be coming by to pick it up. Hey, give me a half hour or so to get cleaned up and we can all head into town in REB's truck. I have to rent one until I can find another, as mine is going back to the Police Department."

"Hell, we have a busy day ahead of us! I'll get that old Shovelhead out for you and give it a once over, and you can use it as long as you're here! If you want, take it for a ride, while I'm in the shower! There's an Iron head Sporty in there too if you want to go along with her kid." He said, as he led them to the garage and opened the door.

I think they both have a full tank of gas. He was about to go check them over for them, but stopped. Hell Foxy, you are a wrench and Cal here, can wrench with the best of them. The keys are on that rack over there. There are some helmets up on the shelf! Enjoy the ride, I'm heading to the shower!" At that, he turned and walked back to the house, with Zeke at his heels.

The warmth of the water cascading over his body soothed and relaxed him. It was an almost euphoric, and he found himself just standing leaning against the tiled wall with his eyes closed almost ready to fall asleep. He heard a soft knock on his door and looked to see the door open slightly and Calamity's slender arm reaching in a depositing a small bottle of mouthwash on the vanity. "Try this stuff and let me know what you think!" She said through the door as she gently closed it again.

"Thanks, I will." He shouted back and continued with his shower.

He could hear the sound of the two bikes fire up and depart and listened intently as they made their way down the street. They sounded good and strong as they accelerated, they were shifting almost in unison and he listened until the sound faded and he could hear them no more but Zeke with his keen ears was still hearing them and he was his ears were twitching and he was following their progress.

Dan shaved and brushed his teeth out of habit, almost grabbed the bottle of mouth wash that he hated. He pushed it aside and twisted the cap off the bottle that Cal had given him to try. He poured some of the dark green liquid into a paper bathroom cup and first gave it a quick sniff. "Hmmm, smells decent, he emptied the glass into his mouth and swished, gargled, and spit into the sink! He smiled at his reflection, reached over and picked up the bottle of the old yellow stuff, opened it, and poured it into the toilet and flushed! It looks like piss, tastes like piss, let it end like it was piss! He then unceremoniously, but triumphantly, pitched the empty plastic bottle into the blue recycling box.

By the time he finished dressing he saw Zeke's head suddenly lift, his ears twitching and a few minutes later, he heard the distinctive bark of the Shovelhead's shorty exhaust as it came up the driveway, He could also make out the note of the Iron head Sporty and they both sounded good. He didn't ride either of them near enough and was happy that they got a decent little run. Cal, was an incredible rider and she could ride circles around a lot of guys he knew, himself included!

Both her and Gypsy competed in the Biker Games, at all of their own Field meets, as well as those hosted by other Motorcycle Clubs, these were open field competitions where women and men competed against each other and, quite often one or both of them, came away as the winners. Sometimes the ultimate winner, had to be decided in grudge contest between the two women, having eliminated all the rest of the competition. It was always a toss-up who eventually won but winning was always secondary to having fun, riding and competing while improving and honing their individual riding skills.

There was getting to be some serious competition and the number of lady riders was increasing rapidly and many took their riding very seriously and a lot of men were looking over their shoulders and stepping up their game!

There was however, another lady, a pretty, petite, blonde with massive dimples who was tough as nails and was also a fixture at all the bike rallies. She rode a full dressed, bright yellow, Harley, that seemed to be twice her size but she could handle that bike like ringing a bell! She would always give everybody a run for their money and lot of trouble! There was a lot of good-natured rivalry and serious competition, and a lot of tremendous riding skills were on display! There was no cakewalk to the winner's circle for anyone, male or female. You, had to earn a win. These ladies inspired a lot of other women to get more seriously involved and they earned respect as riders, not just decoration for their Ol' Man's bike!

Leaving Zeke in charge of home security once again. The three, headed into town in REB's Black Ford F150. This truck, other than his old Knuckle was his pride and joy and it was decked out to the hilt, with a custom paint job, reminiscent of the Harley-Davidson truck, that Ford, used to produce but even nicer. The interior was all custom upholstered and it had a sound system that was out of this World. This was a pleasure to drive!

They finished in town, Dan was able to rent a truck and they took it back to his place to drop it off before heading back to the Clubhouse again. The road check was still in place and they were pulled over. A cop who Dan recognized, came up to the driver's side window, and looked inside. He spotted Foxy in the passenger side, acknowledged him, smiled and said to Dan; you two look in better shape today than you did last night. He then looked at Calamity in the back seat, who he obviously recognized, smiled, and said; "Calamity, with all due respect, I'll bet you couldn't look bad if you tried! Sorry but it had to be said." He then winked, slapped Dan on the shoulder, and said "You all, have a nice day!"

Dan drove off down the driveway and glanced in the rear-view mirror to see Calamity, her mouth agape and full-on, blushing and at a complete and total loss for words! Two things, he or anyone else he knew, had never seen or heard of or even dreamed were possible!

"Looks like you have a fan Darl'n!" Dan said with a wink. There was nothing but silence from the back seat. Young Foxy just sat there grinning. He told Foxy about the time when he had once asked her, when she took a pause from talking long enough for him to ask, "I wonder if for you, talking, is like a shark having to keep swimming or they would drown, and if you quit talking, would your lungs just collapse or something?" Everybody else, had thought it was funny. Calamity; not so much, but she has forgiven me, I think! He glanced again in the rear-view mirror to see Calamity smile and stick out her tongue, just before she playfully, smacked him in the back of the head.

They drove down along by the pond with Foxy, trying to remember where he and his crew had parked and found them in the midst of cleaning their bikes while enjoying a couple of cold beer. They stood up when Foxy got out of the truck and started unloading his beer (Cans) and his old beat up cooler from the back!

"Send a guy for ice and he shows up the next day with company!" One of them shouted good naturedly. "We heard he was in good hands! Did he cause you any trouble?"

"Naw not much, other than he sure can eat!" Dan replied and heading over to shake their hands and introduce himself, along with Calamity who had now regained her composure as well as her ability to talk. They passed on their condolences about REB, and said that they had been up to visit him at the Clubhouse early this morning. This place is filling up fast, they said. It's been a steady stream of bikes all night and all morning.

Just then, a dozen more bikes rolled in and were in search for a spot to camp. Dan knew some of them and they exchanged waves as they headed towards what looked like a suitable looking location.

"He turned to Foxy and said; "I'll look for you later tonight, at the bar in the CH tonight, and I can finish that story. The 50 is on me!"

Foxy nodded and smiled and went about explaining to his companions what had happened.

Dan and Cal carried on, down to the house.

Linda greeted them as they came up the front steps. The Lawyer is here and he wants to speak to you two. They followed her to REB's office where the remainder of the original "Bakers Dozen" were gathered. Linda quietly closed the door, as she Dan and Calamity took a seat at the large table.

He began; "First let me express my deepest and most heartfelt condolences." He smiled and continued. "This is the last will and testament of Robert Edward Baker. It is fairly short and to the point. To his wife Linda, he leaves the house and the property it sits on along with all chattel. The ownership of several other properties and businesses will also be transferred to Linda Louise Baker, along with all his Worldly possessions, other than specifically, his 1947 Harley-Davidson, Knucklehead motorcycle, along with a dozen or so other motorcycles all listed here, along with his shop, his tools and equipment, all parts and accessories contained within his shop also itemized, and his 2018 Ford, F150 Pickup Truck. These are his words; "I love you my Dear Linda, with all my heart and soul! My regret is that I couldn't have lived longer, and enjoyed the warmth of your smile and the tenderness of your touch through eternity. Slán a fhágáil le mo ghrá., Go dtí go mbuailfimid le chéile arís (Goodbye my love, until we meet again.)"

· · ·

"The truck and my 1947 Knucklehead, as we discussed over the past while, You've got plenty of cars and never really liked driving the truck, and I know you won't ever ride the Knuck, and I don't want just anybody's ass sitting on that saddle, so I leave these items to my friend and Brother, Dan O'Reilly. They meant a lot to me, and I know they will mean a lot to him. He always liked that bike and it runs good and it will likely take him forever to finish that old Panhead, especially now that I'm not going to be there to do all the work on it! And the Truck because he's going to need one if he gives up being a Top Cop! The shop and parts and the rest he will appreciate more than you Darl'n. He adds, enjoy them Mo Chara! At that, Dan was handed some documents to sign, and an envelope containing ownerships, bills of sale, and keys!"

The 100 acres that the Clubhouse sits on, the buildings and all chattel, I leave to the remaining Members of the Bakers Dozen, Baseball Club. It is free of all mortgages, liens and encumbrance's other than a 99-year lease that I'm attaching to the property in the name of the Bakers Dozen, Motorcycle Club. The officers of this Club, will insure that through Club dues and monies earned through events, that the property is maintained and the taxes paid on time and in full. You Members, being the landlords will ensure that these terms are complied with. The title will be transferred jointly into each of your names and in the event future deaths of any or all of these Members, those names will be removed from the ownership of this property with no renumeration to the estates of these persons. In the event of all of those listed, the title will revert back to my family with the stipulation that the lease to The Bakers Dozen Motorcycle Club be honoured."

"There is more as to distribution to family but that doesn't concern anyone in this room at present, other than Linda Louise Baker. Any questions? Okay, I have some documents for those concerned, to sign, have a good day, and again, accept my condolences, I loved REB too!"

Those involved went through the signing process, while Dan left the room and went to go outside but instead went to the large bar, that was extremely busy, stopping at the sewing table where the young lady that he'd given his patches and his vest to, caught his attention and as he approached she handed him his vest with the awesome new patch sewn on. Congratulations she said as she helped him slide into it! It looks fantastic she told him. He tried to give her more money but she wouldn't accept it. You've been more than generous she smiled and went back to the table! He stood there looking at his reflection in the nearby full-length mirror.

Someone came up behind him, slapped him on the back and handed him an ice cold 50. Young Foxy was standing there beaming! "Congratulations man! Great looking patch, and that vest is none too shabby either. Man, you have to try some of this stuff! Fucking wicked!" He held up a bottle of Pure Old Panther Piss." They say some really hot lady, from BC makes it in her own still! That is just too cool to believe!" He was obviously having a great time!

Dan noticed that he was no longer wearing his Labatt's 50 shirt but one of the Support the Dozen shirts and when Dan commented on it he spun around showing the back too.

The front had a small image of their support logo and the back had; In memory of REB, Founder, The Bakers Dozen MC in a nice script font above a large image of REB on his old Knuckle and below that, it said in Sept. 12, 1945 – Sept 12, 2020.

"Fucking REB! he was always thinking and planning ahead! Even printing his own memorial shirts! No doubt, something else he did as a donation without approval! He would have been some pissed if he had lived until the 13th. That conniving old fucker, thought he was Babe fucking Ruth, calling the date of his demise like the Babe pointing to where he was going to hit the ball out of the fucking park!" He laughed!

"Yeah. They have patches, stickers and pins too! I got the shirt but I'm running low on cash! Maybe I can get you to send me one of each of them too. I'll send you the money, or I can come back for them, (which is what he really wanted to say! Fishing for an invitation to come back.)" Foxy said excitedly!

Just then Calamity joined them. "You two becoming an item? "she asked with a mischievous grin.

"He picked up a bottle of Panther Piss and is pretty impressed, he says it is made by some hot chick from BC."

"You don't say?" she said playfully "Is she here?"

"I don't know? They had it at the bar and it looked and sounded really cool, so I picked it up. It was a little pricey, but I have beer again, thanks to Dan here, and I think I have enough gas in the bike to get back home again. They say she's got some killer weed and shrooms too!"

"No shit! Hey Cal, don't you live out in BC? I hear

rumours that you run a little shine from time to time and how does, your garden grow?" Dan asked with a big smile!

Foxys' jaw dropped to his chest. "No fucking way? You?"

She laughed and told him not to worry, and palmed him a couple of envelopes she had taken from her jacket pocket. Foxy tried to give her whatever money he had. She waved him off, saying it was payment for keeping her ex Cop friend company when he needed some! She handed him some money and said; "Here take this and pick up three of every-thing the have in the way of Swag, don't worry about The Panther Piss, I have plenty. I'd might as well get you some too, Dan the Man!" She said laughing!

"I'll catch you in a bit my friend." Dan said to young Foxy! "Cal and I have some catching up to do." They left him there, having a good time. He had made a big impression on both he and Calamity and he heard Tramp commenting to a couple of the other guys over at the CH about the wild young redheaded kid who seemed to be having such a great time and what a great attitude he seemed to have, how they'd found him and I passed out amongst a whole heap of 50 empties and they had to transport us home and tuck us in!

"It's too bad this is such a sad occasion, as this has been fun! I don't think I've felt this relaxed or at peace in I don't know how long! I'm glad we bumped into each other, and thanks for putting me up and it felt so good on M's old shovel this morning, that tribute you painted on the tank was pretty special! I loved that old fart! I saw that and I almost cried. Thanks!"

She took his arm and they wandered off to find a quiet spot. He looked at Calamity and smiled. He was really enjoying her Company. They just strolled along arm in arm in no particular hurry until they found a nice spot. "Well I guess I can return that rental truck." he said as they sprawled out on the grass in the shade, under a large oak tree.

"He started to say something else, but Calamity interrupted him by suddenly leaning in, and kissed him full on the mouth! He was caught totally off guard, and didn't quite know what to make of it, as they rarely even hugged one another, despite the fact that they had known each other for years.

Her lips were softer and more tender than he could ever have imagined. The scent of her delicate perfume, rose deep in his nostrils as he drew in a quick startled breath. It was almost intoxicating and combined with the complete surprise of her action, Dan's head was spinning! He could feel her lips part, and could hear her draw another breath. Now her tongue was now probing his lips, they parted and her tongue slipped delicately into his mouth.

Then she pulled away slightly and looked directly into his eyes smiled, before leaning in and kissing him again in much the same manner, but longer and lingering. She then sat back, her lips had now formed a sinister grin, she reached out, placed her hand delicately on his chest, then slid it slowly, and deliberately down his body until it reached it's intended destination, which was, his now throbbing, groin! She gave it a gentle squeeze and momentarily, her fingers gently caressed and rubbed him intimately and she could feel his member growing hard and straining against the fabric of his pants.

"OK then! I see that works she said, coyly glancing down

at the bulge in his pants, smiling sensually, then she looked him square in the face again, as if gauging his reaction!" Just checking to see if you still function. She said. "Actually, I've wanted to do that for years, but the opportunity never presented itself. You want to go grab something to eat?" She asked quickly, hopping to her feet.

"Dan was totally flustered and it was his turn to blush, again!" He stammered a bit, but managed to say. "Give me a minute or two!" She just laughed and reached down and grabbed his arm, to help him up! "Don't worry, we have a bit of a walk ahead of us, and it isn't that noticeable," She gave him a sweet little grin, and added, "Yet!" At that, she reached in front of him and with a quick, playful, flick of her wrist flicked her long slender fingers, struck him sharply, but not hard, right on the affected area sending him doubling over, grimacing with a muffled moan!

"See that? That big, hard, nasty thing is all gone!" She giggled. "Calamity Jane giveth, and she can taketh away! Just like that!" She snapped her fingers and then mimicked the flicking motion that she had just applied to Dan's groin, laughed again, and ran ahead, just in case there was going to be retribution or retaliation. She didn't want to get thrown into the pond or anything. Dan just laughed it off, but his mind was spinning!

They went back to the barbecue pit, and Cal made them both a couple of monster-sized, roast beef sandwiches, out of some of the excellent, freshly sliced, beef that had just come off of the huge roast that had been cooking on the spit for hours. She had included a couple of cobs of nice freshly roasted corn, which she slathered in butter and salted and a baked potato, also saturated in butter. Dan was off getting a couple of cans of beer, from one of the many beer tents that were scattered throughout the property. He came back with young Foxy in tow and the three sat, laughed and talked as if they all had known each other for years!

There were some great old tunes being played over the fantastic sound system and the DJ was really mixing things up, with some Blues, some Southern Rock, and some good old Rock and Roll! There were several bon fires going at various fire pits that were almost as plentiful as beer tents and the orange glow they cast on the dark sky was a welcome sight and a beacon, that could be seen for miles, as new arrivals were rolling in steadily and would be throughout the night. The rows of porta potties were being cleaned and sanitised at all hours as they saw plenty of action.

I met a bunch of your guys down at the beer tent and got to talking to them. They are thrilled being part of an actual Club now. They said that they have always loved this place and the people involved and this guy REB seemed like a great guy! I wish that I had gotten to know him."

"So, are you going to finish the story or what?" Asked Foxy as he returned from a trip to the beer tent with a box full of 50 and several Coors light for Calamity! "They wouldn't take my money he said in disbelief!"

"Yeah I told you I had it covered! But you are going to be the runner, OK?"

Foxy nodded his agreement. Calamity leaned in to listen as well.

"OK where did I leave off? Oh yeah, the baseball team."

"So that was the baseball days. That pretty much is how and why this Club came about. The Club has been going strong ever since.

"So, I became a Cop and my ascent to my goal, was complete and I could torment Robert Edward Baker to my hearts content and I was content. I was fine, right up until when, Chief of Police, Stanley Marshall who was wanting to retire, told me he had been considering me, as his replacement. This thrilled me! But then he challenged me with some absurd statements and questions! Among other things, he said he had doubts about my fairness, and said that I had serious prejudices. He was concerned that I was treating Robert Baker and his biker friends unfairly and I was wrong in doing so.

I told him exactly what I thought of Robert Edward Baker and all his biker buddies, and I, as much as told him to go fuck himself, and told him to shove any promotion to Chief up his ass! I stormed off in a huff!

Then he did it again while, I was in the Hospital recovering from injuries I had sustained in an accident that saw myself and my entire family crash and plunge into the lake in our car. I didn't remember much about the accident, as I was mostly unconscious and I didn't see who saved us. When I came to, in the Hospital, the Chief informed me that REB, his wife Linda, and Bakers Dozen Member, Tramp Jackson, were the ones who had saved the lives of myself, and my family as well as our little dog!

I couldn't believe it! REB hated me as much as I hated him, or so I thought. He would be the last person on Earth that would save me. The old Chief had a somewhat different take on things and didn't sugar coat any of the stuff he laid on me. There was no storming off this time however, and I was in for the full treatment! I was thoroughly pissed. But I had heard what he said, and not having too much else, to do while cooped up in Hospital, thought long and hard on it all and gradually it started filtering into my closed mind and some light was able to penetrate to some of the dark reaches. Once some light found its way in, and illuminated some things, it allowed other thoughts to grow and I began to realize some truths as others saw them.

That was my turning point and there was no turning back, I flung back those curtains and had a good look around and discovered things about myself that I couldn't be proud of. Was it too little, too late? Had it gone too far? Could I make things right and start over? I was about to find out!

I got out of Hospital and was still mulling things over and this whole thing with REB was really bothering me. I couldn't sleep, so sat outside, nursing a cold beer or six, and that is where I woke the next morning, sitting by the swimming pool with a row of empty Labatt's 50 bottles lined up beside me.

I gathered up the empties and deposited them on the kitchen counter.

"Have a good night's sleep?" his wife Nancy, asked sarcastically, as she slid a cup of black coffee in front of him.

"I slept some! Had some thinking to do." He replied, sipping the strong black coffee.

"I got the day off. I think I'll go for a ride." He announced.

"OK, where are you off to?"

"I think I'll scoot over to REB Bakers place!"

I heard the plate she was drying fall into the sink and smash, but didn't react.

"I'll give him a call and make sure he's free, but I think it's a ride, that is long overdue!" He told her matter of factly. He then turned to see the shocked look on her face!

"Yep! That's what is on tap for today! According to what old Stan Marshall has been telling me, they might be serving crow!" He smiled and reached for his phone. This was something that he had been considering for a while now and had already programed REB's number into his phone, even gave it a speed dial assignment!

I dialed, and heard REB's gruff voice answer.

"REB?"

"Yeah! Who's this?"

"Dan O'Reilly!"

There was complete silence for a full minute!

"Yeah what do you want?" REB finally asked, very curtly!

"Are you going to be around this morning, I was thinking about riding over that way to talk!"

"Talk?" was the skeptical response.

"I'd just like to try and clear the air between us!"

There was another long silence. "That's a lot of fucking air Dan! A lot of years! A lot of history! That could take a while! He paused again. "Yeah I got some time. I'll be at the CH all day, come on over! I'll let people know that you are coming. Hey but listen! No lights and siren! Respect our fucking neighbours! And he chuckled!"

They hung up and Dan turned to Nancy with an astonished look on his face. He actually made a joke and chuckled!" he said incredulously to Nancy. "That is a start!"

CHAPTER TEN

WHAT GOES GOOD WITH CROW?

IT FELT good to get out on the old Duo glide it was running great and it was eating up the miles to REB's property almost too quickly. I was hoping to have a little longer to figure out what to say and how to say it. I didn't know what kind of reception I would receive or if we could ever get past the animosity, the mistrust or the bad vibes that I had created but I had to try. I didn't know if REB would even give me a chance to change or not.

I knew where the place was, every copper around knew where it was, but I had never actually been here before. Dan came to the driveway entrance and followed the dirt roadway to the end where it opened into a large field where some old buildings and various old cars, school buses, trucks, campers and some old farm implements formed a perimeter. At the end stood a nice looking, decent sized shop. Just beyond that was a large pond with a huge fire pit in front of that. I could see how it had been opened up down to the

Lake as I had heard that they annexed the three properties into one.

I could see the Clubhouse and it too looked respectable. REB, and his family lived at one of the adjoining properties. As he was buying up whatever land as it became available in the area and had compiled quite a few properties over the past ten years or so. So along with the properties that his parents had left him, he might even qualify as a small, land Barron.

REB appeared in the doorway of the shop and motioned me to come on up. I rode forward and parked right by the front door. Kicked the side stand down and climbed off.

I was getting some strange looks from the others who were hanging around either working on a bike, a car or something. Dan's arrival caught their interest once they started to realize who he was. Reb just waved them off! "Beer?" he asked.

"Sure" I can always go for a beer!"

"What do you like? We got Ex, Red Cap, 50."

"50 sounds good to me!"

He pulled a cold 50 out of the cooler and extracted a bottle of Guinness from a case on the ground beside the cooler. "No room in the cooler for the Guinness?" I asked.

"Hell, man, are you some kind of a fucking savage? You don't chill Guinness like you do with that Moose piss your drinking!" At that, he laughed, and opened his Guinness. He raised the bottle towards me in a toast "Slainte" they clinked their bottles together, then raised them to their lips and I watched from the corner of my eye as REB held the bottle in that position for a second and suddenly chugged down the entire bottle!

I was unsure if this was traditional here, or the way bikers drank or whether if it was a challenge, and followed suit with my bottle of 50!

"Hah! Always up for a challenge eh, Dan O'Reilly? That tasted just like another one!" He said with a hearty laugh, while passing me another cold 50 and grabbed another Guinness for himself as well. Slowly this time, like gentlemen, not heathens!" He laughed again!

He had a magnificent laugh! Full of gusto and it was indeed, pleasant to hear!

"So, Let's get down to business Dan O'Reilly!" He said, slapping a large right hand on his thigh! "Excuse me for being curious, but what brings you all the way out here, on this fine day? Or are you just out for a ride on that lovely old motorcycle and thought you'd drop by for a pint? We haven't been anything that could be described as friends for the last 30 odd years. You've never seen fit to drop by before, although several of your associates have dropped in unexpectedly on occasion! I notice that you are not armed, so I'm assuming that your intentions are peaceful." REB stated things quite plainly, and to the point and he fixed those ice blue lasers that he called eyes on my eyes, looking for some indication where this visit was leading! He always tried to be direct and to the point. There was less chance of truth getting mired down and obscured in bullshit. That was his thinking.

Truthfully, although knowing him all these years, I had never heard Robby Baker speak that many words at one time, before, ever. In school even, he seldom spoke in more than short sentences. When he'd been pulled over at Police stops, he only muttered what was absolutely necessary, nothing more. Mostly one or two syllable answers to any questions that were posed to him. I was taken aback at the eloquence of his speech, his speech patterns, vocabulary and demeanor. It was a bit unnerving, yet refreshing, much different, then what I was expecting. In fact, I didn't have any idea of what I was really expecting, but it was different than what I was now experiencing, and it bothered me somewhat. Like I said, he never said much of anything, to me or any other cop! Any interaction I'd had with him for years was at Police stops, and he had always remained silent throughout them, letting us get on with what he considered to be; "Total Bullshit!". He'd wait until we either gave him his paperwork back and let him go on his way, or arrested him and he'd call his Lawyer. He always seemed to be totally indifferent and uninterested, in the whole process.

"Well, I guess first off, I want to thank you, your wife Linda and Tramp for saving me and my family that night and for looking after our dog too!" There aren't enough words to express my gratitude." I extended my hand, and while he looked at it, it was left hanging there, so I retracted it.

He continued to fix me in his unflinching stare, his eyes, locked on mine, his face, void of expression. "That, is what people do, Dan. You help, or try your best! You do what you can! That is all we did, the best we could. We are glad, for the sake of you, and your family, that we were there, when we were, and were able to help and our efforts were successful.

Now, you extended you hand to me just now, and I didn't

take it. I only shake hands with friends and people I respect. As I already stated earlier, you and I could never be mistaken for friends. If you want to extend your gratitude for what happened that night, you have now done that! Thank you, will suffice and Linda and Tramp will be appreciative as well. Happy Birthday by the way! I guess that was our Birthday gift to you!

Now, you mentioned on the phone, that you wanted to clear the air between us. Given our history, I don't know if that is possible, but I'm willing to try. Considering the dynamics, we will probably, never be the best of friends, but it would be nice to be civil, and maybe work all the way up to respectful, given the chance. You had the guts to ride out here and seem open to change, I respect that. So, Dan O'Reilly, let us start with a hand shake and work up from there!

We both extended our hands and shook firmly! REB started to squeeze just a bit harder, and could instantly, feel me start to react, by increasing my grip as well. REB let go, and I looked up into his ruddy face to see a huge grin, formed behind that red beard and mustache!

It was, yet another test, as REB, was always wary, ever cautious and always alert for even the slightest hint that something was off, or the slightest whiff of deception. Old Tony had drilled that into his head from those early days. "Deception and dishonesty have a distinct smell to them." He would say. "Learn what they smell like, and keep your nose in the wind!" So far, with Dan, he could smell nothing, but he was still a Cop, and that was never good when you are a biker, but he would play out the hand and see which way the game would go!"

"See! Still always up for a challenge O'Reilly!" He then let out one huge laugh and slapped Dan playfully on the shoulder!

"Now let's go over and take a look at the bucket of bolts you call a motorcycle."

That was it! No animosity! No attitude! They weren't the best of friends, but they now, at least, had the basis for a respectful relationship, which is a far cry from what they had before. After checking over the old Panhead, they wandered down by the pond, taking two more beer each with them, so they'd have something to drink there and, on the way, back. This place did have a nice vibe to it and Dan felt at ease. They found a couple of large rocks to sit on and watched, as several large trout, breached the surface of the water catching a juicy bug for their dinners before disappearing again into the dark water, leaving slight ripples in their wake. It was peaceful.

"So old Stan wants you to take over as Chief?"

"Yeah! He needs to retire soon so he can enjoy his retirement! I wouldn't have believed the kind of workload he has shouldered all these years! He's way past, over-due! "He is a real straight shooter and a totally honest individual, and he has given me quite and education over the past couple of months. A lot of history and a lot of truth about a lot of people and a lot of things!"

"You figure you're up to the task? You got some awful big shoes to fill!"

"You know someone said earlier today, that you just try your best! I will try my level best!"

Reb just winked and nodded in agreement.

"Well Dan, it has been nice sitting talking, and enjoying a pour or two but I've got a "to do list" as long as my arm that Linda had prepared for me and expects me to complete, so I'd better get at it. Come back again some time, and bring the family if you want. Just don't come in a Cop vehicle or wearing a uniform! We have a reputation we like to maintain and plus, we need time to hide all the drugs and illegal guns, so give us some warning OK." He cautioned with a big smile.

REB walked him back to his bike, and saw him off. When he disappeared down the driveway he turned to the few, that were now standing around him. "Well I guess we'll see were this all goes. At least he didn't shoot my dog and nobody got taken away in handcuffs." Every body laughed as REB fired up his old truck to get on to Linda's list and everyone got back to what they were doing!

I rode home, satisfied that he made the first step and very happy with the outcome.

I got home parked the bike, and went inside to find Nancy bursting to see how it went! I gave her a big smile and a huge hug! "You know what? I asked. "That was first taste of Crow wasn't too bad, but not my favourite thing to eat! I guess I'd better acquire a taste for it though, I think its going to be on my plate for a while! Damn! That was a long time coming and it felt good! Except the man drinks warm fucking Guinness!"

"I was happy with the outcome and progress that was made. I had managed to swallow my pride and suppress my ego, two things that I have to keep in check. I thought that it might may have been very strained at first. It wasn't. I rode my Harley over as I hoped it would show that we had at least one thing in common, plus I just love to ride and will use any excuse to throw a leg over that thing."

"I thought about our meeting and analyzed it and what transpired over and over. I really had no idea of the kind of man he was, as I had never been interested in finding out. I found him to be a little cold, and cautious at first, he had every right to be, and what else should I have expected? Our previous interactions, were always one sided, and forced upon him.

I had no idea what his voice was like or if he was even literate. I went to school with him and played on the same Hockey teams as him but didn't associate with him other than when we fought. He was mostly, a person of few words, around me at least. He was a complete stranger to me yet I'd known him for more than 30 years. I had, literally, no idea of what to expect. I was in for an education.

When I first heard him speak that day, I was amazed at his eloquence, his diction, annunciation, his vocabulary, his speech patterns and phrasing! His voice resonated and carried well, as did his laughter. He had a magnificent laugh and I can't recall ever hearing it, before that day.

I was also very disappointed with what I found this man to be, or rather what I found out he was not! I had always vilified him and pictured him as a bit of an imbecile, and a dolt! I thought he would be an uneducated boor, devoid of any intelligence, humour, or any positive attributes. What I discovered was, that I couldn't have been more wrong about him.

Instead, I found him to be sincere, warm, kind, loving, with a tender streak that was a mile wide and twice as long. He had a tremendous sense of humour, a captivating smile and infectious laugh that could resonate through a room like a breath of fresh air. He was highly intelligent and extremely talented!

I was more than a little surprised as I didn't think I could ever even like this man, whom, I had hated so long with all my heart! Having Now, actually met the man, my opinions changed and this time they were formed and established by my actual honest assessment of the man. and what was immediately evident and not based on my biased, distorted, perception of him. I realized that my previous assessment had been formulated by lies, innuendo, and prejudicial remarks by some of my mentors, peers, and instructors.

Based on the man that now sat with me that day, I couldn't imagine ever having an ill thought towards him. I was deeply ashamed of myself. I didn't discover all of this, all from that first serving of crow, but over time. But the seeds of friendship that were sown that afternoon over some cold beer.

I became aware of the fact, that much of my attitude, and many of my prejudices, were engrained in me by my father, who had these things engrained in him by his Father, peers and mentors. Prejudices and attitudes can easily be passed down, from generation to generation, and are hard habits to break and large obstacles to overcome. As well, many of my attitudes and convictions were taught in the Police Academy as truths about bikers, biker lifestyle turned out to be falsehoods and prejudicial.

Many of the methods and outlooks that are presented and taught to these young and women who chose a career in law Enforcement are outdated, and do far more harm than good. They teach disrespect for individuals just because they are bikers, and do not give these people credit for any morals and, or, humanitarianism. They treat them as if they don't recognise them as citizens, who pay taxes, raise their children teach, love, or any of the human qualities simply because they are bikers. For a guy who prided himself on being fair and open minded, to find that I was anything but, was a rude awakening.

There are not enough Cops like Chief of Police, Stanley Marshall who looked at life and formulated his judgements based on what he found to be true, through actual evidence and his honest analyses and observations, rather than conjecture and the opinions of others. Opinions are only opinions, and he took the time to formulate his own and gave truth, the opportunity to present itself! Unfortunately, there are too many Cops like Dwight Higgins Sr. and sadly, Seamus O'Reilly as well. I hoped Dan O'Reilly would fare better. Stan Marshall was respected and trusted because he was respectful and gained trust through his actions. Big shoes to fill indeed!

I rode home that day, very pleased with the outcome. We weren't the best of friends by any stretch of the imagination, but door had been opened and perhaps a window or two as well. The light and fresh air could get in now and we would see what would grow from it!

There is more to the story but it will have to wait for another time as we have other stuff that needs to be done if we are going to bury our Brother.

It will all come out soon my young friend, trust me.

Foxy was now seeing an entirely different side of Dan O'Reilly, he was starting to see the side that Robert Edward Baker had come to know and love and he was starting to like him a lot too.

Calamity, too, had been listening in, and it was obvious that she was not aware of the whole story, and she looked positively astounded by some of what she had just heard and had a different understanding of how two men she truly admired, could form such a strong bond and make the journey from being Worlds apart, to being Brothers.

Her opinion of REB was based on her experience and knowledge of him over many years. She had always found him to be honest, and forthright and he had saved her from the abuse of others on more than one occasion and from herself and her own self-destructive tendencies, on many more. She owed him so much, that she would never be able to repay! She would carry those debts to her grave and her love and respect for him would be eternal.

Dan, she had known for years as well, and wasn't particularly fond of him in those early days, as she was more than a little aware, of the bitter feelings between REB and he. When REB and Dan buried the hatchets, she, and everybody, were more than a little skeptical. But, as the friendship between the former nemeses, became evident and respect and the trust seemed to grow right along with it. She, and the others just sort of accepted it, because they trusted REB and respected his judgement and if it was good for him, who were they to question it! They treated Dan as he treated them; well and with respect, but he was still a Cop and many were always wary. You see a rattlesnake, it might seem docile, but it is still a rattlesnake!

The friendship had evolved into something real and sustainable and it was a bond that would never be broken.

Until just then, she had never heard the whole story. Dan O'Reilly had just elevated himself in her personal evaluation of him. She had long had a physical attraction for him, now her respect for his honesty and integrity grew as well. She too, could see the man that REB saw when he looked at him and now had a better understanding of the bond!

CHAPTER ELEVEN
LET THE LESSONS BEGIN

AFTER HE GOT out of Hospital, still recovering from the accident at the lake, and having had sufficient time to think about what the Chief had said, but with no opportunity to discuss it with him further, he was still running many different scenarios in his head. He never discussed any of it with Nancy as he felt it was something that he had to work out for himself.

He was off work for eight weeks, doing physiotherapy to strengthen his arms and legs. He hung out with Nancy and the kids a lot and played with the dog when he wasn't doing light yard work.

He looked up from weeding the front lawn, and was happy to see Chief Marshal's Cruiser pull in the drive. He had gotten over the verbal assault that he laid on him in the Hospital and they were now cordial, but had never had the opportunity to talk further about the incident since. He was trying to find the words and the nerve to say them.

"You up to taking a ride?" The Chief asked.

Dan said sure, went to the front door, stuck his head in the door and told Nancy that he was going out with the Chief for a while.

He climbed in the front seat with him, and noticed some large file folders that had been sitting on the passenger seat but were now on the centre consul, between them.

"I have to go and pick up some folks over in the next Township and bring them back to a place near here!" The Chief explained.

They were on the road for about an hour, before pulling up in the rear of The Police Stationhouse, and drove into the large underground parking garage.

This all seemed rather clandestine, like something out of a movie where illegal deals went down, snitches were met, drugs or money was exchanged and all the rest of those scenarios.

The Old Chief looked at him and smiled, as he seemed to know what he was thinking. "You won't be needing your gun." He then brought his cruiser to a stop beside a large RV got out, motioning for him to do the same!

"We switch vehicles here!"

Dan noticed two men exit the front doors of the RV. and recognised them both, as soon, as their faces came into the light. One was Walter Brown, Chief of Police for the district that they were now in, the other, his Deputy Chief, Charlie Andrews. They were both well respected officers with long and distinguished careers.

They stopped briefly beside the RV and exchanged short pleasantries. Chief Brown handed Chief Marshal a file folder which he opened, examined the contents, signed and handed back a couple of forms, and they separated, Chief Marshal and Dan climbed in the RV and the others boarded an unmarked Police vehicle and abruptly drove away.

Dan heard some stirring in the back of the RV and spun around to check it out. The Chief told him to relax and he would explain what was going on. He handed him the big file holder and instructed him to take a look. "It won't make much sense to you at this point, but it will soon enough."

Tearmann sábháilte was written across the top of the page, listed as destination.

"It means, Safe Haven in Irish, said the Chief. It is the code name for the destination of a safe house, which is in our district, he explained further. We are taking the family in the back there to escape extreme domestic abuse from a father and his three Brothers, who are alcoholics and all have a history of methamphetamine use. As well, one of the Brothers is a registered sexual offender who hasn't reported to his parole officer for three weeks now. They are from a Town in South western Ontario and need safe refuge until other, permanent arrangements, can be made."

"These safe houses operate in total secrecy and anonymity. There are only one or two of us in the department usually The Chief of Police, and who I trust to be on board as well as the heads of Social Services, who know of their existence and who runs them. This one that we are going to today, has been one of the best and longest running, safe houses in the Province!"

"Before we proceed further, I take it, that you have had time to think over what I had to say to you, in the Hospital." He asked.

He looked the Chief straight in the eye and responded; "Yes, I did, and what you left as food for thought, turned out to be an entirely different diet to what I'm used to. It seems to be agreeing with me though."

"Nancy and the Kids went over two weeks ago and picked up the dog. They ended up spending the day there and had a ball. I rode over yesterday and sat and talked with REB even drank some beer for a couple of hours and seemed to get along. No punches were thrown, and I didn't have to draw my gun even once, no dogs died during the course of the meeting and nobody got hauled away in handcuffs. So, I think we made some progress. Oh yeah, and he invited me back but no police vehicles with lights or sirens because he doesn't want to lower the property values or piss off all his neighbours!"

"Very Good! Given the chance, I think you two will get along just fine!" Said the Old Chief! "

"Dan, I want to retire! I need to retire! I would like to have you replace me but, for the reasons I mentioned previously, I am cautious and will proceed cautiously. I want to be sure that you have resolved or are resolving those issues. I would like to propose, that effective immediately, you become Deputy Chief, and as such, we will work closely together every day for the next two months and I can bring you up to speed on current events and situations. If everything is satisfactory during and by that date, I will officially retire and you can become Chief of Police for Swanton Harbour!" Is that agreeable?"

"Yes sir!" Dan affirmed.

"OK Deputy Chief, Daniel O'Reilly, we have some work ahead of us! This is not just a position, it is a job! Tedious and demanding, frustrating and infuriating but if done right, it can be satisfying and fulfilling as well!"

At that, they shook hands, Chief Marshall handed him an envelope containing his new badges, patches and pins, and paperwork outlining his new pay structure and benefits plans.

They were now back in their own district, and made their way along some rural roads, Dan hadn't really been paying absolute attention to the roads and various turns but the road they were on were familiar to him. The Chief slowed and pulled into a long driveway.

"This is just North of RE…" intending to say REB's place as he thought that REB and his family lived on the same property as the Clubhouse,

But the Chief held up a hand, put a finger to his lips and said quietly; "No names! Total secrecy! Get used to using code names only! He cautioned."

Dan nodded to say he understood!

This wasn't REB's place though. It was probably on REB's land but this wasn't his house as far as he knew. The Chief guided the RV up to the front of the house and backed it up near the front porch. He motioned for Dan to come with him, and the two men exited the vehicle and walked up the front steps across the wooden porch to the door, which opened before they could knock. It was obvious that they were expected!"

Linda Baker was at the threshold, but was obviously expecting only Chief Marshal and was obviously startled to see Dan O'Reilly there as well. She turned and looked behind her as Robert Baker strode up to stand beside her, temporarily blocking the entrance.

"I just made Dan O'Reilly my Deputy Chief, and tentative replacement as Chief when I retire in two months."

Reb looked him straight in the eye and gave him a look that said; OK we'll see how this goes, then he quickly moved passed the two Lawmen, to gather what belongings had managed to arrive with the family.

The Chief and Linda then went down to the RV and gathered up the occupants who Dan hadn't seen until now. There were three kids, two girls, probably six or seven years old, and a boy of about three, a woman who was in obvious physical distress as her face was bandaged and her arm was in a sling! They all looked scared and confused! Linda ushered them all upstairs while, Dan stood awkwardly by himself on the porch!

REB gave Dan a sideways glance and asked; "You think you're up to the task?" As he took the large file folder from the Chief, signed what was required of him to sign and handed those papers back to him! He smiled, and curtly said; "Good night then!" and promptly closed the door.

The Old Chief slapped Dan on the back and said; "Trust is going to take a while, when so much effort has gone into destroying it, it's going to take some time, and effort! The longest journey, starts with a single step my friend! You took that step, is a start! It is a start!" They then returned the RV to the parking lot they got it from and swapped it out for the Chiefs car and headed back!

It was now late and the Chief was showing the signs of wear! "Let's stop in up here and grab some food and a beer or two." Announced the old man jovially! He actually seemed pleased with the evening's outcome!

The Chief was indeed starting to fade and after one beer, and fighting partway through a burger and a plate of fries and gravy his eyes started to droop and he looked like he could fall asleep at any time.

Why don't I drive you home? Dan suggested? I can take a cab home!

"Yeah OK, but drop me off, and you take my car, you can pick me up early in the morning, 6:00 AM, we have a lot of work to do, Deputy Chief O'Reilly!"

"Yes sir." Was his reply and they headed off to complete their mission for the day!

So, it went, Dan was now, Deputy Chief, assistant, chauffer, trainee and body guard for the Chief. He'd pick him up each morning at 6:00 AM sharp, including Saturdays, Sundays, and Holidays, this salaried position started to look not quite as rosy in reality, as it did on paper. They would start with breakfast which the Chief insisted he pay for each and every morning! It was a breakfast special, $1.99 each. Dan ended up paying for lunch and occasional dinners, and the Chief ordered al le carte!

Their days, as forewarned, were long, and could be tedious, but Dan was learning from an old experienced hand, who had been doing this a long time and could provide history and frames of refence that would mean something to him and he could put it all in perspective. He was the perfect mentor, because he loved this job, and these people. He had class and style in a time, where class and style were going out of fashion, quickly!

He would also answer questions directly and honestly, instead of avoiding certain subjects or topics or glossing them over He was the type of man where; if you couldn't handle the truth, don't ask the question! He wouldn't sugar coat anything!

When Dan often asked about his father, the Chiefs accounts, were never what he wanted to hear, but they were what he needed to hear, or he wouldn't have asked the question. He was probably, the first and only, totally honest man, Dan had ever met, in his life!

One day in his office, Dan asked him about the unsolved murder of Dwight Higgins and how if Robert Baker was the Prime suspect, why did he hold him in such high regard, instead of just a suspect in the Murder of a Police Officer?

The Old Chief sat back in his chair, carefully organising his thoughts, so that what he was about to say to this young man, whom he was grooming for his job, would be satisfied with. It was a fair question, and deserved a fair and accurate answer.

"Yes, Constable Dwight Higgins was a member of the Swanton Harbour Police Department and he was indeed murdered. Of that, there is no doubt. Robert Edward Baker, was indeed a suspect, a prime suspect. He certainly had motive to do so, and was quite capable of performing such an act! Of this, there is also, no doubt! Were there others in the Community with equal motive, opportunity and capability? Absolutely!"

"Officer Higgins, your father, and several other officers who were employed as Peace Officers, by the Town at that time, rather enjoyed having these young men and women from the Dozen at their convenience! These young people, who much of society found to be undesirables were available to these officers, to tease, torment and bully, pretty much at their discretion!"

"They could even do so, in front of witnesses who didn't give a damn about these hooligans and riff Raff. They did so, in the name of Law and Order and making an example of these thugs and hoodlums and the Community as a whole, had been conditioned to think that that was perfectly alright!"

"If nothing much was happening one night, they would often lie in wait for one of these punks and they would spend hours tormenting and harassing them and REB was one of their prime targets. But, were the bikers the only targets of these over-zealous officers? Not a chance! They were full on, bullies with badges and thanks to the Blue Wall, where even, other Officers who were appalled by the behavior of the few bullies, covered up for them because of this so called, Policemen's Code of Honour."

"I also heard rumours that these officers. often beat REB and others into unconsciousness, sabotaged, their motorcycles and other vehicles and then, left them bleeding in a ditch. I couldn't substantiate these rumours, and they just died away, as just that, rumours and inuendo. Of course, REB and his crew had by this time, adopted the Biker Code, where you didn't Rat, or Punk out, you never talked to Cops. You didn't co-operate and you didn't use the legal system because it was always rigged in the Cops favour!"

"Officer Higgins, had also recently shot and killed REB's pet dog, while conducting the raid, that he had initiated and orchestrated, for no other reason than; he wanted to, and could. He claimed the dog tried to attack him and while many disputed that claim. I eventually, had to take the word of my officer, because none of the bikers would speak to me."

"Also, an unsubstantiated rumour; had your father striking Officer Higgins on the wrist with a truncheon as he was allegedly in the process of drawing his weapon and was about to shoot Robert Baker for striking him in the face, in retaliation for the shooting of his dog!"

"I know Officer Higgins did suffer an injury to his right wrist, as I have hospital records and accident claims to prove it, but by his and other officers' accounts of the incident, say he suffered the injury due to a fall while performing his duty and applied for and received Workman's Compensation for eight weeks. Again, none of the Bikers were talking!"

"Robert Baker was brought in, along with many others in his "gang", who were providing an alibi for Mr. Baker and questioned thoroughly. They claimed that he was with them at the estimated time of the murder and also covered the hours long before, and long after, the murder took place."

"They say they were all together, working on a troublesome motorcycle at that time. They had also taken delivery of a pizza, during the evening and the delivery driver concurs that REB was among them and that he was even the one who paid and tipped him generously! There was no evidence that placed Mr. Baker at or anywhere near, the crime scene and eventually we just let the matter remain in our unsolved crimes file. Yes and Mr. Baker and the rest, all retained council through the philanthropy of a Mr. Arthur Johnstone, a very successful local businessman who knew the accused and wanted to see them properly represented."

"I was also aware of many very disturbing rumours concerning Officer Dwight Higgins, which, while I was also unable to substantiate them at that time, these rumours, were persistent and consistent and could not, simply be ignored. Some of these rumours suggested that several of our officers were engaged in accepting bribes from local bookies, loan sharks, bootleggers and several Brothels in Town and that one Brothel in particular, was owned and operated by Officer Dwight Higgins and officer Seamus O'Reilly!"

That statement, set Dan back on his heels! "You weren't ready for that eh?" He said, looking directly at Dan, one thick eyebrow raised and a slight grin on his face. "Don't ask questions if you don't want to hear or can't handle the answers! Your Father was no saint! We were investigating these claims when we started to uncover evidence of perverted behavior and rumours of production of pornography, some involving children all linked to Officer Higgins! Our investigation ended when Officer Higgins was murdered. There was evidence of projectors display screens and all films and individual pictures were completely destroyed in the fire along with the body! They were totally obliterated by the flames and useless as evidence!"

"I had suspected for quite a while, previous to his death, that Officer Higgins was a bad Police Officer, and perhaps, a bad person as well. I observed, that most other Officers avoided him and nobody ever invited him to parties, get togethers, barbecues and the like. When he did show up unexpectedly, the wives of other officers, would avoid him like the plague and no children were ever allowed near him. To me, that speaks volumes!"

"Was he a bad cop and a bad person, guilty of perverse acts and worse, thanks to the fire, I lack proof and solid evidence, so I'm left with "No", but between you and I, my Cop's instincts tell me yes! I cannot proceed on my instincts or gut feelings! I am bound by the Law! Having exhausted my investigation with no positive results. I relegated the case to the unsolved files! Perhaps, in someone's mind, Justice was served!"

"Do I think he deserved to die like he did? My personal views of right and wrong and what justice represents, and my belief that all, and any, murders are wrong. I would have to answer no! Obviously, someone felt differently and their moral compass took them down a different road, and their own brand of justice prevailed!"

"Do I feel Robert Edward Baker could have murdered Dwight Higgins? Possibly! I have recently heard an interesting and quite plausible, rumour and theory, to the effect, that Mr. Baker killed Officer Higgins because of perverse acts that were being committed against many young girls who had mysteriously disappeared from this Community. One name in particular, was listed as a possible victim, that could have invoked this kind of action by Mr. Baker. But that name is unimportant now, as they are just rumours. These unsubstantiated rumours say that Robert Baker snuck away from the Club property, made his way to the Higgins property, where he confronted and killed Mr. Higgins and made his way back to the property, where he returned to working on that troublesome motorcycle and nobody noticed his absence, keeping his alibi intact! Plausible? Feasible? Still, no proof! It remains, a mystery!"

"There are always things about certain cases that really piss me off and bring out that "Old Cop, curiosity and instincts" when something doesn't quite fit! It is like an itch that you can't reach to scratch. There was a pair of local characters who claim to have witnessed the murder that night, they even claim to have seen the murderer, as well." He said thoughtfully, scratching his chin as he talked.

"Yeah they were camping on the land right beside the Higgin's property. They, admittedly, were enjoying a few beers and a few tokes as well as some "magic mushrooms." They heard this loud shrill screeching sound, that sent a chill down their spines, and looked over at Higgins cabin, as that, was where the noise was coming from. They saw a tall figure, wearing a long black shroud that had some kind of a red image down the front of it, that they say resembled an ugly woman screaming! A Banshee is what they claimed it looked like!" Anyhow, while they didn't see the murder itself, they said they watched this shrouded figure set fire to the place, throw a baseball bat inside the burning cabin and then disappear into the woods carrying some object by its straps.

"Wow! I never heard that before! Did it pan out?"

"No, those two tended to go hard on substances and booze quite often and they freely admitted that they had drank a lot of beer by that time, plus a few joints, and a couple of shrooms apiece, so the credibility factor dropped well below the point where I or anyone else were taking them seriously! They always have some outlandish tales to tell. They've been abducted by Aliens at least twice now! And we were expecting them to tell us that they regularly hung out there with a few sasquatches, and that they saw it too, but didn't want to come into Town with them to tell us about it! So, we just wrote them off as crackpots! But they really seemed to be bothered and shaken up, and I somehow, partially believed them, it has always bothered me, and still does."

"Would I arrest and put to trial one, Robert Edward Baker, if clear, substantiated, evidence, came to light that would prove his guilt or involvement, Absolutely! You don't take justice in your own hands! That is not justice, that is murder and murder is wrong!"

"Does that satisfactorily answer your questions? I suspect not! I do feel that what I have just told you, may bring a couple more to mind. Was your father's implication in the bribery, and other activities not becoming a Police Officer, going to result in charges being laid against him. Yes! It was shortly after the investigation started and he got wind of it!

He became very distraught and subsequently, suffered a heart attack and died! Did we pursue or will we pursue charges posthumously? No! We felt it would serve no purpose to besmudge his memory or name and embarrass his family. We dropped the investigation."

"Do I feel that your father was involved in Mr. Dwight Higgins' perverse acts and actions? No! Not even for a second. There is no reason to even suspect him of such things!"

"Does that cover it? More food for thought, perhaps?' He asked, looking Dan directly in the eye!

"Expect to get flack, that is part of the job. Don't be afraid to make mistakes! Mistakes will happen, that is part of being human! No one expects perfection but they do expect and are owed honesty! That is what you are paid to be; honest! But, always be ready to own those mistakes. Don't try to hide them or cast-off responsibility, that is dishonest!"

At that, the Chief rose from his chair, walked to the wall behind his desk and removed a couple of old framed photographs from the wall. He handed them to Dan to inspect. It was a picture of a much younger Stan Marshall with several other men of the same age. All were in uniform and posed with old military motorcycles.

"These men were part of my unit during the war. We were motorcycle despatchers and many of those pictured here perished in action. Some who made it back also live in this Town or at least come and go. These two here, owned a motorcycle shop in Town. This fellow, was a Ukrainian by the name of Tony Boiko and he died from Cancer many years ago, the other is Art Johnstone, they were partners in that motorcycle shop and best of friends. If you are not familiar with these names now, you will be, as they were huge factors and influences in the formation of what is now, The Bakers Dozen."

"Old Tony, came to me after he was approached by these kids, for help with and old motorcycle and he wanted to tell me about them and what a great bunch they were. I was thrilled, as Tony and his crew would be great mentors for them and keep them on the right path."

"Then Tony died, but Art Johnstone took over where Tony left off, and the rest of their crew were really fond of these young folks. Art keeps in touch, so I know more than you may think I know, but I never betray a confidence!"

"After Dwight Higgin's murder, they were giving the Dozen Crew a pretty rough ride. I tried to get them to back off, but this was a pretty high-profile case and there were other Law Enforcement branches involved. Somehow Art Johnstone was made aware of what was going on and got his Lawyers involved!"

"Old Tony, once told me, that when I was unsure of myself and decisions that I had made or was making, to look at the person that looks back at me from the mirror and if I truly and honestly, like the person I see, I'm doing OK. If you don't, you have some work to do! You have to like yourself before someone else can. Now, I think I've had enough for one day, can I get a lift home? Tony was an incredibly wise man."

"Wow! That was a lot of information to absorb." Dan said to himself as they wrapped up work for the day!

Dan dropped the old Chief off at home, and then went home himself his head was spinning.

The next morning, he called the Chief to see if he wanted him to pick up something before going to pick him up as he had mentioned he needed a couple of things the night before. The phone was answered but the voice on the other end was almost inaudible. "Chief are you OK?"

He heard some mumbling coming from the other end of the line but couldn't distinguish what was being said.

"Fuck!" Hang on Chief, I'm on my way!" He ran from the house to the car explaining to Nancy that something was wrong! He the roared off, lights flashing, sirens wailing and called in to 911!

He got to the house just before the ambulance and charged in to find his old mentor sprawled across his living room floor. A tray, a cheese sandwich that hadn't even had a bite out of it, a plate, along with his cell phone, and a spilled mug of coffee all strewn across the floor, told part of the tale. The coffee was still hot, indicating that it must have just occurred. This is all important information in establishing a timeline for the medical team. Dan checked his pulse, he was alive! The EMS Team arrived and took charge and established that he had a probable stroke and quickly got an IV going loaded him in the Ambulance and were gone. Dan was in pursuit and chased them all the way to the hospital. A concerned neighbour, shouted to Dan, as he jumped into his truck, saying that she would clean up the mess and lock the place up as she had a key.

They were able to get Stan stabilized and were setting up all kinds of tests, but he had survived.

The next morning, they established that he had indeed, suffered a stroke but was cognitive, although some physical functions on his right side, seemed to have been affected.

"I guess your going to have to step up a little sooner than we expected!" Were his first words when Dan walked in the room. They weren't clear, as the stroke had affected his speech somewhat, but they were decipherable. He was sitting up in bed, looking alert and smiling, albeit a crooked smile, as the right side of his face was drooping, and his voice was somewhat garbled and his speech slightly slurred. "I'm feeling pretty good!" he said other than things on my right side doesn't work so good right now! The doctors are saying I've got a really good chance of a complete recovery. Thanks largely, to you for getting me here so quickly! Time is important in these matters!"

The old Chief was smiling although, just on the left side of his face. He gave him a thumbs up, "Sometimes it takes a while!"

Just then, the nurse came in and shooed him out! "I'll drop by later! Apparently, I have Chief of Police stuff to do, now that you've decided to slack off!"

The chief gave him a weak wave as he left.

So that was that, he was now Chief of Police for Swanton Harbour. The adventure that would last for the next Forty Years, was about to begin! Judging from his recent decisions, and new roads to explore, it looked to be an interesting ride.

CHAPTER TWELVE
MOVING FORWARD

FOR DAN O'REILLY, things were moving forward, his meeting with REB, set many things in motion and in a direction that he hadn't foreseen. None could have been happier than Stanley Marshall, who never completely recovered from the stroke, that ended his career, which probably occurred at the right time as it was time for him to do so! He lived for another ten years and was able to watch with satisfaction as Dan blossomed into the kind of Police Chief that he knew he was capable of being and the kind of presence that the Town needed!

His faith in him was vindicated and he would be the stabilizing force that would counter the influence of the up and coming Dwight Biggins Jr. in the local Political spectrum. He wasn't afraid to challenge him on any issue, at any time, and he was fully capable standing his ground and of beating back the bully tactics that Dwight Jr. was becoming known for.

Dan's new-found friendship with REB was growing into something solid, tangible and real and it was having a stabilizing effect on both men and those around them. They came to love and respect each other.

REB too, was becoming increasingly comfortable around his former nemesis. He found his company to be stimulating and they could relate on so many topics, even things they disagreed on, that could spark lively discussions and debates, from which they could walk away from, sometimes just agreeing to disagree but never again, a fist was raised or a punch thrown! It was refreshing!

He did get some heat from some in the Biker World, as Cops were not trusted or welcome in their midst, and it was only because people loved and respected REB, that most condoned him, with many, acceptance was a stretch would take some time to breach, and with others, would never happen, in this life, or the next as the mistrust and hatred ran that deep!

Dan considered that to be fair enough and totally justified! He had walked that walk and even had the t shirts and would stand up to anyone and could admit when he had been wrong! He made sweeping changes in the Department's policies and practices, in an attempt to bridge the gap, but stereotypes and prejudice run deep and hard to overcome and the obstacles are abundant! But he was doing the best he could. Many Cops didn't like the fact that he hung with these Bikers either and the Mayor Dwight Higgins certainly didn't agree and tried his best to create problems for everyone. He eventually got his Son; Walter a job as his personal assistant.

To see them together was like looking at Tweddle Dee and Tweddle Dum, and in fact, that was what everybody in Town called them behind their backs!

The two families had bonded as well. Linda and Nancy were the best of friends and their kids played together constantly.

Then Dan hit a bad patch when in 2012, his wife, Nancy was diagnosed with cancer and while she was fighting the disease and going through the treatments that would wrack her body with excruciating pain. Their Son and Daughter then aged 19 and 20, respectively died, when out with friends at a graduation party, and had indulged in some Marijuana that had been tainted with Fentanyl. That was a blow from which, Nancy could not and would not recover! She just seemed to give up! She stopped all treatments and passed away, two weeks after the kids died!

For Dan it was beyond, too much to bear! The losses, arranging, and attending three funerals in such a short period of time, was devastating and it was almost the end of him! If not for Robert Edward Baker, he would not have survived. Dan had turned to booze as a crutch, but it was fast becoming an appendage. His mental state had plummeted and was at an all time low! He was drunk 99.5 % of each waking minute! Plus, a well-intentioned Doctor prescribed some drugs which were supposed to help. They did not, instead he had developed a dependence to them and when combined with the liquor was catastrophic! He, couldn't eat or sleep, and he was suicidal! His work suffered and he eventually was forced to take, a leave of absence, which, was far better, then the solution, that Mayor Higgins had decided on, and he was trying to ram through Council, which was termination with no benefits and reduced severance.

Reb showed up at his house the night, after Nancy's funeral, confiscated every drug or pills other those that he needed to keep healthy, and poured every ounce of liquor and beer down the drain, hid all his guns, drained the swimming pool and someone was with him 24/7. He was never alone, not even in the bathroom! He had brought Tramp and Linda along for back-up. They refused to leave as he commanded, and they disconnected the phone system and took his cell phones away. They had, ultimately kidnapped him, and held him a prisoner in his own home, but they did so with kindness and reassurance, and in doing so saved his life for a second time!

They put their own lives on hold and stayed with him for over two months. Why? Out of friendship and Brotherhood, which they had a firm grasp of, and he was brought kicking and screaming into the fold, and the realization that there were good people out there who do the right things simply because they need to be done!

Dan eventually was able to win a hard-fought battle, resume his life, and he was able to look at things from different perspectives and strive for real solutions, rather than band-aid, temporary fixes, that often, ended up being made permanent! He recognised and found in REB, source of knowledge, of reason, a consultant, a devil's advocate, an advisor, a champion, a confident, and a true friend!

The one-way street of hatred was now designated a two-way thoroughfare of trust, understanding, mutual respect and love.

The Clubhouse bar, was always a busy place on a Friday nights and people would drop by on a regular basis. One Friday, Reb and Dan dropped in late in the afternoon, after a long ride, to find the parking lot full of bikes and the bar absolutely packed. They waved at everybody as they came in and went directly to the bar where they had a cold 50 already pulled from the fridge for Dan, and a warm Guinness from a case behind the bar for REB.

From the moment they walked in, they noticed an old indigenous, man immediately look up and stared directly and unflinchingly at REB. It wasn't a menacing stare, but a stare none the less but it was troubling to REB and others who were noticing as well. It was obvious that it was annoying REB, as he kept glancing over at the old man and even gave a sort of shrug as if to say WTF? The old man was sitting at a table with Tramp and several of his family and friends and Tramp also noticed what was happening and spoke to the old man, as he could see that REB was clearly bothered by it all. He got some sort of reply but the staring continued relentlessly!

Finally, REB lost it! He sprung from his chair, sending it crashing to the floor and stormed across the room and was now standing directly in front of this old man, his fists balled up and ready for action. Tramp quickly sprang to his feet and tried to get between them.

"Am I wearing your fucking shirt or something old man? Why are you fucking staring at me? He hollered!

The old man, reached out his hand, drew Tramp in close

to him, and whispered something in his ear, while still continuing to stare.

Tramp looked confused, but turned to REB and explained. "He's my Uncle! He is a Shaman, a medicine man, a seer and a visionary. I asked him not to stare at you, but he has been drawn to you! He calls you Banshee, and asks to see your birthmark." Please don't hit him, please, please, please! Pleaded Tramp, hoping he could appeal to REB's sense of fairness and stop him from punching this old man!

"My birthmark? How does he even know I have a fucking birthmark?" He yelled, now inches from the old man's face. The old man, never changed expression, not anger, or fear, just a blank curious stare. He never flinched or backed up even a fraction of an inch. He stood his ground and just looked right into REB's piercing blue eyes, and raised two fingers to his lips, in sort of a shushing gesture. Everybody, thought that that would be the final straw and that, old man or not, Tramps uncle or not, Shaman, medicine man, or not, REB would knock this old man into next week! REB surprisingly, took it differently, as it seemed to have a calming effect on him!

He suddenly stepped back, and ripped open his shirt to reveal his birthmark. The old man looked at it, then resumed the thoughtful stare into REB's eyes, he reached out and gently placed those two fingers directly on the birthmark. He closed his eyes and just stood there! REB just stood there as well, not knowing what to make of all this, as did anyone else in the room. You could have heard a pin drop, as there was absolute silence for at least three full minutes.

Suddenly the old man's eyes reopened, and once again

stared deep into REB's eyes, he tilted his head slightly, then nodded, but did not look away, while he removed an amulet from around his neck, leaned in towards an unflinching REB and put it around his neck and fastened it! Banshee, this Talisman will bring you peace and protect you! I have seen, and you no longer bear the burden alone, be at peace! He then smiled, hugged REB, and went back to his beer as if nothing had transpired. From that day forward, no one had ever seen REB without that Talisman.

Rose Marie and Big Bill Johnstone, who had moved into a relationship, were two, of many, who were mesmerized by all those road stories, but they were the first of the younger bunch to make it heir chosen way of life! One day, they were sitting over breakfast with REB and crew of others. Someone mentioned how great Alaska was and was telling stories about it. Rose Marie and Big Bill simply looked at each other, nodded and smiled, then looked around the table at their friends and announced that they were leaving for Alaska.

The rest looked at them in wonderment and Calamity asked; "When?"

"Right now!" they said simultaneously. At that, they rose from their seats, gave everyone a big hug, picked up the tab for the table, walked out the door, mounted their bikes and off they went. That was the end of Big Bill Johnstone, and Rose Marie Fitzpatrick, they would henceforth, be known as "Gypsy" and "Wandering Bill". They came back almost a year later, in the spring, picked up some work for a while and did some maintenance on their motorcycles and then were gone again, six months later, in the fall, following the migrating birds and chasing the sun. Heading south, no real destination in mind, just a direction, south.

They toured around down there for about a year together. Then one morning, they were eating breakfast, Bill announced that he wanted to head to Texas and check things out down there. Gypsy said that she wanted to go to California and see the whales.

Hmmm! Was all Bill said. They got up walked out to where their bikes sat side by side, Gypsy gave him a big kiss and a hug, they fired up their bikes and took off, he, bound for Texas, and her, to Southern California.

They'd still bump into each other from time to time, as their paths would cross occasionally, and when they did, they picked up right where they left off with the same intensity and passion that they always had. They pretty much barricaded themselves in a tent, a cottage, a motel or hotel or whatever was convenient and you wouldn't see them for days, sometimes a week!

Their love for each other remained strong, but the wanderlust was stronger. They were a special breed, and knew that this was the life they were meant to lead and neither would even consider trying to tie the other down. Not yet anyways!

As for Gypsy, the road, the relationship, and the experience had a calming, healing, nurturing effect on her. It made her strong, self confident, and self assured. The things that had tormented her all those years, she had now overcome, and had she was able to file them away in the dead files, along with all the stuff from her past which would have eventually destroyed her. Those things, may well have affected and infected her early years and they made them a nightmare but she didn't allow them to define her life and dictate who she was and who she was going to become.

One day as she was riding up the Pacific Coast Highway she stopped for gas and noticed a rack of post cards and grabbed one. She addressed it to REB and wrote on it. Enjoying my new life! Thanks! She didn't sign it, just put a stamp on it dropped it in the mail box just outside the door, and carried on with her journey to wherever.

Reb gathered the mail from their mail box as was his custom when coming back from wherever. He examined the post card and smiled. No signature was necessary as he recognised her handwriting and he understood the meaning of the message. He smiled contentedly, took out his Zippo lighter and quietly burned the card scattering the ashes to the wind once the flames licked his fingers and thumb he ground the ashes and embers into the gravel with his boot, and went on with what he was doing.

As for the Club, it kept on, keeping on, as a gathering spot and a place where the bikers could be amongst their own. If you were having a problem, there was usually someone there, who could help you out. Injured, there was someone who could help you in whatever way was necessary and would go cut your lawn, pick up groceries or medications or get you to appointments or whatever task you couldn't accomplish. It was a family when you didn't have a family. They cared! In, some cases, they cared more for you than their natural family ever did.

REB didn't want the place to become a dump or a junk yard and really started cracking the whip about getting all the derelict vehicles out of there and it kept a few of the guys with tow trucks, busy for a month hauling them off to the scrap yard. They started building some small shacks or bunk houses, down near the pond where people could crash for a night or more if need be. They were well constructed but weren't fancy. They had guests coming in from out of town and It gave them shelter and a bed and that is all some needed. There were portable toilets that they maintained regularly. If people didn't respect the property they were quickly, told to leave and directed to the exit. It started to resemble a small town. And it was good.

Those early years were probably the absolute best! Everybody was young, exuberant, and full of piss and vinegar. The parties were legendary, and life with the Club was extraordinary!

They did things, had adventures and rode their motorcycles. None of them had any money to speak of, but they didn't care! Many of them, kick started their motorcycles, rode miles and miles, on old rigid frame motorcycles, many held together by wire and tape and whatever they improvised. This wasn't to be cool, or "Old School" it wasn't to create an image, it was living the life, riding what they had and they making the best of it. Many times, they ended up working on their bike at the side of the road in the middle of nowhere! They didn't have CAA, but if they had a friend, especially one with a pick-up truck, they made a call and while it might be in the middle of the night, you can bet your ass that he or she, was on his way. You might have to pool your money to get enough gas to get back but you got it done and had another story of another adventure to tell.

Other times, other bikers, would spot you and stop to see if they could help. Complete strangers, would do what they could and help you fix it or get you someplace or to somebody who could. But all good things sadly, come to an end. We age, and some of us not so well, or at all. Old ways are discarded and those who still respected and lived by the codes of conduct, became non-existent, or extremely rare.

Nowadays, there is a trend to ride bobbers and choppers and the youngsters, call it "Old School" or "Old Skool" or whatever, like they invented it, and if you aren't riding one of them, you aren't really a biker! Those bikes, still look fantastic and many improvements and refinements have been made to them, over the old rattletraps that were our rides back in the day. Then, they were quite often, held together with wire, duct tape, and lots of hope, back when it was, ride what you got, and make the best out of it, but ride!

The old school, was the education you got, trying to keep them on the road! The bikers of those days weren't all blessed with large amounts of cash, and real mechanics, were often considered to be, something of a luxury, many of them, couldn't afford. The backyard variety of mechanic, along with your own two hands and your friends and initiative were what got riders through!

If you wanted to ride, you just made do with everything and anything, from Honda's, Yamahas, Suzuki's, British bikes or anything and then rode the wheels off those things, but Harleys, were the desired bike of preference for many. Guy's used to break down on the way back from a run one day, and work all night, fixing it, so they would be ready to go on another run the next day! For many it was learn as you go and trial by fire or by trial and error!

As time went by, things got better, jobs improved, times got better, and money became more plentiful, life changed and so did the motorcycles. Aching joints, dictated, that it may be time to look at something with suspension and perhaps some creature comforts! Rubber mounted, air shocks and cushy seats, replaced hard tail, bone shakers. Many refused to get rid of those old buckets of bolts, with outdated, under powered motors with quirky temperaments and glitches, as they loved them dearly, but other than a short blast, they no longer suited their regular riding needs.

These days, there are highly educated, well trained motorcycle technicians, as everything new, is computerized and many shops consider an EVO to be "Old Crap" and they won't even look at them. Back then, you might get kidded over your choice of ride but it was all good natured and everybody was just happy that you were able to show up.

Then snobbery started replacing, many of the good-natured, parts of the lifestyle. That was when things started to deteriorate within certain motorcycle circles, when people were being judged and pigeon holed, by the make, model and style of their motorcycles, rather than their character and personalities of the people who ride them. It was becoming more superficial.

Still, those hard tail choppers that became trendy, are great to look at and are fine for young bodies, complete with young knees and other younger joints that can actually still take a beating as the ride, of a hardtail where the only suspension and cushioning from the bumps and potholes was the air in the tires, They are not particularly kind to older bodies and far from what old farts, can now endure, especially when you like to put on more miles, than the distance to and from the local hangout!

Some now ridicule the old farts on their Geezer Glides and Trikes and whatever they use to keep themselves in the wind and many say that they are not cool. Many of these old farts, were cool long before cool was discovered and many of these old guys and gals actually invented it. These old geezers had learned over the years, that the purpose of riding, was to enjoy the ride, and that the only one that they had to please with their choices of rides, was themselves! DILLIGAF what someone else thinks!

Riders used to appreciate the work that goes into putting a bike on the road and keeping it there. They used to ride what suited them, not what suited others! They understood and appreciated the love, that they knew other bikers had for their motorcycles, and for the lifestyle. Their motorcycles weren't just a possession to keep pristine and hardly ever ridden. Those bikes were not just decoration or something to make you look cool. They weren't something to be traded off when a new model came out.

Those motorcycles, whatever make or model, if they are what blows wind up your kilt, you shouldn't have to qualify or defend your choices to anyone! Bikers used to pride themselves on individuality and free choices in what they did, who they did it with, and when they would do it. If you prefer a Honda over a Harley, that is your choice. If you like a sport bike over a cruiser. Ditto, knock yourself out!

If a Decker, or full dressed touring motorcycle, is your

preference and what suits your needs and riding style, over a chopper, or bobber, you do what suits you and your needs better! If you like to have your stuff in bags that mount to your motorcycle rather than trying to cover long distances on a bike on which you are uncomfortable and carrying all your stuff in a backpack that is your choice and no one else's.

CHAPTER THIRTEEN
TAKING CARE OF BUSINESS AND THINGS LEFT UNSPOKEN!

ALONG WITH ALL THE good things that came from this place and these people, and thinking and speaking about them can bring back fond memories and perhaps prompt an unconscious smile, just at the memory of those precious moments in time when things were simpler and times were better.

But things, in reality, are seldom, absolutely perfect, and on closer examination, what appears perfect, is usually found to have some flaws! Such things are often multi faceted and some of those facets are often classed or identified as; good, bad, black or white. But what of all the other colours and shades of black and white exist and what of the variants of good and bad and what of evil? Is that the flaw? Is evil just a different shade of black and white, or is it an entity all its own?

There are filters that can remove certain colours from the spectrum, that are visible to the human eye, but the reality is, even though you can no longer see them, they are still there.

The old saying that what you can't see, can't hurt you, is a fallacy. If it exists, it can hurt you and the fact that you can't see it, just means you just don't see it coming, often until it is too late!

Good, bad, and evil can all take different forms and there are different degrees of each and dealing with them differs from case to case.

Weeds and bugs in a garden, can be considered, to be by gardeners and farmers, bad in these cases, can be dealt with such methods as plucking those offending plants from the midst of the garden, or using various products such as insecticides or fungicides to deal with them. You must, of course use products that do not do more harm than good, but those weeds and noxious plants must be eradicated, if your garden is to grow.

In nature there are wolves, foxes, coyotes, weasels, eagles, hawks, all predators, that exist and survive by doing what nature intended and they feed on other things like rodents and other creatures that are lower on the food chain, but can be considered as bad or harmful, thereby keeping the pest populations in check. That is natures way. They, however, can't distinguish between domestic animals such as small dogs and cats, or animals that are being produced as food for humans, such as chickens, sheep, cattle and other livestock. These creatures do not do evil, they are merely fulfilling their natural purpose, by instinct. You can, try to dissuade or discourage these predators by putting up fences and blockades or building structures to keep your creatures safe or try to. But many of these creatures are sly and cunning and can usually figure out how to circumvent whatever solutions you think you have found. Sometimes you have to use harsher methods of controls, like poison, guns or people trained and equipped to provide humane, or sometimes, less than humane, but effective solutions.

Cancer and other diseases are also exampling of bad, and claim millions of lives, cause untold misery, to both humans and animals. A cancer must be removed from the body or the host will die. A cure would be the ultimate goal, but until a cure is discovered, you must deal with the disease, one case at a time. Cancer itself, will move on to infest and try to destroy other parts of the host if it isn't removed or eradicated by means of lasers, chemotherapy, medicines or other methods. Surgeons and specialists, learn and teach how to cure and save lives as best they can. Scientists work tirelessly, to find a cure and while progress has been made, they are far from defeating certain forms of cancer and until then, the Dr.'s and surgeons are our only hope.

Bad in people, is another situation entirely, but can and can be dealt with in a number of ways as well. Bad can be dealt with, with punishment and people and animals can be taught right from wrong, bad from good, and what is acceptable and what is not.

Evil, however, is like a cancer and can spread rapidly and insidiously and must be eradicated, quickly and decisively, with resolve, using whatever means are at your disposal. Many people can live their entire lives and never be knowingly, exposed to or ever had to deal with pure evil.

Most human beings, are not prepared to do what is

necessary to combat true evil. Evil, unlike bad can't be treated, it doesn't respond to punishment, or therapy, or reasoning. When your family and what you hold dear, is threatened, and what is good, and innocent is put in peril, by evil, how far do you go and what extreme measures, are you willing to take to protect them and the sanctuary?

To whom do you turn when faced with pure evil?

We, as a society, elect people to political office, to run the day to day operations of the Country, city, towns, Provinces and so on, and give them power and authority, to make decisions, pass laws and such on our behalf, and they, in turn hire and fire people who are charged with enforcement of these laws and rules.

Thus, we have Police, hired to protect us and enforce laws. They are supposed to be the protectors and caretakers and they work well in most cases. However, there are many times when they are restricted as to what they can and cannot do. They are equipped to deal with bad, but are ill prepared and lack the knowledge, methods and resolve when and where pure Evil is concerned.

There are also times, when those charged with the protection of society and its innocents, are not up to the task. They are given, by virtue of the job itself, an amount of power over the ordinary citizens! Power, however, can be as intoxicating and as addicting, as any alcohol or drug. Power can be absolutely corruptive, and absolute power can corrupt absolutely! When the thirst for power and authority becomes overwhelming it can over-ride whatever sense of duty and honour and best of intentions some people may have had in the beginning.

There are some, who truly honour, the power that they are given and the faith that has been placed on them, to do their jobs as custodians and protectors, to the best of their ability. There are others, for whom, the menial tasks of serving the public no longer excite them or satisfy them. They consider those tasks to be demeaning and below the station, that they feel they are qualified and destined for. They want to rule not to serve! They feel that they are above the laws by which the rest of society lives.

So, to whom do you turn when threatened by pure evil, the Police? What if the Police or segments of it, are the source of that evil? What do you do then, and to whom do you turn?

We are all capable of extreme violence, it is in our nature, however, most of us, are equipped with a mechanism that helps us suppress and resist urges, and keeps us from stepping over the line. However, as nature dictates, there are those among us, who are walking that very thin line and on occasion will, and do veer off from it. They exist, mostly unseen, in the shadows of ordinary men and women, those dark shadows, where many dark secrets, are kept, that few if any, even know about, let alone speak of! Things and deeds, that are best left alone and unspoken. Those shadows don't appear any different than any other shadow cast, but in fact, they are a little darker, a little longer and able to obscure what lies beneath.

In life, things aren't always pleasant, beautiful, or uplifting. Beneath all that is beautiful and pleasant, often lurks brutality, ugliness and things that are best forgotten, and deeds unspoken, if you can! There are things that happen and things that must be done, if you, and those you love are to survive.

In Society, there are malignancies of a different sort, but just as deadly with equal ability to destroy, that sometimes, elude whatever safeguards, Society, has put in place to protect us from unpleasant or distasteful things.

Like a surgeon tasked with removing a malignancy in a body, there are those who take on the task of removing those cancers from Society, to heart. Unlike the Medical surgeon, there are no accolades, or big paycheques. There is no notoriety, if the job is done properly. No reward, other than the knowledge that that particular cancer will spread no further, or cause any more pain. It takes a certain kind of person to do things, that in their mind, have to be done, because right or wrong, justifiable or not, it is still a burden, that can never be shared, and the secrets must ultimately, be taken to the grave.

The fewer who know the truth and the facts, the better, so it is a solitary undertaking. They shoulder the whole burden, wondering what the consequences will be, because in life, there are always consequences and uncertainties! Perhaps, that is punishment enough, the waiting, the not knowing? The guilt and the torment of second guessing, and hindsight, that can cast serious doubts as to whether or not the proper actions were carried out!

The fact, that these acts are often meant to be born by one, is little comfort to a troubled soul! One, who will answer for things that they felt had to be done, deeds that were committed, for what may be all the right reasons and in the name of justice or what was right! Because something was done, for the right reasons, in reasonable people's minds, does not make them truly right, or forgivable, as they are still crimes against humanity and society and society demands, that someone must be held accountable! If the truth comes out, and if, there is a time of reckoning, they are ready to stand and be judged and suffer whatever the consequences might be.

The Dozen's property, had become a place sanctuary of for many of these older, hard core veterans of wars who were left to deal with their own personal dilemma's and demons and now they would do there best to guide these young people who seemed to come with the package, as best they could. This was not a plan or a conscious decision on their part but was perhaps their destiny.

In a perfect World, a sanctuary, should not be necessary for a pretty fifteen-year-old girl. She should need no shelter, protection or someone to avenge her. Her parents should provide all that. But in the real World, bad things happen to good people and still worse things can happen to bad people!

Rose Marie Higgins was acting very strange for quite some time and of late, she seemed even more troubled. She would hang around very late and often ended up staying at the property over night and getting whoever was around to drive her to school in the morning. She would have unexplained bumps, bruises and marks appear on her body, from time to time. She was very self conscious and nervous and would over-react to anyone who dared ask her what was wrong! She was moody and depressed most of the time. She was avoiding going home and that was obvious to all of us.

REB tried to get her to talk to him and she shut him out as well!

Being the daughter of one of the Town's Cops, brought the whole group under the scrutiny of the local Constabulary, in general, and Officer Dwight Higgins Sr. in particular! It was not a good situation. Higgins, felt he was a shoe in, to be the next Chief of Police of the Town, as soon as the old fart that had held that position for years departed or died. He was out to impress, and, to his thinking, if he could show that he was tough on crime and criminals, and wasn't afraid to go up against thugs like a local Motorcycle Gang, as proof that he could rise to the occasion and mete out punishment to those who deserved it. He knew Rose Marie had been staying there overnight and often for days at a time, and he wasn't the least bit pleased. He used that as a partial excuse for his next actions!

He organised a full-scale raid on this property where his step daughter had been hanging out and was obviously being led astray by these evil, unsavoury bikers, he also claimed to have reliable information from unsubstantiated sources that there was large scale drug dealing going on as well as a possible meth lab! He gathered up every available officer and they moved in on the property, fully armed.

They charged in, shouting commands with fully automatic weapons, locked and loaded and looked really impressive, in his mind, as it was he who was leading the charge and barking orders as if it was the Battle of the Bulge!

They had the whole bunch of them surrounded and they were now lying face-down on the ground, waiting to be handcuffed and taken into custody, while his officers tore the place apart looking for contraband or some evidence of wrongdoing! They found none, other than a dozen or so bottles of beer, a couple of small roaches and perhaps a half a gram of marijuana in some unidentified person's jacket pocket.

Dan's father, was also on scene and looked totally disappointed at the outcome of this raid and as he was relating this to officer Higgins, REB's dog, a small, very friendly, extremely intelligent Border Collie walked up to him. Officer Higgins, gave it a look of total disdain, drew his gun a shot the dog in the head, killing him instantly! "He then yelled, "That dog just tried to attack me!" He had a smug look on his face as he started to holster his pistol! Dan's father was in absolute shock at what he'd just witnessed, as was everybody else!

"Cocksucker!" was the only word uttered by him, as REB rose quickly from the ground in one fluid movement and was in full stride when he lashed out with his right fist striking the fat Cop squarely on the chin then, briefly, standing over him, he managed to get a solid kick in to his face before being restrained and soundly beaten by a phalanx of Cops! The were able to overlook the totally unnecessary act that a fellow officer had just committed because he felt entitled to do so, and throw a beating on someone who protested! Many of the Cops present, later admitted that they were horrified and appalled by the shooting of the dog. Some of them were just petting and playing with that dog just before he was shot! Yet, in their official reports, they backed up their fellow officer unconditionally!

Higgins went down like a ton of brick, and lay there for a

few minutes, while other nearby cops had grabbed and were trying to restrain, as well as beat, a struggling, furious and near hysterical, Robert Edward Baker.

Officer Seamus O'Reilly, saw Higgins, get up from the ground and saw the set of his jaw and the intense hatred flaring in his eyes, as he glared at the now fully restrained, Rob Baker, his revolver was being drawn and about to be pointed at REB, and he knew what was about to happen, he lashed out hard and quickly with his truncheon, striking Officer Higgins on the wrist, thereby disarming him, thwarting what would have been a killing for certain, and it would be extremely difficult to cover up, given the number of eye witnesses present! He didn't need that kind of aggravation. He moved in tight to his fellow Officer's face and hissed menacingly "There will be no more of this shite!"

Higgins backed off, but not before ordering his men to completely trash the place and arrest everybody, including his stepdaughter on some bullshit charges that were thrown out of court on their first appearance.

This, just seemed to increase Rose Marie's anxiety levels and she became even more alienated, reclusive and reserved. Her emotional state was at an all time low!

Other than that, things were relatively quiet for the next Month or so. REB did some time in the bucket for the assault on Higgins until their Lawyer once again got involved and he was released.

Then, late one afternoon, REB was riding home along this remote stretch of road, he spotted a young lady walking along the roadside in obvious distress. He thought to himself as he came up behind her "That looks like Rose Marie, but what would she be doing way out here?"

She heard his motorcycle coming up behind her, spun around and he could see blood flowing from her nose and mouth. She had recognised him too, but instead of coming to him she sprinted away, as if in fear! He killed the motor and let the bike fall on its sturdy crash bars and took off in pursuit on foot, catching her just before a ravine. He held her fast, despite her resistance! She was clutching a large brown envelope.

He then escorted her back to his bike, up righted and started it back up, and ordered her on the back. They rode in silence and she clung tightly to him as they rode to the property. Instead of stopping where everybody else was gathered and joining them, he stopped, grabbed a half dozen cans of beer from a cooler, stashing them in the front of his jacket, remounted and rode off to the seclusion of the far side of the pond!

He shut off the bike and guided her to a big rock where he sat her down, handed her a cold beer that he'd just cracked open and sat across from her on another rock and opened one for himself.

He took a long swallow of the cold liquid, as did she, he looked her straight in the eyes and said; "Enough bullshit! What the fuck is going on with you? It is just you and I, and what you tell me stays between you and I!

She looked at him plaintively, then the tears and the words started to flow, as if they were dammed up inside her, just waiting to be released! She told him everything, between heavy sobs and gasping for breath between them! He took an old shop rag from his hip pocket and handed it to her. Not much of a hanky, but it would have to do!

She told him of the physical abuse, that both she and her Mother suffered at the hands of her stepfather and how, for the past several years, that he was now sexually abusing her as well! He would take her to his cabin, not far from where he had found her! He abused her and would film and take still pictures of her naked. He forced her to do things and told her that he was soon going to bring some of his friends up to meet her and that she'd better be nice to them. She knew that he had other young girls that he was using as well, because he showed her their pictures. She didn't know what to do or where to turn because he was a Cop and he would brag about how he could get away with anything!

"I'm so fucking ashamed! How could I let this happen to me? How could that man force me to do those kinds of things? I really like Big Bill Johnston, but what will he think of me?" She again, erupted in big sobs and the tears once again started to flow uncontrollably! He took off his t shirt and handed that to her as the shop rag was sopping wet from her tears. She told him that she had even considered suicide on many occasions! This place was her refuge and the people here, were the only things that kept her from doing it!

"Today, I found these!" thrusting the envelope at him.

He opened the envelope and removed a dozen or so large pictures! His heart stopped for an instant! A torrent of emotions swept over him, as he examined the contents of the envelope! He sat there slack jawed and silent at first! Shock, was the initial reaction, then sadness, then anger, then he was dead quiet, lost in thought, dark thoughts! His face was now emotionless, his eyes gave no clue as to what was going on in his mind!

"You looked at these?" He finally asked, holding the pictures out in front of him before throwing them on the ground in disgust! They depicted depravity but it wasn't the activity but the subjects, that made him truly upset, one petite little brunette, one diminutive blonde with excessively large breasts each with a small, distinctive, green Shamrock, with a red heart and a 13 in the centre tattooed just above the left breast.

She nodded.

"You know who they are?"

Again, she nodded and the tears once again flowed from her eyes.

"That Mother Fucker!" He hissed. "That low down cock-sucker! Snuff films! That sleazy fuck is making snuff films! Those girls didn't deserve that! Nobody deserves that! He must have fucking killed Jingles too!"

He stuffed the pictures back inside the envelope, took a Zippo lighter from his pocket and set them ablaze, holding the envelope until the flames licked his fingers and thumb and he was sure the contents were completely destroyed. He then ground the ashes and cinders into the dirt with the heel of his boot.

She was done talking now. They were done talking. Rose Marie had finally found a release from what she had bottled up inside her and collapsed in his arms still sobbing until she fell asleep. She awoke an hour later still snuggled in his arms. He was, wide awake and still, deep in thought! Sensing that she was now awake, he suddenly stood up, helped her to her feet, and then kicked over the Knucklehead, they mounted up and he rode her around the pond to where many of the others were gathered around the shop. Calamity was there, as was Big Bill Johnstone. He called them aside and handed Bill some money. Take Rose Marie here, into Town, go to a movie. Keep the stubs. Go to someplace for dinner, and just hang out, close the place, make some noise, be noticed, stay out late, and take her home, the later, the better. Make sure people see you getting her home! They nodded and asked no questions.

He pulled Rose Marie aside and told her; "Rose Marie this ends tonight! You have to cast it all from your mind! Everything! All of it! We never talked about any of it! Understand? No one else knows of this shit! Keep it that way! Your new World begins tonight and we never, speak of any of this again! He held her by the shoulders and held her directly in front of him so she could look right into the depths of those ice blue eyes!" Understood? Nothing ever happened to you, ever, nothing! Can you bury that shit, yes or no? Never speak of this again!" She nodded in agreement and they parted company!

She, Bill and Calamity Jane went to the movies and a late dinner, while REB and several of the guys went to work on a troublesome motorcycle. They had some beer, ordered some pizza, and the work continued. REB went into the shop and locked himself away in the art studio/office/bedroom to complete some stuff he was working on, which was not at all, unusual. He often had ideas that came to him, and he had to at least start or get his thoughts on paper or he would forget them. He had his silk-screening equipment in there as well and he was known to stay in there for hours on end! He was a very creative guy and examples of his art could be found everywhere, in frames on walls, on t shirts and in hundreds of doodles that would appear anywhere and everywhere. He came back out, about five hours later, and rejoined the crew working on that damned bike.

Later that night, Dwight Higgins was in his cabin, dressed only in his boxer shorts his hand pushed down the waistband and pleasuring himself, while watching the results of his afternoon's filming session. He was startled by an extremely loud piercing shriek and wail coming from just outside. He leaped to his feet, grabbed his revolver from out of the holster that hung on the back of the door before whipping it open! He was then immediately, confronted by a large figure clad head to toe in a black shroud with the image of what appeared to be a Banshee on the front!

He started to raise his gun but a baseball bat struck him hard on his wrist, knocking the gun from his hand and it clattered to the wood plank flooring. He was then pushed back into the cabin and the bat was applied to each knee in quick succession before it came down, several times on his head. The movie projector, viewing screens along with reels of film, film canisters, still photographs and every chemical that was used in the evil productions were dumped on top of his body as was gasoline before a Zippo lighter ignited some paper that was then thrown into a pool of volatile liquid and was soon fully ablaze.

The next day, Big Bill, Calamity, Gypsy and REB gathered at the local diner for breakfast. The news had just broken, about the fire and it was now the talk of the Town. A body had been recovered from the smoldering ruins of the cabin, but they had to wait for the Coroner to determine identity and cause of death. It was suspected, that Swanton Harbour Police officer Dwight Higgins had perished in a fire at a remote cabin, and that arson and foul play was strongly suspected! The foursome, all expressed the same shock and disbelief as everyone else, that something like that could happen in their quiet little Town! Rose Marie's first reaction was one of horror and disbelief. She rushed to the pay phone to call her Mother.

The whole Town, attended the funeral, other than members of the Baker's Dozen and their followers. The Club; through spokesman Robert Edward Baker, did make a statement that was printed in the newspapers, both local and National; that Higgins had shown them no respect, and that they had none for him, in life or in death! While, they sympa-thised with the family, especially young Rose Marie, as she was a friend of theirs and she was taking the death of her beloved Step Father very hard, as was her Step Brother; Dwight Junior. It was a major event attended by Coppers and Politicians from all over Canada and the United States as the murder of a Cop is big news. They all wanted to make statements about their personal outrage and shock that such a heinous Criminal act could take place and how much of an honoured and well-respected Police Officer Dwight Higgins was and assured everyone that the perpetrator or perpetra-tors, would be caught and brought to Justice!

The Police were now desperately beating the bushes, looking for clues. They brought in everyone with a possible motive and of course Robert Baker and his crew were at the top of their lists! The questioning and interviews, went on for just over a year. It would be quiet for a while then, acting on some new lead, or rumour and they would be called in again. Finally, the case stalled altogether, and was eventually sent to the inactive investigation, files.

Then there were hints and rumours that during their probes, investigators had overturned information that the Police were keeping quiet about until they could probe deeper. Persistent rumours of possible Police Corruption and worse were starting to make their rounds. Dwight Higgins name was being attached as the subject of these subsequent investigations. Dan's father died of a massive heart attack and since he was also apparently being investigated, his death, ultimately those investigations went nowhere as well.

The Police lacking any real hard evidence other that a charred body that had been according to the Coroner, had been severely beaten as it showed evidence of crushed skull due to several heavy blows as well as legs arms which had also been broken presumedly from blows by the same baseball bat as one burned baseball bat that was found with the body, is suspected as being the murder weapon. Also found, at the scene were remnants of movie projectors, viewing screens, movie cameras as well as several still cameras, film canisters, piles of photographs and films all completely obliterated by the fire! Having no other physical evidence, they managed to piece together a theory of what went on that fateful night with Officer Dwight Higgins. They speculated that sometime during the evening, a yet, unknown assailant, or assailants, had come upon Officer Higgins who was occupied watching some home movies, that appeared to be his hobby, given the number of cameras and darkroom equipment and chemicals found at the scene. Everything was rendered totally useless as evidence, by the fire which appeared to have been intentionally started as an accelerant was used! The case was sent to the cold case file where it still sits unsolved!

Gypsy; AKA; Rose Marie Fitzpatrick, formerly; Rose Marie Higgins;

Gypsy's recovery from years of abuse by her Step father was a slow process, but she was getting there, because she wanted and willed it to happen. It might all be what shaped her, but not what would define her. She was the master of her own future and destiny! The damage done, might, well, haunt her for years to come, but she was strong willed and determined to get her life back on track on her terms. She was determined not to let the past, determine her future.

She had a tight-knit group of friends there who supported her although no one other than REB knew the story as she, and he had told no one. Her and REB had not spoken about what happened that night or what had gone on before or since. With REB, she was assured that her secret was safe, and although she could only speculate as to what transpired that day, after they parted company, she knew the outcome, and she stayed true to her word, she already knew his commitment.

She had grown up initially, in as near perfect a World as you could imagine, with a wonderful father and a loving mother in what was a near perfect family! Then her father died in a car crash and her World came tumbling down.

There was no insurance and the death of her father was crippling to the family.

Her Mother took a job waitressing at the local diner, where she caught the eye of a young ambitious policeman by the name of Dwight Higgins. He courted her and promised her and her daughter a good life. He had been married before, but got divorced within two years of marriage and he filed for and received custody of his son Dwight Jr.,

It didn't take long for the bliss to fade from the wedded part and then the abuse began!

It was sad for Rose Marie to see the life and the love, fade from her Mother as she was now being used as something of a whipping boy, when Dwight would come home in one of his foul moods, which was often! He seemed to despise the sweet little girl who used to be the apple of her real Daddy's eyes. She was now just an expense and a pain in the ass as this beast disguised as a man, preferred his son over anything else and made it clear who was his favourite and he doted on him. Then when she started to mature and developed breasts, she became an object for his lust and abnormal sexual preferences.

She was never sure if her Mother knew of his late-night visits to her room or not, where he would force himself on her, first, she was made to satisfy him with her hands, then orally and by the time she was thirteen he was having full on intercourse with the terrified child! Then came acts of sodomy and soon she was subjected to anal sex and he had started photographing it all! Then he got the cabin, and he would drag her up there and do what he pleased with her, and she didn't know what to do about it.

She tried to talk to her Mother about it, but she too was terrified to do or say anything, as he would beat her unmercifully and lock her in a room, like a prisoner. There was no life and definitely, no love in that house!

When she met REB and hooked up with The Bakers Dozen it was like a breath of fresh air to her, it was a release from the horrors she was facing at home. But she could not speak of any of it, as it was embarrassing to her and she was terrified of her Step father as she knew what he was capable of and as a Cop he seemed to be unstoppable! She could not speak of the things that were forced upon her and the things she was forced to do by a man, a police officer, who was supposed to be protection for the Community, for kids like her and people like her mother from people like him! Instead, he was what people needed protection from! It made no sense!

Then that day, she was put through the same depraved rituals, except this time, he laid out all the pictures of many of his other victims, many she knew, friends, young friends, how did he get his hooks into them? How many, and for how long, had this been going on? To whom could she turn? Who would believe her? Who could stop him? She saw the pictures of sweet Little Lisa and Dominique. She knew the state they were in and who was responsible! She recognised other photos, as others who had just disappeared from the property, as well.

She hated him, and hated herself, for all the things she had done and were done to her! She had run off from that cabin that day, and heard him taunting her as she ran; "There is nothing you can do about this! Come back and suck my cock you little whore! I'm a Cop and I can do whatever I want!" He believed that, and she believed it too! She felt she was trapped and helpless!

Then she chanced to meet up with REB that afternoon and was finally able to unburden herself, it made a huge difference. REB truly cared and when he held her, looked her directly into her eyes and told her that her World was going to change that night, she truly believed him! There was something in the way he said it, perhaps it was the look in those ice-cold, blue eyes, that was reassuring, yet disturbing, and she knew that if it was really going to change, she had to do her part, whatever happened! She did! Her life changed instantly! She swore, that she would never again be used or abused, by anyone!

Her Mother received the insurance payments and the more than generous benefit packages and pensions that Dwight's job had provided and dyeing was by far the best thing that he had ever done! She fixed up the house the way she wanted it. Dwight Jr. moved out on his own when he was sixteen, and Rose Marie did as she said and would never set foot in that house again. She was unsure if her Mother was aware of what had been happening to her, but she had done nothing to stop it if she was. They never spoke about any of it, ever, and in fact, they never spoke again!

After the charade of a funeral, where people were giving accolades as to how great a policeman he was and how his passing was such a loss to the community and heaping praise on an abhorrent creature who deserved none of it! What should have been said that many little girls in the Community could now sleep safe in their beds. But she wept and smiled on cue and waved at the fresh grave as they walked from the gravesite. Rose Marie, however, only waved one finger.

When her Mother died, she took her share of the proceeds and donated it all to "The Victim's of child abuse!" She no longer considered herself to be a victim, and didn't want compensation!" She was, thanks to Robert Edward Baker, a survivor, and she would never forget him!

There were other tales and rumours of how things were sometimes dealt with and scores settled by the Club that were certainly not common knowledge. No one in the Community, and even most in the Club or their followers, knew anything about that stuff, as it was never discussed. Guys like Dan and other Cops could only speculate as these things, were allegedly always handled by the crews, within the Clubs themselves and seldom, if ever, were brought to anyone's attention, let alone, police attention. Other than occasionally, dealing with the aftermath, and having no witnesses or clear suspects, the investigations usually went nowhere.

But rumours are still, only rumours, and mostly, they remain that way but they do, quite often persist and for a Cop, it is like an itch they can't scratch. People could buy stories of fights and beatings and such as that was minor league stuff that Bikers are known for anyway. Fights and disagreements happen everyday! These, were mostly just kids, mostly between 16 and 22 years old. Murdering a Cop was what the heavy hitters did! The rumours of corruption and involvement with Organized Crime and Gangland retaliation, made more sense to most people than a bunch of kids doing it!

Nicky was always a wild card and a bit of a loose cannon. He remained with the Club until his death but he also got involved with some hard-core people whom he had met in various Juvenile detention centres and jail when he got caught and through contacts that he was making on the street. He never brought his shit around the Club, because he knew REB wouldn't allow it. However, he always had some kind of hush, hush, deal going on, but he was also very greedy and always kept whatever he had going, on the down low as he didn't like to share too much, if any of his pie!

However, he was a solid, stand-up guy who; if he had your back you knew that you had not much to fear, unless someone, changed up the rules and brings guns into play, like that hot August night back in 1995 when Nicky and a few others were leaving a local Strip Club, when a black Cadillac pulled up in front of them and a couple of guys, unloaded a few, fully automatic weapons into the group killing three including Nicky on the spot and wounding one other, who later died in Hospital.

Dion, also met his fate that night! Apparently, none of those involved in the shootings had a single thing against Dion. He, like the other two, who were just friends and hang-arounds, were just in the wrong place, at the wrong time and were collateral damage! Nicky was the target all along, over some deal that went wrong or someone he pissed off somewhere along the way! There were rumours, that the one who led the attack was the hot-headed son of some high-level gangster, who asked that there be no retaliation or retribution, as it would start a war, that the Club could not win. The father was killed several years later and found stuffed in the trunk of his car, so all bets and assurances were now off in regards to his son.

There was no immediate retaliation, for the shooting, even though, everybody suspected who was behind it, and there were no arrests. After that, there was noticeable tension and rumours of "Bad Blood" between certain members of a family who were allegedly connected to organized Crime, and the Dozen, as well as other Clubs, who were more than a little aware, of the facts, persisted.

When those, suspected of the shooting, mysteriously disappeared, without a trace, exactly thirteen years to the day, of the killings, some read into it, or presumed, might be a slightly more, than, cryptic message. Those, presumably in the know, immediately speculated, who, was responsible. No arrests were made, and no further retaliation came from the incident! The slate had obviously been cleaned and a draw had been declared!

Calamity Jane, survived a childhood that might have scarred a lesser individual for life! She never talked about it, but it wasn't a happy upbringing, to say the least. She never dwelled on it, or at least, not to where anyone else was aware of what she had been through, other than REB and now Chief Stan Marshall that is, They, became her only confidants. If she was scarred, she hid it well from all others. Seemingly, her only flaw was her choice in men, as she had a knack for finding only the absolute worst ones.

She was born out of wedlock to a Mother who was a cheap whore, drug addict and alcoholic, who wanted no part of this scrawny brat. Jane was left alone most of the time in the squalor of a rundown bachelor apartment and was thrown into a dark closet, whenever the mother would bring home some trick, who she would service before she was punched in the face and robbed of what little she had and the low life would just split!

She was six years old, and came home from school one afternoon, to find her mother and some john laying on the bed, naked, both stone dead from an overdose, her mother, with the needle still in her arm. What followed was a long string of Foster homes which turned out to be disastrous.

She knew of plenty of Foster Homes that were great, with great people who were truly there for the good of the children. Unfortunately, she was never placed in any of those kinds of homes. Hers, were what many horror stories are based on!

Even at that early age, she had inner strength and self preservation instincts that she tapped into, and that saw her through a veritable minefield of only the worst kind of people! She managed to get through it and when she first met REB and the Bakers Dozen she knew she had found a sanctuary and she didn't even know what a sanctuary was. She found it by accident one day, when she was eight years old walking home from school, at a baseball diamond. That diamond still shines for her.

She was eight years old and living on the streets, after running away from yet another abusive foster home, sleeping in the woods in makeshift shelters, sometimes, in abandoned cars parked alongside the road at other times. She would scrounge food from dumpsters, behind restaurants or steal food from stores, and did her best to stay out of sight as the Cops were looking for her, for an eight-year-old, she was very resourceful and resilient. The hard existence that she had living with a callous, cold mother had somewhat hardened her and made her self sufficient, because she had to be!

When she started hanging around the baseball diamond, because there were kids having fun and she had never really known fun, but it looked, like, well, fun. REB noticed her and took an interest in her as he knew something wasn't right. She was dirty, her clothes were tattered and she seemed to be extremely troubled. He approached her cautiously and started talking to her. She trusted him and confided in him. He then introduced her to someone he trusted, who may well be able to help were without breaking the confidence she had placed in him; Chief Stanley Marshall, and he promised that he would personally make sure she found a safe environment. He moved her into his own home temporally, until they could find a place that she could call home. The Chief personally interviewed all candidates. That changed her life but she was going to suffer more trouble for years to come. Her weakness was men!

Those foster parents, were wonderful but they died in quick succession of each other, when she was sixteen and REB found her a place to live that she could afford, as she had dropped out of school, and was holding down a couple of jobs waitressing, and working part time at the Dominion Store in Town while studying to be a hairdresser.

You might have thought that anyone with the kind of self assurance, confidence and inner strength that she possessed and displayed, would never be led astray or demeaned by anyone, let alone be put in compromising positions! Yet, time and time again, she got taken in and taken, by some absolute waste of skin and she wouldn't listen to what the rest of them recognised, instantly, as serious red flags, and someone who should be avoided at all cost! Love is blind and can cause you to let your guard down, and ignore sound advise, from those who actually love and care about you. Such was the case with Calamity Jane!

More than a few times, it got to the point where people from the Club, had to intervene and get her out of the jack-pots that she found herself in. Generally, those tasks fell to Nicky and it usually took only a visit and a strong warning, and occasionally a black eye or a broken bone or two to persuade the individual to move on! Sometimes, as soon as the low-life would hear that Little Nicky was looking for him and he'd head out of Town as fast as he could, leaving Calamity with a broken heart.

The worst was back in 1985 when she got hooked up with this piece of shit, drug dealer, by the name of Vinny Balmoral, who was using more than he was selling. He moved her away from her friends because he knew that they were on to him. They moved out near London. One day "Gypsy" happened to be going through the area. Gypsy was out, living up to her nickname and maintaining her reputa-tion as a wandering soul! She was constantly putting thou-sands of miles on her motorcycle, travelling aimlessly, throughout Canada and The United States. She had even ventured to Europe a couple of times. This time, she was coming back from one of her many trips to the States and decided to drop in on Calamity for an unexpected surprise visit.

She was shocked by what she saw and what she heard. This scumbag had tried to rip off a bunch of would be bikers, rough necks and rounders, for some drugs, and he got caught. They were going to kill him but decided a good-looking bit of trim like Calamity could earn, and pay off his debt to them. They and this scumbag, somehow convinced her to go along with it! She, was now working as a dancer and would turn tricks, work Stag parties and whatever else they wanted, to just to keep this worthless maggot alive, and now, they considered her to be their property and refused to release her.

They threatened Gypsy as well, when she tried to inter-vene, but she managed to fend them off with a large buck knife that she carried on her belt! She then hurried right back and made a full report of what she'd found to REB. Tramp and some others, who happened to be around the CH!

There was no discussion, they immediately put together a crew of four. Reb, Nicky, Tramp, and Dion. They all knew what was being expected of them and never hesitated or even blinked! One of their own, was in trouble, and the Calvary was on their way. A large heavy satchel was loaded into the trunk of the car and within an hour they were halfway to London.

Mindful of protocol, REB had made a call to a couple of his contacts with a couple of MCs', out that way, to let them know they were coming to their Town, as a heads up and a courtesy, but made it quite clear, that they weren't asking permission to deal with them. They were merely informing them of shit that was happening on their turf. These Clubs knew, who they were after and had no problems with them taking care of business as it would save them the trouble, as these guys were already on their radar and were about to be dealt with, anyway. They even told them exactly where to find them.

The crew, rolled up on this property, in the industrial district and stopped in the laneway behind the address that they were provided. It was now late and the whole area was quiet as a tomb. They then opened the trunk and extracted a couple of shotguns, some baseball bats, rolls of duct tape and some rope from the satchel, before making their way silently to the back door opened it and quickly entered the building.

There were some loud protests from the inhabitants who tried to scramble for weapons. The protests, were soon stifled, by the brandishing the shotguns to the unsuspecting bunch. They separated them from their guns and knives. A few of them started talking trash, about how they would hunt them down and kill each and everyone of them and the tall, skanky, bitch too! These comments were duly noted, Tramp, delivered a smack in the mouths of a couple of the more vocal ones with his baseball bat, acknowledging that they had heard them and assured them, that while they had their full, and undivided attention, talking, on their part, without permission, was not permitted!

There were eight of them in the room, not counting the piece of shit boyfriend. They were told there were nine and Calamity was no in the room! Vinny, apparently was the designated punching bag for the evening as he was already duct taped at the ankles and wrists and suspended from a big hook in the ceiling that ran through the duct tape and rope on his wrists. It all looked like good sport and REB and the others each took a swing or two at him. They decided to just leave him hanging there.

They lined the bunch up against a wall and made them kneel down. REB, who had gone off in search for number nine, and found him and Calamity, naked in a back bedroom. REB clobbered him with the butt end of a shotgun across the bridge of his nose as he stood up to protest, he threw Calamity her clothes, and ordered her to get dressed. "We are taking you out of here now!" He barked! She complied without hesitation.

REB then kicked this lowlife who was now bleeding profusely from his mouth and nose, continuously and repeatedly as he crawled, naked, down the hallway on his hands and knees, to join his friends, kneeling against the wall.

One of them started to speak and Nicky spun around and without hesitation, fired his shotgun into the wall next to the man's head. This hapless bunch now realized that this bunch was totally serious and that they were in a lot of trouble. Tramp came over and clubbed the asshole, square in the face with his baseball bat.

"Were you not listening when we told you guys; No Talking?" Blood and urine now covered the floor, and these heroes were now crying and pleading to be left alone.

"Fuck! Nicky hollered! What is that awful smell? Did one of you fuckers, shit yourself? That is fucking disgusting!" He figured out which one it was and walked up and shoved the barrel of the shotgun right against his fore-head! This caused the guy next to him to follow suit, with a loud stinking report escaping from the man's butt!

"Fuck! He hollered again. "If you guys survive this night, you should see a Doctor! You obviously can't control your bodily functions!

They then turned their attention to Vinny, who was now, pretty much, in a full-on panic. They had stripped him naked cutting his clothes off and, his mouth was still taped shut and they had his ankles were also taped together.

"Cal. You may not want to watch this!" REB suggested. Calamity shook her head, glaring at the guests of honour with an intensity that only added to the anguish, these mangy pieces of shit were going through!

"OK then!" Let the fun begin!" and he moved in, bringing a bat to bear, in a short, level swing directly on Vinny's right kneecap! You could hear bones breaking quite distinctly even over Vinny's muffled screams! "Wow! That was a solid hit! What do you think Brother?" He asked Tramp who was standing back a bit.

There was muffled screaming from behind Vinny's duct taped mouth. Tears flowed and mixed with the blood that was dripping on the filthy floor. A couple of those against the wall now feinted and collapsed into a heap.

At that Tramp said; "That was good but I really think you should put more hip in the swing!" He moved in and brought his bat down hard on the other kneecap!

"Point taken! I will work on my swing!" REB replied trying to be heard over Vinnies' high pitched yet muffled screaming.

Vinny lost consciousness at that point and had to be revived so they could deliver the final message. You know who we are, but if we get any Police coming around, there are more of us, that will find you, wherever you try to hide and do you a whole lot worse! Am I understood? Vinny nodded vigorously in the affirmative! REB then turned to those against the wall who were still capable of hearing him and understanding. You do not treat one of people the way you've done! Understand?

They and Vinny all nodded frantically!

"Now, you, assholes, can do what you want with this piece of shit! We have what we came here for, and we are here, with permission from those who are in a position to give permission! Understood? There were again, vigorous nods of agreement. It is my guess, is that you, assholes, are finished in these parts anyway, and should move, quickly, and far away! If you dare rat, or retaliate in any way, shape of form, our next meeting will not be so pleasant! I'm also spreading the word on you guys, so be aware of where you decide to go next and what you do when you get there!"

At that, REB handed the bat to Calamity who took a hard swing, hitting Vinny square in the groin and then spit on him.

"Great swing! You haven't lost your feel for a bat!" REB quipped, as she tossed the bat back to him.

Vinny, tried to double up but couldn't, as his legs wouldn't bend he started convulsing and tried to puke but the duct tape across his mouth held it in and he started to choke on his own vomit!

"You guys should cut him loose and get that tape off his

mouth, before he dies or just find a place to hide the body! It's up to you!"

At that, they turned, filed out, piled into the car, which now had one more very appreciative passenger, and left, without looking back. They never heard anymore about it, and no one spoke of that incident again.

Sometimes you just have to deal with things as they arise. It is the ability to deal with things firmly, decisively, effectively and efficiently that sets you apart! It is establishing that you as a group, or individually, are ready, willing and capable of doing what needs to be done and willing to face whatever consequences come your way from establishing, to all that there can be severe consequences, when you mess with them! In life you can choose to be a Lion, or a sheep! They preferred to be lions! They were known and respected as such, by other Clubs, as word does get around.

However, some, were either terribly brave or incredibly stupid and refused to listen or take heed even when stern and final warnings were issued. Such was the case with one, low-life, drug Dealer, by the name of Vinny Balmoral and a group of his associates. After the severe beating they had taken at the hands of members of the Dozen, in London, four of the group including, the then, leader split from the rest, and Vinny was taken in as part of that crew after he was released from Hospital, even though he didn't walk too good and he had really developed a serious drug dependence and was especially, using opiates heavily. They left London and had moved around the Country, East Coast, West Coast, and everywhere in between trying to set up shop but, true to what he told them, the word that REB had put out about them, caused problems for them, wherever they went and when the heat, particularly from Motorcycle Clubs proved to be, far too intense! They kept on the move for a while, before settling in in a small town about 40 miles from Swanton Harbour, where they tried to keep a low profile, which is hard to do when you are also trying to promote products in territory that wasn't theirs! Their main product was marijuana; however, they did dabble in other drugs like crystal meth, ecstasy and some opioids as well.

Some unscrupulous dealers, in an effort to make their product produce a stronger, more memorable, experience, with a longer lasting high, as well as increasing the addictive tones of the drug, they laced it with Fentanyl. They wanted to have a reputation of producing "Killer Weed" and that is what they did. It was unclear, if the tainted weed was the direct result of purposeful actions, or if mishandling and poor storage of their products was the cause.

But, when five high school students, including the Son and Daughter of the Swanton Harbour Police Dept., Dan O'Reilly, died from an overdose, on their product, the heat was on, as was the search, for those responsible! It was not only the Police, by who were looking, but others who also take an interest in such matters. The word came back to REB, through Tramp, who began his report with; "You aren't going to believe who is involved in this shit!" the name that was provided made REB's blood boil! He thanked Tramp for the information and they parted company!

The crew of ner-do-wells, knew instantly, that serious shit, was about to hit the fan and they decided to split. However, they didn't move fast enough! They were busy packing up their stuff and loading it in whatever they could get their hands on.

They were interrupted and the air was shattered by an eerie, high-pitched wail or shriek that curdled the blood in their veins! Two of the crew, who were packing the stuff into the vehicles were the first to be confronted by the large figure cloaked in a black shroud with the image of a red Banshee imprinted on the front! That terrifying image would be the last thing they would see! Several rapid heavy blows to their heads from a baseball bat ended their night, and their lives.

The others, came scrambling out, guns drawn, to see what was going on and walked right into the full blast from two sawed off shotguns fired at point blank range, three dropped and died almost instantly, one, was severely wounded and was doing his best to get away.

The figure stepped over the bodies of the dead and dying and followed the scrambling terrified individual, while reloading.

It was obvious that the beating that they had delivered several years earlier had diminished Vinnie's mobility substantially, and the blast from the shotguns slowed him still further! The cloaked figure quickly caught up to a hysterical Vinny who was now crying and begging for his life!

He had turned to face his attacker and stared up, at the black shrouded figure and looked into two unforgiving, piercing, ice blue eyes. "You don't listen and you don't learn! Our little visit back in London, was a stern warning, you earned a beating and got one.

Now you and your poison, has caused the deaths of five nice kids. You have five deaths to account for! Unfortunately, I can only kill you once! That will have to do!" Those were the last words Vinny was to hear!

The wailing stopped and the figure disappeared into the night.

CHAPTER FOURTEEN

THE FUNERAL

IT WAS AN ABSOLUTELY gorgeous late summer day, it was quite cool in the early morning and they had been forecasting, possible, heavy rain, high winds and even a risk of tornadoes which is just what you want to hear when you're setting up for an event this.

The property and the Clubhouse, lent itself nicely for the funeral and they set the front porch up for the sound system and ran speakers out into the yard so that all would be able to hear and filled the space in front of the porch with chairs. There were going to be a lot of guests but could not be certain as to how many, so they set out two hundred. They knew that many of the guests would be sitting on or standing around the motorcycles anyway, so they would just do the best they could with what they had and Bikers who are used to improvising and making the best out of any situation, would certainly understand.

They had motorcycles form a semi circle around the

perimeter which was a loud and lengthy noisy process and the lawns took a real beating, but it looked like it was going to work just fine as all were co-operative, seasoned riders, who could handle their bikes and could take direction well.

There were some who had been involved with many similar situations and their input was vital. It is preferable to have an event such as this remembered for the event itself and not because it was a giant cluster-fuck! The other Clubs were more than willing to help and everybody was assigned specific tasks so everybody was aware of who was doing what, when.

Actually, in the few days leading up to the funeral, there were several meetings with various Clubs providing their best people to be involved in setting things up and with their input, they planned everything out from start to finish. There were lots of moving parts to this plan, so co-ordination and organization was key to its success. There were no egos displayed, with a too many Chiefs and not enough fucking Indians, which can happen and that usually results in the Cluster Fuck scenario that they were hoping to avoid. Everybody did the job they were assigned and everything went smooth as silk!

Dan was the obvious choice to co-ordinate with the Police for the procession to the Cemetery as to approximate times, route, and an approximation of the size of the pack. The Cemetery had been advised to be prepared for a larger than normal turnout so they could advise other funeral parties to schedule their affairs around this one. This would be one very large pack as there were already over three hundred motorcycles here and more were arriving all the while.

The Club had called on and old friend; Hank, who, for years, ran a fantastic looking Motorcycle Hearse, from out in Brantford Ontario. It was a real beautiful set up that used a Harley-Davidson trike with a fifth wheel set-up on the back that connected to the spectacular hearse trailer rig. He had moved to Tucson, Arizona, several years back to run a great little bed and breakfast. When called, he instantly said; on my way, loaded his hearse rig onto a custom-built trailer that he used to haul it from place to place and was indeed, on his way! He and his wife Marsha, arrived early that morning and were now set up and ready to go.

They had brought REB's casket out, and set it up in the centre of that large front porch along with all the floral arrangements, surrounding it. REB's old orange knucklehead chopper, his cut, and other pieces of his gear were set up on either side of the casket. It was quite a sight.

REB had insisted that this would be a non-religious affair as he had not attended Church since his early childhood and while he supported and respected people who were devout followers of the religion of their choice, he chose and rode his own path. He felt that it would be hypocritical to interject it into his funeral. Some, might be critical of that decision, but he simply said; too fucking bad, it's my fucking funeral, not theirs!

The guests took their seats or stood at the back and the service began. They hired someone to perform the service, but Dan delivered the eulogy as requested;

The Eulogy

Robert Edward Baker - Sept. 12 1945 – Sept 12 2020 – R.I.P. – G.BN.F. – L&R – A&F.

"Robert Edward Baker – Born September 12, 1945, died September 12, 2020, may he forever, rest in peace, he may be gone but will never be forgotten, and it is with the utmost Love and Respect that I deliver his eulogy at his insistence, simply, because he wanted to humiliate me just one more time!" We shared the same birthday, and we had known each other for 72 years! The first 30 of those years we hated each other with a passion fought often and constantly. For the past 40 years we loved each other and cherished each others company as Brothers. A subdued, and uncomfortable murmur could be heard waffling through the congregation. "REB was perhaps this most spontaneous and totally real human, being that I've ever met in my life!

"Linda asked me to do this, saying that the request came directly from the crusty old fucker himself, saying it was the last request he would ever make of me, and if I didn't he would come back and haunt me! So here I stand! Quite frankly, I had no idea what I was going to say, not a fucking clue!

Then a couple of days ago I met a brash young man wearing a Labatt's 50 t-shirt and matching ball cap, toting around a large cooler full of Labatt's 50, as advertised, I happen to drink that particular brand, and somehow, he got me talking. I got drunker than I have in 50 years and I opened up to him about a lot of shit I have not talked about in years, or ever!

Until two days ago I served as Chief of Police for the Town of Swanton Harbour, my father was a Cop, and his father was a Cop, before him, and I just followed in those footsteps! He was justifiably, curious as to how that went together! A Motorcycle Club and an event such as this, so respectfully attended by some very distinguishable and distinguished Clubs from all over the Country and an ex Top Cop, without an escort. I started to explain it all to him, until our tolerance for beer failed to surpass our supply. But we did our best though! Since he is in attendance, I will finish the story I was telling him as I'm sure there are many of you who may be wondering the same thing! It is a story of Brotherhood, tolerance, intolerance, interpretation, misinterpretation, truth, lies, respect and lack of respect. It is fairly long, but I hope you will bear with me!

Over the past two or three days, time flies when you drink as many 50 as we have put away, this young man has learned more about me and the relationship I had with this gentleman here, again pointing to the casket, than even I realized! I may have to kill him! He said with a big smile.

Laughter erupted and Dan waited for it to subside, before he started speaking again, and with these words, he then began his tribute to a man he despised for so many years and loved for not nearly enough!

"I have nothing written and nothing prepared, and I really hope that you aren't expecting religious overtones from me, because I'm not at all, what you could possibly class as religious! For that matter, neither was my friend REB here. We had always tried to do what in our hearts that we knew as right, but righteousness and religious would be stretching it a bit!" More sporadic laughter ensued.

" My first meeting with Robert Edward Baker was when we were both just three years old, and resulted in me suffering a wound to my forehead that left scar that I have carried most of my life and will be there when I die! It marked the start of a misunderstanding, or, perhaps, a personal war or conflict, might be a more appropriate term, that lasted between us for more than 30 years. We have long since, resolved our differences. I still have this scar, that is now a constant reminder, that I'm not always right, or just! I am human and subject to the same human failures and all and any of you here today. For, years I used to regard it as a sign that I had a score to settle! No longer! It is now a badge of honour and a reminder that he was here and this was his mark! He offered to autograph it more than once! His passing, now, leaves a wound that will never heal and another, not so visible scar that will remain on my heart and in my soul until my last breath and I truly believe it will be there until eternity, I will feel the pain and anguish forever, as I feel it now, to the very depth of my soul! That scar will serve to remind me to look for the good in people, not the bad, and to value true friendship when, where and if you are lucky enough to find it.

REB said it to me, just before he died, that it is a pity that we wasted so many of those early years hating each other, because it was such a waste of time and energy that could have been better spent loving each other as brothers and friends. He spoke the truth!

Robert Edward Baker, was no Saint and never professed

to be! He was however, as decent a Human being as any of us could hope to be, and in my personal estimation, better than most! More so, he was a humanitarian as is Linda.

I can speak of this now, as the House, has long stopped operating, but, Unbeknownst to most everyone, and myself until I proved that I could be trusted with the information along with a very select few who had to know, that he and his wife Linda operated a safe house in our community for many years, in total secrecy. They took hundreds of desperate and destitute Women and children into their home. They provided them with food and shelter and protected them from extreme domestic violence! Sometimes in the middle of the night, they would get a call or hear a knock on the door, and a desperate family would be brought in, unannounced and they would be accommodated without question.

This wasn't done for recognition, because, as I previously stated, it was all done in total secrecy. Not for money, as much of the time, they ended up paying for much stuff out of their own pockets and were never reimbursed. They just did what they knew was right!

There are many, who are here today, who consider, these kind folks; REB, Linda, and their five daughters, who made space in their home their rooms and in their lives for those in need, to be part of their families and hold them in a special place in their hearts!

There were, and are other safe houses, such as what REB and Linda operated here, scattered throughout the Province and not surprisingly, many of the people who ran them were often from the Biker Community as well. There is one that operated up in the Sundridge area years ago, that has become quite well known, because the daughters now do an Annual Tribute Ride for their Mom who was called Ms. Dazzle. That is the kind of notoriety or recognition these people truly deserve, but do not want or expect! They just knew that they did the right thing, when it was needed and the feeling they got from doing it, was all that they wanted or expected!

I guess the turning point for me, started, when I did a ride along with a kind old gentleman by the name of Stanley Marshall, who was Police Chief of this Town at the time. He had wanted to recommend me as his replacement as Chief of Police but was uncertain, if I was the right man for the job because, according to him, I had certain deep routed prejudices, and treated certain people and groups unfairly!

"He said that he needed someone who could think with their own mind and make decisions that are fair based on knowledge and facts, not opinions, conjecture, myths and falsehoods! He stated this, emphatically!

I couldn't believe what I was hearing! I had always thought I was totally fair in my treatment of all citizens, Aboriginal, black, brown, women, homeless I could see no justification for labelling me as prejudiced or racist or anything other than a fair and Good Cop! I honestly always believed that I was a good Cop! I thought I was an excellent Cop!

"I have always thought with my own mind and made my own decisions based on what I know or believe to be true! I have no prejudices! I'm no racist or fucking bigot!" I told him.

The Chief continued and I was getting angrier with each

word he spoke. "I've watched you since you joined the Department, and you have real potential! But you need to think for yourself! Be yourself! Form your own judgements based on truth and reality."

"I do! I always have!" Was my stern reply.

The Chief persisted; "No! Most times you sound just like your father! I loved your father, I liked working with him for all the years we spent on the job together! Your father, was also a hard man, with tendencies to step way over the line! He thought of his badge as a privilege, with the authority to stray where he wouldn't allow ordinary Citizens to go. He thought that because he was a Cop, those same laws didn't apply to him. Your father could be extremely mean and brutal at times! He and Dwight Higgins, another officer, who was a thorn in the side of The Dozen, and shared many of the same ideas. I did not agree with them or like their methods but they were hard to keep in line! Thanks partly to the Biker code where you don't talk to Cops I couldn't press charges or pursue action against Bad Cops, and thanks to the Blue wall where even good Cops won't speak against the bad ones even when they don't like what the bad cops did.

This was the first time I'd ever heard anyone speak ill of my father to my face, and I was none too pleased with the direction this was going! I started to get my back up!

"How about bikers? He asked. How about guys like REB Baker? How do you feel about him and his bunch?"

"They are criminals, thugs, thieves, and drug dealers! I despise them! How do you think I feel about them?" I replied, in none too kindly a tone either!

That statement certainly got an immediate reaction from

the congregation! There was a definite buzz in the air and many a dirty look was cast in his direction as well as many one finger salutes!

He acknowledged the expected reactions; "Duly noted!" He continued.

"OK, so, you are telling me that you know for an absolute fact. that all of them have long criminal records, and have been arrested for more than some of the fictional bullshit that you and some of the other cops in this department, cite them for, just to make their lives' miserable, and you can then brag about how you showed them that we aren't putting up with their kind? Is there a contest for the best creative writing of a citation that I don't know about? So, you actually read their criminal records, or just assumed that they had one?" The old Chief countered.

"Look! I know an asshole when I see one!" was my curt reply! "If it walks like a duck, talks like a duck, it is a fucking duck!" I told him. "REB and I have been sworn enemies since we were three years old! He's a low-life, always has been and always will be! Don't try to convince me that he is not! I Ain't buying it!" at that, I stormed out of his car and walked away! He was, in my mind, attacking me personally, and questioning my ethics, morals, values and my character, not trying to make me examine myself from a different perspective as he claimed!"

Now the audience was really reacting! Angry comments could easily be heard; "What the fuck kind of eulogy is this? Who the fuck is this asshole?" Along with some much worse, were being muttered or worse from everywhere in the room! He looked down at Calamity and she looked as puzzled as everybody else. Big Tramp and other Club Brothers too, looked unsure as to whether they should move in to protect him, from an unruly Mob or to grab him themselves, find an appropriate length of rope and a low hanging branch and help lynch him!

Dan quickly continued speaking a little louder so as to be heard over the din that he had provoked. "He passed me over as his replacement, and instead, stayed on for five more years. Five long and very hard years, and the job took its toll on the man and his health. He must have still had a glimmer of hope for me. He had failed to reach me this time, but wasn't giving up!" He certainly hadn't convinced me that I was wrong, but he did plant the seeds of doubt! Those damned seeds! I knew about planting fucking seeds of doubt!"

In the time that had passed since our last chat, I had reconsidered what the old Chief had told me and re-examined my methods, and motivations, many times, and while it was food for thought and reflection, however my opinion of Robert Baker and his band of misfits, steadfastly, remained the same.

Then one night, something happened, that along with another subsequent, conversation with the old Chief, gave me cause to think, about maybe changing my opinion. I discovered what other people that knew me, had long ago, figured out; along with other things, I was stubborn. There are pills and medication you can take to cure or control for all kinds of maladies and ailments and ills, but you can't take nothing for stupid or stubborn.

Now I was only aware of some of this, as, I was going in

and out of consciousness through much of it, and a lot of the details were supplied by the police report and witness statements. To the best of my knowledge, this is what transpired on Sept, 12, 1998 at approximately 10:00 PM.

On that evening, my whole family, wife, two kids, and the family dog and I were heading home from an evening shopping and a nice dinner at the local diner to celebrate my Birthday. It was a rainy night, the roads were extremely wet, slick and slippery. We were just rounding a sharp bend, when suddenly, a couple of large deer jumped out from the brush on the roadside, directly into our path. I was able to avoid hitting one, but the other, I hit dead on. The hood of the car folded up around the windshield with the deer's head coming through, striking me in the face and head! Stunned by the impact and the suddenness of it all, I went hard to the brakes, locking them up, and the resulting skid, sent us careening down the embankment, into the lake.

The car was partially submerged, the passenger side was completely under water. I looked around and could not see my wife I felt for her and tried to free her from the passenger seat, while trying to also find my son and daughter in the back seat at the same time. The dog was panicked and was wildly trying to escape the car. I was dazed from the crash and also panicking!

Suddenly the rear door of the car was ripped open by someone who quickly plunged his head and upper torso into the very cold and murky water. I saw a hand come into view and grab the dog, who was impeding his efforts, by the scruff of the neck and fling her out of the car and into the water in one shift motion, and it quickly swam to shore. The hand was once again back in the water feeling frantically until it came upon what he was looking for. He reached back again and drew a large knife from the sheath on his belt and then plunged it into the water. Seconds later I saw the body of my son emerge from the water and also being flung back out of the car. I couldn't make out who it was as it was pouring ran and very dark but he had no sooner extracted my son and his whole upper body again plunged back inside and came out with my daughter and she too was thrown from the vehicle. I knew he was not alone as I could hear frantic voices and movement in the water coming from outside of the car. The car was rapidly sinking and I was now up to my chin. I drew a breath and plunged my head under trying to free my wife from the seatbelt. She was not moving at all., my left arm was useless and stuck at an odd angle and was bleeding profusely. I knew, as well, was right leg was broken. My injuries greatly hindered my efforts to free Nancy from the seat belt and the confines of that vehicle, and I knew, that despite my best efforts I would never be able to muscle her from that wreck! I was frantic and felt totally helpless and ineffective! I felt strong hands grab me and I was pulled from the car and I then, felt other hands grabbing me, and I being thrown over huge strong shoulders like a sack of potatoes, and quickly moving towards shore.

"Please! I pleaded! My wife is still in there." I could make out the form of the large man who was still with the vehicle, bracing his legs against the door jamb of the now almost, completely submerged car to try for some stability! Suddenly, the car slipped completely, below the surface of the water just as the man once again plunged his upper body into the interior of the now totally submerged, car, in a desperate effort to save a life. I watched helplessly, while I was being deposited roughly on the bank and saw the hulking mass of a man immediately turn and was wading quickly back to where the other man had just surfaced with a limp female form in his arms! He was already performing CPR on my unconscious wife as he started to wade for shore. The bigger of the two men was now carrying her while the other continued to try and resuscitate her.

I heard a child coughing and turned to see my son sitting upright, spitting and coughing up water, but alive. There was a woman who was now bent over the body of my daughter, compressing her chest rhythmically while breathing into her mouth. Suddenly, she too, was revived, scared and confused but also, alive.

The two men had reached shore with my wife's limp, life-less body. She was definitely not breathing. The woman now turned her attention to her. They quickly deposited the body of my wife in the bed of a pick-up truck, while the woman, jumped in with her and continued performing CPR. They operated as a synchronised team, no words were spoken, as the three just did the right thing, as it needed to be done, almost like they were choreographed or did this type of thing regularly.

The men threw a large tarp over the two women to protect them from the rain as best they could under the circumstances, weighted it down with some rocks and other heavy objects to prevent it from blowing off when they hit the road at speed. They turned their attention to me and scooped me off the ground as if I were weightless, and stuffed me excruciatingly, into the passenger seat of the truck. My two kids were put in the cab of a second pick-up truck, which immediately tore off in the direction of town and the Hospital.

I was in and out of consciousness, which was merciful, as there was bone protruding from my left arm, and my right leg was obviously broken as well as it sat at a strange angle, but my comfort at this point was not even a consideration for these people, saving mine and my wife's life was the only thought on their minds, as they raced off down the rain-soaked highway. If I had been able to remain conscious, and if I was even asked, I would have agreed!

This was long before cell phones so there was no calling ahead. They just tore off towards the Hospital hoping that they, themselves would be able to control their speeding vehicles on these treacherously wet and very slippery roads.

As they approached a roadside diner, they spotted a patrol car parked in the lot out front. As if operating with one mind, the lead truck with the two kids, had turned in and slid to an abrupt stop out front! The driver of the truck I was in, knew exactly what his friend was doing and just kept going.

The other driver had leaped out of the barely stopped truck, ran inside and barked his orders to the Cop who was sitting at a table, about to start his meal. "There has been a bad accident. We have Dan O'Reilly and his family! I have the kids but Dan is in really rough shape and his wife is not breathing, we are on the way to the hospital. Radio ahead, and let the Hospital know we are coming, now!

He turned, ran back to his truck, leaped in, and took off

again, as fast as that old truck could go! I came to again, and saw the flashing lights of the cruiser come on and knew that the Cop was on the job and in pursuit. Now it was just going to be luck and the skills of the Hospital staff that would determine whether there would be a happy ending. But they had a better chance now than they had less than twenty minutes earlier. I knew that these three people had done all they could as best that they could and I hoped it would be enough! I again lost consciousness and didn't awaken for perhaps fifteen hours in a hospital bed.

The Hospital had teams ready and waiting to take the patients from the would-be saviors. They moved quickly, first taking Dan's wife from the bed of the truck and that team hustled off inside the building. Another team extracted an unconscious Dan from the confines of the cab. Yet another team, was tending to the kids who were dazed and confused but seemed fine.

They were kept busy for the next hour or so, answering questions for the Police reports. But had received no updates on the family's condition.

Just then a door opened and a doctor along with several nurses came outside to have a cigarette. They looked tired, but satisfied, and one of the nurses called out, asking; "Are you the ones that brought the family here?" She asked.

REB nodded.

"They are all going to be fine! The wife just came around and she seems OK but we will run some more tests on them all. They will be here for a day or two, especially the father. He has some nasty injuries but should be fine! You three did a great job and saved some lives tonight! That family owes you big time!" She told them.

"Good news! All's well that ends well" REB said with a grin, and added to his two companions; "This ought to really piss Dan off when he finds out it was us!"

There was one more survivor of the whole mishap. There was a stirring from under the tarp and a very wet and bedraggled, shaggy haired dog, emerged from under it. Confused but wagging his tail in delight at having survived the ordeal. REB, had spotted her and threw her in the back of his truck before they left the lake. Linda, now, had her in her arms and was doing her best to comfort her.

She asked the very relieved, and grateful Cop, who had chased them here from the diner, what he thought she should do with the dog. She volunteered to take it home with them, and they would care for it, until the family could reclaim her.

That would be fine with him he said but asked. "Does Dan know you, and where to find you?"

REB, Linda and Tramp all smiled at each other. He replied. "Yeah! He definitely knows that! Tell him REB and Linda have her. Tell him he should drive more carefully on wet roads or somebody might have to report him to the Cops! He can come by anytime, and he doesn't need a warrant, if it just to pick up the pooch!" He laughed and the three walked out into the night. REB and Linda wrapped the shivering dog up in a blanket that he kept behind the seat, and it rode home between them in the old pick up truck. He had thrown another blanket over the seat, so as to not get Dan's blood all over them.

Dan paused, as there were very few, who had heard these stories previously and there were many mixed reactions to what he had just related to them.

"When I came to, I realized where I was and had a very vague idea as to how I got there! I looked up to see Chief of Police Stan Marshall sitting in a chair by the window waiting for me to come around."

Our conversation went something like this; "It's OK! You're gonna be OK, Nancy and the kids are OK, even your dog is OK!" he said reassuringly, in comforting tones! "The deer and the car, not so much!"

"So, you celebrated your birthday with a bang! Most people, just have a second piece of cake, you went out hunting for venison!" He said jokingly, the big smile that spread across his face wrinkled his weathered skin, that just seemed to fold into a permanent, familiar, creases of a face, he was used to wearing one! His eyes showed the relief that he felt at seeing his young officer regain consciousness.

I was struggling to piece together memories of the previous night, but there were so many blank spaces, and it just confused me. "Those people, the two men and a woman! They were incredible! Do you know who they were? I have to thank them!"

The old chief looked down at him with surprise and asked; "You didn't recognize them?"

"No, it was dark, raining too hard and everything was happening too fast! I kept fading out! Everything was a blur!"

"It was the Bakers!" he replied.

"The Bakers? As in REB Baker? You have to be kidding

me! Why would he want to save me and my family? He must not have known it was me!"

"He knew it was you alright! There was REB and Linda Baker along with Big Tramp Jackson. They were also at the diner celebrating his birthday, and left right after you and your family did. They saw the whole incident and they were the ones who fished you and your family, out of the lake, performed CPR and drove you here!"

"Wow! I don't know what to say"

"Thanks, would be a great start!" Muttered the old Chief!

"But he hates me! Why would he risk his life and work that hard to save someone he has hated for so long?" I protested.

"Are you certain that that hate street that you talk about so much, is actually for two-way traffic?" He offered. "Maybe you should look at the signage and again. Take a closer look, it may be one way traffic!"

He explained; "I've talked to REB many times over the years and it is clear that he doesn't like you much. You've given him little, or no reason to! But he doesn't hate you, never did, even though you have given him cause, more than once!"

"Son. You have to know that I'm an old man who has lived in this town my whole life, I've observed some things. You know, I came out to all the ball games. I coached your Hockey teams and I witnessed first hand many of those fights! Over the years, I've been called to the schools, from Kindergarten, Elementary School and High school as a cop, to intercede in fights between the two of you. I've hauled your young asses out of skating rinks, movie theatres, amusement parks and even Church a couple of times!"

"Yeah, if we were anywhere near each other we would fight!" I told him.

"You sure it was we?" he asked.

"I looked at him like he had three heads! What do you mean am I sure? You were there, everybody saw those fights! It was a constant battle!"

"You know, I've been a Cop a long time, I've been a father to my three boys and a coach for Hockey, soccer, baseball, and football and I like to think I was good at it! I was analytical, and that was my strength and I still am. So, I'm now going to be analytical about you and REB and the fights you've had over the years, right now.

"In all those fights that I saw between the two of you, I saw one boy fighting and the other boy fighting back! Each and every time! Bar None! I saw an attacker and a defender. You my boy, were the attacker, Robby Baker just fought back! He was defending himself against a bully!"

"I just sat there, totally speechless! How could he say such a thing? The old man had surely, lost all his marbles!" these were just some of the things running through my head! None of them kind, or in agreement!"

"You will, no doubt, disagree with the statement that I have just made." He said.

"Son, I am not the only one who holds that opinion! The other coaches, people in the stands, even players on ours and the other teams knew it. Either, no one else has ever told you this or you didn't listen! I think it was the latter in your case! You don't even want to listen now!"

"I have film footage that shows it, plain as day!" In Hockey if you were on the ice and REB Baker stepped on, you made a bee line, straight for him. No other players, only REB."

"I was now, in a complete pout, like a spoiled child who had just been punished, and took absolutely nothing away from the experience, other than he didn't like being punished, no misgivings, no awareness of any wrong-doing on his part, just more bitterness! I hoped this old man would fuck off, and leave me alone. Senile old fool!"

He wasn't finished; "Now do you remember the All-Star Games, when I had both you and REB on the same team and I put you on the same line. The other coaches thought that I was nuts! REB played Centre and you were Right Wing. For some reason, you were able to put your differences aside during the course of the games, and you two were like magic. Lightning in a bottle! There was automatic chemistry, between the two of you, and all the other players got caught up in it too. It was like I'd just mixed a magic potion or waved a wand! I now looked like a fucking genius, not a maniac!

He continued; "The two of you were there to play hockey, and you both knew what needed to be done, and you knew how to do it properly! It was Hockey 101 for two players that already knew and had long mastered all the fundamentals and were capable of some great play. Previously you were playing with players who weren't in your league and couldn't keep up and play at your level, they couldn't, and didn't, think like the two of you!

Now, you were both top calibre players, with real skills.

You had just never gotten the opportunity to utilize them, with a player with the same talent and instincts! You might not have cared much for each other, but you liked but these other guys less. For once, you had a mutual enemy that you two could focus on, together! When a pass needed to be made between you two, it was made, mostly through instinct, you guys clicked. You were like a matched team of horses! You humiliated the other teams!

Our team, kicked some serious ass that day, in more ways than one! When things got chippy, as the other team, didn't much like being beaten by a bunch of hicks, Micks and misfits from Swanton Harbour! When the fight, that everybody knew was going to happen, finally broke out, it was great to see the two of you fighting shoulder to shoulder and back to back for a change and you both fared well!

"Then the game ended and we went right back to the status quo. That was disheartening!"

"Now I think I've said quite enough, I can see that you are angry and I know you don't agree, but think It through, and watch for those signs, I think you may have misread them! A good Cop should know the difference! This Town doesn't need another bully for a Cop, we've already been down that road. It certainly doesn't need a bully as Chief of Police! Like on those Allstar teams, you have all the skill and know all the basics, you know right from wrong, you just need to realize how good you can be! I can see your potential, but Son, you haven't reached it yet! Open your eyes and your mind Son!"

At that, he left, I was left there to sulk, stew, and think, I fell asleep, and dreamt, woke up, still, fully pissed off, and thought and stewed some more, and was still pissed off. "Me, a bully? Bullshit!" I shouted, out-loud and threw my pillow at the wall and then regretted doing that, as I couldn't yet, get up to retrieve it, and would have to wait for a nurse and I was now uncomfortable and pissed off. That just pissed me off even more!

"Stupid Old Man! What does he know? Fuck him!" I cursed and fussed like that, for a couple of days.

Sometime after the second day, it occurred to me that Old Stan Marshal, had been considered by many, to have been one of the best Coaches in the Province! Perhaps his views had some merit, perhaps I should look closer at his analysis? Those fucking seeds of doubt again! They, didn't give participation trophies back in those days, you earned them, and Stan had a trophy case full to overflowing, plaques and certificates covered every inch of wall space in his office and there were pictures of him with superstars of the game. He had even had offers from Pro teams to come and work for them, but he chose the Police Department.

I remembered how happy I was when he got to play on Coach Marshal's team. I also remembered how good it felt playing those All-Star games and actually having plays work that had never worked before! I figured I was perhaps just having an off day all those other times! They should have worked, as they were good plays in theory, but in practice they always came up short! I would make a pass and no on was there to receive it or I would be in perfect position to take a pass, that never happened!

With Robby Baker, those plays clicked, without preplanning, with no communication, just pure instinct and when playing with REB, together, we did kick ass!

"This was hard for me to swallow! This was hard for me to even consider! Fuck! Maybe I was the asshole!"

"I reflected on the story of how REB and I first met and how I tried to take the hammer away from him he resisted, I punched him, he fought back and I walked away the loser. I tried to look at it from another perspective. And damn it! That made me the bully! It made me the aggressor. Maybe that scar I've been carrying should have reminded me not to be an asshole or a bully. Maybe the old Chief was right, I had seriously misinterpreted signs. I looked back on other incidents as well, and discovered that I had some serious thinking and re-evaluating to do. Sometimes it may take a while to consume and digest, what has been put on your plate. Even if it looks like inedible and unappetising. Sometimes, if it is prepared just a little differently, presented as it had never been presented before, it is a meal worth eating, not just food! Maybe I wasn't the only one who could plant seeds?"

So, with those seeds firmly planted, I tried my best to nurture them and keep the weeds cleared away and see what kind of a crop I would get.

I rode over to see my nemesis, Robby Baker, one day, not as a Cop, but just a guy who finally realized mistakes had been made. I was expecting at best, to eat some crow, and maybe move on from there, or be physically removed from his property and I knew now, that he had every right to do so. Instead, I was surprised by his humour, generosity, warmth, intelligence, talent and humanity. All qualities I admire, but I honestly, didn't expect to find them all wrapped up in a person I had despised for so long! To say I was pleasantly surprised would be an understatement.

I now realized how easy it is to create false images of people and things through misunderstanding and misinterpretations. I discovered that you have to look past the outer appearances and see what lays behind things, not what appears obvious. I learned that you had to make judgements based on your own evaluations not on what the others opinions happen to be. Proper evaluations are harder to achieve and a lot more work, but they are worth it.

I thought I knew a lot, it turns out I had a lot more to learn and my new education was about to begin, now that my eyes and my mind were fully open and my ears tuned to listen to more than just what I wanted to hear.

REB and I, surprisingly, became fast friends, and found that we had a lot in common and together, our minds were stimulated and we developed things together, that we couldn't do on our own as individuals. Together, it was like playing hockey together on those All-Star Teams; we just clicked. I was in search of that missing piece that would complete the puzzle, that was my life, and it was right there all along in Mr. Robert Edward Baker! Some, of what we were working on will soon be revealed and I wish REB could still be here to unveil it with me!

How I wish that on that first meeting, when we were three, that we could have smiled at each other played together with those fucking hammers and been friends from that point on. What a team we could have made!

But then, fate has its own agenda, and leads us where it wants, when it wants and decides what paths we will follow and when those paths should intersect and continue on as one line. There had to have been a reason. Perhaps just so we will really appreciate it when it, whatever it happens to be, finally gets there! That is all I have folks! What REB told me on his death bed was true, the times we spent embroiled in hatred had been such a waste, it was a one-way street after-all!

One other thing that REB told me, was that the "Once a Cop, always a Cop thing", would haunt the relationship between the two of us forever. He had trouble getting his head around it and I the same. Many of you, I'm sure, also have serious doubts, and you would be right to do so. There is a distinct division that was established over many years and for many, that division will always exist.

It has taken me decades to learn to seek out truths and realities. What I learned from my mentors; Tony Boiko, Chief Stan Marshall and my dear friend and Brother; Robert Edward Baker, along with experience, was that you have to ride your own motorcycle on your own paths. You have to be accountable to yourself first! You decide what is right and wrong and be prepared to defend yourself. You have to always, be yourself, first and foremost!

Perhaps, most importantly; Give respect and you will get respect in return, if not, fuck them, and take it from there!

He turned to face the casket gave a light tap on the top and said; "Slainte Mhath, Mo Chara go deo! I did my best!"

He turned looked out into the sea of faces, spotted young Foxy, and said directly to him; "Does that cover it?" Foxy nodded solemnly.

At that, he stepped away from the podium, took his seat

next to Calamity and just sat there staring at the casket wanting to just break down and cry but resisted, for fear that if he did, REB would burst from that casket and punch him square in the face, or worse!

Then the podium was then offered to people would like to speak it was a long list as REB had touched a lot of people and lives!

They then closed the casket, and he would be carried to the Hearse, with Tramp, Gypsy, Calamity, Chuck Taylor and Moise, who, were all of the remaining Members of the original Bakers Dozen Baseball Club, acting as Pall bearers and loaded him into the hearse.

They would then form into a pack with Dan riding the Knucklehead immediately behind the Hearse. He would be packing Linda and the rest of the immediate family, were each assigned a rider who would take them to the Cemetery and the pack would start out slowly and the rest would dovetail in and form a procession riding two abreast that would stretch for a mile behind the Hearse. Helmets would be a personal decision for the individuals to make. Most did not wear them. The Cops were excellent, and co-operated fully, blocking intersections and motorcycle Cops escorted the ensemble to the Cemetery and hung around during the funeral to perform the same task in reverse for the trip back to the property for the Celebration of life afterwards. I thought to myself, this should be the norm, not the exception to the rule.

REB was laid to rest next to his parents, in a large family plot that REB and Linda had expanded as their family grew. It was a beautiful spot on a hillside overlooking the Lake, near the road that Dan rode often and he would give the throttle of that old Knucklehead, a twist, and offer their traditional salute with his left hand, as he rode past the Cemetery, in case his old friend could hear it!

The funeral went off without a hitch and the celebration of life afterwards, was something that anyone in attendance will remember for the rest of their days. Tons of food and gallons of beer and alcohol were consumed and the party actually went on for days. The last of the guests finally rolled out late Wednesday afternoon and the Club guys, and particularly the new Probates, were able to finally get some much-needed rest. The final clean-up could take place over the next few days.

CHAPTER FIFTEEN
TURNING THE PAGE

Foxy and his crew stayed at the property that night, and had headed back to the London area, the following day. However, when he got back there he found that his boss wasn't very pleased with him for taking time off, and fired him. He called Dan and told him about it and Dan invited him to come work at his shop on the Club property, and also told him that he could stay at the house. He was thrilled and immediately started planning to move and within two weeks, he had a new job and new home and great new prospects for the future.

Calamity and he, had stayed around until long after the funeral and rode home, he, on the knucklehead, and her, on the old shovelhead. They would bring the decker back another time. Dan, had left Zeke with some friends down the road and when they heard that he was coming back that night, they brought Zeke back home, and he was waiting anxiously, to greet them as they came through the door, as if they had been gone a year.

They turned on the outside lighting, opened a couple of beers and sat out back by the pool. It was an absolutely gorgeous night the pitch-black sky was full of stars and the air although a touch on the cool side was refreshing and it was nice to be able to relax after all that had transpired over the last while.

"Do you mind if I go for a swim?" Calamity asked.

"Go for it! Mi casa, su Casa." Dan told her.

Much to his surprize, she stood directly in front of him, and slowly removed all her clothes, folded them neatly and placed them carefully on a chair, while looking Dan straight in the eye the whole time. She knew the effect that she was having on him, but seemed totally casual about it. Dan sat there, totally mesmerized by the beauty that stood, totally naked, before him.

She was a sight to behold and he couldn't really believe what was happening! It was like a dream. He had long pictured her, and speculated, but never dreamed that he would ever get near her! In fact, he hadn't been with a woman since Nancy died. The encounter a couple of days ago, had certainly surprised him and caught him completely off guard, and even given him cause to think. But nothing had happened since and they never discussed or even mentioned it again so he wrote it off as simply a tease or a good-natured joke. In all the years that they have known each other, there had never been any real indication that she was interested in him.

Sure, there was the odd tease or comment that she would

make but he passed it off as kidding around. He felt she that she knew that he was attracted to her, but most guys were attracted to her and she could have her pick. What could she possibly see in a 75-year-old? He, had always liked her and felt very comfortable with her and was happy to have her just as a friend. Now after the other day, it looked like it could be more than just friendship. Still, as it hadn't been spoken of again, he didn't want to jump to conclusions, it could be just some British Columbia tease kind of thing! He never considered himself to be a ladies man and had never been one to mess around and had never strayed during his entire marriage despite the fact that there were always opportunities to do so.

Now, here she stood, she was like a vision, tanned toned and in fantastic shape, she could easily be mistaken for a thirty-year-old. She reached down grabbing him by the hands and pulled him to his feet.

"I don't want to swim alone!" she said in that sultry tone that stirred his soul. She had a glint in her eyes as she moved purposely towards him. She first removed his vest folded it neatly, and lay it on the chair. Then she pulled his t shirt over his head and removed it, but in the process, she inadvertently, brushed her ample breasts lightly against his chest. Her erect nipples seemed to be electrified and Dan actually quivered at the touch. She felt it, and stepped back, gave him a surprized, quizzical look, smiled the most enchanting smile he had ever seen, and in the raunchiest of tones, she purred; Easy Tiger, just relax, this could take a while and we have as long as it takes!"

She kneeled down in front of him and pulled off his

boots, and his socks, still kneeling, she reached up and her long, slender, fingers, deftly, unbuckled his belt, unbuttoned his jeans and slid the zipper down. Then grabbing the waist-band of both the jeans and the undershorts pulled them simultaneously, both down to his ankles in one smooth movement. He stepped backwards away from them. Calamity then rose smiling, slowly scrutinizing the naked body of an extremely nervous, ex Chief of Police who wasn't feeling the least bit in control of this situation. She smiled coyly while carefully folding the jeans and underwear and placing them on the chair in a pile, alongside his vest and t shirt and then placed his boots and socks with them.

She then, turned quickly and suddenly, sprinted to the edge and dived into the pool. He followed, and the two swam underwater the full length of the pool, he watched in awe as her lithe body glided effortlessly and gracefully through the water, her dense mane of hair, flowing freely behind. She was flawless! They surfaced in the shallow end and now just stood there looking at each other. Dan was speechless and could only stare in disbelief as this beautiful woman, now waded purposelessly towards him and locked him in an embrace and a long, hard, passionate kiss. The exotic scent of her perfume rose in his nostrils and stirred his senses even higher. The warmth of her firm, wet, body pressed tightly against his, as she slowly and assuredly, stepped forward, guiding him backwards to the pools edge where she posi-tioned him on the edge of the pool, his feet and lower legs, still in the water and lay him back on the cool concrete slabs, her straddling him.

What happened next, was a blur to Dan, but he recalled

being very clumsy and somewhat less than suave. He remembered apologising when he fumbled and displayed all the style and grace of a virgin, teenager, rather than a full-grown man. He started to explain that he hadn't been with any woman for a while, but Calamity quickly brought a slender finger to his lips and in her silky, sultry, husky, voice told him; "Shush, Dan the man! I got this! You, just lay back and enjoy the ride! I will go slow and take it easy on you." She paused, and added "This time!"

She was a very energetic, enthusiastic and motivated lover, to say the least, and she proceeded to take him to dizzying heights, to which, he had never been, utilizing her, mouth, tongue, hands, legs and breasts in slow, deliberate moves and in ways that he didn't know were possible. She brought him pleasure that he never realized existed and in ways that he had never experienced. He had his eyes closed, much of the time and he quivered and shivered with each; tickle, touch, tease, caress, lick, nibble, bite and kisses that would be gentle and soft as a whisper, then instantly turn to hot and passionate! No part of his body went untouched in some way. She was confidant and in total control, much, in the same way she rode her motorcycle and was able to get maximum pleasure out of the experience.

It was an experience! Dan, had always felt that his sex life to this point, was always satisfying and full filling, however, this was different, so different! He felt he was floating, one instant, and then in almost anguish, the next, as she playfully, skillfully and sensually took where she wanted to take him. Then, finally, mounting him, taking him inside her, when she, ground, gyrated, and thrust herself against him leaving him gasping for breath, straining as he tried to drive himself deeper inside her, until he could finally take no more, he reached for and finally ascended to found the release point, and mind numbing relief that occurred in spasms until he collapsed, totally spent and satisfied beneath this exquisite enchantress.

Cal just lay there atop of him for what seemed like an eternity, languishing in the rapture of what had just taken place, her long hair still wet from the pool, cascaded over his face like soft, soothing fingers, and she kissed him ever so gently. Her lips, touched, soft and sensual, against his, the delicate scent of her perfume lingered and hung in the air like a velvety mist that seemed like you could see and physically touch. She slowly rose and rolled off of him and just lay there beside him on the concrete patio slabs gently running her fingers delicately over his body while he just lay there, not wanting to break the spell she had just cast on him. Cal stood, helped him to his feet then led him, upstairs to his bed and they fell asleep together, locked in each other's arms. He was amazed, as this wasn't his first rodeo, but he had never experienced anything quite like what had just occurred. The only other comparison he could draw, was playing hockey with his usual teammates and then playing with REB on those Allstar teams, years ago when things, just clicked!

"Wow!" she had remarked just before they fell asleep, "That was long over-due! I've wanted to that with you for many years, but Darl'n I don't knowingly, fuck married men, and you never struck me as someone who fucked around on his wife. I always knew you were attracted to me and I know you never hit on me! I always respected that. We can't let you go so long between oil changes again!"

Dan, was still speechless and totally spent, and fell almost instantly, into a deep, restful sleep!

Gypsy, having rekindled the relationship with Wandering Bill, soon headed back on the road with her old road partner and Skooter the dog, in search of new adventures to share and things to see and experience. They would keep in touch, and from time to time make it back into Town, but the road was their true home and where their hearts were.

The Club was thriving, and enjoying a resurgence of energy and it was showing. The new Clubhouse and the increased membership, that it brought with it, new probationary members and ultimately, more members to share the workload and the extra dues went a long way in fulfilling the financial obligations! As well, the income from support merchandise and the open nights at the bar, when guests could come in and enjoy themselves was making an impact on their finances as well. Tramp, was elected President, and Big Jake Connor was VP. And others were being groomed for future leadership roles.

The large kitchen was put to good use as well, as many Members and their wives and some girl friends, not to mention, sons and daughters, displayed great culinary skills, and prepared all kinds of snacks and trays of delicious foods that just added a welcoming touch to the Clubhouse. Time spent there, rivalled any time spent in any bar, anywhere, anytime, if you were a biker! It was a joy coming here! It was always decorated in the spirit of whatever the Calendar dictated, be it Christmas, New Years, Easter, Halloween, Cinco de Mayo, or whatever.

The rooms and the space were well utilised as were the cabins that had been constructed down by the pond and the lake. It was becoming a destination with bikers from all over and when Dan Introduced phase two which he and REB had been working on, it was an instant success. It was a complete Biker Town that was put together by them on property that had already Zoned for use as a year-round campground that was adjacent to the Clubs property. It was set up with small cabins all with electricity, and running water with attached toilets, electrical and water hookups for RV's as well.

They also ran motorcycle tours of the Province from there and were booked solid for the entire season.

It was now, also equipped with a pool and a community centre with a large stage and bar and a small general store. They had also set up some of the cabins as small stores where crafts and custom products could be sold, or tattoos or any number of small visions and dreams could be realized. Some of the best artisans in the Country were looking to set up on the Property.

REB's visions and dreams were brought to life and his spirit and influence would live on here. Linda and the girls could see it as well and they knew that REB would be at peace.

Foxy had come back to Town and moved in with Dan, Calamity, and Zeke, at the house. It was just supposed to be, until he could find a spot of his own, but it felt like he was in the right spot as it was, and he just stayed. Dan had put him to work at the shop and he was proving to be a real asset and he had lots of repeat business. That told Dan that he was creating happy Customers with satisfactory work and what more could you want from a business?

Dan welcomed the company, and the help, as Calamity also stayed on and volunteered to assist as a mechanic as well. Dan knew that she was a highly skilled wrench but didn't know that she was fully licensed and accredited, as well. This helped immensely as Foxy was able to finish his apprenticeship under her tutelage.

Another thing, Dan was to discover about Calamity, was parts of her dismal track record and lack of luck, with men! In yet another, failed previous relationship, she had hooked up with yet another complete waste of skin, who, at least, was a licensed mechanic, which is about the only asset, or positive anything, that he brought to the relationship.

They had used her money, plus whatever money she brought into the business by twisting wrenches, to open and operate a Motorcycle shop out in the Guelph area. He, being, a licensed mechanic and she was able to do her apprenticeship under him. She had a natural aptitude for such work, which had been evident from those early days on that concrete pad, and did great work, including performance stuff!

She then built a great reputation, as a top wrench, and business was booming. Thinking that they were building the business together for them, and their future, they bought a lot of high-end equipment including a dyno test unit, using, of course, mostly her money as he was apparently spending his, on wine, women, and song!

She then found out, he that he was screwing around with

some stripper from one of the local strip clubs and lavishing her with extravagant gifts, like a new car. Calamity freaked out and a fight ensued! He blackened her eyes and threw her out, and claimed that all the equipment and tools were his and she was to leave with nothing!

She had once again, retreated back to Swanton Harbour, with her tale, and related it to REB and those at the Club House. One-day, Calamity, REB, Tramp, Little Nicky and Calvin, drove over to the guys shop with a large truck and some sports equipment and paid him a visit. They pointed out the obvious flaws in his thinking, his math and his strange ideas of what was his property, and what wasn't! Legalities and rightful ownership were brought into question and discussed thoroughly and it was explained, that Calamity had all the receipts, for everything.

All that aside, it was also pointed out that baseball bats can be used for hitting more than baseballs and when applied properly to kneecaps, it can be very painful and recovery time can be very long. They didn't have to explain any further as the shithead had heard rumours about a visit this crew had made to London and a demonstration wasn't necessary!

They came back to Town with the truck loaded full of tools, lathes, milling machines, and other parts and accessories as well as the Dyno testing equipment and other high-end stuff. They left the schmuck with some things to remember them by, but little else. He decided that he should move on, closed the shop and was not, heard from again! The stripper left him too and is enjoying her new car!

The stuff was still all in a storage container not far from

the shop in Swanton Harbour and she would gladly donate it to this new enterprise and it was all put to good use!

She admitted to Dan that along with all her strong points, she had horrible luck with men, she didn't elaborate and he never asked her to. She was going to say something, like third time is the charm, but couldn't figure out the actual number would be. She said instead; "I've made so many mistakes in my life! The difference was, with all the others, my friends were all trying to warn me to not go there! This time around, they are all for our relationship.

Even REB, just before he died, suggested that I should see if you fit my fiddle. So far, we harmonise pretty well, and haven't hit a sour note yet. Unless you've been able to con all of them, and me, this just feels so fucking right! If this goes South, and you turn out to be just another asshole, I'm going to jump in front of a fast-moving, fucking train, cause my back-up crew are dyeing off and I'd have to kill you myself and I'm not much into digging graves!"

She and Dan were hitting it off, really well, and while the lusty sessions had quieted down slightly, after they got the first hundred times or so out of the way, and their libidos quieted down some, to try and fit their age, but their age, didn't entirely fit their libido's so they just winged it and they settled in nicely.

She still had a thriving business and interests back in BC, that was being looked after in her absence by trusted friends, and after a few months, she went back to BC and stayed for a while before coming back again, for a while. So, it went, until Dan figured he could leave Foxy in charge, Zeke loved him and he and Calamity could revolve freely, back and forth between Provinces together! It worked well for all of them! Plus, they were free to go on extended trips and motorcycle tours whenever the whim hit them.

Dan had never heard about some of her other less than stellar relationships, like the one in London or her childhood or any of the stuff that was best left in the past. That page had also been turned and another chapter was unfolding.

Linda and a few of REB's and her daughters looked after the campgrounds and they employed many of the Members and Probates as guides for the Motorcycle Tours and other duties around the place, from landscaping to maintenance and repairs.

Foxy who had now been made manager, as well as head Mechanic after he completed his apprenticeship. They had hired a couple of wrenches and an apprentice and the shop was doing a good business. He had also joined the Club, first as a Probate and was now a full member! It was a good fit!

Dan thought it only fair, that Foxy and Calamity should be made equal partners in the business, that they all played a part in making a success, and had the Lawyers draw up official partnership papers!

One day, they were cleaning up REBS old studio and burning a bunch of old papers and other clutter, as REB was accomplished in many things, but being neat and tidy wasn't one of his strong points, and had managed to accumulate quite a bit of crap, along with the treasures. It fell to them to rectify the situation and make the space inhabitable for the new office space.

They were digging through piles of stuff, when Foxy

pulled a box out from under some other shit. It was sealed with tape.

"What do you think is in here." He asked. "it has some weight to it.

"Why not open it and find out!" Dan replied.

Foxy pulled his Buck knife from the sheath that hung from his belt and sliced at the tape holding the box closed, pulled open the flaps and looked inside.

"What the fuck do you think this shit is." He first pulled out a large black sheet all neatly folded, set it aside and then extracted an old police siren that used to fit on Police Bikes. It was attached to a board about a foot long and had a couple of leather straps, to supposedly to carry it with. There were wires running from a switch to the siren and connected to a large battery, that was hooked to that switch by some other wires. One of the wires had been disconnected from one post of the battery. "This is a strange set-up!"

Calamity had come over and picked up the black sheet and unfolded it and looked puzzled by what she saw "Wow, What the fuck is this all about?" She asked and held it up for Dan to see. It was appeared to big a shroud, as it had holes cut out, obviously as eye holes, and there was some sort of red image that had been silk screened on one side. She further shook it, to open it fully and looked even more confused by it.

Just then, Foxy had reconnected the wire to the terminal of the battery and flicked the switch on. The siren emitted an extremely loud, shrill, and ear-piercing shriek! It was like a woman's scream or wail. Dan spun around and stared at the shroud that Calamity held in front of her, the red image of a large Banshee had been silk screened on it.

Foxy had already switched it off and was just shocked and baffled by the sound and he hadn't seen the image that was on the shroud. "What the fuck do you suppose this is about?" he stammered.

"Just some shit from REB's quirky side I guess!" was what he offered as an explanation. Dan quickly, grabbed the black sheet from Cals hands, and stuffed it back in the box, he disconnected the battery wires once again, undid the bracket that secured the battery to the board set the battery aside and then stuffed the board and the siren in the box with the black fabric. He opened the shop door and walked directly to the fire pit where he threw the box and its contents into the flames. He stood and watched it burn and occasionally stirred the embers and ashes with a stick and poked the siren deeper into the flames, which had now ignited the board and the leather straps and those flames licked the metal surface of the siren, turning it from silver to black and thereby, destroying it.

"What are you doing?" Asked the pair in unison.

"Just turning the page, he replied! Starting a new chapter!

Calamity seemed to catch on to something, but, nothing, then, or ever, as she knew when to leave shit alone. Young Foxy was still puzzled but thought, WTF, and got back to work.

Dan, thought about the box and its contents many times, from the first shrill sounds and then staring at the image of the Banshee, he had instantly, pieced together what it was, as well as what it meant, from things that the old Chief had told him. He was puzzled, however, as to why REB had not destroyed it. He wondered why REB would leave it, where he knew it would be discovered, and that it would be he, who would discover it. He would have to have known, that Dan would have enough inside information, that he would easily figure it out!

Was this another test to see if the Cop side of his life had truly been abandoned. Could he handle the truth? The truth, that would hurt many, who, thanks, to the intervention that had taken place in their lives, had been able to move on with those lives! To reopen those old wounds, would certainly bring a lot of needless pain for a lot of people and create divisions in their personal lives, as well as within the Club and the Community.

The inquisitive side of his being, and those old Cop instincts and curiosity being somewhat satisfied and mysteries had now been solved, at least in his mind, and he figured that would have to suffice! While he didn't have all the facts, the results were satisfactory. He could finally reach and scratch that elusive itch. He imagined, that the old Chief, had long suspected the truth as well, and that is why, he related the story of the two campers, who had witnessed the goings on, at Dwight Higgin's cabin all those years ago.

Dan had also figured that this Banshee, had probably appeared to the drug dealers that were responsible for the deaths of his kids and indirectly, the death of his wife. He didn't share all of his predecessor's views on justice and what should or should not prevail if justice was to be truly served. He could live quite contentedly with that possibility! If there was a heaven and he was to meet Chief Stanley Marshall there in the afterlife, they could get in a debate about it then, before he walked away, with his beloved Nancy, his two kids and REB agreeing to disagree.

He had drawn out a small image of the Banshee that had been on the shroud and identical to the birthmark that was on REB's chest. He stopped into the tattoo shop that was on the property, and had the artist tattoo that image on his left chest in red, just above the nipple in a small banner above the Banshee that read, the page is turned, on the right side in the same position above the nipple was the Clubs logo. These were his first and only tattoos. He figured since he was to bear the burden of the truth for the rest of his life, he would also bear the mark. That, the scar on his forehead, and the silver and turquoise Talisman that he never took off gave him peace. Then there were the memories which would come flooding back especially when he kicked over that bright orange Knucklehead and took it for a ride! He always felt that REB was close at hand!

They were just settling up the bill, when one of the other artists rushed into the room and zeroed in on the Television set on the wall. "Holy fuck! That's just down the road from here!" He announced loudly, while frantically, fumbling for the remote, to turn up the volume!

The story, was being done live, on some property that is owned by Swanton Harbour Mayor, Dwight Higgins Jr. They went on to explain that this was land, that he had inherited from his late father, Dwight Higgins Sr. a Swanton Harbour Police officer, whom had been murdered decades ago on this same property.

Apparently work crews hired by the Mayor to build a

new house on the land made the startling discovery. While excavating for the foundation they unearthed the remains of what appears to be multiple bodies from several unmarked graves. The area had been cordoned off, and Police were waiting for forensic teams, cadaver sniffing dogs, and sonar equipment to arrive and aid in the search as they apparently expect to find more. The Mayor has no comment at this time!

"I guess, sometimes, it takes the chickens some time, before they finally come home to roost!" Dan stated matter-of factly, to no one in particular. He then strode out and gave the bike a once-over before, bringing that old Knucklehead to life with one, smooth, well practiced, kick! He then mounted that bright orange chopper, kicked her into gear, and with a gentle rumble pulsating, from the exhaust, eased her out of the parking area onto the roadway, before a quick twist of the throttle saw them heading off into the country-side! He was one with the machine and his thoughts. The thought that he was happy that he was no longer, Chief of Police, brought a contended and satisfied, smile to his face.

Manufactured by Amazon.ca
Bolton, ON

32432624R00214